PENGUIN BOOKS

THE HOUR OF MAXIMUM DANGER

James Barlow was born in 1921 and educated in Leamington Spa, Stoke-on-Trent and in North Wales. He became a gunnery instructor in the R.A.F. in 1940, but the following year he underwent prolonged treatment for tuberculosis and took to writing technical articles for *Flight* and *Aeroplane*. In 1948 he started writing for *Punch* and published his first novel, *The Protagonists*, in 1956. He gave up his post as a rating inspector for Birmingham Corporation in 1960, and now devotes all his time to writing. His publications include *The Hour of Maximum Danger, Term of Trial, This Side of the Sky* (all available in Penguins), *One Man in the World, Liner, Both your Houses,* and *Burden of Proof* (successfully filmed as *Villain*, starring Richard Burton). He also wrote a non-fiction book, *Goodbye England*, in which he explains his reasons for emigrating to Tasmania. In fact, he and his family only stayed there two years, and he now lives in Ireland with his wife and three children.

THE HOUR
OF MAXIMUM DANGER

JAMES BARLOW

PENGUIN BOOKS
IN ASSOCIATION WITH
HAMISH HAMILTON

Penguin Books Ltd, Harmondsworth, Middlesex, England
Penguin Books Australia Ltd, Ringwood, Victoria, Australia

—

First published by Hamish Hamilton 1962
This revised edition published in the U.S.A. by Simon & Schuster 1963
Published in Penguin Books 1963
Reissued 1973

—

Copyright © James Barlow, 1962, 1963

—

Made and printed in Great Britain
by Hazell Watson & Viney Ltd
Aylesbury, Bucks
Set in Linotype Times

TO ROGER MACHELL
WITH RESPECT AND
GRATITUDE

CONTENTS

PART ONE

*

In the War in which we are engaged, no man can pretend to say how long it will last.

WELLINGTON

Each day the crises multiply. Each day their solution grows more difficult. Each day we draw nearer the hour of maximum danger, as weapons spread and hostile forces grow stronger. . . .

PRESIDENT KENNEDY

1

ESCAPE

THE atmosphere was like fire: it clung to the dirty suburban buildings as if it had been poured over them from a jug. The man called Antonov did not approach Naples in the manner of the posters, across azure water sparkling in the sun and a horizon to catch the eyes: bays and islands and stately ships – the rich of the world playing with summer, brochures materialized – but entered through villages of baked stucco squares, squalor, tired dust, carts overloaded with straw and asymmetrical tomatoes, women at the roadside selling melons.

He wanted to see Naples and *not* die. He was not a tourist, he had no wish to see gaiety, old churches and museums, aquarium or beautiful green bays, only to find a ship, escape, seek sanctuary in England. He had never been so hot in his life. Moisture poured out of him; he could smell the sweetness of his own sweat, and his clothes – at variance with summer, he wore the clothes of one attending a Conference of Spherical Mathematicians in Florence – his clothes stuck to his back and his knees and genitals. His hair, not thick, was nevertheless wet, saturated by himself. He was beyond caring about this. He was prompted by terror; he knew what he had done. A flash of bravery had taken him out of the Hall of the Five Hundred. Malinski and Pervukhin, so-called 'interpreters' to explain their ignorance of mathematics, hadn't noticed for whole minutes. He looked meek, unlikely to do anything. He'd been lucky: a lift in a Belgian Citroen all the way to Rome, from Rome a ride in a British Ford with some schoolteachers as far south as Foggia. Now, three days beyond the decision, stunned by lack of sleep, confused by unfamiliarity with everything (language, place, food, even laughter) and with fear propelling him in the stunning heat – so that he walked quickly at three o'clock in an August afternoon, drew slight attention to himself – he approached the city.

Alexei Antonov was small and as weightless as a bird. His

thirty-year-old face was serious, sallow, tired, creased too much for its age, and it was framed by ears rather red, so large that they were embarrassing. A turnip-shaped head and an exhausted, frightened look: the face of the victim, the dial of the slaughtered, a mass-produced, unimportant appearance. He could be an artisan at highest, a technician, a second-class soldier, but never an aristocrat, never, one presumed, in charge of anything.

As he came beyond the squalid inner suburbs and into the city near the railway station he knew they'd never find him. The whole place was packed; there was no privacy in this entire small word. Garbage on the road, paper and pulped lemons lying about in millions, a great shouting and confusion, dirty houses next to palaces, hands seizing him, pleading voices wishing to sell trash. It was as if war had just passed that way; lines of washing hung across streets like signals of surrender. Youths tried to sell him cheap binoculars, cigarette lighters, shoes. Horse-drawn carriages clattered by, dung among cardboard boxes, and the oranges and lemons squeezed dry. It was crazy. They'd never find him; if he saw them a hundred yards off he could vanish in instants; the noise alone would stun them, reduce initiative. Music blasted the air: hurdy-gurdies, accordions; in the uproar a man even sang; no one gave him money, but he was undeterred, happy perhaps. As each tram went by it seemed to spread a wash behind it: people gesticulating, a shoeblack moving on with his gilded stool, the vendors of drinks, peanuts, trash, tortoises. The shops, too, in the maze of streets that were like smelly corridors, had their own splendid confusion: strings of lemons, vegetables, sausages, figs, black olives, Provolone cheeses, anchovies; fish of unutterable ugliness lay on the slabs: squids and octopus, eels and lobster, things he had never seen. His nostrils, too, were assailed: the hot sweet smell of watermelons, spurting under the knife like heads in a revolution.

He sat in the *galleria*, sweating under glass, drank coffee, but the people still bothered him, who was as poor as they – cameos and corals in this more sophisticated part. American sailors walked by, some with girls, one or two already drunk.

He stood by some hotel as formidable as a fortress on the

Via Partenope, overwhelmed by the size of the harbour, inde-
cisive – where did one enter, find a ship, plead? The traffic,
more sure of itself, roared by in half a dozen lanes, and he felt
the nibble of panic, a solitary figure on a spacious promenade
by a sea. (Was it the Mediterranean or the Tyrrhenian? He
wasn't sure, and how could you escape on a sea you couldn't
name? They'd laugh.) He breathed deeply and there was no
pleasure in the scent of tropical flowers. The waiters stood on
doorsteps, villainous, like bandits in clean clothes, picking their
teeth, examining cars, women, ships, him. There were several
impressive ships anchored: an American aircraft carrier and
attendant destroyer, steamers, merchant ships, and a barge
moving gracefully not far away, smaller boats fussing around
it, much coming and going.

'You know who that is?'

The voice had an American accent but belonged to an Italian,
a young man with curly hair and navy-blue suit (in this heat,
but he seemed cool enough). He had passed Alexei twice on
his scooter and now was hopeful. On his head he had a peaked
hat, but it was meaningless, to convey a half-hour impression
of being employed, an authority on the subject, any relevant
subject from currency to prostitutes. He spoke in English, would
never know how well he had guessed.

'Who?'

The man was small, agile, thirtyish perhaps, or twenty, but
aging fast.

'That barge belongs to a film star.' He named her. 'You
know her? I screwed her two years ago. You don't believe it?
Listen . . .'

Alexei listened. He was apprehensive, a victim; although he
neither liked nor trusted the other, he had secrets, needed help.
If this man went to the police, said, 'There's a Russian having
a look at the harbour,' what would happen? At best he would
be sent back to the conference.

Now the man's motives were clearer, for he asked, 'You want
a hotel? Listen. No use walking about here. Expensive. I can
get you a good cheap place – how long you stay? Two nights? –
near the station, half, quarter the price. How much money you
want to pay?'

'I have not much.'

'Okay. Then no use staying here. You get on the bike.'

Alexei was without initiative, had been caught off guard. He sat on the pillion seat and the scooter raced back through the city and stopped in a chaos of buying and selling from stalls, kids running, boxes, white-clothed policemen sorting out the traffic mess. The Italian parked his scooter and moved rapidly, beating off beggars and peddlars and *sciuscias* like an employee at a cake shop knocking down wasps. Alexei followed him down alleyways of stone cobble; girls stared, children pleaded, tourists came out of an entry, loaded like Guardsmen. The Italian talked his way into corridors, lifts, and in minutes had a conference with a fat man on the eighth floor of what was called a hotel. The fat man took his feet off his desk, eyed Alexei, but did not seem to think him worth picking (no case, for a start). But he shrugged, handed over a key, returned to a magazine and his rested feet.

In a small room the young man said, 'You like it?' and Alexei acknowledged, 'Yes,' to be rid of him. 'A fine view, not expensive?' And indeed through the window was a small balcony, and down below was Naples and in the distance Vesuvius. It was difficult to deny that it had value.

'You a student, eh?'

The Italian did not believe it.

'Sort of.'

'Student of life?' the man said with a sly smile.

'You could say that.'

'You want a woman? A young signorina, juicy as a peach. What time? He arrange.' And a delicate ponce's hand waved toward the door, the corridor, the resting feet and the pornography (so much better than reality — it didn't answer back, demand a percentage).

'Not here,' Alexei explained with a rush: 'I have principles. Religious principles.'

'Oh, sure. We all have. I'm a good Catholic. Except when it's dark, eh?' The face, innocent at a standstill, creased into age and experience when it laughed. 'Listen! I got a wife, four kids. You know, in my job I meet women, beautiful. I'm only small, but I got what they want . . . One a night. I can get them.'

Alexei did not like this man but could not get rid of him. He now began to give details of a tour. 'Four thousand lire. A complete day, Capri, Amalfi, meals, steamer, no tips.'

'I have work to do.'

'Don't gimme that! What you do if you won't go on a tour? Look around Naples, you get tired, hungry, you eat, catch a bus, a boat, you go to Sorrento, Pompeii, all those places. I tell you, you pay twice, three times as much, and you see nothing.'

'I can't go tomorrow. I have no money. Tomorrow I go to the bank. Then I decide about the trip.'

'Okay. Don't worry about me.' He was slighted, hurt; the little runt had feelings: he was in love with money and Alexei had none. 'It makes no difference to me. I don't get anything out of it.'

'It was kind of you to help me.'

In two seconds the man had gone.

Alexei stood on the balcony, and the lights came on in the sulphurous dusk and the ships were garlanded with illuminations. Down below Naples was still a roar of noise, bells, engines, voices, trams, music; somewhere began the old Neapolitan custom of throwing bottles against walls. A man is never so alone as this, when he can see and hear a hundred thousand people and is afraid of all of them. The roar of engines, half identifiable, scooter, Fiat, Volkswagen, always driven hard, noisily; females screamed. A hammering somewhere, many car doors slammed, brakes, tyres squealed, heard even up here, any one could be *them*; their opinion, dislike, so-called justice, could reach anywhere on earth. Voices, laughter, shouts, endless music, the shattered glass. People in opposite windows, flats, hotels, a woman ironing, two girls half naked on a seventh floor, aware of him, tittering; who were all these people? He had assumed responsibility for all of them. It was too much. He was acutely depressed. As if to reassure him, bells began to plead; some were solemn and magnificent, others in a panic. After a while, being exhausted, he relaxed on the bed and waited for night. He was still hot, and when the first aches had left his body he decided to have a shower. He left his jacket (with its pitiful few hundred lire) in the room and, locking the door, went into the adjacent small room. The fat man with the tired feet was not in his office ten yards away. Somewhere a baby began to cry, and some floors below laughter, harsh, unkind.

It was a dirty small room, with someone's washing on a string, and the residue of the last shower still there, and the window was broken and a spider on the wall, making quick darts at a wasp with its fine mesh of death. The water was cold but ecstasy.

Naked, quiet, he was drying himself – the lift noise, voices, a girl's laughter. Then some American voice, 'Y'got smooth arms,' and a giggle and then the same voice, 'Hell, no, I'm just curious,' and a repeat of the giggle, maturity achieved in bed. Alexei was nearly dry when he heard the lift again and the voice of the fat man with the tired feet, and then, petrifying, so that his heart pounded and sweat broke out, a knock on a bedroom door, *his* door, and the same voice, 'Are you there, signor?' and another voice, male, to be afraid of, Pervukhin's, 'Can you not open the door?' and the rustle of notes and then a key and a third voice, Malinski's, scarcely bothering with hypocrisy, 'He has gone out.' Pervukhin said, 'He has left his jacket; he will be back,' and in satisfaction Malinski said in positive identification, 'It is the one he was wearing in Florence.'

'You can wait in my office.'

'No. It is better here.'

'You are so busy –'

The door shut and someone's feet moved away. Outside, bottles smashed, an accordion, a whistle, and up here a row beginning, complaints in furious, accelerated Italian. The moon rising, but unromantic, Vesuvius hidden in dust or smoke, a mere ugly lump. There was no way out. Alexei was wet again with fear. And no money. There was no question of meeting his 'friends', recovering the jacket, having dinner together, some rough wine and a fine Neapolitan pizza. He examined in his mind the geography of the place, as he'd arrived with the tout, as he'd seen it in indifference, moving from that door to this, and after a while he knew that he could not go downstairs without passing the fat man's office, nor could he use the lift, but it was possible to ascend – the steps upward were opposite his room. Even so, when he stepped out of this shower (the light mercifully out of order – a miracle) the fat man had only to turn his head, hear a sound.

He waited a long time, half an hour, completely unnerved, before he even thought of the keyhole. He took the key out, saw an empty corridor, the illuminated office, the resting feet (did he never tire of *that* posture?). The place was livening up, girls, old people, consultations, a phone ringing. He inspected through the tiny aperture again, and Tired-feet was just coming out of the office, turning.

Alexei put the key back, turned it, ventured out as weak as water, hot; the silence from his own room (in darkness, itself ominous) was so absolute that the quiet movement of his feet was like football boots on shingle. Going up the twenty steps to the bend of the staircase his body had the fragility of glass. He expected it to be shattered by a mere word.

On the ninth, and top, floor, the lift had just gone down, and there, escorting two girls with small suitcases (but not carrying anything for them), was the tout. His gallantry, in opening a door, was crude – his hands had to touch as far as was permissible, the waist, the hip – and through the opened door Alexei, sweat rolling down his face, his neck, heard the patter: 'You get tired, hungry, you eat, catch a bus, you go to Sorrento, Pompeii, all these places . . .' and the girls' voices being polite, waiting for him to go.

The lift was moving, but the wrong way. Alexei prayed in an earnest whisper, 'Oh, God, save me, so that I can serve You . . . His escape had a terrible unreality; it seemed out of his control, and if it was in the control of others, what hope was there for him?

Someone was staring at him and he turned quickly. A child. She was small, a mere thirteen or fourteen, curly black hair like shiny rope, and a rough skin, lips slightly Negroid, a dirty dress, bare feet, but tender eyes, beautiful, all of humanity in the eyes. She was smiling at him, smiling, carrying some bottles of aqua minerale in a straw basket, smiling – no, it was impossible, not a child this young – this, surely, must be hell. He stared her out and the smile died, but it was true. Impossible – no, he looked at her and again the leer that was without experience; it was as if Christ had tittered.

The lift came and, being small, there was no room for others. She pressed the button for *terra*, and as they neared the eighth floor the tired feet came into view and the fat man was standing there, satisfaction, importance – see, when I press the button the lift comes. As it passed him he protested, but the protest faltered and became a cry, courtesy, guests remembered, 'Signor, your friends have come!' And Alexei, reduced to a victim without initiative, pleaded as the fifth and fourth floors passed, 'Please help me to hide' – surely the rarest request made in this building.

He spoke in English, but whether she understood or not he did not at first know, but certainly she pulled him by hand along the stone and cobbled corridors, and in the crowds, still there despite the hour (when did they tire?), she led him in a zigzag up a hill, past men drinking at tables on the pavement, a prostitute, very fat, shiny as a balloon in a pale-blue dress, a blonde (imported or home industry?), half a dozen children, younger than his escort, who questioned a solitary tourist, 'You Deutsch? Americano? You want a signorina? No. Give us a cigarette then. Lucky Strike.' Every street was hot, packed to make it hotter, noisy with laughter and music; faces stared from shutters, turned on scooters, and he hurried through the litter of a million squeezed lemons into a building old like the rest, stale, crowded – no one took any notice – and into a room, and there she lit a candle, in shyness perhaps, or in shame at the squalor of the place, or because there was no electricity....

'What have you done?' she asked. 'Killed a man?'

'No.'

'Nothing bad?'

'Nothing at all.'

Clearly she did not believe this. 'Stay here,' she suggested. 'No one bothers here.' She began to strip, said with nervousness, 'I've never done this before.' She made it sound like a failure, a confession that she wasn't yet up to the standards of Naples. 'That's why it's only five hundred lire.'

Someone sniggered, and Alexei saw that two boys were watching, had opened the door, found this initiation too funny for silence.

She shouted at them in Italian. Feet scampered, but only

temporarily; they would be back. She was aware of this, blew out the candle (but they would listen, deduce, their minds find that even funnier; it was, presumably, an occasion, her first).

Alexei said quietly, 'I have no money anyway,' and her silence was hopeful, pain and degradation postponed. 'But he will want money.' It was as if they were both conspirators in a plot to save her virginity and yet find five hundred lire.

By now she was close enough for him to hear her breathing. Here was someone in the world more afraid than him, with a future more pitiable. When he touched her he found she was shaking with fear. Her smooth skin meant nothing to him; he suffered with her, was interested in her problem, although it was, he suspected, hopeless.

'Do not be afraid,' he whispered, keeping his voice almost as quiet as thought; the boys would hoot with derision if they could hear this, put it down to impotence, fear. 'I believe in God.'

The word 'God' was understood, caused anxiety, silent tears. Hands produced a crucifix. There was no longer any question of sex; they had innocence in common. He caressed her, standing there in the stunning heat, the sour smells of dirt oozing out of the building, the world fingering with the door. Her skin was warm, her back bony and slender.

'How old are you?'

'I am fourteen.'

'Can you not run away?'

'It would be the same.'

'You have been to school?'

'No.'

'But you understand my English?'

'Yes, am I not good?'

'Where did you learn English?'

'My mother's friends,' she told him with childish brutality. In the appalling silence she at last ventured, 'You do like me though? It is not because I am ugly?'

'You are very beautiful.'

'That is wrong, silly.'

'Do you have a name?' he asked in great tenderness, and it even occurred to him that she might not.

'Yes. It is Alessandra.'

'What can I give you, Alessandra?'

She said nothing but was interested. She wanted something to be given to *her*, not bartered, not a reward, not a percentage, something for the I-am-Thou.

'I want to go to London. I can send you something.'

'Send me a picture,' she at last requested. 'A picture of London.' It would be fascinating – someone on the other side of Europe thinking about *her*.

'I want to find a ship,' he told her.

'Which one?'

'I am a refugee,' he explained. 'I want to get to England.'

'Why England?' she asked, puzzled. Why should anyone want to leave Italy, go to a country that was cold, wet, law-abiding?

'It is a question of politics.'

'Anything is possible in this city,' she said with the certainty of a fourteen-year-old, 'if you have money.'

'I have no money –'

'Nothing is possible –'

'I have a wrist watch, see?'

She could see the illuminated green figures of the dial: forty minutes past eleven.

'It is a good one?'

'Very good. The seconds, the minutes, the hours, and the days. Automatic –'

'It is a long way to England.'

'It is worth fifty thousand lire.'

'Give it to me!'

'Your wrist is too small.'

'I will find out.'

She was dressing in the privacy of darkness. The boys could hear it, presumed satisfaction, laughed aloud, asked questions in Italian.

He trusted her but not others. 'They will steal it.'

'They?'

'Whoever sees this watch.'

'Wait,' she instructed.

Alexei heard her only yards away: inexplicable, frantic dialogue – it sounded like a row; a man's voice, full of disbelief, anger, contempt, but finally interested.

He was small, plump, cheerfully aware of his own weaknesses. Alexei did not remove the watch but stretched out his left arm for the man to inspect; the very gesture confirmed the value of the watch. After a while the man could not resist it. He grinned, laughed, and there was much dialogue between him and the girl. The girl smiled, like one being congratulated – her first man, brilliantly successful, big business!

The man spoke excitedly to her on a different subject, and then the girl translated: 'A Spanish ship, he knows. It would stop at Gibraltar for you.'

The girl talked quickly to the man, like a newly promoted partner in a company, who mentions uncomfortable things such as insurance, fire exits, new vehicles, expensive but necessary. The three of them went out into the humid, crowded night, and within two hours Alexei was on board a Spanish ship. Five days later, in someone else's clothes, he was in an aircraft of the Royal Air Force, heading toward England.

2

ALEXEI ANTONOV

IN England the churches were empty and the mental hospitals full. There was no morality, but endless criticism, no right or wrong, only right and left. Discipline had come to an end, for it was no longer possible for a man to be wrong. Authority was tolerated but no longer accepted. The very government that had been legally, democratically elected was ignored and instructed and harassed by anyone, from trades-union leaders to schoolteachers, from playwrights to racing-car drivers. It was the decade of the committeeman, the clubman, the expense-account man, the sycophant. Corruption, although not overwhelming, was substantial and present in all ranks of society, even touching the medical profession and the arts. Such philosophers as existed had the wisdom of contempt, limited to words: meaningless words in books and arrogant TV interviews; and if they were ignored it was as well, for their private lives were without integrity, full of arrogance, dirt, vanity, nothing that could be valued. Cultured and sophisticated values could be summarized: all that was honest and clean was naïve; only evil was significant, of interest. Freedom existed but staggered under abuse.

The incidence of V.D. among fourteen-year-olds was described by a leading physician as 'not serious'. An actor arrested for importuning outside a public lavatory was described by his friends as 'very tired and overworked, but a man of complete integrity'. The Teds and their bewildered girl friends were dancing to a new one called 'Kiss Me Chicken, but Not Down There', which was regarded by a bishop as 'immoral in intent, serious in implication'. The cultured of the metropolis were crowding nightly to a new play in four dimensions (believed by one critic to be 'brilliance almost beyond bearing' and by another to be 'yet another load of nonsense by yet another scatologically minded provincial') about a blind nymphomaniac and a blancmange salesman. The new Veall sports car could develop 363 b.h.p. and travel with two persons at 162 m.p.h. A washing powder had been developed which, when used, was claimed to produce 'not whiteness but the colour of your big blue eyes'.

The portrait on one wall was of Winston Churchill, 1940, the impish grin, the day of glory, the voice that caught at the throat, could make the heart leap: 'I can offer you nothing but ... And amid the ruins, quiet, confident, bright and smiling eyes, beaming with a consciousness of being associated with a cause far higher and wider than –'

Disraeli had leaned on the desk ...

Wellington had stormed out of the room.

The Permanent Under-Secretary had carted a Halifax over Berlin, Hamburg, Milan, Mannheim. He belonged here. Two hundred feet away dry rot was crawling, destroying the building as others were destroying the tradition.

Stranger people than Alexei Antonov had been welcomed here: exiled princes, couriers, ambassadors, spies, heroes ...

Mr Babbington apologized, breathless, 'Traffic jam in Oxford Street.'

'There is always,' the Permanent Under-Secretary explained with a smile to Antonov, 'a traffic jam in Oxford Street. It was designed for them.'

Mr Babbington accepted the sherry. 'And may I say, Mr Antonov, how I admire your courage ...'

They were like men being polite with creaking care before getting down to business.

'Vodka,' contributed Mr Babbington further, 'gives me a lousy head.'

'A lousy head?'

The little man with red ears, the tired face, agitated hands, clearly believed in forms of insects.

'He means a headache,' explained the Permanent Under-Secretary. 'An exhausting session with Immigration?'

'They were very polite –'

'I suspect you are, too, Mr Antonov.'

Polite, meaningless laughter.

'Seven hours,' said Antonov, 'with a meal in the middle.'

'The price of freedom.'

'I do not,' claimed the odd, nervous, shy little man, 'believe in unqualified freedom.'

'Quite, quite.'

'I believe,' said the Russian with a warm face, 'in humanity.'

'Immigration gives you a fine report,' said the Permanent Under-Secretary vaguely.

'I have acted on my beliefs,' claimed the little man.

'Indeed you have –'

'I told the spies –'

'Spies? Oh, police. We call them police –'

'Everything I could.'

'Everything relative to their work,' suggested Mr Babbington.

'The point of your escape –'

'What we want to know –'

'Sorry –'

'I have come,' said Antonov, 'because I have information.'

'Exactly.'

'What is this information?'

This was better. This was ideals in application. In the end that was what won. It was complicated. Millions died, had passions; buildings were shattered; it seemed irrelevant, but in the end – the achieved, sour, disappointing end – the ideal won. Usually. The Permanent Under-Secretary had put his twenty-year-old ideals into action from March 1942 to August 1944, when he'd been shot down over Augsburg. His were not the ideals of anger or hatred of others. They were ideals that had been battered by time and experience and had survived the failures of several decades. (It hurt, though, in the sleepless night, caught by music and word, a noise, it wounded to remember the youthful faces, all dead, burned, buried, mere crosses of wood in cemeteries all over Europe, while the generation they fought for had the ethics and principles of the motorcar salesman, the bingo hall, the representative with the french letter ready in his wallet. All we heard now were the voices of louts, demanding, insulting.)

The thing was called Platform and it had been launched, Antonov told them, from Baykonuv in West Siberia. It had an aggregate thrust of 3,000,000 pounds, equivalent to 64,000,000 horsepower. An initial thrust of 1,830,000 pounds in the six engines of the first stage; 1,036,000 pounds in its second stage; and a third and final thrust of 292,000 pounds. It had H_2O_2 for operating the stabilizing jets, beryllium heat shield, infra-red scanners, three-axis position control, retrorockets. It weighed 7,000 pounds, had a height of 200 inches and a diameter of 150 inches. It was called Platform because, at present, it was used to photograph to an accuracy of forty feet, and it was in orbit now – he had the frequency, the orbital path – circling the earth unseen, unannounced, within the earth's shadow at night and the sun's glare in the day. It could be used for other purposes – control of intercontinental ballistic missiles, radio, weather forecaster. On and on the little man talked, tireless, slightly hysterical: timer sequences, attitude sensers, electronic stabilization devices, horizon-sensing units ... At present it was merely being used for reconnaissance, photographing or identifying every installation in Europe and America down to the accuracy of cranes, hangars, concrete installations.

It was espionage on the magnificent scale.

They had shot down the U-2 aircraft. Quite rightly. But the effort involved to destroy this thing – and there were five of them in existence, it seemed – involved a political decision.

'We have an answer,' said Mr Babbington.

'More sherry?' asked the Permanent Under-Secretary. 'Have a biscuit?'

'If you have an answer,' Alexei Antonov said, 'then for God's sake use it.'

He told them about the intended, possible – no, probable – use of distributed crop poison. His father, now disowned, had worked on the mathematics of that, explained that it could be done: with Platform out there watching the vast movements of weather, and Platform to redirect rockets, explode them, dissolve them, or whatever, so that poison floated –

'Is it manned?' the Permanent Under-Secretary asked.

It was. It had a crew of three.

That made the decision harder, the risk greater.

There had been no objection to the anti-missile missile for some years in theory . . .

This was one stage beyond that, but they had an answer, slightly beyond theory, rather more, in fact, than drawing-board stage, to the thing called Platform.

The question was, should they now use it? Must they use it to prove that the balance of power was not in favour of the Platform?

There was no question of identification. Current radar could identify, electronic machines could work out in seconds the trajectory, speed, all the details. The question was: should one fire?

The Permanent Under-Secretary believed, in view of what Alexei Antonov told him, that they should.

The answer to Platform was not merely a rocket that could get within a mile of it, meeting its 20,000 m.p.h. orbital path with a reverse trajectory of similar astonishing speed – they had the rocket all right, solid fuel, warheads, all the rest of it. In addition they had the secret thing called spatial impulse selector. This was an electric brain in miniature. It was a cylinder about five inches in height, one and a half in diameter. Its nerves were wires as fine as cotton, hundreds of them, so that it was like a furry, dangerous little metal animal. It could think, select, change its mind, move on, select reality from decoy.

There were problems.

The Permanent Under-Secretary enumerated them.

Antonov said, 'You must use it. They will never be quite sure. Loss of Platform could be caused by many things – meteorites, oxygen failure, disintegration, the unknown factor.'

'If we destroy one it could be the accident of oxygen, the elements,' Mr Babbington contributed eagerly. 'If we destroy two it will show awareness ... That, however,' he concluded, 'is the political problem.'

'What about the Americans?' Antonov asked.

'I don't know, Mr Antonov. It spreads the risk of secrecy. The Americans tend,' he added with the smile, 'to print their secrets in *Popular Mechanics*. We can keep secrets in this country, Mr Antonov.'

It was necessary.

The world, the world, this strange, absurd, beautiful, cruel place still worth saving. The world that was so fascinating because it depended on courage, whimsy, chance, love, charity, intentions, hatred, the unexpected ...

They were, reluctantly and under pressure from fools, giving them their 'freedom' six thousand miles away in yet another country. The white man was being thrown out in haste, in a litter of murder, rape, burned-down buildings, chaos, disease, bombastic interviews, dishonoured contracts. A man named 'Terrible Tom' Tupoka, whose name had never been mentioned in politics before, with seven thousand men, had raided a village. He hated his cousin and lusted after his wife. He slashed the cousin to death, not satisfied until each limb was hacked off, the face mutilated beyond recognition. Then, naked and gleaming with blood, he pursued the screaming wife, killed the children who clung to her, and raped her. It was insufficient merely to have emptied his loins, more satisfying, completion, to slaughter her, too, to indulge in bestialities until satiation came and he could return to the politics of the situation. The village was then burned down. The smell of flaming flesh and blood hung over the trees in the sun, vultures wheeled in ecstasy, sly animals smelled the scent of meat seven miles away. It was five days later, with fifty thousand men, before Tom was too exhausted to continue, was satisfied to limit himself to sniping at buildings, massacre the odd few hundred men sent to control him, explain the potential, the risk of the Third World War being detonated. This, had said the opposition in London, is a country which is adult, wise, and must be given freedom to decide its own destiny. But that was last week's cry, forgotten, wrapped around fish and chips. Today, anything rather than the honest humility, 'We were wrong' – anything, so great was hatred of the other party; and so the public, cynical (for in this country no one had been wrong for twenty years), indifferent, heard some fool in the House ask the War Minister whether he could give assurances that British troops would not use violence in this area which must have the freedom to be what it wished.

Two hundred miles from London two sixteen-year-old schoolgirls had been found in a room with ten Pakistanis. All were naked and the police said that – But, more amusing, the parents said the girls never reached home before seven. No, they hadn't worried. The Pakistanis were baffled, annoyed. The girls were willing, it was claimed, so what was wrong?

A landslide in Gazilia, five thousand miles away, killed four thousand people, destroyed three villages. A relief fund was set up in Cambridge, and Britain's fifty million contributed £4,613 11s. 9d.

The well-known brewery owner, Mrs Trenchard-Wax, had died. Her estate, valued at £313,479, was divided thus: £100 each for the eleven servants; £1,000 for Miss Cutler, her secretary; the balance for a dogs' home in Sussex.

It took two hundred hours to break the anger, strength, and intelligence of Alexei's father. He had been completely ignorant of his son's motives, religion, principles, but now he broke down, admitted guilt; further, he admitted that on a day in 1943 he had helped a wounded German soldier. He lost five stone in weight in three weeks. Each day they allowed him to hear the firing squad, to see the military ankles through a barred window. He spent a week in a cell before he even knew what his crime was. His first confession was not believed, and he was beaten up for insolence. In the end he had to plead, laugh. An endless conveyor belt of men questioned him for two weeks.

Some of them shouted; some were polite, a few even intelligent; others just repeated one question for six hours, irrespective of what he said. Now and again he fell down, unconscious. Sometimes he was allowed ten minutes in which to eat an enfeebling meal, urinate. At the end of the three weeks he was laughing and weeping, talking rubbish – 'I am guilty,' he shouted (or thought he shouted). 'I can prove it' – and at last the examiners were interested.

Two corridors away Alexei's mother had lost control of her faculties and functions and was a babbling idiot. They had to destroy such a filthy animal. Mercifully Alexei knew nothing of this.

In a temperature of 120 degrees in the shade the man hung by the hair about two inches off the ground, his arms and legs in a crucified position, roped. The executioner could not slash off the head with one blow and the crowd roared disapproval. The executioner became angry, and his final blow was so strong that the hairs broke and the head shot off at a tangent and landed in the crowd amid much laughter. A mile away armoured cars began firing and the sound of a mob screaming in panic could be heard; it approached in a condition of dust. Dirt and the stupefaction of drugs and children selling themselves, disease and squalor and thieving, but they were beyond caring and they had nothing to lose. You couldn't drink oil.

The 4.06 train from Charing Cross to Folkestone was fourteen minutes late, and Lady Charlotte Slinger wrote to *The Times* about it.

The world, our world, this bitter, dirty, beautiful place. A restless world, all talking, none listening, full of philosophers whose wisdom was contempt. The world that depended on courage, love, charity, on rain, sun, soil, on tyre pressure, bromide paper, radar, lifts, postmen, string ...

The fashionable eyes of Sheila Haward stared down from the climbing Boeing 707 as it turned over New York, the stalagmites of concrete beyond Battery Park, the steel of Manhattan and Brooklyn Bridge, the transatlantic piers she was too hurried to use. The elegant, long fingers pressed the button, summoned the stewardess. 'Darling, a drink of something?'

Nineteen-year-old Maggie Preston took two aspirin – the earphones gave her a headache sometimes – and greeted for the five thousandth time this week or month, she didn't know, 'World Mechanical; can I help you?' Her mind was nevertheless in no condition to assist anyone; even if she'd possessed technical knowledge of World Mechanical's jet engines, explosives, rockets, refrigerators. It was, as usual, planning. Do I go out on Saturday with Mick or with Ray or *both*? Is it my turn or Vera's to cook tonight? I'd better get sausages. Eggy likes those.

Geoffrey Sumpster saw a photograph in someone's abandoned newspaper, a girl, flesh; he was on his way to tea; an erection made him hot, uncomfortable, a different appetite. The mind, superior surely, struggled hard, work, think, go on the beer – oh, God, I'm fed up.

In his studio Max Stuhler was finishing a photograph of an alderman, fixing the monorail camera, a new adjustment, idea. The face was like a pudding, without dignity, but Max's technical mind intended it to become a photograph, skin, flesh, pores, in two colours; heads would turn. It was not important, conceit on both ends of the camera. The round, foolish clubman's face said with City cunning, 'Forty guineas! You can't be worth that much.' Max's technique overcame reluctance, probed vanity, won, as usual: all were fools. 'Ah, but the point is, *you* are!'

The half-past-twelve siren blew and the men and women rushed out of the factory in the hundreds, filled the road, swarmed on buses, entered hot, shabby cafés and pubs, and Charles Filmer, forty-seven, fixed his bicycle clips and adjusted his spectacles and rode down the main road.

Dieter Buechner, blond, twenty-two, lively, amusing, bitter, posted the letter and returned to his red Volkswagen. It was only when driving that he could forget himself, his hatred of the world. He drove with skilled, reckless fury past pine trees and timber mills; he overtook lorries on corners deliberately, to see if death was coming the other way. Inside the hour he was in Karlsruhe. In a café the soldier was waiting, a simple, thick, good-natured boy of nineteen. 'Coffee,' Dieter ordered, without a glance at the waitress. The soldier grinned and whispered eagerly, 'Dieter, listen. The 112th are moving.

They're going to Hamburg.' Dieter responded impulsively, 'Darling, how clever you are,' and flushed at the arrival of the waitress. He said to her brusquely, 'I said a pot of coffee, not two cups. Am I a tourist to be overcharged?' The waitress – a superb fair specimen, with eyes slightly mascaraed, mysterious, and a splendid body – smiled, knowing how safe it was to do so.

None of these people had met. They had, at the moment, nothing in common except dissatisfaction. Alexei Antonov had never heard of them. Mr Babbington and the Permanent Under-Secretary did not know of their existence. They moved on shoe leather, tubeless tyres, a Number 8 bus, unaware of each other's existence.

It was a two-hundred-acre disused gunnery range, still owned by the Royal Navy. During the war matelots had fired rifles and machine guns here. It was assumed that 'normal' guided-weapons establishments would be under some surveillance by the Communists, if only from a passing car. But anyone wandering around this particular range would be very conspicuous. There was a village three miles away, a town nine, but hereabouts was a mere scattering of coastguards' cottages, with tiny barren gardens, a lane, and a farm two miles away. On the north side was shingle and the sea.

On the site itself were a few small brick buildings, saturated by heavy rain and time, coils of barbed wire, boxes, crates, a flagpole, some dustbins, and a notice, faded and flapping which stated that this was the property of the Royal Navy and when the red flag (unconscious irony!) was flying the risk was upon the visitor who ventured near. The whole place was surrounded by inadequate chestnut fencing and barbed wire.

On this wet day in September, the place, including the shore, was flooded and dirty, the few small trees bent in a high wind; there was spray on the dull sea and rain blew into the ears of the hundred or so persons standing about anxiously. On a wet concrete base stood the rocket which had the code name Billiards. Soldiers were crawling around it, getting very wet. Inside its intricate guts the spatial impulse selector's hundreds of furry wires were attached to other instruments and to the warhead. There were a number of lorries and very expensive cars parked about haphazardly. In one of the cars the Permanent Under-Secretary talked to the Minister and Mr Babbington, and all ate a sandwich lunch.

The rocket would be ready to fire at three o'clock, and it was anticipated that at four Platform would pass quite close (ninety-three miles high), being then not only conveniently over the Atlantic and British waters but also at or near to perigee, in which condition it would be appreciably slowed down by the rarefied atmosphere despite its one-millionth of normal density. The choice had been made. This was similar in the protection of national sovereignty to the shooting down of the U-2, but the risks and possibilities were proportionately larger. It had been a very difficult political decision and one the Opposition knew nothing about. Indeed, several members of the Cabinet were unaware of what was intended.

The rocket contained 1,750,000 electronic components inside a frame only eighteen inches in diameter and forty-three feet long. Its various parts had been manufactured in great secrecy and assembled in the government laboratory. Of the hundred soldiers in attendance only four knew that the target, the living target several hundred miles away and ninety-three miles high, would not be of friendly manufacture.

The problems of firing the rocket and causing it to proceed and meet an oncoming small object moving in reverse trajectory at 20,000 m.p.h. were as great, if not greater, than those involved in estimating the behaviour of Platform. Platform, it was now known, had been sent off with the rotational advantage of the velocity of the earth. Its speed, orbital path, stability, and temperature were known. In use for the first time was British radar of unprecedented power and capability. This radar had a final valve which was eighteen feet long and which produced enormous long pulses of 100-megowatt power (say, one-third the power of an atomic power station). A jet of electrons rushing through the tube at four-fifths the speed of light would be matched exactly in speed with a radio wave which would pass in the same direction along the tube. The electrons would gradually slow down, giving up their energy to the radio wave and thus amplifying it. The pulse would last a hundred-millionths of a second, and the returning echo would be squeezed into a much shorter time.

Thus Platform could be found in the sky. The problem of the artillery (as it was still called) was to send the rocket Billiards to a meeting point, bearing in mind the sweat on a thumb might cause an error of a mile. (A mile in fact was not an error: it was brilliant shooting.) The actual firing, then, was related to information given by the superb radar. The mathematics of it would be coupled to a remote-controlled electronic computer and firing system; the computer was capable of 300,000 operations a minute. The problems fed to the machine (in the form of radar answers, mathematics on perforated tape) allowed for the orbital path of the earth itself, its rotation, infinitely varied problems of weather, wind, barometric pressures at all levels, the curvature of the earth, the gravity-held orbital path of the target, its other characteristics, and the delay in the electronic and mechanical actuation of the control mechanism itself. The largest and least controllable degree of error was in the propellant fuel. Solid fuel was more predictable than liquid or gas, but even so, each load had an incalculable behaviour beyond which it could not be manufactured. This was the risk, the enemy's proportion of luck.

At three o'clock the edges of the sky began to clear and the rain stopped. (Not that it mattered to the rocket, only to the saturated soldiers.) The sea still ran heavily despite the cessation of the gale.

The Minister and the Permanent Under-Secretary and Mr Babbington and a general strolled anxiously on the shingle.

'How good the air smells ...'

'Absolute secrecy. Nothing in writing if possible, not even at the highest level ...'

'If this thing is going into volume production ...'

'Components, many of which indicate nothing ...'

'Danger is where assembled ...'

'Someone has to be trusted ...'

'They have troubles, too ...

'This fellow Antonov ...'

'The time, what's the time?'

'Over Kansas City now ...'

'General, do you think ...'

They were haunted by the memory of Fuchs, Pontecorvo, Blake, Lonsdale. A man's mind could ignore his own signature over the oath of secrecy. There were no values of patriotism now if a man was a Communist; it was his 'duty', in fact, to betray patriotism, God, country ...

'A lot of bloody seagulls around here ...'

There were indeed. With five seconds to firing, some of the birds seemed as if they were about to fly over the rocket at its moment of departure, which might cause minor error or major disaster.

The solid fuel gave a more rapid send-off than liquid would have done; it was like a child's rocket on November fifth, but a million times more powerful, a million, no, fifty million. There was a terrifying flash and roar and a shock wave that spread and was not dissipated until it had spent its strength eighteen miles away. Things died. The seagulls were blasted about like bits of tissue paper in a gale. Fish were stunned. Tiny things that lived below the turf died by the million in high, unbearable temperature; so did minute things in the air. A perpendicular signal of smoke stood two hundred feet high until the air began to remove it, absorb it.

Men exhaled breath several hundred yards away, talked, laughed, lit cigarettes; a sergeant's voice commanded; the ears began to lose their odd behaviour, hear again in normal fashion.

Minutes passed, people walked about, a quarter of an hour, drinks of tea; tension began to accumulate for the second time.

Then a telephone rang in a hut; the general walked across the shingle and told the Minister, 'Platform is no longer in orbit.'

The Minister said, like a schoolboy in excitement, 'Thank God for that, General. As from this afternoon, we resume our status as a first-class nation. That will give them something to think about.'

It already had....

The destruction of Platform was an alarming confirmation in Moscow of rumours which had begun with a British soldier lying in the grass in Somerset making love to his girl friend. Neither of them were Communists. They were simply in love with each other, he in eagerness and she in ashamed, tender reciprocation. Both were anxious about his departure to a place he didn't wish to mention. The girl was uneasy because the soldier had talked of marriage in his love-making and now he was going away and she didn't know where. He talked of secrecy, which was ridiculous – there was no war; they were in love. She began to weep, reproach him, protest that he had told lies in order to fondle her, remove clothes, do what he wanted.

The soldier was very hot and bothered. It was all terribly remote, this secrecy. The birds sang above his head; the hot sun shone on her thighs. He had every intention of marrying her, was in fact afraid she might seek a similar pleasure elsewhere now that her sensual appetite had been roused and satisfied. He knew she was safe – she was going to be his wife. He'd seen the village school, the cottage where she was born. She'd cried out in a hot-and-bothered tenderness that was entirely for him and had done so in an accent belonging to Somerset. She was as English as apples and beer and roses. So he told her where he was going and, as far as he was informed, what for and how long he would be away. And when he'd gone her face betrayed her and her mother knew she'd lain with him and there was a quarrel, and when the girl, weeping, talked of love and marriage, the mother was angry and contemptuous and protested. 'D'you think you'll see *him* again?' and laughed bitterly when the girl said, 'Yes.' So that the girl, anxious to prove the lad's good intentions, told her mother where he had gone with his artillery unit. And since a girl of seventeen, country bred, gentle, foolish, unsophisticated, wanting in the world only love and children, could not force or even request her mother to keep a secret, the mother mentioned it in pride in answer to malice and gossip, a proof of the boy's eventual return, approaching betrothal. The vital information, the curious information, meaningless to civilians, that a rocket, whether a standard one or not, should be fired from a disused site, with a general in attendance, was mentioned in all innocence on a telephone, in a hotel, on a train, until, in a rather vague form, it reached an embassy.

Ten days later photographs of the site, taken from a camera that looked like (and in fact was) a cigarette lighter, in a 'passing' car, were on a desk in Moscow. In many ways they were disappointing, conveying no technical secrets. But the nature of the concrete, the marks of scorched grass, the cranes not yet removed from the area, at least indicated the nature of the problem. There was no association yet between the disappearance of Platform and the photographs which indicated a secret rocket test, but there was suspicion, anxiety, even some alarm.

It was necessary, the Minister and his technical advisers thought, to build about three hundred Billiards rockets. Manufacture had to be broken down and spread throughout Britain – a complicated programme to build billions of minor parts which would then be assembled into the larger sections: nose cone, spin mechanism, three-stage motors, helium spheres, junction boxes, pitch and yaw jets, electronic equipment, including spatial impulse selectors, battery, fuel tanks, explosives, the frame of magnesium alloy 27/10,000ths of an inch thick, miniaturized instruments, and the larger items for handling – the gantries, cranes, motor vehicles. Each Billiards would cost about three million pounds, but before manufacture could take place certain factories had to be extended, a few built specially for the task. The programme was secret, but it was also urgent. There was a date line for each contract, and now other difficulties began.

The date lines carried a penalty of several hundred pounds a day to the contractors, that is, for every day beyond the date line the contractors would have to pay this sum. The tradesunions and the building employees knew this, and the temptation was too much. They were also aware that the work was 'for the Government', and therefore money was meaningless. There had already been bribes of various natures among building contractors, quantity surveyors, some officials, and now the workers demanded dirt money, danger money, spot bonuses, a shorter week, a longer week, more overtime and less. Men who were caught stealing and sacked had to be reinstated because the possibility of keeping the contract date lines was receding, and with receding date lines overtime became vital, price no object. These men were not traitors any more than the surveyors and builders who met and fixed their prospects over a drink, a meal, a game of golf. They were men of good humour, courage even, but they lived in a society which had replaced God with money.

It took a few months for the Billiards project to get under way. Inevitably there was some loss of secrecy. Factories being extended can be examined from a moving vehicle or across a road. But the Soviets could not know what was being made inside, why, where it would go from a particular factory, or of what other structure it would become a constituent part, what was the purpose of the final object. There were not many Soviet spies in Britain to carry out the innumerable visual inspections. Members of the Soviet Embassy in London are limited in their travels to a radius of thirty miles. A skilful examination of newspapers and technical journals could explain a surprising amount, but what was needed was help from within. They were cynically confident of obtaining it in a society they had condemned as decadent, selfish, pleasure loving, without a dynamic such as they had.

PART TWO

*

It is one of the ironies of our time that the techniques of a harsh and repressive system should be able to instil discipline and ardour in its servants — while the blessings of liberty have too often stood for privilege, materialism, and a life of ease.

PRESIDENT KENNEDY

An accursed thing it is to gaze
On prosperous tyrants with a dazzled eye.

WORDSWORTH

The English are decadent, but they do not know it.

MR KHRUSHCHEV

1

SHEILA HAWARD

THE satisfying, assured mechanical scream of the Boeing's engines, almost unheard inside the aircraft, the hard cauliflower edges of cumulus clouds thirty thousand feet above a sea, equally unreal, dull pewter; the passengers crumpled slightly after hours in the air; an old lady saying even now, never tired of it, 'If it's God's will that we crash, then so be it,' in an American accent, a formidable, remarkable old lady who had already been to Japan and India and still incxhaustible, undis-turbed by strange diets, about to 'do' Europe; and sitting near her the young woman who, after seven hours, still had a poise that was elegant, untired.

The stewardess, an attractive girl, rather heavy by the side of the passenger, said in a friendly, shy transatlantic voice, 'Miss Haward, did you know you were on the cover of this month's *Bizarre*? I just got it from a passenger. I sure wish that woman'd stop acting as if this plane was about to disintegrate. I've done this trip seventy-nine times already.'

Other things called her away, and Sheila Haward held the heavy glossy magazine in her hands and stared at the face. She remembered the day and her wide, rather thin mouth smiled secretly: outside the Villa Aldobrandini at Frascati – a perfect day, thirty photographs, of the clothes, not her, and then one of her, her face, and Miss Sylander had decided – and one of the photographers had been sick and they'd missed a Viscount from Rome and waited hours. What a day, but here was the end product, the face staring with fastidious arrogance, or, at any rate, technical superiority, over the entire feminine world. The picture had been taken in February – it was one of the hazards of the profession that summer frocks were modelled in February, fur coats in August; once she'd modelled one in Mombasa in a temperature of 120 degrees.

The portrait on the cover of the magazine was almost un-bearable, too theoretical to belong to a human, too beautiful

to be real. This, surely, was the success and tragedy of such
a face: such a person could not live a normal, humdrum life, at
a sink, in the stale smell of steam; everything must be significant, elegant, not by the wish of the mind inside the face
but in a certain inevitability. She would never belong to
ordinariness.

Sheila Haward was a functional machine of absolute perfection: a fantastic arrangement of nerves, sinews, blood vessels,
pores, eyes and hair and bone structure. One of God's most
beautiful creations, it was almost a pity she had to think, have
the responsibility of a mind and heart. For in them she was,
like all of us, fallible. She was not arrogant but was unaware
of her own perfection in its ultimate sense – viewing it, not as
God's miracle, but the thing in the mirror. She did not contrast
her beauty with the emaciated of the earth or the misery of
the deaf and dumb, the timid, the sick, the unsuccessful. She
could not have survived in her profession if she had. Confidence was essential. The slightest doubts, the smallest lack of
seriousness in the profession of vanity, would be to falter and,
in the camera's eye she must not falter. In fact she had no
qualms at all – except the waiting problems of old age, skin deterioration, false teeth, spectacles. These would be disaster as
far as she comprehended it. Yet she was capable of pity – but
strictly in her own world: a friend ill, a dress torn, an opportunity missed, a girl pregnant, a jinx on the camera. The margin
of error between her perfection and its downfall – a tyre valve
faulty, fog at an airport, a corner too fast in someone's two-litre,
an instant's confusion at a cross-roads – those simply never
occurred to her. She was, in fact, at times bored within her
own perfection; life become too dull between excitements ...

She could be generous, impulsive (but, again, within her own
territory; all was related to the known and admired, never to
the unknown, the despised). She had poise, elegance, wit,
temper, and courage, a long memory of kindnesses, a short one
of jealousies, the malicious remark, later regretted. She liked
and expected people to have fluency, ability in the everyday
things. That an old lady should be terrified to use a telephone,
or a workingman be ill at ease in a restaurant, or that a young
man or woman should be ashamed to expose their bodies on a

beach and let the equally imperfect world see them, was beyond her comprehension, or, to be more accurate, outside the time she could spare.

Professionally, Sheila was five foot nine tall, weighed eight stone eleven pounds, was a slender 34–20–34, had blue eyes and brown hair. She was ageless in appearance – a beautiful, fashionable woman – but to meet her, talk to her, was to obtain the impression she was perhaps twenty-nine and wearing well. In fact, she was twenty-three years old, had been a model for five years, and was now one of the top forty in the world. Much was expected of her because of her elegance and competence, but at twenty-three much could be excused, forgiven. At that age, even with her Cheltenham education and Swiss finishing school, she could be expected to look down from perfect health and tremendous energy and observe with perplexity or even disdain the distresses and weaknesses of her elders in the certainty that she would remain different. She would grow old, yes, but not like that. She would marry, yes, it would be delightful, but *she'd* never make a mistake like that ... She had no religion or politics; those things simply didn't enter her life; they were too boring and she was at full throttle. A great deal of her day was devoted to self, before the mirror or camera, across the restaurant table, being attended to or complimented by others. She lived in a small, slick flat in St John's Wood, rather far from her work and other models, but it was peace when she wanted it, a haven, with only the wretched telephone to interrupt. She had been seduced when she was sixteen by a married man who had wrecked his own life, identifying that exceptional beauty, unable to resist seizing it while it was still in his ordinary world. Sheila had never quite recovered from that foolish passion. There had been some subsequent affairs. Morality meant nothing to her, nor did immorality; she sought neither. Men were interested in her – they were a bore, often a nuisance – but only occasionally did they get beyond the penetrating scornful isolation that she could, if she wished, obtain.

She flicked the pages of *Bizarre*, recognizing some of her friends – Ann, Heather, Suzie, John, Vivian – and after a while sought the stewardess. 'Darling, what's for breakfast? I'm famished.'

Some hours later she walked about the air terminal, stared at, she knew, and found a telephone booth.

A female voice answered, a touch of Continental in the 'Hello?'

'Janine, darling, it's me, Sheila.'

'Oh! We weren't expecting you . . .'

We. Sheila smiled inside the dirty air of the phone box. A man, of course. Naughty Janine, using the flat like that. 'Oh well,' she explained, 'you know these airlines. They do crazy things with the clock.'

'What was it like?'

'Fabulous. And the money – four times London.'

'Where are you?'

'Kensington.'

'Listen, I didn't know, you see, Sheila, and I asked a friend for lunch –'

'I'd love to meet him. But more than anything, Janine, I want tea, buckets of tea. Can you cope? And then sleep. My God, I'm so tired. I thought I was tough, Janine, but New York took off a stone.'

'There is a plane to Paris this afternoon.'

'Don't rush away because I'm back.'

'I'm due back tomorrow anyway.'

'There's a dear little man waiting anxiously for the phone.'

There was so little English currency in her handbag that Sheila travelled by tube train, carrying her heavy case along platforms. She breathed the hot dusty air, observed the corset advertisements. She never did those; she was above them, in editorial, perfumes, costumes, frocks, hats. As usual, men were staring – little men sniggering without hope in groups, damning her as some kind of superior slut because they could never make her, and some heavy businessmen (I don't usually travel like this; I have a car) smiling tentatively. She had long since acquired the art of not seeing them, although she still disliked public travel. Her profession and her own startling beauty had long since driven her to the safety of taxis, other people's cars, her own baby Fiat, expensive restaurants, night clubs, country pubs. . . . It was not so bad in certain streets of central London – the famous and fashionable strolled almost in crowds – but in suburbs, on buses and in dreary provincial cities, they stared as if she were illuminated; her only privacy was the absurdity of the film star's smoked glasses.

It was an eight-storey block of flats, new, handsome, expensive (her rent was eleven pounds a week), very pleasant and quiet, with an excellent restaurant on the ground floor. The porter greeted her as she went in. 'Hello, Miss Haward. How nice to see you back.'

She warmed to the welcome – that he should remember her so easily after four weeks.

'It's nice to be back,' she answered.

In the lift the inevitable rude stare – she wouldn't meet the opposing eyes, was only conscious of the man's electric stiffness; a new tenant, presumably.

Janine, dark, tall, superbly beautiful, heavily made up – green eye shadow, artificial lashes, cream, nails like fluorescence, a beautiful mouth covered with the fashionably pale ·651 lipstick (it meant that whatever the pressure of application the result was a pink film of ·651 mm., so you couldn't go wrong), Janine, pleasant, promiscuous Janine, greeted her affectionately, 'But how wonderful you look! Where did you get it?'

'Off the peg, Janine.'

'I don't believe it!'

'Honestly. It was such a dream thing I couldn't resist it. Fifty-eighth Street. Or was it Fifty-second? These American streets . . .'

They conversed very rapidly and in extreme technical pleasure for long moments, other things forgotten, until a man's voice complained, 'Am I not to be introduced?'

Laughter, and then Janine, slightly conscious of that slip of the tongue over the telephone, 'This is Peter. He's been sweet to me, even speaks French. This is Sheila. Isn't she just like I told you?'

'Better, I'd say.'

He was good-looking, thirtyish, large, heavy, curly-haired, kind of cheeky in a permissible way.

'There are stacks of letters for you,' Janine informed her. 'You did say you were tired, didn't you? So I didn't think you'd want to go out. I'm preparing lunch here. Do you mind?'

'That would be perfect.'

All the time Peter's eyes were staring, having a look, were interested. It was very complicated. He knew that she knew and also that he knew that she knew – oh, God, this was ridiculous. She talked about New York, fashions, photographers, traffic, hotels, while her eyes and her mind examined the letters. From a woman: 'I think you look so charming and wish you would tell me the secret of poise, and what, oh what, do you do to your hair, it is so natural . . .' An income-tax demand for £563; it didn't hurt too much – her accountant had told her it would be 'about £600'. From a man, writing unknown – who was it? Lord Duguid? – 'You were introduced to me at the Cotton thing and I am wondering if I may be so bold . . .' Letters from David, George, Ian, and Mr Harley. One from Mummy: 'I hope it was all exciting and interesting for you and that you return safely. I just don't like airplanes. I went in one in 1932 and I remember . . . Fomes is being a little difficult. I really don't know why Daddy keeps him on . . . General Brand came to see us on Thursday, Daddy was so bucked . . .'

'It's such a pleasant flat and the view –'

'I'm sorry,' Sheila said, startled.

Peter was probing, she knew, wanted to come again, without Janine – a party, a dinner, gramophone records, any excuse; his eyes betrayed him just as easily as he was prepared to betray Janine. Still, he was terribly good-looking. It was impossible not to be satisfied that within seconds he was prepared to jettison Janine.

'She's doing the lunch.'

'Yes, I worked that out,' Sheila told him. He was just a bit too confident, successful. 'Are you on the stage?' she asked. His good looks and confidence had a touch of theatre.

'Hell, no, I'm in insurance.' He laughed, and interest faded. She liked men to be exciting, but *insurance*! Terribly morbid. 'Marine insurance,' he supplemented, rather quickly as if he'd said inside his head, 'Even in insurance we have our little snobberies.'

'What's the news in London?'

She meant trade news, or social gossip, but he answered, 'Another little man's gone out into space, and a few thousand people have been murdered in another African crisis.'

If there was a touch of criticism in his voice Sheila did not notice it.

'It's such a bore.' She sighed. 'I can't *think* why there's all this fighting.' Meaning that there were more important things to attend to: tra-la-la pyjamas (sweet delights for steamy nights); the enchanting new Woof! perfume, made, packaged, and sealed in Paris; new, dramatic, and simple, in white, navy, lime, ice, écru, lavender, mushroom: wool with a scarf-collar of a bias jumper, by Charles Leonard. White straw sombrero by Michael Rebé. Worn with today's face: creamy, dreamy, pallor, pale lips, pearlized colour at the eyes . . . She was so acclimatized to freedom that it was impossible for her to take seriously the world of ideas, emotions (so absurdly out of control, stupid) not concerned with things or the love between individual people. 'Still, perhaps it's good for the insurance business,' she concluded.

'You did ask –'

'Oh, not you, Peter. You're a darling. But they are terribly silly, aren't they?'

'I'd like to be terribly silly,' he told her quietly, outrageously.

'You must be insured against positively *everything!* Or is it for? For or against. I wouldn't know.'

'You should be insured –'

'Oh, don't turn dreary . . .'

'I was just concerned. You are superbly beautiful –'

'So is Janine . . .'

'You were terribly generous . . .'

'Absurd. It's a practice among Continental and London models.'

'Such generosity should be repaid. May I take you to dinner perhaps?'

'It was generosity toward Janine.'

'But she returns to Paris.'

'I'm going to be awfully busy for weeks.'

'May I phone you then?'

'Well – you can try!'

'You're not engaged or anything?'

'I'm not engaged. I wouldn't know about the anything.'

Lunch, and further impertinence impossible. He would phone and she would make up her mind then. But insurance – heavens, what next?

She was exhausted, not merely by the night flight but by four weeks of concentrated living. They were packing – an absurd pretence that all the cases belonged to Janine – and she was yawning – rare, for she had tremendous stamina, but New York . . . well, she could take Paris and Rome in her stride, but New York, God, what a place!

'Be a darling, Janine, before you go,' as she rubbed hands together with cream, 'and phone Maurice for me. My hands are a mess and my hair's out of Macbeth. Oh, and if he can manage tomorrow, make it afternoon because I must see my agent in the morning.'

They went out in a breath of coats and perfume and Janine's ·651 which was sensual, collision-proof, and Peter's eyes delighting in past guilt, present intrigue, future hopes . . . Sheila slept, woke at five, lifted the pink telephone and spoke to her agent. She could hear the girl saying, 'Sheila's back,' and again the warmth of belonging, being needed. 'Audrey, yes, I am indeed back,' and a long, excited technical conversation, what's happened and who wanted her, the Grandchester Hotel on Tuesday, Hanover Square on Wednesday, Globe Place all day Thursday, Grosvenor Street Friday, the distinguished list of the most fashionable people in London who wanted *her* face, her hands, her form, her feet, for the most exclusive items in the feminine world.

The phone rang at seven. David. 'Darling, how nice to hear you.'

'I've got a new Jag. I thought perhaps you'd like to –'

'Do you mean *really* new?'

'Well, no. Fifty-eight model.'

'David, I'm pooped now, but in a day or two –'

'Friday?'

'Splendid.'

And at nine Ian rang.

'Did you get my letter?'

'Yes, Ian. It was terribly sweet of you to welcome me home like that.'

'What was New York like?'

'Marvellous. A real dream place. But exhausting.'

'I suppose you'll be as busy as hell for days ...'

Ian had this curious habit of being dejected before he started. 'I expect so, Ian.'

'It was just that I've two tickets for Friday's –'

'Oh, what a shame. I'm engaged Friday.'

No explanation offered, none requested.

'How about next Tuesday?'

'What had you in mind?'

'Nothing special. I just wanted to see you.'

'Well, think of something, Ian, and I'll see. Can you phone me again?'

She was like this with all of them – quite frank about the value of her time. She was in love with no one, nothing, except the pleasures of living.

'You're using your hands,' complained Captain Dean. 'The foil handle is so designed that it can be controlled by the fingers and thumb. Hands are too heavy, too slow. Even small ones like yours,' he added quickly. 'Let me show you again.'

He demonstrated, manipulating her fingers. If it was an excuse for touching her hand – but no, even she didn't think it was. It was rare for Sheila to feel clumsy, but she did now. 'I'll drop it,' she protested.

David said, 'You won't, poppet. It's so light.'

'Try it again,' urged Captain Dean. 'Try to make a straight thrust. I shall be in the line of engagement and will remain partly covered to start with.'

Instead of doing as she was instructed, Sheila passed her foil over his in a quick cutover, but he defended easily despite the unexpected and parried with a semicircular movement, deflecting her blade and scoring a hit in his riposte.

He was a little ruffled.

'Don't be in a hurry, Miss Haward. Learn first, show your skill afterward.'

'Sorry,' said Sheila. 'That was rather silly.'

'Five minutes,' David pointed out. 'All that's allowed for women.'

'Ah, but Miss Haward is no ordinary woman.'

'I was quoting the rules,' David said rather disagreeably. He was anxious to be elsewhere, alone with her. This was a bore.

'Miss Haward is still under instruction,' Captain Dean explained.

'Are you tired, Sheila?' David asked pointedly.

'Don't be ridiculous.'

'All right,' said Captain Dean. 'Now, let's try some more.'

He was a short, plump man of about forty-four, with an absurd blond moustache, but on his own territory he had something; outside it, he would probably be a boring clubman, coarse jokes and the next drink. Despite his mask, she knew perfectly well that he was a little disconcerted by her, being more used to public-school boys and film actors who needed the instruction for some part. He was very intent on business – it was obviously the one thing in the world he knew very thoroughly, of course – but he was aware of the waiting David, languid and handsome, and would have preferred him elsewhere.

'Now, this time I shall have the right of way and you must defend.'

Sheila was a fraction hesitant; he took it so seriously. She took the on-guard position.

'If you can parry my attack,' said Captain Dean, 'then carry on with the riposte.'

'Do a Hollywood in fact,' David said sourly, but Captain Dean clearly didn't like this droll commentary on his profession.

Sheila held her head high, thought she could see the opposing expression through the captain's mask: shyness, concern, sensuality, interest. She was determined to win this small engagement, although it was ridiculous, only her fifth period of instruction. Captain Dean extended his sword arm in line with Sheila's left breast, at the same time raising his right knee and extending his left leg behind him. His left arm dropped in stiff theatrical parallel to his left leg as his right foot stamped the ground, and he lunged slightly upward and the point of his foil touched her breast, stayed for one arrogant instant. She had watched this in such fascination that she went to pieces, forgot everything, failed to counter him at all, and for a dreadful moment felt the nervous urge to knock his foil aside with her free hand.

Captain Dean removed his mask. 'That,' he said with a slight, comfortable smile, 'is known as the development. I think you had a fit of nerves.'

'Yes, I'm sorry. David puts me off.'

The captain was pleased now. He'd won, proved something, could now be magnanimous. 'Don't be sorry,' he said. 'I think you'll be fine very soon. Will you stay for a drink?'

David said, 'We're rather late. We've got to get to Brighton.'

The captain's face suffered very slightly as if David had said more than this. 'Well, see you soon, Miss Haward.'

'Yes. Thank you.'

Sheila strolled from the *piste*, conscious of other admiration, the captain, slightly humiliated, standing there, not knowing what to do. (They didn't usually refuse a drink. They were eager to spend an hour in the bar, talking, analysing the game; it kept him in the position of expert.) She was supreme now in *her* element, clothes and form and poise; she was wearing a white, divided skirt, but somehow it conveyed an impression of fashion, expense, something better than the regulations required.

'Clever little beast, isn't he?' David said outside the stale air of the club. His Jaguar was parked among crates of beer bottles, small trees and shrubbery, all very untidy, water heard not far away in some small stream, an impression of countryside, although a hundred yards up the rough track was a dual carriageway and seven miles away London ....

She had changed back into her slacks and jumper; she lit a cigarette now and said, 'Oh, I don't know. What was all that about Brighton? I start at ten tomorrow.'

'Just to irritate him. I hate these men who paw you with their eyes.'

'They all do,' she said with unintentional vanity.

David smacked her lightly on her bottom. 'I'm guilty, too,' he admitted, but there was hope in his voice, expectation.

'It's a beautiful monster,' Sheila said, looking at the Jaguar. 'Have you done the ton in it?'

'Give me a chance. I've been in town ever since I bought it.'

'Let's do the ton, David,' she pleaded. 'Let's go to that little place –'

'The Cock and Pigeon?'

'Yes. I'm ravenous.'

'Have to raise the tyre pressures.'

'I wonder,' said David in irritation five minutes later, 'what all these silly little people are doing?'

Seven o'clock in the evening of a mid-September day. The sun going down on their right, causing trees to glitter. It was warm, but the amount of traffic was inexplicable. Why weren't silly little people where they belonged – in front of their TV sets or in the local or putting dreary kids to bed?

Ten minutes beyond this, however, David, cruising at seventy, tense with interest, Sheila smoking by his side, said, 'This is better. There's a Porsche up ahead and the bypass in a mile. Let's move!'

They were doing ninety when they passed the Porsche, itself moving at eighty or so. Sheila stared at the occupants of the smaller car and then, waving, said, 'It's John and Vivian.'

David asked with slight worry, 'Who the hell are they?'

'Ex-actors, darling. Not to worry. They're male models.'

'They're coming up in quite lively style. Good little bus, the Porsche.'

The bypass came up. David stepped on everything for the damn silly roundabout that slowed all traffic down. Just over half a minute later he said excitedly, 'The ton, Sheila. Where's the Porsche?'

'Stuck behind some dreary little man in a Zephyr.'

David laughed, forgot the German car, and concentrated, almost by will, on urging his own car faster.

'A hundred and eight,' he shouted above the shriek of air, the pounding cylinders.

Sheila was not the slightest bit intimidated. She loved it. It was their world – dependence on metal, the tyre pressures, piston area, compression ratio, castor angle, valve timing, revs per minute, disc brakes, tiny exploding drops of petrol. She under-

stood the specification, knew David, relied confidently on both.
It was the same technical confidence that kept her at the top
of her own world – ·651, and Maurice in Bond Street and the
creams, powders, colours, scents: the perfection was in maintenance as well as original design.

On the road ahead David saw, nearly a mile away, some fool
in an old Singer going from lane to lane – farting about
courageously at fifty-five. Woman driver, he analysed, with
contempt, meaning middle-aged, not like *her*. He began to
slow, perfectly aware that the driver ahead wasn't looking in
her mirror at all, and, sure enough, it *was* a woman driver
and, just as expected, she began to pull out (for no reason what-
soever) into the right-hand lane as David shot by at eighty-five.

'She nearly had kittens,' Sheila commented dryly.

'Ouch!' David hissed, looking in his mirror. 'She nearly
pranged your friends.'

'Not friends,' Sheila pointed out. 'Business acquaintances.
Terribly amusing, for all that.'

'For all what?'

'You know.'

'Oh,' said Sheila, ten minutes later, 'how disappointing.
They've enlarged the place.'

'How dreary,' David agreed. 'Suburban.'

He arranged for their dinner and they strolled into the bar.
It was low, of stone, an impressive grate with inglenook, lanterns and beams, wood and thick, soft carpets; coloured lights
over the bar shone on labels from France, Italy, Holland, Germany. A few people were dancing in a larger, adjacent room.

'People dancing –'

'Terribly old-fashioned, though.'

'Shall we?'

'One or two, then a drink?'

People, middle-class, heavy, without the local accent, had
turned to look at the tall girl in slacks; one or two women
may even have identified her as the face on this month's *Bizarre*.
The air murmured with approval. Very few were critical, even
in the tiny ballroom, of her slacks. There were a few peasants
(who'd be eating elsewhere – fish and chips for two bob while
David paid a guinea or two) and these were frank in approval,

while the young people who'd come in their hotted-up Minis
glanced with sly interest. Girls' mouths tightened with annoyance as male heads turned. Sheila heard a peasant say, 'Christ,
see that?' to another youth in passing and a tiny exhalation
of approval. But not to notice, that was the thing. Nice, for
all that so long as they didn't make claims – 'I've seen your
face' – or become a nuisance. David was superb – he was a
natural; they fitted perfectly, were made for each other, as the
recorded song said, too loudly. All the same, they mightn't be
here again : a new landlord, very much the peasant; the types
were rather grim. Not to worry. David as smooth as his Jaguar,
and she was tireless, tireless, tomorrow Globe Street and those
darling matte jerseys in drip-dry trincotate plin-lon, styled by
that heavenly little man – what was his name? – awfully difficult, pronounced with a sneeze, spell it Grzimek. Why hadn't
Ian rung? He would. Hurt little thing. This was pretty corny,
though, after that spot on East Fifty-sixth Street, so painfully
correct and ashamed were the English in their pleasures.

'On duty tomorow?'

'Afternoon,' David said.

'Where to?'

'The Rome trip.'

'Wish I was coming.'

A new record on now. Time for a drink. . . . The music was
too sweet for them. Stared at again, a little dislike in it somewhere, the desire to humiliate such competence, arrogance, and
the Negro girl sang from a box :

> Hate me,
> Disintegrate me,
> But don't never, never underrate me,
> 'Cause I've got a mind o' my own.

In the bar, leaning on it – a professional kind of lean, as if
the camera wanted a man leaning on a bar, but not to sag –
Vivian and John.

'Hello, there.'

Introductions by Sheila.

'Did you do the ton?'

'God, yes, we were doing it when that clot in her Singer
moved over . . .'

'Sheila, poppet, what'll it be?'

'Martini, David, terribly dry.'

'And you?'

You couldn't really tell with Vivian. He was big and clumsy and confident and asked for a pint. He was terribly droll, especially about his work. But with John you identified (not, strangely enough, on bromide paper, only in the flesh), and he knew it, poor lamb, and suffered, even blushed, especially out here where these things weren't understood, taken in their stride – the present landlord's dropped eyes, a face turned too quickly, a snigger somewhere as John asked, 'A gin and tonic. No lemon, please.'

She could tell he *adored* Vivian, doted on him utterly. Poor darling man. Terribly amusing, though, to realize that he modelled golf clubs and big cars and tweed suits for *men*.

> Accost me –
> Defrost me –
> But never, never double-cross me,
> 'Cause I've got a mind o' my own.

'Yours is a 3·8, isn't it?'

'Alas, no, only 3·4.'

'Awfully sweet, though. Went past us like a bomb.'

'What d'you get out of your Super 90? It is a Super 90, isn't it?'

'Alas, no, a mere Super 75.'

Laughter . . .

Sheila's thin wide mouth smiled enigmatically. What, she wondered, do they actually *do*? Who makes the first tactile move? Whatever and whoever, it would be highly interesting to find out. The delicious absurd moment of climax – trousers were the ultimate absurdity. She felt her own flesh slightly warm with electric sensuality, remembering one very naughty night in New York (God, how drunk the man was), the slide of clothes and her own wonderful body, a bit skinny, she supposed, but . . . She was wearing slacks herself tonight. How very awkward. Oh, dear, David was going to try something, she felt it in her very bones – or somewhere. Should she let him? Such a clever boy, piloting that enormous aircraft. So smart, he had the heater on in the car for twenty minutes and, although she knew damn well why, Sheila asked, 'Why the warmth, David? Growing plants on the rear seat?'

'You know damn well why!'

'Such a considerate boy, but overconfident.'

'Darling, you've been away ages . . .'

'Yes, I know, but in a car! Awfully untidy!'

He parked in some lane, lights out, pleaded a bit; it was awfully hard to refuse him. It wasn't quite love, but he certainly was the one she liked best of them. The warmed air and the awkward posture and David terribly eager and the pangs of it, a flicker of sensuality, moments when she forgot everything, became crude, like a shopgirl, and then all over, rather embarrassing, sorting things out, and then David, a new David, worried, on his own, no engines or pounding cylinders to pull him . . .

'Darling, why not marry me?'

Her eleventh proposal, but it shook her, quite unexpected, even though David was rather special.

'David, don't be a bore. Can you imagine me at the stove, the washing? Isn't this fun enough? Marriage is so binding, so humiliating for the woman.'

It wasn't that at all. She was in search of permanency just like the shopgirls, but something indefinable, fierce, painful, hopeless, total. He was nice and had an exciting job, but at heart, despite the Jag and the Viscount at thirty thousand feet, he was the boy next door.

'It doesn't matter. Sorry if I was a bore.'

But it did matter. He was hurt; this had been accumulating. While Sheila was in New York he must have thought –

'When I'm old and grey ask me again,' she told him lightly.

He seemed relieved, as if this last was a hint that no one else was involved. It was all rather complicated, or would be. What would happen now? Would things be as before? No. There'd be a new relationship, the small hurt in his face, the humiliation, rejection, every time. How would he treat her? She'd been rather crude tonight. A weekend in Rome and another in (of all places) Düsseldorf and a crazy one at Brighton and some heavy petting, permitted in her flat, but those all had had an air of sophistication, an affair. She should have refused him tonight. Would he now regard her as just one of the girls he could paw on the seats of his Jag? Inexpensive, not worth a hotel bill? Someone he nearly, but not quite, thank God, married. Very complicated. Never the same after a proposal.

'Turn the lights on, David, sweet. I must do my hair.'

'Would you like to try the Jag.'

Sheila kissed him. 'You are a darling. I'm sorry I'm so mean. I'll think about it.'

It wouldn't be complicated. *Status quo.* She could tell that he had relaxed, that was the way he wanted it. He was helling around with one of the most beautiful girls in the world. It was a status. She supposed he mentioned it to his co-pilot, navigator, even the stewardess. He wanted the *status quo,* to try again in a year or two.

She drove the Jaguar as fast as her courage, unfamiliarity, and the darkness would allow. After a while she became completely confident but even so came up to one or two corners too fast and without the time to change to a lower gear. The car wallowed and she had to struggle with the wheel. On long straight stretches she did not exceed seventy miles an hour because of the dark and thus came around a long bend in the road well under control, to find a policeman standing in the road, some vans at all angles, two cars locked in metallic destruction, and glass all over the road like spilled sugar. One of the two cars was the Porsche.

'Stay there,' David suggested. 'I'll go and see what's happened.'

Sheila was conscious of the cool night air, the voices, a silence that had brutal finality. Then an ambulance arrived. A quarter of an hour went by before David returned to the car.

'I'm sorry, darling. They've taken your friends away.'

'Are they all right?'

'I'm afraid not.'

'I see.'

After a while she asked, 'What happened?'

'Oh, they came around the bend and – well, you can *see* – those three post-office vans were parked there, doing a repair – *three* vans just around a fast bend! I ask you – if there'd only been one –'

'Someone was coming?'

'Two old fools in a Morris Minor or something. Panicked, of course. Just braked; didn't do a damn thing with the steering wheel despite the six-foot verge.'

Not their fault.

Two old fools in a Morris Minor.

'Can I do anything?' she asked.

'They've taken them away.'

David spoke like someone in a war. 'One of our cars is missing. Pranged by two old fools in a Minor.'

Not to worry.

It happened despite the technical excellence and the maintenance and the human skill. Law of averages or something. There were fools in the world, people who panicked.

Other people.

Vivian had been terribly funny about the time he modelled string vests.

I must phone Audrey, tell her about it.

She'll be fascinated.

She hated the sight of him.

An hour later, David departed, his smoke still hanging in the flat like a depression, Sheila stretched out her perfect, elegant, unshaken hand for the pink telephone but hesitated. It was, after all, midnight. It would keep. The perfect digits sought a gold cigarette case. One more and then sleep. Rather tired. Very emotional evening. Love in the heated car, the hunger pangs that made her thrust her thighs upward for long, crude moments; David's proposal, her eleventh, not counting the several score from strangers, through the post; that beautiful Porsche wrecked and Vivian and John, two people from *her* world, killed because – None of it really touched her.

The phone rang and she jumped, not wanting to be bothered; she'd had her quota for the day, now needed, more than needed, the proportion of sleep so that tomorrow she would face the cameras in flawless subtle vanity. It rang and rang. It would be Ian or Mr Harley or even David. Not work.

She had to answer, become involved, because it would inevitably be relevant to that vehicle of perfection, herself. The only people who knew this telephone number were people who had the privilege of being given it. The long slender left arm reached for the pink instrument of communication, and the mind that operated the limbs and the eyes, pivoted the perfect neck, rejected everything previous to this moment and became fascinated and absorbed in the extant now.

2

GEOFFREY SUMPSTER

THEY were discussing Geoff Sumpster as he entered Barton's room.

'I've had a bellyful of him. You know he was around my neck for two terms.'

'You can't even be rude to him.'

'Is it an inferiority complex or a superiority?'

'Still, he knows his history –'

'Oh, my God, no. He thinks Deverson's the ultimate.'

'Deverson's pretty good.'

'Christ, George, Deverson's just a bloody journalist –'

'They've always got him on TV.'

(A sure sign of decadence, lack of scholarship, the fatal mistake of being a popular historian.)

'It's his bleeding poetry that gets me.'

'Has the *New Statesman* rejected that one about solitude?'

Laughter, dying gradually as he entered.

All he heard was the word 'solitude', but their averted eyes and silent tongues conveyed the antipathy. The rejection was in his pocket, no letter, just a printed thing; Christ, it was unbearable; he'd suffered writing that thing. They wouldn't understand. The herd. They all grinned now and made careful insults, but alone, and sometimes they were alone with him, it was, 'Yes, Geoff,' or 'Well, Deverson's certainly accurate,' or, 'I'd like to write poetry, but there's bugger-all left to write about.'

He was nearly six feet tall and heavy, a good boxer, an intelligent mind, but something wrong in the assembly. They didn't like him because he said what he thought and, honestly, he thought, he *knew*, he'd have poetry in every London rag before long; it was just a question of getting past the bloody London name pressure. And they were so gutless, without ambition, and (in the herd) they sneered and took the mickey (but with caution, in awe of the fists) when he said he'd be a headmaster before he was thirty-five. Christ, what did they want to be teachers for? He was a solitary, too individual for them, that was it. Well, he was tolerant, generous – they couldn't deny that. He was big, but that didn't mean he wasn't sensitive. He was very sensitive; he'd had to resort to the psycho boys, and even now the little red pills were there when depression got him.

Herd unhappiness – he didn't belong to a herd, but he must suffer the herd process, the machination of becoming a teacher. They never doubted that would happen though they often doubted themselves; that proved he was good. Later, being a solitary, he would find his own pattern and framework within which he could live. But at present he *must* live in college with a lot of people who didn't understand him, who teased him, hurt him. Not that he was unpopular – he was wanted for every social, drinking session, party, dance – and it wasn't because of his money. (Though some of them, the unwashed, hated that canning factory in Capetown.) And they were nearly all nigger lovers. He had to be careful about that. Once or twice he'd flared up because on the subject of apartheid and the Union they talked a load of crap, just like a rag-bag newspaper . . .

(He wanted to be popular, but neither the psychologists nor the canning factory nor the money nor the singsongs – nothing could do it. He was assembled badly.)

They welcomed him in bitter camaraderie.

' 'Morning, Geoff.'

'Here's the man of the moment, the budding poet laureate, the power behind the throne . . .'

'See Joan last night, Geoff? Where d'you get to?'

He was young enough, despite previous experience, to feel some of it was genuine interest.

'We went to that French film at the Galaxy.'

'Did she get steamed up?'

'Joan'd screw any time I asked.'

'When y'going to ask, Geoff?'

'I went to see it. I thought it was a load of crap.'

'I didn't like it much,' admitted Geoff.

'Did Joan hold your hand?' (Said with three other implications.)

The door of the small students' room swung open violently; paperbacks fell; faces, as desired, all turned. A bearded, stocky student, a ferocious Christ, pullover in holes, slacks without a crease – he'd obtained the desired attention. Lively green eyes above the beard, this was Jack Tharp, seducer of women, drinker of pints, ex-Navy, who (via no logical process) was liked as much as Geoff Sumpster was despised.

'Gentlemen! Time for tucker.'

'What's on, Jack?'

'Bangers and pigs' earholes.'

'It's too late for hall anyway.'

'Then along the road to Geraldine's, eh, gentlemen?'

'Can you lend me one and ten, Jack?'

'I was about to ask you the same economic question, mate.'

'Geoff –' (Prove your popularity, earn it, pay for it; we'll try to stomach you.) 'Can you?'

He was anxious to oblige, to make a friendly gesture, obtain obligations, camaraderie. He knew he'd never get it back, was even aware he could never buy or obtain their friendship, but he went on trying. (A solitary, but in need of something, affection, admiration; whatever it was, he rarely had it.)

'Thanks, Geoff.'

But spoiled straightaway by another student: 'I wish I was rich and had a pa who owned a factory in South Africa.'

Jack, impartial, with the wisdom of a lunatic, reprimanded, 'Don't be such a miserable bastard. Amen. Geoff doesn't have to give his pa's money away.'

In the room, the simple bed, suitcase, mountain of textbooks and paperbacks – Kafka and Lady Chatterley and T. S. Eliot and Lucky Jim and nine hundred pages of Deverson and (on the floor, soiled to ribbons) *Sex Sense* – a hopeless pursuit of important minds and lost values. What am I? What

may I be, do, obtain? Mixed with the confused urges and dis-
comforts of crowd process and uneasy thoughts of the future.
I believe in nothing, can respect no one, yet I am to teach.
(One in five was a homosexual, one in twelve a Communist, one
in six a Catholic.) In college the lectures and the sports and the
communal everything (the toilet was the only aloneness); in
their spare time writing (a few typed), and learning, the perusals
of respected opinions (the *Observer* on Sundays, various on
weekdays, an occasional surrender to pornography and TV
values). An insatiable craving for music – sadness and despair
and frustration identified, lost, overcome in the scratching
symphonies from someone's transistor. They were silent then;
eyes didn't meet; they smoked and picked at fingernails. Music
was the only emotion permissible (except for the queers who
had a club – the subject of much sensational conjecture – a
few streets away).

Out of the room, the linoleum corridor, ranks of other
rooms, showers, toilets, iron staircases, old lecture rooms and
laboratories, tired bits of grass and a million tissue-paper brown
September leaves and slender, dejected trees and a high wall
like a prison or a monastery (the chaplain had a nice pink-
brick modern house) and a main road. The foreign cars and
the grey buses taking people to London Airport and the
glamour of the rest of the world (the green and blue and brown
of *The Times* atlas). An area of old pubs and greengrocery
shops and people who were straight from *Pygmalion*. A few
transport cafés, and one of them was Geraldine's.

It was empty.

'Morning, Geraldine.'

'Oh, hello, lads. What y'having?'

A happy, exhausted middle-aged face, a world removed from
their experiences, but no resentment. Live and let live, I always
say. I've had my fun, laughter, alcohol stunning the appalling
memories of degradation and poverty and childbearing and
disappointment and humiliating ill-health. So long as y'can
smile.

'Beans on toast.'

George, who had a knack of saying the tedious inevitable:
'Every little bean has the right to be obscene.'

'And coffee?'

'Fine, Geraldine, fine.'

'Nice morning.'

The hard tar macadam and the endless stream of steel; litter on every yard of the pavement; old dirty walls and buildings as far as the eye could see, the mind reach; a sense of defeat, reality. This was reality; theory was in the newspapers, the lecture rooms. They lived two lives, what was intended and what was here, in the way.

They were talking about Deverson, couldn't get away from him; he was like a sore: they must scratch, refuse healing. Deverson was important – on television, six books to his credit, on committees – and yet he mixed with them. Some therefore wanted to take him down a peg, prove him mortal, as they were; others admired him, were in danger of being sycophants.

Sam said, 'Speaking for myself, I think Deverson's a prick. Nothing personal, Geoff, it's just my opinion.'

'Deverson happens to be a historian of twenty years' experience,' said Geoff. 'You are – what are you? – starting your second year's study of history. Right?'

The same remark was true of himself, but conceit overrode that. He had the frontal, non-debatable habit of bringing discussion to the point where either one agreed with him or risked his fists.

Sam countered weakly, 'I was talking about Deverson, not me.'

'But are you qualified to talk?' demanded Geoff. He had to rub the other's nose in it; that was his weakness, why he found friends hard to keep. He could see the fright in Sam's face and the evasive eyes of the others, ashamed, he believed, of Sam.

Tharp stroked his beard, had the final word, restored order, as usual. 'Anyone who goes in for history must be a nit. Deverson's not a bad bastard ... Got a paper, Geraldine?'

He looked at the already tatty newspaper.

'God, look at this bit of talent.'

'I could use twenty-five minutes with her ...'

(The meaningless longing for sexual perfection; no relation to reality, the half-aroused girl friends or the solitary thoughts in bed.)

'There's more bloody trouble with Terrible Tom,' said Tharp. 'Anyway, United Nations is going in. That ought to be good for a laugh.'

'We were fools to get out,' said Geoff.

'We?' queried George. 'I didn't know South Africa had a part of this.'

'I referred to the white man.'

'You think white men are superior?' asked Sam scornfully.

'Yes,' said Geoff. ' 'Course they bloody well are.'

He was red in the face, had had apartheid thrown at him for nearly two years.

'You'd kick 'em around, let 'em live in shanties, shoot 'em?'

'It's a question of education. They've a hundred years to catch up, two hundred.'

'You think we are so superior, we whites, with H-bombs, concentration camps, war, and all that?'

'You've never seen those *tsotsis* running around.'

They didn't understand a damn thing about South Africa. They looked down their moral noses (in between pornography and hypocrisy) and squeezed the Union out of their bloody empire. They thought of all Africans as one man, and that as a man sitting in some lecture room, polite and sweet and earnest and not smelling too much of nigger. They thought if they sat down in Trafalgar Square and were carried about by poor bloody policemen who couldn't be goaded anyway that they'd seen life, they were doing something. Once, in Jo'burg, he'd seen six thousand of them, drunk on destruction, leaping in the air in an ecstasy of disorder. Thirty-seven people had been killed, and killed in a way that made one sick. He remembered a crowd of them coming out of a dance in Cape and they'd swarmed all around him, hot, greasy, and he'd been scared by a sense of uncontrollable mob, a happy mob (he'd realized that, despite his fear), but one prey to emotions just like a child, ready to smash and destroy buildings, glass, cars, people, fruitlessly, like a kid's toys. Equality! My God, they didn't know what they were talking about.

But in words, in safety, in theory, they could, of course, corner him, prove him wrong.

'Well, why not educate them? Why stick 'em in prison and refuse 'em rights?'

'You don't understand,' he said wearily.

'Make me understand. Explain it to me.'

Sam was getting satisfaction, with the other four on his side.

'We're giving them rights slowly as we're giving them education. Time will make a difference.'

Not that he wanted to see that day. His prejudice was too deep, from birth, and he knew how with the smallest concession they'd find loopholes for more; they were bombastic on the smallest authority, just as they were drunk on the act of destruction.

'How much time?'

'A hundred years.'

'A long time to wait.'

He tried to enlist their sympathies, demonstrate how difficult the problem of sympathy was. 'My mother looked after a nigger once. He'd been slashed in a fight and left at the bottom of the estate. She nursed him for three months. He'd have died otherwise.'

'I hope she made him comfortable,' sneered Barton.

Geoff said, 'Don't be so bloody dirty minded. You don't understand. She had him *in the house*. The white people wouldn't speak to her for two years afterwards.'

'She was a Christian, wasn't she? She was obliged to help him.'

They didn't *want* to understand, that was it.

'Have you had a coloured man living in the home?' he asked, and they hadn't. 'Well, you see, this one was a kind of criminal.'

'How do you know that, Geoff? How d'you know he wasn't just waiting a hundred years for his education?'

Laughter, eager, offensive, against him. They didn't want to understand. But he needed them, couldn't stand alone, and ended it, not altogether weakly, by saying, 'Oh well, you've never lived it, that's the difference.'

'Who's for a game of badminton?'

They wanted him then, because he was useful to have on their side; he'd probably win.

'Ta-ta, Geraldine.'

Over the dry dusty pavements, waiting for rain, and sour-smelling sexless women looking at vegetables and today's headlines in four versions clipped in vertical rows above the coloured sex magazines (invariably disappointing) that one of the students sometimes circulated; through a different gate that was nearer the badminton court, and there, parked in the side road (the college fronted on four roads, two main ones and two minor), there was a taxi, and out of it stepped a little man who looked confused. He had large red ears. Geoff had a tiny memory of having seen him before but thought it must be because he belonged here, and, rather surprising, there was Simpson from the science block to meet him.

Vague dialogue as they passed.

'The impartial frontiers of science . . .'

'You are very kind.'

'We shall be proud to have you in our midst, Mr Antonov.'

'I am glad to be here.'

Beyond that Tharp said, 'I've seen that little bugger before somewhere. Christ, Simpson was practically kissing his arse.'

'All these science bods look like experiments that went wrong!'

Laughter . . .

For forty minutes he, Geoff, was one of them. Not a barbed remark. But in the library afterward he found two more, who crucified the silence by examining *The New Statesman* with deliberate malicious care. 'Don't see your stuff in this week. Are you writing under a pseudonym?'

'Oh, wrap up,' he said angrily.

'Did I say something nasty? Sorry, Geoff. Had another rejection?'

'For Christ's sake shut up,' he told them. 'Don't you ever get tired of your own mediocrity?'

'Oh, God, what a big word!'

He knew they'd repeat it in amusement elsewhere. 'He thinks we're all mediocrities!' There was nowhere he could find comfort. He could be sure of no one's confidence. For two years he'd been Sam's best friend, but now Sam, he suspected, retailed all his confidences to hysterical laughter. The fact that they had similar individual problems wouldn't stop the laughter. He squirmed when he remembered what he'd told Sam about his poetry, Deverson's occasional kind remark, his feelings for Joan.

The windows marked by pigeons shut out the blue sky of September and London's dirty air. Why had he come here? He'd been so eager to travel, see London. Travel broadens the mind; it also broadens the bottom. Thousands of leather-bound books in here, all the thoughts of yesterday, and on the magazine rack the views of today. Angle lights and current literature, an immense library of minds, the people who cared. But no explanation of *this*: the barbed remarks, the rejected poetry, the hatred of South Africa, the loneliness – no one ever came to sit by him at breakfast, lunch, or tea these days; he always had to go in late and sit by them or seek a crowd to drift in with. He was big, but he was sensitive. He hated them, feared them, despised them, wanted them.

They'd been to a symphony concert and sat now in a crowded bus. In theory he was taking her home, but in fact they didn't know what to do, were filling in time.

'I thought the recapitulation was poor,' Geoff said. 'The development was technically perfect, and then that fool sneezed –'

'You're very clever, aren't you?'

He didn't realize it was sarcasm, a whispered rebuke with the implication: don't talk such arrogant rubbish on a bus and don't talk so *loud*. He was conscious that one head had turned and stared with idiot vacuousness, but it didn't put him off; he was trying to impress and interest Joan, not some lout who'd be outside his life in a couple of bus stops.

'Oh no, not clever,' he insisted. 'I'm sensitive to music, that's all. People think because I'm big I'm not sensitive.'

'I think you're clever, but I'm only a girl who works in a shoe-shop. I never went to college.'

(Meaning, although she didn't herself identify it, you only like me because I'm pretty and I wear clothes that arouse you. All you want is what Tom Inman told you about. The indefinable longing for college boy's status without this one's insufferable superiority.)

'Is something the matter?'

'Not more than usual.'

'Didn't you enjoy it?'

'I was bored stiff.'

'So was I,' he acknowledged, but too late: he'd committed himself with several opinions already; she had been very slightly humiliated, unintentionally perhaps, simply because he wanted to impress her. The concert had been her idea, not his, which made it baffling.

'This is where we get off. Want a drink of coffee?'

'I wouldn't mind.'

'What does that mean?'

'If you do.'

'I asked *you*,' he said.

He was beyond understanding that Joan was on edge because she, a nineteen-year-old salesgirl, had felt ill at ease in the concert hall, her first concert.

In a coffee bar Teds stared boldly at her, sniggered from a distance. Music blasted forth from the steel-and-glass monster in a corner. Everywhere were mirrors so that the crowded space seemed treble its own size. Noise and steam and the consciousness of being stared at reduced conversation between them to the proportions of actual embarrassment. They, who had been out together six times, became as strangers. Geoff could see her in the mirrors – half a dozen views of her bored face, sagging, complaining body that autumn clothes couldn't hide. It was failure. Vaguely he'd thought music would condition her; she'd wilted quite a bit the last time, dropped hints about future delightful prospects. Now it was going cold on him; he was no longer sure she even liked him.

'Let's get out of this dump,'

'Your idea,' Joan said.

He was blamed even for the apportionment of the district's Teds. It was her district, not his. He held her hand going across the main road, and although she didn't reject it, Joan complained petulantly, 'I'm not a kid, you know. I can cross roads.'

'You're mad with me.'

'I'm not mad with anyone.'

'You wanted to go to the concert.'

'All right! We've been. Thank you very much.'

'What's the matter, then?'

'Can't a girl be fed up?'

'What are you fed up about?'

'Oh, you wouldn't understand.'

He propelled her from the main road down a back lane, a cul-de-sac of cinders, concrete garages, a few parked cars. Before they'd proceeded many yards, obtained a silence, privacy from public lighting, passing vehicles, other people, he pulled her to the utter darkness of a hedge. It scratched the back of his neck, but he was heedless. His eyes saw a few back windows, illuminated, some upstairs, some downstairs. No voices, not a dog barked; there was poetry in this, Geoff decided. He glowed slightly in the certainty that he could extract beauty from this which, in daylight, would be hideous. He could hear the faint scuff of Joan's feet on cinders, smell her various scents. The voluptuous warmth of her was beginning to excite him.

'Hell, Joan, what's the matter?'

'Nothing, Geoff, really. Just a busy day at work, I suppose.'

'Well, then, don't get moody.'

(Kissing her, opening the autumn coat, five guineas off the peg. Hands around the warmer, firmer waist inside.)

Faint protests. 'I didn't say you could do that.'

'Go on! You like me, don't you?'

'I don't know.'

The doubt in her voice was genuine, alarming.

'What's the matter with me?'

A giggle. 'You're a bit queer.'

(He flinched, misunderstanding, remembering those weeks and months with Sam, a thing he'd worried about. He'd felt an affection for Sam. She's got to let me, he pleaded to himself. I can disprove *that* right now.)

He stroked her breasts. There were thicknesses of material between his hand and the desired flesh, and she scarcely responded.

'There's nothing queer about me. You'll see.'

His hand now up her stockings – the legs firm and the nylon unbearably smooth, sensual – but she closed her knees quickly.

'Geoff, not here!'

'Where, then?'

'You only want me because you think –'

'What do I think?'

'I'm cheap or something.'

'I love you,' he insisted.

(Not aroused sufficiently, he decided. *Sex Sense*, Chapter IV, pages 87 to 93, the ones that got him steamed up. His hands returned, the left to her waist, an exploration below the hips, and the right had difficulty with buttons.)

'You love yourself.'

'Christ, what does that mean?'

He found it quite funny.

The right hand explored below the brassière, but Joan said, 'I don't feel like that.'

'You will in a minute.'

'Geoff, I shan't see you again.'

He was stunned in the very blood.

'Joan, what the hell's up? Tell me.'

'I don't want to hurt you, but I don't think we've anything in common.'

She sounded shaky, a little frightened of his possible reaction.

'But we like each other.'

'I know, but, well, I've got other boys . . .'

Geoff was appalled, but in the middle of his shock was the bitter knowledge: *they'll* find out; they'll ask about her; it'll be something else to laugh about – Geoff never made her . . .

And he wanted to, the urge inside his clothes was like fire . . .

His hands returned to the more sensually desired legs; they weren't going to wilt in pleasure for him.

'Joan, go on, be a sport, just this once.'

'I don't want to.'

'You went with Tom Inman before me,' he accused, pointed out, pleaded, justified.

'Tom Inman's got a nasty mind,' Joan said.

He was caressing her now, kissing, tight together, recommencing at page 2: a woman needs tenderness more than anything.

'I love you,' he persisted, but it sounded feeble, false. Was it true? She was certainly beautiful. Hot thoughts had come into his mind the first time he met her, but hadn't he sought an introduction because of the very hope of her body?

'I'm very sorry,' she answered.

There was no chance now of ever doing it with her, no hope of reciprocation – there was death and finality in her voice – but desire and pain were like a fever, so alone, in the darkness, hard against her breasts and stomach, he was taking her, unknowingly, he thought, in her clothes, standing up.

'You can stop that,' Joan said, stepping away.

He became angry.

'You're mighty pure and innocent all of a sudden.'

'Don't be mad with me.'

But he was, inevitably, and more so as he deduced that she not only wanted to get rid of him; she wanted him nice and polite, available at some future college dance as a success symbol or something.

'Good-bye,' he said with angry finality.

'Oh, are you turning nasty? Good-bye, then, Geoff. I can see myself home.'

And he had to wait until she'd walked along the cinder path to the main road. He saw the distant, desirable silhouette turn right, and when he followed he turned left.

The physical urge was still in his body, hotter with the rejection, and he knew wretchedly how it would end. If only he could find an easier wench to be rid of the ache in his groin. Then he thought of the blonde barmaid, always very friendly to the college lads (but no one had tried anything with her), Barbara, who looked, despite her mere twenty-three years, as if she'd done plenty. He looked at his wrist watch. There was plenty of time; it was not long after nine. Almost as if the thought could become the actuality merely by moving toward it, Geoff ran for the bus.

Desire died twenty minutes later when he entered the pub, two hundred yards from Geraldine's café. It was packed. Desire had forgotten about other people. It was a small bar, one of three. Smoke stung his eyes as he entered; conversation and laughter stunned the senses. Barbara's face, illuminated by small coloured lights (Christmas was only three months away), and her blonde hair reflected in a long mirror, her young/old face (things learned outside college) turned in curiosity to see who had entered. There was interest in her eyes to welcome him, and when the face had to turn back to the monologue of some old woman it did so without indifference.

Bottles and glasses and the blue issue of smoke and the smell of humans, money noises and liquid, yawns, laughs, a small dog, a party in the centre hanging on to every word of a middle-aged woman of the district, fingers overloaded with jewellery, hair and face treated with all that science was at present capable of, but uselessly – nothing had happened; money couldn't make her anything but what she was, a woman of a poor (in the cultural, spiritual senses, plenty of lolly, of course) district, and as if she had heard she offered an immense laugh (thirty guinea teeth, none of your National Health stuff) and said in magnificent confidence, unawareness, 'Me, I wouldn't be anyone else.' And Geoff had almost reached Barbara – to at least enjoy words; words were permissible in a crowd, and she was a mistress of words; she could say ordinary things, make them and him sensual; she could have had a love affair of extreme passion entirely on words – he was almost there when he saw them, five in a discreet corner, their eyes moving, malicious observation; they must almost have read his thoughts, the disappointments and hopes . . .

'Early tonight, Geoff.'

'Been out with Joan?'

'We went to a concert. It was lousy.'

Martin, one of the queers, asked, 'A bad performance, old man?' and the others laughed at his implications.

Geoff reddened and growled, 'What would you know about performing, Martin?' which shut him up, pale and angry, but only temporarily: Geoff knew damn well the hatred these bloody queers could harbour.

Barbara leaned her breasts and jewellery over the bar.

'What's for you, Geoff?'

'He needs a tranquillizer. He's browned off.'

But George's remark was taken at face value by Barbara, who held his hand. It was all relatively meaningless, Geoff was aware, but the fact remained that she only did this sort of thing to those she liked. 'What's the trouble, Geoff? Tell Auntie Barbara.'

'Nothing much,' he said. Her hand was small and warm but rough from hard work. He felt the luxury of pity. Like a bloody nigger's, he thought, although he'd never held a Negro's hand. 'Girl trouble,' he said. 'She wanted too much,' he explained vaguely.

Barbara's eyes became coy. 'A girl can never have too much,' she said. He wondered if she just made these meaningful remarks to satisfy the customers or if she really would ... Like the woman still holding forth in immense platitudes, Barbara was laden with bits of jewellery. Trash, most of it. 'That's an interesting bangle,' he said, still hands-entwined, but fingers exploring the loop around the wrist above.

'All gold,' she explained. 'Every little thing made of gold. It's my security.' The heavy collection of medallions and coins rattled as her arm moved, withdrew. 'We're awfully busy. What tranquillizers did y'want?'

Geoff could not resist the urge for camaraderie. 'What are you lot having?' And they all, even Martin, were prepared to accept pints.

Tharp said, 'What about a game o' cards?'

'All right,' agreed George.

Martin was now eager to get away. 'No money,' he explained. 'Anyway, I'm off to the club for a drink on credit.'

They walked out into the cool air, discussing him.

'He'll be in bloody trouble before the term's over, you see. He's knocking around with an actor.'

'I wonder what they do at that club.'

'Drink, mostly.'

'He'll come back as pale as death, you see. Drinking doesn't do that.'

'It does if you're sick.'

Presumably they talked about him, Geoff, like this when he was elsewhere. There were no secrets in college, no privacy. They knew all about his visits to the psychiatrist and the red pills that kept him happy, all about his morning exercises and soaps and lotions and extreme, fussy cleanliness. And they'd notice when, because he couldn't bear to see it, he removed the photograph of Joan from his cupboard door.

He was winning. He was rather good at cards and usually did win. Now George was looking very anxious, had already lost thirty shillings, and Geoff taunted him, 'What's the matter, George? Scared of losing your money? I thought you were the brainy lad,' and George had nothing to say.

But an hour later he, Geoff, made a bad mistake and they analysed it endlessly until he could scarcely bear it. 'All *right*, so I made a mistake,' he half shouted, but now he was flustered, aware that even his partner wanted him to lose. It aggravated his desperate unhappiness, reminded him of Joan. Not a happy moment in the whole day. They all hated him. *Why?* It was terrifying, filled his stomach with despair, and he longed for the comfort of a red pill.

'I'm going to turn in,' he declared.

'What's a matter?' George asked. 'Scared of losing your money, Geoff?'

He was so angry he shouted, 'Watch it, George, or you'll be for a thick ear. If I want to go to bed I shall go to bed. It's nearly midnight, isn't it?'

They stared at him, not a word out of any of them. There was at least that satisfaction : they couldn't face his violence. Even Tharp didn't stick his neck out.

'Goodnight,' he said breathlessly, and they mumbled a return, their communal blast of laughter and Tharp strumming his guitar, but five yards down the linoleum corridor in darkness he heard and he felt the weak urge to weep.

Solitude. He took a red pill and knew that in twenty minutes he'd feel happy. He hated them. They didn't understand. He felt an unutterable loneliness in London – the roads around the college, dirty, useless, an endless roar of traffic and people who knew what they were doing. It was hard even to convey it in poetry. Perhaps there was no poetry in it. It was too materialistic. He recognized that. His verse ought to be bitter. He'd do one more, just one, as bitter as he knew, everything in this lousy country. There was no beauty here just as there was no God.

He'd prayed to God, earnestly, petitioning Him, but the pain and insults and rejections went on. It was ridiculous to keep turning to a God when you prayed and prayed and nothing happened. (The other people, who never prayed, spat in the face of God, always won, without effort; there'd never been the thought of losing.) It made you feel a fool. He'd talked to the chaplain about it once, and the smooth nigger-loving bastard had an answer. They always had an answer; it was their job: some crap about intensity of prayer and the desirability or selfishness of what was sought. Implying that whatever he, Geoff, prayed for would be selfish. Well, he'd prayed for peace in the world and he'd meant it, and look at the balls-up the world was in! And the chaplain, very interested to hear that he was South African, had started to chew the fat about that, held him, Geoff, responsible for the whole bloody continent. He'd been shocked when Geoff had been truthful (rude, he'd called it) and asked him what he knew about it.

In the darkness and warmth of bed he grinned at the memory of that victory – the smooth prick had gone red, gasped like a fish, couldn't really take argument. No more trouble from *him* – he stuck to soothing the consciences of the queers and such-like problems. It occurred to him – and it was funny, damn funny, so that he giggled in his bed – that he hated England. What a country! It was dirty and it rained and there was only smoke to breathe and everyone was arrogant on the subjects they knew nothing about (especially niggers). You couldn't tell 'em a bloody thing. They knew it all. Well, to hell with them. Once he was back in the Union – if he ever went back, and he would – they could have their bloody atomic war and blow England off the map. A lot he'd care. He'd had a bellyful of the English.

Very slowly he relaxed, ready for sleep, and his mind explored ahead, as a human being's always will, in hope of alteration. Barbara would be impressed. She didn't know he had a lot of money, could buy the lot of them. He'd be kind to her and in return . . . He fell asleep with a slight smile on his face – a boy of twenty, large, fit, and intelligent, but something wrong in the assembly.

CHARLES FILMER

THE twelve-thirty siren blasted the sky and the men and women downed tools, switched off, physically and mentally, they rushed out of the factory, two thousand of them, full of their noises – laughter, grumbles, discussion – and over the main road stamped their way, some of them, on to the waiting buses. Some tooted their way through the crowds amid ribaldry, on scooters; others walked in groups, entered cafés, the quick hot meal, the menu chalked on a board: cottage pie and chips, one and nine, apple tart eightpence, cuppa for three-pence. The humid atmosphere of steam and fat, the shouts across tables for salt, sauce, pepper, and the impertinent examination of any girls present, even a bit of cheek: ' 'Scuse me, love, I need a bit a' pepper,' and the implications under-stood, two or three or four pairs of eyes responding, and the one addressed would make a reply as quickly as could be mus-tered, 'Wanta heat your blood, do you, or start sneezing?' and the other girls would laugh and that would be that unless some-one wanted to take it seriously, prolong it into something else. Afterward, hundreds of them would sit about on walls, or even in the factory grounds, or venture into the nearby park, play football for half an hour. At one-thirty the siren blasted again and like a swarm of bees they went back, laughter, foot-ball talk, newspaper being folded, the last bit of the cigarette sucked to nothing. And in their absence one heard the traffic and the children in a school playground, and after a while the mothers wheeled prams into the park, the pubs closed, and there was a feeling of afternoon, even of the end of the day. Thousands of people adjusted their lives and their clocks by the siren.

One man was different. All men are dissimilar, but whatever it was that all two thousand employees of the Electronics Division of Mayger Electrics had in common, Charles Filmer was without it. He was strange, perfect, too disciplined, without laughter, without coarseness; he had a will of steel; he belonged to some society they who knew him thought was crazy: God on pamphlets, door-to-door arguments. He was not popular – the moral, serious people within a society never are, only the clowns, the beautiful, the weak, the successful. He had no weaknesses except hatred. The hatred was confined within justifiable bounds: he hated the right things, or, rather the wrong things, those that it was necessary to hate: promiscuity, laziness, blasphemy, dirtiness, coarseness, vulgarity. He was clever enough to realize that he hated and that his prejudices, although on behalf of good, were judgements, and it was not for humans to judge. Therefore he did his utmost to control them, said little outside his own family, only exhibiting by his behaviour that he was not on the side of evil. He worked steadily and without pause, a humourless man with rimless glasses and white hair, forty-seven years old, small, pale, opinionated eyes, and a frame thinned down by the burning within – possibly the most dangerous man in the world.

The half-past-twelve siren blasted the October air, scattering birds; the men and girls stopped work and the roar of machines and hundreds of ticking and pulsing and drilling noises were replaced by the human kind.

He could not catch Bull. He had the feeling that Bull, a shop steward, wanted to avoid him, wasn't interested in his pitiless, logical complaints simply because he wasn't interested in Filmer. He was, Filmer knew in icy dejection, not going to do anything for that miserable fornicator (Filmer) who didn't give a sod for the world of beer, football, vulgarity, who was, by gestures and silences, above it. Bull would have the entire electrical industry out on strike for one of *them*, to eat sandwiches, or drink two teas, or go to the toilet, or earn a spot bonus, or go to a match when it was on the way to the Cup, but if he, Filmer, pointed out in his cold, logical clarity that machines weren't fenced or that the mechanicals were doing a job that should be carried out by the electricals, Bull wouldn't stir a yard toward the management. And it was, as Filmer pointed out, his job to approach the management.

Filmer fixed his bicycle clips and adjusted the rimless glasses and cycled past the crowds and out of B Gate and on to a main road. He cycled in the same manner each day – in mechanical, disturbing precision; irrespective of wind, traffic, his pace was the same – steady, sensible, something more than slow, so that he arrived at the hotel in the slightly better suburb without becoming hot, breathless.

He despised alcohol and the weak people who drank it, couldn't even converse without it, but came to this same place every day because he was entitled to. He did not enjoy it – but then, he did not experience enjoyment at all as others did – but some of the management came here and he was better than they, or at least as good, and as he ate his lunch, alone, never talking to anyone beyond a 'Good morning' or a complaint shared in regard to the food or service, he listened to them who did not recognize him, know of his existence, although they paid him. And certainly some of the things they said had the sound of carelessness, indifference, selfishness. They were heavy men mostly, who got red in the face with alcohol and laughter and self-importance, who ruthlessly sought out or obtained by bribery the comfort by the fire if it was a cold day. They obtained prompt service by money and indifference and had no respect for the waitresses who grovelled at the shrine of money and on behalf of the money endured (or perhaps they enjoyed) the coarse laughter, the lewd, unanswerable remarks, the attempted fondling.

'I've been here twenty minutes,' he said on this day when the room was crowded. There was no temper, no row impending, a simple statement of fact, her stupidity, inefficiency, acceptance of bribes by others.

'I'm sorry, sir.' (The 'sir' was technical, meaningless.) 'We're very busy today.'

The excuse made every time the place was anything more than empty. She knew him all right – he'd been coming here for three years – but hated him because he never tipped. He had the right change and put it down on the bar counter every day. He was not mean but didn't think the meal was in any case worth what was charged, let alone a tip. Principles. He was full of them, and if his life was made uncomfortable at least he could be sure he hadn't faltered, given way to pleasure, sex, happiness, in place of those principles.

'Rice pudding,' he demanded ten minutes later.

'Yes, sir.'

And he sensed her snigger as she passed the other waitress. They were fools who were prepared to accept their environment. He wasn't. He knew what a fraud those others were. Birth had put them on the Board, in their Rovers and detached houses with lawns and the high hedges of privacy.

He cornered Bull just after the siren recalled them.

'A trades union isn't a trades union any more, it's just a union,' he told Bull. 'Before the war you had to *earn* your way into a union, to prove your skill. Now you don't do anything.'

He was bitterly conscious that the cunning, truculent Bull was at least ten years younger than himself, was equally aware in humiliation that if he had been asked to do Bull's job he'd be afraid to do it. He, Filmer, had the brains, but it needed a dim tough like Bull to go and argue the toss with the management. And Bull perhaps knew this, too, for he had no respect for skill or age and said, 'Yeah, we know all that crap. What's the bellyache this time?'

'If this country was run properly a man'd get his proper wages, what he was worth.'

Such a lot of men talked like this that no one noticed it was a remark tending to Communism.

'Is that your grumble? What am I supposed to do?'

Bull sounded bored, fed up with Filmer's long-winded reasoning, and his eyes that dodged about were an illuminated rejection: the sod belongs to the Christian Doorstep or some rubbish. He don't belong to *us*.

'No,' said Filmer. 'It's about this new job.'

'What about it? Christ, I'm sick of hearing you lot bellyache. We're starting on it Monday.'

'Yes, but what *is* it?'

'What the hell do you care?'

'It's an instrument of war.'

'You don't say.'

'We should be informed.'

'All right. Yer fornicating well informed as from now.'

'We make transistors and things for peace. Now we're going to make parts of a rocket.'

'Who the hell said that? Who told you?'

'Isn't it true? Am I a fool who doesn't know what miniaturized equipment is for?'

'Listen, Filmer, you just do your bleeding work and let the fornicating government worry about what they do. You're a skilled man,' he said in sudden concession, appeasement.

He knew it was hopeless but concluded, 'But the Christian Doorstep's rules forbid us to partake in war.'

Bull said, 'I can't help the fornicating Christian grandmothers. This is a bleeding factory, not the Salvation Army, and we've landed a government contract.'

Filmer gave up. He felt the bitterness of a skilled man among fools who, within a world situation that needed this unqualified, mass-produced skill, believed that *they* were the qualified, he was an old has-been, a moaner belonging to the thirties. They were completely without ideals. They pleaded just after the war for a forty-hour week and then, having obtained it, began this cunning stranglehold on industry. They began to do overtime on Saturdays, finding that they 'couldn't manage' on a forty-hour week (manage the work, that is). So having made Saturday work a necessity, they demanded double time for it (as well as time and a half for overtime on other days). They then over a period of time built up their standard of living so that they *must* have plenty of overtime and were in financial difficulties without it. They then expected the management to comprehend and sympathize with this view and, if the work was such that it could be managed within forty hours, to 'arrange' that work was 'necessary' on Saturdays and even Sundays. The ramifications were now so hopelessly confused that if some lout shouted about injustice it was difficult to dispute him.

As well, Filmer, who had learned the electrical trade before the war, now had lads and apprentices working alongside him who were paid very nearly as much per hour as he, because the voices that represented them had the capacity to cripple the industry unless even its most inexperienced young men could be held by money, which was today's God, today's patriotism.

All of this had crept into his life slowly and he accepted it,

but the question of whether he could on principle work on instruments for a weapon of war had worried him, filled his belly
with depression and fear since he had heard about it. He had
worked at Mayger Electrics since 1938 and was unlike the
young men who moved from job to job. He had roots in this
suburb. He would ask Dawson about it. Dawson should be
able to advise. In the meantime, he'd see what Violet had to
say, if she was prepared for a change of job, of district.

It was raining when the siren signalled the end of the day,
but he rode home still at the same uniform pace. He lived on
an estate in a small semi-detached house with a neat garden.
Behind were other houses, lines of washing unclaimed in the
rain. A few trees and a hedge were all that divided the back-to-
back rows of gardens. Across the road were similar houses, a
parked car here and there. Between the houses, if he had
turned his head as he cycled the last hundred yards, he would
have seen the immense structure of the local vehicle works, a
cinder square of ten acres covered with diesel lorries and tiny
figures moving in the rain. It had taken half the value off his
house when that factory had been built in 1946 and was a
factor that trapped him in the locality. Violet grumbled,
but he didn't think she really minded. She had friends,
that was the difference. He burned alone, without any sym-
pathizers.

A small house, so small that he could stand at one point on
the ground floor and see into all the rooms at once, into the
road and back garden as well. Small, and therefore full, even in
the bedrooms, of the smells of frying sausages, rain, polish.
It did not matter. His ambitions were not of the kind that de-
mands. God watched, saw everything, waited. Principles – they
were what mattered.

'Is it still raining?'

Surely Vi could turn her head; there was a plenitude of windows, too much glass, in fact. It was as if the builder had
cheated, saved bricks for some other dwelling.

'Yes, pouring.'

'I'll have your coat. What about your trousers?'

'Never mind them.'

She was heavy; they were like Jack Spratt and his wife. She

would be fat in ten years' time, had a round, jolly, senseless face. No brains, he knew, but it did not matter. He had long since forgotten love, but there was companionship, problems shared. They had Brenda in common. It was incredible. Neither of them handsome, yet a daughter of extreme beauty. He loved the daughter more than anything in the world. Nothing could really hurt him because he despised the world, knew its vulgar greed, but if the world touched Brenda, claimed her, enticed her, ah, that would hurt, break his rigidity, cause him to cry on some cross.

He said to Violet, tentatively, to see her reaction, to test his own mind, 'They're going to make parts for rockets at the factory.'

She identified the something exploratory in his voice. 'Charlie,' she pleaded – she was the only person who called him 'Charlie'; he was Filmer or Charles to the rest of the world – 'you won't do anything silly, will you?'

'Silly? Do I ever do anything silly?'

'I mean, you won't throw up your job?'

'I could get another one.'

'We'd have to move.'

'It's a weapon of war.'

'I know, I know, but think of Brenda, me.'

'I shall do what is right,' he said, not even qualifying 'What I think is right,' so sure was he of principles. 'A man's principles are the only things of value.' It was true, must be. 'I can't compromise.' But his heart heard the knock at the door, the excited double knock, Brenda, and he knew he could compromise; little lamb of God, it is thee that I love . . .

She was rather tall, red in her smooth tender face from hurrying; her blue raincoat splashed rain about, and her hat was thrown somewhere carelessly. Brown hair and brown eyes, ordinary colours, tall she was, and beautiful; from whom – God, yes, God's most esteemed gift. Magnificently unaware of herself. Nothing in her voice or mind or heart about money, war, unions, pay packets, vulgarity, greed, selfishness; a purity of intention; the very act of staying alive was, with her, splendid, *clean* . . . His bitter whatever-it-was melted each day, stumbled awkwardly in her presence. His heart was mellowed because each day she hurried home, eager to be home, to talk excitedly.

It was like a love affair without the dirty touch of things claimed, desired. He desired nothing except that she should exist, be this same being with the original touch of God in her . . .

'What did you do today?'

'Oh, you know, the usual stuff.'

Her mother's voice, blind to the superb innocence, presence of Creation, complaining, 'You've made the hall a mess. Why didn't you shake your coat in the porch?' Not waiting for a reply, orientating this life around what she stupidly thought was a more important one, her own. 'Get your mack on again and go to Harris's for some Swiss roll.' The pretty face lost excitement, was humiliated; it struggled, protested. 'Oh, Mum, it's pouring.' And then, for him (who acknowledged its importance, agreed it was more than his own; he was just the vehicle of its creation, one of them), Brenda giggled. 'I *hate* Swiss roll!'

'Did you do history?'

The perfect voice slightly exasperated. 'Yes, and geography. You *know* I do on Wednesdays. Dad –' in a different voice, the world's – 'Can I go to a dance on Saturday?'

He was frightened, hurt on behalf of her, who was perfection, as God created; he remembered the voices in the factory, not a drop of innocence left; they wallowed in dirt like pigs. He wanted to please Brenda, surrender, give her things, but sometimes she asked for what terrified him.

She wasn't a child, of course. Filmer had loved the child, the baby, the small thing that was not involved in the filth and greed of the world. But now she was fifteen, a girl, wanted pleasures. He must not be mean. Pleasure meant nothing to him, but she could not sit about, be sad, disturbed, on behalf of principles. You had to see, encounter evil before you worried, and so far she hadn't been involved. They had nourished her, preserved her.

For what? he wondered with fear.

She would marry young, of course. She was beautiful and it hurt to know (that because of him, his nothingness in the world? Surely not. Principles were more than what money could bestow), it hurt, then, to know that she was defeated before she began. He had done all he could, but she still lived *here*; this was her environment, her world. The only things available, unless she was lucky, were the mass-produced youths who went to the coffee bars, the football match, whose ambition was a motor bike and a night with an actress; the youths who hated the other half of society, but not hard because it hadn't hurt them; they couldn't really be bothered to dislike it seriously, because of its evil, only half-heartedly, begrudgingly, with envy of the bigger cars, houses, money. And they placed no value at all on God, love, innocence. If they could they would soil her and pass on.

This was the concern that showed in his face as he asked, 'Who with? You're very young to go dancing.'

'Mum says I can.'

'There's such a lot of nasty youths about.'

'Oh, I'm not scared of them.'

'Is it a school dance?'

'Not exactly. But it's all right – it's in the church hall.'

'Oh well, then.' (Relieved, God, in the person of the clergy, would protect her.) 'It'll be all right. What time does it go on till?'

'Just after eleven.'

'That's very late.'

'It's a Saturday.'

'Who'll see you home?'

'I'll be with Molly and Ann.'

His mind, at ease, returned to his own problems.

'Listen, Brenda. Before you go for the cake ... They're going to make parts for a rocket at the factory. That's a secret. Do you think I ought to leave? You see, it's an instrument of war.'

He saw that her face was worried for a moment, lost purity, wanted the environment unchanged.

'Your mother thinks it doesn't matter, but I think principles are involved. What do you think?'

It was almost a plea: think differently from your mother. She's good, but she's a fool. You're only a child, but out of your simplicity, your purity, comes truth, wisdom without motives.

'Somebody'll make it if you refuse to,' Brenda pointed out.

'Ah, that's evasion,' he chided. 'We must face if it's right or wrong.'

'What's the rocket for?'

'I don't know yet.'

'Well, then.'

How wise she was, how innocent and decisive. He would have to find out what the rocket was for, see if it offered an innocent solution.

The urge to touch her hair and bonny arms and slender neck was pure, perfect, without sensuality. She understood, of course. She was the tiny child who had overwhelmed his frozen heart years ago. It was a kind of secret between them. Little lamb of God, I love thee. Violet was practical, would laugh: you big babby, you're going daft; so it was all in secrecy, a moment's affection when night or goodbyes permitted, understood only by God. His soured blood and disappointed heart were saved from bitterness and despair by this secret the world didn't know about, couldn't touch.

Saturday night. A fire burning and the room warm. Violet drinking tea, watching television: the man went into a night club, hit someone, two toughs stood at a door, a girl with most of her breasts revealed was singing . . .

'What's the time?' he asked.

'You've got a watch,' Violet answered, eyes not turning from the blue box.

He couldn't believe it was correct. It informed him: half past eleven.

'Where's she got to?' he asked, pleaded, aloud. 'It's half-past eleven.'

'It's Saturday. The dance goes on till one.'

Terror flushed his belly like a bad drink.

'When I was a kid --'

There was a pause. The singer had stopped; the two men had killed someone. Now it was time for the refrigerators and whiter than whites; Violet could spare him two minutes.

'You never had a proper childhood. Things were different then.'

'Better,' he said.

'You're like an old woman worrying –'

'What do you know about it?' he snarled quickly. 'You didn't meet me until you were twenty.'

'All those prayers,' Vi tittered. 'I'll have another cup.'

The sound of the teapot was obscene, insulting. She re-minisced, 'What a young fool I was,' as if she had made a mis-take marrying him; only a young fool would do it. 'When I think –'

Filmer fulminated in silence. The punishment of being work-ing class (one of *them*) was that you had to marry girls who were ignorant, who'd done nothing, been nowhere, understood only knitting . . .

Brenda came home at eleven forty-five, So tiny was the house, so without privacy the whole road, their whole world, that they could hear her feet and someone else's, and laughter, and hissed cautions, and a 'Good-bye' and another one, louder, as he/she who had brought her home went further away. The gate banged, and the hand was near the bell, but by then Filmer was at the front door, confronting her whom he loved but who in dread he feared would learn to love the world, despise him, or, worse, forget his existence.

'What d'you slam the gate for?'

'Sorry, Dad,' she said penitently – she was prepared to be abject, recognizing the signs of his anger. 'I didn't mean to.'

'You're an hour late,' he said, inside the house.

'Want a cup of tea, dear?' her mother asked, confusing his demand.

'No, thank you, Mum.'

'Your dad was worried.'

'Will you be quiet,' Filmer ordered. 'You're talking like a fool. You're an hour late,' he repeated. He had, almost without knowing it, accumulated anger in his anxiety, and now it poured over her. 'An *hour*. Twenty minutes I could under-stand, but an hour is deliberate disobedience.'

'I didn't mean to, Dad.'

'Why did you, then?'

'We had something to eat.'

'You didn't *have* to eat.'

'The others all did.'

'Are you a sheep to do as others do?'

'No, Dad.'

'Then why not do as you're told?'

Brenda was now presenting a face that was sullen, alien, without comprehension, a face that said *he* was wrong, a face that was prepared to wait until he'd finished, then go to bed, think, remember brighter moments. What was the matter with happiness?

'I'm sorry, Dad.'

'You won't go again,' he half shouted, not meaning it, but wanting to penetrate, hurt, make her realize he existed, worried.

Brenda began to weep, and he was more wretched than she, but he never wept, for he was among the right, the mighty.

'Who was that you just said good-bye to?'

'You're not fair,' she cried hysterically. 'You never let me do anything.' And the impact of this lacerated him because it was unintentional; only in hysteria would she dare to release such opinions. It had uneasy implications, which were ... But he was frightened to examine the implications. They might mean whole areas of communication were meaningless, in his mind only. They might mean he was almost nothing in her sight.

'I only look after you.'

'I can look after myself.'

'You're only a child.'

'I don't know what you're on about. It was only a dance.'

This had the uncomfortable air of truth. The complications and anxieties were all in his mind, of his creation. It was hard to warn her against the world when she had not encountered the world.

'Brenda, you did promise to come home at eleven.'

She identified the conciliatory tone and excused herself. 'Honestly, Dad, I don't remember exactly saying that. I'm sure I only said it would end at eleven, and actually it did, only – Besides,' she justified herself, 'if I'd left early I'd have had to come home alone.'

That prospect terrified him. It all had the uneasy permutations against which he was powerless. You sent a child to a
shop and she saw another across the road who waved and one
of them ran in excitement and a car killed her. You allowed a
child to go to a dance on a condition that she'd be back at
eleven, but before she was even on her way the condition was
misunderstood, so you, who operated by that condition, might
have gone to the police in the event of disaster and started
them off on a hopelessly mistaken basis: yes, she'd have been
on her way back at eleven. A child was like a pure white ball
in an electric game. It ran about confusedly, innocently, and so
long as it bounced against white markers it was all right, but
if it illuminated the green or blue ones it became your oppo-
nent's point, and if it touched and lit up the red one you lost
everything . . .

'Brenda, who did bring you home?'

'Dad,' she chided, smiling now, 'you don't mind if I have a
boy friend?'

He did, he did. It hurt, not because he had some curious
urge for sole ownership, the secret love, but because he was
afraid. He knew this district. He heard – they gave him no
option but to hear – their filthy talk: girls and women were
a device to use. Love, it had nothing to do with love; it was a
kind of masturbation, with some a score card. There were no
exceptions that he knew of in the Electronics Division of
Mayger Electrics. All of them over eighteen talked like a police
case quoted in a Sunday paper.

He loved her and didn't wish the world to be 'good' to her.
The world's tongue was most persuasive to a girl with beauty;
he didn't want her to heed it, be corrupted. She was a small
child who had diluted the acid in his soul, who had held his
hand in the terror of night, who had asked 'Dad, who is
God?'

She told him now about a boy at school, and her analysis
and comprehension remained as innocent as that child's; the
boy, too, sounded a world removed from the louts of Mayger's.
Filmer was warmed by her account, even anxious to promote
this other tender affection, while Vi sniggered quietly, without
comprehension, without secrets.

Christian Doorstep met every third Sunday at 10.30 a.m., had what Mr Dawson, its area organizer, called 'a conference about this world and the next' (which meant he enthused, he prayed, others responded), and then at about 11.30 its members went out into the world to convert – convert those gardening, washing cars, doing nothing, ignoring God. They didn't bother with Catholics or Jews but were prepared to argue with the lazier members of the Church of England. Their membership was forty-three, which was quite a crowd inside the dull building which they hired – a dirty pink-painted, grey-asbestos-roofed insubstantial structure. 'The results we obtain,' said Dawson, 'are directly proportionate to the work we do. We are but forty-three but today can influence four hundred and thirty, in a matter of weeks bring four thousand back to God . . .'

They were shabby people with chips on their shoulders: fierce young men with defiant, unhappy faces, a few girls, pious, obdurate, angry with some detail in their original church, or feeling the need to argue personally with the world, convert it, individual by individual, to a particular view. The older men all had something in common with Filmer – a rigidity, a faith based on condemnation ... The pamphlets and tri-weekly texts were printed in Illinois, U.S.A., where the Christian Doorstep Movement was well established, visited hospitals, prisons, was on committees, could bring political pressure, had its martyrs ...

They had discussed their 'attack' on two particular suburbs to be made that morning and had followed Mr Dawson in prayer and were now moving off to work. There were those who wanted to discuss other points, and Filmer was among them. He waited patiently for the majority to go, but privacy with Dawson was always difficult; privacy, in fact, did not seem to interest him.

'Mr Dawson, I have a problem.'

So difficult to get Dawson alone! He was like a popular bishop. The door was open; October draughts blew wet leaves and cold air in. A woman protested, 'Shut the door, *please*,' and Dawson's hand placed books on a scrubbed table. The treasurer said in passing, 'I'll see to that, Mr Dawson,' and looked without expression at Filmer. Filmer was nothing. Oh, he works at Mayger Electric. Yes, yes, Mr Oliphant, but we must welcome *everybody* here.

'A problem,' echoed Mr Dawson.

It would be about contributions, or the district covered, or expenses, or the weather (they were 'realistic' about things like rain), or about the actual burden of pamphlets ('My doctor says I shouldn't carry heavy parcels about'). Even here, among suburban fanatics, Mr Dawson had his little problems; they were his particular cross.

'A problem of conscience.'

'*Ah!*' And the bald head turned. 'You'll cover Wildgate Street, Mrs Booth. I know all about the dog at seventeen, but I trust you to regard that beast as simply a trial. Now about the message, Mr – er?' But he wasn't even sure of Filmer's name.

'It's about my work.'

The frown on Mr Dawson's face was deep, concerned; it continued some way over the forehead into the bald head. It would have been difficult to argue that Mr Dawson wasn't involved. He looked like a man squeezing the entire contents of his cranium on behalf of Filmer.

'At Mayger's we're going to make instruments for a weapon of war. We weren't consulted.'

'We?'

'The workers. And I thought – in view of Christian Doorstep's views on war –'

'What did you think?' Mr Dawson asked, in the manner of someone who needs further explanation.

'That I ought to change my job.'

'You're not happy?'

'Happy?' asked Filmer. What had happiness to do with it? 'Is it *right* to work on an instrument of war?'

'Your most valuable work,' said Mr Dawson, 'is *here*. Does that answer your question?'

Somebody else was claiming his time, glaring at Filmer like a woman kept waiting by gossip in a shop. 'Before I go, Mr Dawson, there's the application for membership from Mrs Hall.'

'Ah, Mrs Hall! A great victory, that!'

Filmer stared at the weak, enormous face, the watery, idiotic eyes, and knew Dawson was a fool, not involved in the world, a little man who was playing a mock game of power, who was fascinated by messages and memberships but not with the world. The shock of it hit him like warmth in his stomach. Dawson and his kind were people the world, quite rightly, laughed at. His own heart thumped in a new alarm, genuine horror, a pitiless and honest revelation: *Is this what I look like before the world? A fool who titters about with words while the world is shattered?* No. He was mocked, true, but *they* would mock Christ. *They* weren't interested in anything beyond Saturday's football, Sunday's beer, the dogs, the value of their time down to eighths of a penny, although they didn't know what to do with time when it was available. No, he wasn't a Dawson. He'd been a fool to serve God and try to alter the world in Dawson's little brigade. There was, indeed, a similar idiotic, useless fanaticism in each of them. He wasn't like that. He was a man with principles, a man who would smash the world if it was evil, a man who would *act.*

He did not know how he would act, but that would come. In the meantime, he wandered outside with his quota of pamphlets and small books printed in Illinois. He didn't bother with explanations, good-byes. It happened quite often: a face didn't turn up again; it was never mentioned by Mr Dawson; failure was impermissible.

His conscience argued that he must do this morning's duty or go back and say he was not going to. It was still raining, and he mopped the saddle of his bicycle with his handkerchief. Before he'd proceeded a hundred yards his trousers were saturated at the knees.

He was too full of hatred to convert. His love was frozen, unconvincing, limited to the words from Illinois, in a hopeless cause. He condemned them even as he tried to persuade: they were idle, unshaven, dirty, lazy, indifferent, insolent. He was thinned down by disapproval of the society he sought pitifully to mend. He was mocked, ignored, lied to, and over the years this had built up a violent antipathy about humans and especially English humans.

This was his last morning at it, but they could still manage to humiliate . . .

In the first suburb – a road of four hundred houses, Victorian – Negroes wandered in the rain, coatless; a child rode a bicycle on the pavement, too fast, through the litter of last night and this morning; hot music blasted through the letter box of the shabby house, unpainted, blinds drawn on the ground floor, a pretty over-painted face looked out around the blinds, examined him with apathy, dropped the blind.

A woman, solid, middle-aged, tough, answered the door, a fag going – a type he dreaded : they knew better than he, than God . . .

'Good morning, madam. Not a very glorious morning? May I ask you to what religion you belong?'

'You can ask.'

'I do ask.'

'I don't see as it's any business of yours.'

'I want to make it my business –'

'I'm sure you do. Good morning, Mr Nosey Parker. I'm busy.' And as the door slammed Filmer heard her (was intended to hear her), heavy in scorn, 'The cheek of it, coming here to tell me how to behave,' and a roar of laughter from others, all evil, all far beyond innocence and God.

At another door a young man, in navy blue, cheap shiny shoes, his face white with indoors and drink and the surrender to any plea his body made. He, too, had a fag going; it was incredible that his hair, saturated in grease, did not burst into flames.

'I want to ask you to what religion you belong.'

'We was married in church.'

'You belong to the Church of England?'

'It was in Sheffield. If you want any money –'

'We don't want money. What we want –'

'Some people think y'got nothing to do but pay, pay. Christ, it makes y'sick.'

'It is your spiritual welfare we have at heart –'

'Y'say that, but y'want money, don't you?'

'No. As I explained –'

'You must be a prick if y'go round in the fornicating rain –' He sniggered, yawned, said, 'I've got to go out now,' and walked past Filmer, slamming the gate so that a piece of iron fell somewhere, and Filmer heard him call to another young man over on the opposite dirty pavement, 'Hey, Sid, watch it – there's a bugger over there trying to save your bleedin' soul,' and they both tittered, proud of their status, among the dung and french letters and bottle tops and broken glass.

They at least had the excuses of poverty, environment, lack of education. The opposite extreme was encountered an hour later. A detached house down a gravel drive between rhododendron bushes. A man washing down a Daimler on a concrete strip. 'The back door, mate.' But Filmer ignored him, went to the front. Did one have to apologize for bringing Christ?

A maid answered.

'I'd like to speak to the owner.'

She looked at his saturated clothes, his bicycle leaning on lichen-covered statuary, and was decisive: 'I'm not going to disturb Mrs Farthingale for *you*!'

Filmer ignored the implication – that he was nothing, an excrescence, something that was of less importance than – well, whatever Mrs Farthingale was doing at that moment – her hair, phoning a friend, cleaning golf clubs ...

'Young woman, do you not respect God?'

She flushed, but not in shame. 'Can't you read the notice? It says no hawkers.'

'Tell your mistress that God is at the front door,' he demanded angrily.

A small wasp of a woman, blonde, smart, cruel, used to power (eight cylinders, committees, chequebook, name), said coldly, decisively, 'What do you think you're doing? If you do not leave at once I shall instruct the police to prosecute for nuisance.'

'Mrs Farthingale, I've come a long way in the rain –'

'Then it's time for you to return,' the arrogant voice told him, and the heavy studded door was closed in his face.

In the afternoon one of his brothers-in-law came. Filmer dreaded his appearance. Ted was vulgar, successful, 'I'm in business' (a pork butcher). Everything he said was brash, immodest; all his opinions were thoughtless clichés.

Filmer sat through the afternoon listening to some of them . . .

'I'm in the Conservative Party when Mrs Hartley-Jones comes in for her pork, Socialist when Henry Wilson collects the Workingmen's Club's meat pies. Get it?'

'I give my accountant an extra fiver or two and he sees to *my* tax problems . . .'

'They oughta chuck out the niggers and Irish and let the British have Home Rule . . .'

Laughter, mostly his. Violet sat in wonder, admired Ted's suit. ('I know a fella, not in a big place, just a little room; he's been tailor to royalty.') Violet (and, alas, Brenda) went outside to admire Ted's new pink Victor Super. ('You got to be smart in business. Impresses people. You can't drive up to Round Table in an old crock.')

A windbag, Filmer knew, but he daren't say it aloud. Ted was generous – he never forgot flowers for Vi, chocolates for Brenda; he was tireless where Filmer was weighed down with the troubles of the time; he was full of laughter amid Filmer's acid silence; he was immune to barbs, comments, indifference; he was overloaded with bonhomie; he never heard anyone speak, so how could he know Filmer despised him?

His wife, Marion, was the same, but quieter. Both of them were, like Filmer, in their late forties but exuded youth, energy, success; they were indefeasible in normal terms. He wondered sometimes what they thought of him and suspected they pitied Vi.

On and on Ted talked his way through the afternoon.

On business. 'You can't have principles in business. You got to get on. There's no morals, when lolly's about. You got to make money or marry it! I made it!'

Laughter, his beaming dial examining the circle of attentive faces, the confirmation for himself of his own opinion of himself.

'I know a fellow who became Catholic just to marry the boss's daughter. It's a fact.' A big beam. 'Got six kids now. Serve him right!'

Which brought him to Catholicism and religion. (He knew all about God, had dismissed Him years ago: He was a stunt by the politicians, the generals, the police. He knew all about priests; not a priest made an error within a range of forty miles and Ted knew about it.)

'They're the worst of the lot' – a laugh – 'except for the nuns.'

Then a dirty joke – but not too dirty because Brenda was there and mustn't be corrupted (or not much, or not just yet). Then another about Jews, then one about Catholics.

On Catholicism, he knew all about it; it was the usual fraud to hold down the peasants. Superstition.

'I know some Catholics who're so meek and mild. They listen to the priests, but the wives go to the birth-control clinic.'

Laughter, again his, and a quick apology, not meant. 'Oh, sorry, Brenda, thought you'd gone out.'

She, whom Filmer loved, was red in the face but not anxious to move away; he saw in worry that she was fascinated by this happy corruption, this storytelling of the world's weakness, this confirmation of what was hinted at in newspapers, films, on TV.

The two women nodded, satisfied with their own perfection in this world of sin. They were impenetrable; charity had long since gone with modesty, and self-analysis had never been one of their capabilities.

It was nearly time for tea, but Violet was reluctant to move and do anything about it. Ted was a tonic, honest, he was, as good as TV. And in truth Vi looked brighter in the face, roared with laughter (she never did that for Filmer), and listened intently, as Ted went on and on, fed by 'Yes' and 'Go on, really?'

'I'm not a snob, but when this fellow says Cyprus wine's better than South African – Don't let 'em fool you. South African is as good as any French stuff.'

'I don't read books, haven't the time. *Reader's Digest* on a train sometimes. To hell with newspapers. All lies. It's a fact, Brenda, don't let 'em tell you otherwise at school.'

Again the women listened, nodded, frowned in attention, laughed.

'If there weren't ladies present I could tell you –'

And, of course, he did.

'We haven't told 'em about our holidays. Ramsgate. What a

place! Honest, it was smashing. Eat? You could eat at that hotel until you were sick. Couldn't you, Marion?'

Marion talked for a permissible moment or two and then Ted asked abruptly, 'Hey, what's the time?' and brought out a gold watch to inform himself. 'Hey, Vi, love, what about a spot of tea?'

Paste sandwiches, tinned fruit, cakes with cream in, cup after cup of tea.

Marion said, 'I think it's clever the way they have them frozen food things. Real cream.'

And suddenly, 'Charles is very quiet,' Ted said with exasperating, observant bonhomie, that made Filmer feel guilty. 'Thinking, Charles, or got the bellyache?'

Filmer said, 'Thinking.'

'You can do too much of that,' Ted pointed out, in the manner of expert, doctor, psychiatrist, one who knew, knew better than Filmer. 'Enjoy yourself. It's later than you think.' And he again brought out the watch. 'Indeed it is. Got a gold watch now, see? Never had it so good! Still making them transistors, Charles?'

'No. We're going on to something else tomorrow.'

Ted said, 'Change of manufacture. Time for a strike. More money. You'd be successful while the management's anxious about it.'

'Some of us have principles,' said Filmer.

Ted pooh-poohed this. 'My God, you'd never do in business.'

You could not explain principles to a fool who had none.

You could not become angry with Ted who was happy and angry with no one.

Filmer was squashed, angry, silent. He had so often retreated into silence rather than argue with fools that when he did speak it was with a pitiful squeak. For he had an unfortunate voice, which suggested femininity, castration, subservience; and it aggravated his hatred of the successful, the vulgar fools, and he even felt a longing for a society in which all men were equal and money and vulgarity and birth were not the criteria.

After tea they sat in darkness and for forty minutes watched Ted and Marion at Ramsgate on a coloured cinefilm.

It was like having Ted multiplied to breaking point, for Ted was not only there, walking about a beach, getting in and out of the Victor Super; he was here, too, talking, talking, never a failure, success all the way. The sweat gleamed on Filmer's head and he hated Ted and Marion and even Vi (for being convinced, overwhelmed by fools); and he remembered with bitterness Dawson, Mrs Farthingale, Bull, the louts at Mayger's. And they expected him to make parts of a rocket to save, preserve, and protect *this* society, perhaps even destroy the other one. He was useless, to be ordered about by fools; any apprentice could open his mouth and be heard, but not the qualified Filmer.

'That's the harbour wall. The other woman is Mrs Bayliss, the one we met at the hotel. A perfect lady – you couldn't hope to meet one like her in a place like this . . .'

'No. That was the woman –'

'Well, it doesn't matter –'

They were perfect.

They were society.

They were without principles or God or politics but reserved the right to condemn the world if it didn't perform as they did.

You'd never do in business.

And when they'd gone the house was very silent and he had a smouldering feeling of guilt, resentment.

Brenda said brightly, 'Gosh, isn't Uncle Ted funny?'

And he snarled, even at her, so that she flinched, 'The man's a damn windbag.'

And Vi sneered for Brenda to hear, 'I notice *you* didn't say much when he was here.'

He went red in the face. 'What's the use? He's not open to other opinions.'

'He's a clever man, our Ted is. He's got on.'

Meaning, Filmer knew, that he hadn't.

What was the use of principles on behalf of a fool like this? What use to expect her to understand that tomorrow he must refuse to work on a weapon of war because he, Charles Filmer, hadn't been consulted?

He squirmed, hearing Ted's views in his mind, Bull's laughter – 'All right, mate, you fornicating well resign' – and the coarse laughter of the louts who'd like to soil people like Brenda. He was a fool in their view; anyone was a fool who didn't cash in on prosperity.

Very well. He wouldn't say anything, wouldn't complain. He would go on working at Mayger's; he had to earn money to feed Vi, cherish and look after Brenda. He would submit to the majority rule. It was democratic. . . .

But in his heart was hatred, a plan, equivocal destruction, balanced, ounce against ounce. If he must work on a thing that was evil he had the privilege, his conscience surely instructed, of rendering it negative.

He was like a hurt child. If the world would not play his way he would smash the world. The Bulls and Dawsons and Teds and Marions and Mrs Farthingales of this world had left out of account those silent, unencountered things: his superior mind and conscience, his principles that they spat on without comprehension.

4

MAJOR IGOR GOUSEEV

NEARLY four o'clock. Igor Gouseev began to increase his pace as he passed the Albert Memorial. It was a fine October afternoon, rather warm, muggy after rain, and a watery sun shone into his eyes, glinted on the vast, endless hurrying procession of vehicles. Very few people were walking, it seemed to him. A sign of laziness or of prosperity? It did not matter.

In Kensington High Street he crossed the road. There were some elegant young women here, and he looked about in anxiety for Mrs Wallace.

It had been a successful party, but he had had rather a lot to drink and it was in that excitable condition that he had suggested to Mrs Wallace that they should meet again. He was, he had excused himself, lonely. She was a woman in her mid-thirties, tall, dark, attractive, with immense electrifying eyes that examined him steadily as he spoke and a full mouth that twitched in secret amusement. He had not met her husband,

who had not been at the party. He had been 'at work'. There
had been the atmosphere that a party was great fun without Mr
Wallace. There was nothing quite like Mrs Wallace in all Moscow. She was, of course, hopelessly decadent, confused, refused
to talk politics ('such an incomprehensible bore'), preferred
music, theatre, gossip. She was not, as far as he knew, in any
way a loose woman. Just crazy. He was not altogether untruthful when he had described himself as lonely. He was described
by the embassy as a 'chauffeur' and rarely appeared at functions.
Therefore he did not move in diplomatic or political circles. In
fact his status was not much below that of the ambassador and,
although he could drive a car, he was never employed as a
chauffeur. The embassy allowed him complete freedom of
movement, and this afternoon he was abusing it mildly.

Things interested him. He did not despise the English. On the
contrary, he was happy to live in such a country. He had no
envy and examined their motorcars and fur coats and fine china
and wrist watches with the attention these could merit. Outside
Bumbles he watched in amusement a young man and a very
attractive girl arrange a window, first covering some nude
models with cloth. The clothes were excellent. He was in a battle
and these were, presumably, the enemy, but Major Igor
Gouseev found them attractive and intelligent. Only in politics
were they without purpose. But, of course, they did not really
believe they were in that battle.

Mrs Wallace surprised him by coming *out* of Bumbles instead of along the pavement. It was as if she must have an
excuse to call this an accident.

'Oh, hello. Why, Major, fancy you standing outside corsets
and fabrics!'

'Good afternoon, Mrs Wallace.'

He was, absurdly, a little shy. She was four inches taller,
beautiful, overwhelming, superbly dressed and a crazy hat over
the black hair. In the open air he saw that her face was older
than the face at the party, but not forty yet, and there was
elegance in her every movement. She was a woman of many
movements: fluttering gloved hands, head turned, legs swayed
gracefully, even when she was just standing, and the eyes, those
eyes, really, he couldn't stare them out.

'Will you have a cup of tea?'

'I'm *dying* for a cup of tea.'

'Here?'

'Oh, well, I suppose so.'

'You don't want to?'

'It was just that my friends . . .'

He understood. 'But we met by accident . . .'

'It won't matter anyway. He's gone. So there we are.'

'I did not know that.'

'All London knows. Bill has left me for a girl who works in a travel agency.' Mrs Wallace giggled. 'Isn't it amusing?'

Inside Bumbles, Major Gouseev moved through the iron-mongery, children's toys (Santa was due), pushed slowly (he was in no hurry) through women in the furniture section, found an escalator, went up to the fabrics and fashion, and very nearly saw a fat lady in a changing room. He was now lost, and Mrs Wallace said, 'You dear man, why not use the lift?'

They waited some time for a lift that was going up and then strolled into the half-empty tearoom. Mrs Wallace looked about anxiously, then relaxed into a soft chair, cushions, where she belonged. She crossed her slender legs and the major was for an instant aware of their shapeliness, expensive stockings, but he was not particularly a sensual man. He sat facing the lifts, which could be seen through glass doors. He did not know why he did this. Habit, perhaps, or a faint guilt. He was slightly infatuated by Mrs Wallace, chiefly because such an attractive English-woman should be interested in *him*.

She was not a contact, and sitting among the cushions and chandeliers and water colours, his belly was warm with silent laughter, joy, that did not crease his face. For no one knew he was with Mrs Wallace. The Soviet Government did not know about Mrs Wallace, and if it did he could explain, truthfully, that her husband worked on a responsible newspaper, drank heavily, and talked carelessly.

The waitress was there, a tall, shy, pretty girl, wasted in this absurd place.

'Tea,' instructed Mrs Wallace. 'Buns? Cakes? Yes, a few cakes, my dear, that sort of thing.'

'Yes, madam.'

'Ursula,' said the major tentatively. 'Can I call you Ursula?' he asked, pleaded, and he was genuinely delighted when she acquiesced: 'Call me anything you like except Poppet. *He* calls me Poppet.'

'Isn't this amusing, our meeting here?'

'Yes.' She smiled. 'Isn't it? Terribly amusing. I'm so glad. I wanted to talk to you. You were *rather* drunk at the party.'

He was slightly drunk now with the intoxication of her presence. The fact that he was working against British interests – obtaining information via persuasion, bribery, impression, and skill – had no relationship to his feelings toward Mrs Wallace, whom he could now call Ursula. It was as if he had two halves of his mind working separately, and Ursula as a British subject who might one day die or be humbled as a result of information supplied by him had nothing to do with the charming supple woman in exotic clothes with the astonishing, bewildered, beckoning eyes and bits of cake crumbs on her fingers, who was clearly enjoying her minor infidelity toward Mr Wallace, her brief encounter. He was very involved with other things but felt entitled to the occasional pleasure of her company; he had no idea where it would lead to; in fact, it could lead nowhere, for he, too, was married and intended to remain faithful to his spouse.

It was their first meeting alone, and they were just a little conscious of it – but not too much; wherever they were going, whatever would be the result, it would come quickly if it came at all. . . .

'I like to drink,' he explained now.

'Shall I serve?'

'I like to drink tea, too.'

'Do you have parties at the embassy?'

'Of course.' He wondered if she were some kind of snob. 'Shall I ask you to one?'

'Aren't they rather dreary?'

She was no snob, evidently!

'A lot of people, certainly.'

Her large eyes made him falter; the mouth smiled very carefully. 'I *hate* a lot of people.'

'What do you like?'

'Oh, I know I'm a silly girl,' Ursula said candidly. 'I like chocolate cakes, music. I think I like vodka. I like big cars. I like parties. I like interesting men. I suppose that category includes you! Am I very silly?'

'You are delightful,' he told her frankly, glad of the opportunity.

She coloured under the skilful make-up and acknowledged quietly, 'It is sweet of you to say so.'

The major said quickly, 'It is not that I am lonely. You know that?'

'I'm happy to know it.'

'I'm not really on the ambassador's staff,' he explained, 'so my social life is negligible.' This wasn't quite true; it would have been more accurate to say, it was a fraud or a professional lie. 'Not,' he qualified, 'that I'm a great one for that sort of thing.'

'You're deep,' she analysed, looking into his teacup. 'You're more important than you pretend to be.'

This was a bit too clever and he flushed. Ursula had the ability to render him careless, anxious to be confidential. This was dangerous, he recognized; it was others who must be careless, not he. That remark of his about not being on the ambassador's staff implied that – But still, if he were questioned about it, he could say that he did not wish to admit to this fashionable lady that he was a chauffeur and therefore hinted at other, more impressive work.

'I'm in communications,' he said.

'Ciphers and things?'

'Things like that.'

She didn't give a damn.

'You walk with a tiny limp,' she told him. 'Does that mean you were wounded in the war?'

This was easier. He could be truthful.

'A long time ago,' he said. 'When the Germans made their first attack. I was in Smolensk.' He did not have to do more than close his eyes to remember those burning summer days, the early confusion, the terror, the brutality. 'We let the German tanks go through and waited for the infantry.' He had a tough memory of shattered buildings, fire, grit, shouts, the moaning of mortar shells, the scurrying infantry, fighting at twenty-feet distances, and then the year of pain, a different man, a man who knew English and was fighting a further war while the final victories of this one were in progress. 'It was then that I was injured.'

'Poor you,' she said. 'I'm sure you hate war.'

'They killed my mother and father, two of my brothers,' he told her.

Silence, and then Igor smiled. 'But do not be sad. That was twenty years ago. I did not meet you to talk about war.'

'Bill was in the Korean War,' Mrs Wallace said, but it evidently did not trouble her. 'He was still in the Navy then.'

'It was a great mistake.'

'Yes. I presume you mean the war, not Bill being in the Navy.'

'Yes, I meant that.'

Mrs Wallace smiled. Hers was not a face that grinned, or she would be grinning now.

'Why do you smile?'

'Quite simple,' she told him. 'We both don't give a damn about *any* war. If more of our people met there wouldn't be a Cold War, don't you think?'

'I do indeed,' he said, not thinking anything of the sort.

'Bill's not a bad sort.' Mrs Wallace sighed. 'I'm not unfaithful, you must know, or anything like that. We're just finished, that's all.'

'I'm sorry.'

'Don't be polite. He doesn't mean anything to you.'

'No, but you do.'

'Do I? I wonder. What do I mean?'

There was a slight edge to her voice, as if she had identified him as a man in search of whatever was going, was easy.

'I don't know yet,' Gouseev admitted. 'I just wanted to see you again and again. What does that mean?'

She laughed. 'Damned if I know . . .'

'I'm serious. It's all very difficult. There is Bill. I am a Russian. And I am married, too,' he concluded. 'So where do we go from there?'

'To the shoe department,' Mrs Wallace said abruptly. 'These new blue things don't fit. I didn't know you were married.'

'She is not like you.'

'What is she like?'

'She is plump and heavy, unsophisticated.'

'But you don't despise her?'

'No. Nor am I a young infatuated fool.'

'Here's the waitress.'

Afterward, strolling toward the lifts, Gouseev inquired, 'So I don't see you again?'

'Do you want to?'

'You know I do.'

'Why, I wonder?'

The lift attendant, an old man who had been defeated by the world, stared at them in something between hate and curiosity.

'You know that, too.'

'I suppose it's all quite harmless.' She said in abrupt amusement. 'I don't even know your name.'

'Third floor,' said the old man impatiently, opening the gate. 'You said shoes?'

They didn't notice him, which proved something.

'It is Igor. Shall I see you again?'

The large, unflinching eyes examined him. Mrs Wallace smiled, surrendered. 'All right. It would be nice. Shall I phone you?'

'It is useless to phone me at the embassy,' Gouseev explained. 'Red tape,' he punned. 'May I ring you?'

She thought about it.

'I think any day before about three-thirty. That's when I go to collect Angela from school.'

'You didn't go today?'

'Detention today, poor lamb. I think,' said Mrs Wallace, 'you'd better leave me here among the shoes. I'm likely to take half an hour.'

It was dismissal, knowledge of her own power, the value of her feminine charm, life.

'Very well, Ursula. Good-bye. And I will phone.'

She had become cold, didn't even turn, and he heard her saying, 'They're terribly sweet but the wrong size.' He walked past dozens of them, young women in their thirties, elegant, beautiful, useless, he knew, but his heart was touched by that particular one. If she was a fool, a silly woman, he couldn't help it;

she had some electric quality that made him equally foolish, and he liked that.

He was still thinking of her as he turned into the absolute quiet of Kensington Palace Gardens and walked along the leaf-patterned pavement, past the parked saloons outside other embassies. The flags hung very limp in the still of afternoon and the whole avenue was in the shade of immense trees. The hum of distant cars and red buses, and a long way off women pushing prams into the park. Some of the houses were immense, ugly; a few were derelict. Overhead the high, impressive scream of a Viscount heading into or out of London, success, money, politics, the world, but strictly this one, not the next.

Outside Number 18 a few Russian and English cars were parked. Two constables stared at Gouseev from across the road. He could hear their radio; perhaps they were listening to a football match. The gardens of the embassy were wild, ignored, so great was the need for privacy. A van was being turned into the avenue and two men were carrying in heavy pots of flowers. Five men in dark clerical suits were arguing earnestly just inside the gate. One of them acknowledged Gouseev.

Inside, tatty rooms, never properly decorated for the same reasons of security. On the second floor the secret room, his. A double steel entrance and windows which had iron bars and steel shutters which were closed every night, irrespective of air or temperature. A steel safe in which were the documents of Military Intelligence, cipher books, telegrams from Moscow, the records of agents, British names that were surprising in number, enormous in potential. Gouseev had his own cipher clerk who, as he entered, grinned and handed him a sheaf of papers with the comment, 'More work!' This cipher clerk belonged solely to Military Intelligence. The other parts of the embassy – Diplomatic, N K V D, Political and Commercial – also had clerks who enciphered messages in individual codes unknown even to each other. Gouseev was responsible only to one of the secretaries of the embassy, and this only for general guidance.

More work . . .

It was difficult to drop the mind's-eye photograph of Ursula Wallace, her fashionable clothes, her frank eyes in the superb, absurd, experienced face, her body that must be full and tall and magnificent despite the apparent slenderness, and the view of the silk legs as they sat on the chair on the third floor of Bumbles and revealed themselves to the top of the stockings as she'd removed the shoes that were 'terribly sweet, but the wrong size'.

More work, secret work, work to defeat Mr Wallace, late of the Royal Navy, and millions of his kind ...

From the Director of Military Intelligence in Moscow, an instruction:

To GOUSEEV. 3192.

1. Answer my last re World Mechanical, especially about radio locators with T-L switches and the magnicoustic locators for artillery. Give details of Pilot Explosive Plant and Ballistics Laboratory here. Find out about Dido, an alternative propellant to nitroglycerin. Have we no one working here?

2. What are they engaged in on the third floor at the Brand Station? There is reason to believe they study and develop detonator capsules and igniting capsules. Believed laminated ND is used with picrate and nitrogushnida. Can Smith's Group be given this task? I am aware of the many difficulties.

3. Obtain details of Jinkabout Mk VII pilotless jet target aircraft. This is used on the range at Woomera but is manufactured at the Marine Aircraft Establishment, where we have contact. This device, originally for target only, is being developed into short-range missile. Try to find out about telemeter control which is new.

4. It is very important to confirm official date of transfer of American troops to USA and Panama areas, also whereabouts of 82nd Airborne Div., 11th Army, 30, 54, 104, and 117th Infantry Divs and 13 and 17th Tank Divs and their HQs. Also, intended arrival in European area of Brazilian troops, supposedly for manoeuvres and experience of European area.

5. Obtain passport in name of Henry Gordon Adams. Age 38, brown hair, blue eyes, weight 117 lbs. Marks: two moles on left shoulder. Photo herewith. Occupation: free-lance journalist.

6. Alexei Antonov.
    (a) Reverse my 3071. Do not eliminate him. It is too risky. He is paraded by the British as a success and must therefore be protected by them.
    (b) He has now begun work at St Hanover's College in London. Find out the nature of his work and how it could be dislocated.

(c) Obtain telephone extension number of his laboratory or place of work, within the college.

(d) If he forms attachments, find out his particular anxieties and what he values.

(e) Obtain information re other scientists, lecturers, research men at the college.

(f) It must be borne in mind that he may be protected.

(g) This matter must not be rushed. He must feel secure, even develop roots. It is essential that he develop friendship or affection or passion for our contact. Find out if his sexual interests are normal or abnormal and act accordingly. Contact used should affect to be religious as Antonov has accepted Christianity.

(h) When contact found and in use, establish safe method of meetings.

(i) Suggest you use Max for this work. He has contacts in high places and works in London area.

(j) Report regularly on this. Do not hurry. It is essential that Antonov is so involved with and concerned for the contact that any later threat or promise made by us concerning him/her would make him work for us. This is the ultimate aim: that, when established, he should supply us with information. If he will not, then we must be in a position to disgrace him, render him useless to the British.

7. Your photographs of 17 September valuable and interesting but do not indicate more than that a rocket of standard type was fired. Have you progressed further?

DIRECTOR

Gouseev examined these instructions with interest and with confidence. It would be easy to deal with Numbers 1, 2, 3, 4, and 5, since it was merely a question of instructing contacts who were already at work in the places concerned. He knew all about Alexei Antonov and was certain that, with care and in time, he or a contact could reduce Antonov to a position of extreme anxiety, subservience, even terror, so that, to regain his Communist status, he'd be ready to do anything. Gouseev was not only trained and experienced in espionage and fifth-column work, in the fomentation and prolongation of strikes, in sabotage methods and barricade fighting, but in political and psychological development methods.

His reply to the Director was confident and to the point:

TO THE DIRECTOR. 779.

1. Funds. Money sent by legitimate channels can be slightly increased as we are in process of 'decorations and alterations' and are buying two motorcars, some cupboards, etc. But we need a secret channel for large sums.

2. Re your 3188. Davis now has complete command of Youth Movement in Cardiff and is in a position of administrative and organizational control. He will at a later date introduce Prosser into a key position. Liaison is maintained with eleven other clubs and some correspondence abroad. Adherence to party is kept secret by both Davis and Prosser. Davis has in fact joined the Conservative Club!

3. Veall Motor Bodies. Bailey says other shop stewards are waiting for the introduction at the London Motor Show of new VM-3 Sports Model before striking. Large orders are bound to be placed. Experience now is that American market insists on delivery date as being part of contract and if not kept order would be cancelled. A strike in six weeks' time would paralyse the company.

4. Your 3192 noted. Will speak to Max.

5. Regret photographs not more useful. Progress is slow on this matter, but will be accelerated once we have the smallest information regarding uses. All known component manufacturers and the relevant trade Press is under observation.

GOUSEEV

He wrote with extreme confidence.

They would win.

How could they lose?

They had a fifth column in New York, Santiago, Liège, Munich, Valparaiso, Seattle, Birmingham, Glasgow, Cairo, Johannesburg, Vienna, Lucerne, Michigan, Marseilles, Istanbul, Bonn, London . . .

There was no fifth column in Moscow.

In all the countries of the world (and, amusing thought, particularly the civilized countries) any idealist who wanted one world and did not believe religion had or would obtain it had only one creed to turn to . . .

In all the countries of the world anyone who hated the established regime could turn to Communism for help. And they did. All the Soviets had to do was promote the fifth column, organize it, use it. There was a streak in every man which delved in secrecy, silent power, unknown might, and another that wallowed in destruction – the senseless destruction of what was most valuable, sacred. Organize these and other urges for Communism. It was impossible to lose. The corruption, graft, and weakness of human nature itself were allies of Communism. There was no one creed in opposition. And those few who acknowledged a God and lived by His rules – fairness, forgiveness, love thine enemies and thy neighbours – a hopeless, useless philosophy in this war. These were so feeble that they were scarcely involved. The difference was that for the Western World the war had no reality; it belonged in the newspapers; but for him, Igor Gouseev and his kind, it was real because they were winning.

5

MAX STUHLER

A RATHER small room, insufficient for manoeuvre really, but Sheila liked it, or, more truthfully, was at ease because the morning's audience consisted of fashion editors and journalists whom she knew, met at parties, shared a language with. An extravagant hotchpotch of furniture. Five slender journalists sat with notebooks on a Robert Adam sofa, four others on a day bed. The fashion editress of *Elegant*, who weighed eleven stone, was comfortable in a substantial Victorian gossip chair. The smaller fry were relegated to shield-back chairs. On a walnut *dressoir* in decorated marquetry stood a bowl of flowers and ferns, arranged with delicate skill by a professional hand, but now wilting in the heated atmosphere of radiators and cigarettes. Tall gilt lampstands with immense shades, illuminating small radii of nothing. On the wall neatly executed water colours by young men who had associations with the world of fashion.

The theme was tartans. It was fun to work with other models; it happened quite rarely, so that when they met there was an excited buzz of news, gossip, trade talk, Sheila wore a long-topped jumper suit and fringed scarf in the black-and-red Wallace tartan. Heather was in a sleeveless jerkin and pleated kilt skirt in yellow-and-black Macleod tartan. Suzé looked marvellous (although hardly Gallic) in trews of the red Royal Stuart tartan, which did not need royal permission. She topped them with a Shetland sweater. Ann was showing a V-necked heavy mohair sweater in MacDonald hunting tartan with a plain skirt. There were a few other girls, not known to Sheila, demonstrating some of the three hundred or so variations of tartan design. In a short while articles would appear in newspapers and magazines with titles like 'Tartan South of the Tweed', 'Gathering of the Clans', 'Over the Border', or the simple, truthful 'Tartans and Kilted Skirts Always Fashionable', and young Sassenach things in Birmingham and Bristol, Kensington and Connecticut would be buying.

No time for lunch, of course. There never was. Sheila ate sandwiches with Heather and Jane Padgham, fashion editor of *The Daily Globe*. Masses of coffee, buckets of it, and a fast, enjoyable dialogue by women who were happy in their work.

'What about accessories?'

'Plain colours, darling, or everything would be ruined.'

'Or an exactly matching tartan.'

'And where are you going to get shoes in Wallace tartan?'

Laughter . . .

'Wouldn't do for party wear at all.'

'It might be terribly clever for New Year, don't you think?'

'What's in these sandwiches?'

'Have you seen Michael lately?'

'Not lately.'

'Oh.'

In the afternoon photographs. Lights, wires, Leica, Rollei, Linhof, Canon, Nikkor; electric flashes; props which suggested a Scottish atmosphere: whisky bottles on a table, a brace of pheasant, rather grisly and off-putting, some heavy paintings of Highland stag temporarily replacing the water colours from Chelsea. Sheila spent half the afternoon in the difficult posture of a foursome reel, while Suzé in the trews had a more easy time of it, pulling vaguely on heavy rope. Buckets of tea, cigarettes, five minutes' flop into a chair, a change back into her own clothes (rather cold after the Wallace), and a taxi to Audrey's.

Her agent's office was above an antique shop. Halfway up,

the stairs of the building changed their character, became fashionable, were covered by different carpeting. Two middle-sized rooms and a tiny toilet. White walls and gilt mirrors, very large. A mixture of umbrella stand, lamp shades, filing cabinets, and pale telephones, two of them ringing. Venetian blinds, soft carpets, books and magazines on a shelf. Pretty girls (but not Sheila's type of beauty) answered the telephones, made endless appointments for Audrey's ninety models.

Audrey was middle-aged, small, with an intellectual face.

'You've been doing the tartans?'

'Yes. I'm just on my way to Maurice's.'

'Can you go to Belgrave Hill next Tuesday?'

'What time?'

'Afternoon. Two o'clock.'

'I was going to Globe Street.'

'I've asked Lize to do that. They particularly wanted you.'

'Well, if you feel, Audrey –'

'I said you would. Naughty of me, but they were so insistent.'

'What is it, anyway?'

'Out-of-doors wear.'

'All right, darling, it'll be a bit of fresh air for me.'

'Thank you, Sheila. I wish they were all as helpful as you . . .'

'Miss Grilli, your call to Brussels is coming through in a few moments.'

'All right, Margaret. Oh, and Sheila, dear –'

'Yes, Audrey?'

'I've forgotten. Oh yes. The Tuesday thing. He's a new one, terribly clever, I'm told. What's his name? Max something, Austrian, I think. *Bizarre* thinks very highly of him.'

'Miss Grilli, they're on now.'

Sheila said, 'I'll try to please,' although it was meaningless. She was in the top forty of the world. Who was Max something to be pleased, coerced? A young one, she supposed, with a gimmick and a good camera. She noted it down in her diary. She would do her best for Audrey. She wasn't temperamental, like some; she was a supreme technician. She could even switch on sleep, which was a necessity for a model, while Heather, for one, was wallowing in pills to make her sleep or be lively. Quite unnecessary, Sheila thought.

It was relaxing to sit for an hour and a half in Maurice's comfortable chair, while he attended to her hair and a girl worked on her fingernails. Warm and steamy so that she was nearly asleep. A nice quiet evening, watching rubbish? Oh, God, no. Peter was taking her to dinner. Ian still hadn't phoned. She had absolutely no intention of phoning him. Why hadn't Heather been seeing Michael lately? Was that off again? She was foolish to commit herself to one man, positively bourgeois. All they had in common was horses.

In Bond Street a woman examined her from some yards off, pinkened, hesitated. Sheila went cold in the inevitability of something and stared beyond her at traffic, buildings, but the woman, stuttering in slight nervousness, said, 'You *are* Sheila Haward, aren't you?'

Sheila said politely. 'Yes, I am.'

The woman was of medium build, middle-aged, smart, absurd. She was very hot and bothered and proceeded perhaps with regret: 'I don't know you, actually, although I do know Yvonne Watson who does know you – I mean, you'll think me awfully silly, but I've seen you so often – if you know what I mean! You're on this month's cover page of *Bizarre*. You must be *thrilled*. But I rather wanted,' she concluded lamely, 'to ask you about facials.'

Sheila just stared.

'I mean, what do you use?'

Sheila was ice-cold, the mild arrogance of perpetual victory. She explained very quickly what she did about facials.

The woman said, 'I'm Mrs Harrington-Smythe. It's so nice of you to –'

'Not at all, but there's my taxi.' She waved a hand at the passing vehicle. 'Sloane Street, please, in a tearing hurry. Good-bye, Mrs Harrington-Smythe . . .' and that lady was left with mouth open, standing by a lamp-post.

Sheila went home, changed into slacks and slippers, unwound. After a few drinks of coffee she started to enter her expenses for the day in a book. She couldn't really remember the taxi fares. How much was the one to Sloane Street? Five shillings. Better put seven – I must have tipped the little man.

The telephone rang. She answered it quickly, almost ran to it;

it was feared and adored, like a lover. Always something interesting.

Ian. Oh dear.

'You did say Tuesday if I thought of something –'

'Did I? I thought Wednesday. I'm absolutely positive I said Wednesday.'

'Oh. Well, I do hope you can change to Tuesday –'

'Ian, angel, I can't be dotted about –'

'– because I've two tickets for that new American musical.'

'Have you now? How terribly clever you are, Ian!'

'I've heard it's terrific.'

'Yes, they were queueing for it in New York. I had to miss it.'

'Will you come?'

'Yes, I'd love to.'

'On Tuesday?'

Ian didn't seem able to believe his ears. Rather small, silly pink ears he had, porcine, and all that.

'Yes, Ian, Tuesday.'

'Will you be able to change your engagements?'

'Ian, don't *interrogate* me. How did you get the tickets?'

'I bought them.'

'Ian, don't be tedious. I know you bought them, but from whom?'

'From the theatre.'

'But, angel, you must have queued for *hours*.'

'Well, yes, I suppose I did. All night, actually.'

'But how incredibly gallant.'

'It was for you, really, not to see the show.'

'Well, it was wonderful of you, and I'll be there.'

Five more minutes to be rid of Ian. Then she considered what to wear for dinner this evening. In the next hour the telephone rang, twice, but on the second occasion she was in her bath and didn't answer.

Dinner in Gratton Street with Peter, Lord Duguid. She decided very quickly that she didn't like him. Not enough, anyway. This in no way interfered with her appetite or conversation. There were other people in the sophisticated restaurant, and it was amusing to see them and be seen, to identify identification. She was glad, despite Peter being rather a bore, that she'd selected this particular dress. Two taxi rides and twenty-five spots of rain would ruin it, but not to worry.

Lord Duguid, thirty-one, about to be divorced, had a proposition, not, alas, like David's, or not quite. He was a well-known lecherous figure in and out of gossip columns, and Sheila had no intention of meeting him again.

Over the *foie gras truffé d'Alsace* Lord Duguid said, 'A superb dress. Tell me about it.'

'You mean what it is?'

'Yes, I'm frightfully interested.'

'Well, it's called, if I remember rightly, a melon-interior jumper-top sheath of tulle, embroidered with crystals. The belt is diamanté buckled and is slightly diagonal – I can't think why.'

'Marvellous, absolutely marvellous.'

'I'm glad you feel it is.'

Over the *scampi frits au cardinal* Lord Duguid, now an increasing pink, reprimanded, or seemed concerned. 'A woman like you shouldn't have to work.'

'But I *like* working.'

He waved a hand that clearly had never worked. 'A woman as beautiful as yourself shouldn't have a care, any money worries.'

'I don't think I have.'

'She should just be beautiful.'

'We shouldn't all be idle.'

'Who said you'd be idle, eh?'

She went cold at the crudity in his voice. He perhaps noticed, for he explained, 'So many places to go to, the whole world to see, and the whole world should see you.'

It does, Sheila thought, on paper.

Over the *poulet à la broche aux herbes de Provence* Lord Duguid, who was slightly drunk, confided, 'Look, I'll put it to you. You're terribly beautiful. I feel you should have security, luxury, anything you want. I can make this possible for you.'

She asked facetiously, 'Have you won a football pool or something.'

'Two thousand a year,' said Lord Duguid. 'How do you feel about that?'

'About what?'

'It'd be tax-free,' Lord Duguid pointed out. 'Don't think I don't know the nuisance tax is to people.'

'I'm not quite following you.'

'I'm offering you two thousand a year to be my mistress,' confided Lord Duguid. He did not even bother to keep his voice down, so certain was he of himself. An old routine perhaps. 'And introductions to the right people.'

Sheila didn't know whether to giggle or be angry.

'Will the right people be interested to meet your mistress?'

He thought she was serious. 'Of course. They're perfectly reasonable.'

She said with sudden anger, 'And you don't suppose I might know the right people already?' (This was the bit that stung: that she should be rated as some tart or shopgirl. The proposition's relationship to her body irritated less.)

'You're angry? No need to be angry.'

'Is it all I'm worth? Two thousand a year?'

'Tax-free,' Lord Duguid reminded her, 'but if you didn't feel –'

Sheila stood up. 'I've an awful headache. I think I'd like to go home.'

'I'll fetch the car.'

'I'm sure there's no need to do that. The man will find me a taxi.'

'He'll get you an aspirin.'

'I've had a busy day,' Sheila said coldly, 'and I'd prefer to go home on my own. You don't mind?'

'You're not angry with my proposition?'

'Your proposition does not interest me.'

'Think about it.'

'I'm not likely to forget it.'

'Shall I telephone?'

'If you wish.'

She had not once called him Peter throughout the evening, a man who expected her to become his mistress. He was even now, as he escorted her over the soft carpet, past an electric spit, people at a stone-walled bar, eyeing other women who were there.

Sheila went back to her flat and read a book. The telephone rang after an hour and she lifted it. 'Hello?'

Lord Duguid's voice pleaded, 'Sheila, how's your headache?'

'Wrong number,' she said sharply and slammed the instrument on its cradle.

Tuesday morning, Sheila called out, 'This is the place,' and the taxi driver cut in mercilessly. Sheila opened the door herself – she was slightly late – and dragged her canvas case out behind her.

'You're an angel! How much was that little ride?'

'Four bob to you, miss.'

'Thanks. 'Bye.'

Sheila hurried into the small, effective contemporary entrance. There was a different photograph on display, one of Ann, rather tired, she thought.

The receptionist greeted her, 'Good morning, Miss Haward,' and led the way to the models' dressing room. 'I'll tell him you're here.'

Sheila sat on a fragile gilt chair amid flawless mirrors and fluorescent illumination. She lit a cigarette, looked in the nearest mirror. Some hair was astray. She stood up, tidied it. A knock. 'Come in.'

'Good morning, Sheila.'

'Hello, Richard. What a delightfully exotic hat.'

'Wrong size, I suspect. Here's the dress. It looks gorgeous and expensive.'

'It certainly is a dream thing.'

'Schneider said to tell you it's a street dress in gold and white silk and wool. Two pieces. A loose Magyar top over a bias skirt with a wrap-over. You'll love it.'

'Is it to be a colour photograph?'

'Alas, no.'

'Darker stockings, then?'

She unzipped the unfashionable canvas bag in which she carried the tools of her profession : six pairs of shoes, jewellery, make-up, different types of stockings ...

'Shoes won't really matter,' the photographer explained. 'I'm thinking of cutting you off at the knees. Very painful!

Oh, and these gloves are absolutely not the colour, but they're pale and will photograph well. Okay?'

'You're serious about the hat?'

'That, too, doesn't really belong. It really feels rather Mondayish around here. But I'm reliably informed that it's Tuesday. It's a light-caramel straw thing. The brim will throw a lot of shadow, practically obliterate poor you. If it's over your ears I still have a white straw sombrero which I think is smaller.'

Sheila said, 'See, it fits!'

'Splendid! Now, very plain props or the striped effect would be obscured. Grey silk curtains, I think, and a chair. One hand to touch the chair and your head turned. No smiles, I think – smiles are for the *inexpensive*! Somewhere between charm and significance. Okay?'

'Make-up all right?'

'Rather paler in the face, I'd prefer. Okay. Shan't be ready for half an hour. The place is a shambles.'

Sheila put on the dress and altered her make-up. She played with the hat and liked it. She was cold now but soon warmed by the electric fire. She smoked three cigarettes in a row and read twenty-five pages of a rude and exasperating, incomprehensible novel. Then one of Richard's assistants fetched her.

They worked for two hours, stopping once for coffee. Richard was hidden behind his monorail camera. The assistants, young men with rather frenzied eagerness, positioned the lights, moved the wretched chair, thought F16 would better define the texture of the dress than F11, diffused the lighting, harshened it, bounced it. Richard used various electronic flash and model lighting, stands and ladders, top lights on booms, spotlights three-quarters behind Sheila, three-quarters in front, themes with intense illumination and themes with subdued or angled.

Sheila was calm, assured, technically cooperative, the perfect human prop. She was aware that every shot was of the material, not herself. Her face would be a vague beautiful something on top of a clearly defined, very desirable two-piece exclusive street dress.

Time passed very quickly, only noticed by an increase in

temperature produced by the lights and used air. She thought how nice it would be to have a cigarette, that she was ravenously hungry, and, because this afternoon, too, she would stand, how fortunate it was, and how pleasing, that tonight she'd sit with Ian and see *Tropicana.* She also decided she hated the shoes she was wearing. Too small. Sheila had large, long feet which one photographer teased her about: 'Constructed in a Clyde shipyard.'

Lunch in a taxi, as usual, and at five minutes to two she was outside the unfamiliar address in Belgrave Hill. She'd heard of him. Duchesses and shipping magnates and theatrical photographs. It was a one-man studio, rather small, with a neat pale entrance into a Queen Anne building in what had once been a fashionable crescent but now had its quota of flats and shops and even a garage. There was one astonishing photograph as a showpiece: taken in Africa, two hundred, three hundred, or, more, tribesmen jumping in ecstasy, with ornamentation and weapons, dust rising in still clouds, the earth baked, and mountains forty or fifty miles distant. A magnificent picture; Stuhler must have an exceptional eye to have taken that.

The receptionist was a dark, beautiful girl with a sad, angry face. 'I'll fetch him for you,' she told Sheila, and there seemed to be some implication – as if Sheila had asked for Stuhler.

He came at once – a tall, overpowering man in shirt sleeves; Sheila was conscious straightaway of magnetism, brute personality. He examined her for several more moments than were comfortable, but it was in no way a leer; it was a rather exasperating inspection.

'You're Miss Haward?'

'Yes. How do you do, Mr Stuhler.'

'Somebody has been taking mere pictures of you,' he said. 'I shall take a photograph.'

'It's really the coat –'

'To hell with the coat,' Stuhler growled so that she couldn't help a small giggle. The coat was why she was here.

'That's a marvellous photograph outside,' she said.

'I was young and impressionable,' he said with curious bitterness. 'Did you notice that they were all naked? Every single one.'

She hadn't noticed.

'What does that prove?' she asked. He seemed to think some comment was necessary.

'About me or about them?'

'About them.'

'Simply that they'd never heard of Manchester.'

He was a little disconcerting; interesting, but with some fixation. Not a young genius with a gimmick either, but forty or a hard-worn thirty-five. A huge beast, fifteen stone of him, pale-blue eyes that were tough, but sensual, with failure somewhere. He had an immense presence, dominating even her who was rarely uneasy. He would not be a man who tolerated fools. She wondered unaccountably about the sad, tall, bitter girl who could be much more than a receptionist.

'What were you doing in Africa?' Sheila asked.

'I'm in love with the primitive,' was Stuhler's explanation. 'I'm only doing this for money,' he confided with rare apology.

'Doing what?'

'Photographing silly little girls and homosexual actors.'

'I only do it for money, too,' she said, stung.

'I like faces, though. There was an alderman here – face like a hippopotamus, but it had texture, weakness. He was an honest little man, said I was a conceited bastard.'

Sheila didn't know what to say.

'I am, of course,' Stuhler affirmed. 'Time's running out. Be honest and to hell with 'em.'

'With whom?' she asked wearily.

'Hypocrites and Philistines and phonies and polite little people. I wanted to meet you because you've a superb face – arrogant and vain and sensual and, I suppose, beautiful. You must let me take a photograph without all those damn clothes sometime –'

Sheila blinked in shock. 'I don't do those sort of photographs.'

'Don't be bloody silly,' Stuhler told her. 'I don't mean smut. In any case, I meant simply without this clutter of props. You're not a prude, I presume. I'd like to get that pride on bromide paper, humiliate it.'

Sheila laughed outright. 'I'm beginning to think your alderman was right.'

'Did I say he wasn't?'

'Aren't we going to work this afternoon?'

'Am I frightening you? You want to run away?'

'I suppose you're rather amusing,' said Sheila coldly.

It didn't squash him, merely earned a little respect. 'I think you're much better than some. You're improving.'

'And I think you're merely rude, not clever.'

Max Stuhler laughed, took her arm. 'Keep it up!' he urged. 'We'll get on fine. Don't be impressed. I'd hate that. It would condemn you.'

'You may talk as long as you wish,' Sheila pointed out tartly, 'and all about yourself, so long as you pay me by the hour. Does it take a long time for you to talk yourself out?' she inquired. She was very angry, had never been treated like this before. Audrey would have to put up with failure for the first time. She didn't ask for V.I.P. treatment (although she usually received it), but any fool with a camera must know that failure was inevitable if the model didn't cooperate, couldn't because she wasn't relaxed.

'Yes, yes, we must conform,' Stuhler said, not at all offended. 'For an hour or two anyway. This is the coat. Collarless, as you see. Useless, I should think. The colour is called opaque green. I call it pea soup. There's a bloody little woman, fashion agent or something, who's handling it, whatever that means. She's waiting.'

'The people who make the coat employ her to advertise it,' Sheila explained.

'You don't like me, do you?' Max Stuhler said. 'I don't bother with charm. My trouble is I'm bored. Nothing frightens me and I ought to be terrified now and again. I like terror,' he confided. 'Crude, raw, with death or blood somewhere about. I can't stand your tame society with press-button death.'

'Not my society particularly –'

'Animals are magnificent. They don't answer the telephone, go to the theatre, write letters, complain of incompatibility. You should go to Africa while it's still there.'

'I've been.'

'Whereabouts? You see – we have something in common. I knew we had.'

'Mombasa, Nairobi, Cairo. I'm sorry,' Sheila conceded. 'It did tend to ice drinks and air-conditioned hotels.'

'You've my kind of honesty,' Stuhler said. He was almost enthusiastic, as if Sheila had to prove something to his satisfaction and was on the way to doing it. 'I'm going to like you. Where else have you been?'

'New York, Philadelphia, Italy, Germany, Switzerland, Paris – the usual places.'

'You like excitement?'

'Yes. I'm only a woman, but –'

'You take risks? On horses, in cars, skiing on ice?'

'I'm capable of those. Yes. I've shot a few things. Why?'

'What are your politics?'

'The usual.'

'Meaning you haven't any?'

'Well, I mean, can one believe in politicians?'

'Or God,' he chided. 'Do you believe in old man God? Are you afraid of Him when you decide to sleep with someone?'

'A little bit.'

'To what do you owe loyalty? Anybody? Anything?'

'My parents, I think.'

'What do you want in the world? Money?'

'I don't know. I hadn't thought about it.'

'Lovers? A husband? Kids? Travel? To live or to exist?'

'I like being alive. I'm a little restless,' she told him, 'as if I'm missing something.'

'Absolutely!' Max Stuhler said. 'You couldn't have put it better. I'm like that. Life is so tame I have to invent excitement, seek out terror ... Everything's been done ... We must work,' he concluded abruptly. 'I talk too much when I find the right one to talk to. Don't think I hate it all. There's a lot to be said for civilization. D'you like American cars? I love them. Vulgar, but splendid, a logical conclusion, not a compromise for country lanes. Powerful. We'll go now with your opaque-green coat and take the photographs outside the American Embassy. That ought to sell the coat. A mere fifteen guineas and it goes with a Cadillac!'

There was a knock at the door. The sad beautiful face ventured around its arc, ready to be insulted. 'Mr Stuhler, forgive me, but Miss Billard is getting anxious.'

'This is Tilda. She has the most difficult face in the world. She insists on sadness, inhibition.'

The girl neither smiled nor flushed, scarcely noticed, but reminded him, 'Who insists on timetables. It will be dark in three hours.'

Miss Billard complained, 'Max, what the hell d'you think you're doing? Excuse me, Miss Haward, but he's no appreciation of the value of other people's time. Only his own. Very rude about his own time.'

'I wish you could frighten me, but you don't,' Stuhler said, quite seriously.

Sheila turned her face to one side to smile.

Outside, in Belgrave Hill, October illumination on wet streets, parked cars; dirty windows glistened; leaves fell with deliberation.

'Do you like the coat?' Miss Billard asked.

'It's a dream thing,' Sheila told her, 'but what about when it rains? Collarless!'

'Rain?' queried Miss Billard, as if she'd just heard of it for the first time. 'Why, I suppose you'd call a taxi.'

Sheila shared her first smile with Max Stuhler.

When they reached Grosvenor Square he soon found a large American sedan, a Lincoln-Mercury. Sheila, slightly stooped, held the door handle of this magnificent monster as if she owned it. They moved on to a Chevrolet Corvair.

'This is a fine design,' Stuhler said. 'Stand in front of it ... Move your legs apart.'

Sheila did so.

'Not as much as that. Like a lady,' he urged, 'not a tart.'

She said in fury, 'Would you know the difference?' and obtained a nervous laugh from Miss Billard. 'He's always like this. A genius or something.'

'There is no difference,' Stuhler said; a stupid, meaningless assertion, but Sheila fulminated, unable to find answer.

Not many people watched them. Stuhler was using flash now, and Sheila stood by a Cadillac Sixty Special. An old lady walking behind stopped and said, 'Excuse me, dear. Did you know the label was hanging down the back of this coat?'

Sheila smiled and said, 'It's all right, my dear. The camera doesn't see that.'

'Oh, are you having your picture taken?'

Stuhler said roughly, 'Madam, your face doesn't go with Miss Haward or a Cadillac. Go and get your tea.'

The old lady didn't quite comprehend but simply said sweetly, ' 'Bye-bye, dear. You are a pretty girl,' and moved on.

Sheila protested. 'That was worse than rude. It was gross.'

'You feel age merits respect?'

'Of course I do.'

'Then you're a sentimental fool. Age is just vegetable stuff. You stick around counting birthdays.'

He merited the most almighty humiliation.

'One day you'll be old,' she said, 'or ill, or in pain. It would be too much to expect your feelings could get hurt, but they'll humiliate your body.'

'Who will?' he jeered. 'God, a hospital, a woman, old age, pain? The only thing that could even embarrass me would be castration . . . Now, then, would you like to eat?'

'No. I'm meeting a friend.'

'How nice to have friends,' he sneered. 'A boy, of course, to hold your hand, tickle you in a car, say how pretty you are.'

She flushed under the pallor of the make-up. 'I hope the photographs turn out satisfactorily,' she said to Miss Billard. 'I can hardly believe they will. Even a Hasselblad camera is useless in the hands of an amateur.'

Four hours later the girls in *Tropicana*, dressed as macaws, danced the new number which was taking London by storm. Sheila had heard it in New York, loved the tune and the cheeky words. Ian offered her a chocolate and, taking one, she thought about Max Stuhler and began to giggle. What a conceited fool the man was! It was a technique, she supposed, to prove to nobility that he was rare. Ian said, 'What's so amusing?' and she answered, 'I'm just happy, that's all.' She could sense his pleasure in the darkness, the belief that the evening was successful by virtue of what *he* had done, was doing and saying.

She went to Paris and worked until midnight for three consecutive days.

Peter telephoned. She knew several Peters, and it was some time before she identified this one as Janine's friend in marine insurance. She put him off, convincing lies or unconvincing, it didn't matter.

Mr Harley took her to dinner, but it was merely a meal.

David did the ton again, this time at night, and it was good fun, but she couldn't bear to be pawed and he was a little angry when the evening ended.

She did quite well in her ninth lesson with Captain Dean, scoring two hits.

She sat in studios and smoked cigarettes and read bits of novels about young men who were angry with the world, because the world was as stupid as they were.

She went home to Somerset for a weekend, the first time for more than two months, and this at least was the same. Home was a small stone house in four acres. It was warm and rich, moist earth and wet grass and silence and a slow sky. She caught Fomes, the gardener, asleep in the rhododendrons. Poirot, the boxer, was a slobbering, devoted, crazy thing. She adored him. She rode for miles on a friend's horse, alone with the ferns and sky and glistening hedges and the steam of the horse's breath. Shots in the distance and birds as quick as light in the hedges. Here was peace, safety, although she knew from five years' metropolitan experience of art galleries, painters, journalists, informed opinion, how naïve were the very furnishings of what had been her home for most of life and how old-fashioned were the views of her parents. 'I worry a bit, you know,' her mother said. 'London's not the same, with all those Teddy boys and people in Trafalgar Square.' Sheila smiled in furtive awareness. She never worried about things like Teddy boys! They had a quick wit when she saw them : 'Careful, miss, your eyes are showing,' which had an element of truth in it, for so skilfully and totally made-up was she that her eyes were perhaps her only uncovered property.

There was a curious unreality about the days. It was as if she were waiting for something. One afternoon she was in Audrey's office and Audrey was reciting a list of forthcoming work: 'And then on Wednesday the Vedette Hotel. The Duchess of Minx will be there. Thursday afternoon Hanover Square for the party dresses. Friday Belgrave Hill. All day –'

'Belgrave Hill, did you say?'

Sheila's voice hesitated, and she was annoyed to feel a weakness, a fluttering in her body.

'Yes, you remember. Max Stuhler.'

'I'm not keen on Max Stuhler.'

'He did a splendid one for Miss Billard. It was in the Sunday intellectuals.'

'I didn't see it.'

Audrey found it for her: a photograph which caught Sheila half turned to the old lady, and the bonnet of the Cadillac not too obtrusive.

'He's a damn rude man and I'm not keen on working with him or for him.'

'That's awkward,' Audrey said. 'He seems to be anxious that it should be you.'

'Send Elizabeth,' suggested Sheila. 'She's my type.'

'All right,' agreed Audrey, and Sheila almost grinned with pleasure. She felt a little sorry, though, for Elizabeth, who would take the brunt of Stuhler's incivility.

She knew that ought to be the end of Max Stuhler and hoped it would be. No. She was too honest and recognized the nature of her hopes, overlaid by pride, and she was perfectly aware that it was not the end, scarcely the beginning.

Days and nights went by and Sheila almost forgot him. Then, one evening, alone for once, her feet up, watching television, the phone rang. It would be David or Ian or George or somebody . . .

'This is Max Stuhler.'

'Oh.' She again found herself annoyably breathless, caught out, not ready for him. 'Who gave you my telephone number?'

'Your agent said if we must quarrel we'd better do it without a referee.'

'Audrey should have respected my privacy –'

'If I seemed rude it was because I had to break down the elements of resistance –'

'And you succeeded, of course,' Sheila inquired, expecting a conceited 'yes' with explanations of technique.

'One never succeeds,' Stuhler told her. 'Not totally. A human being is too complicated. I did manage to remove the aloofness, the not-involved.'

'You only needed to explain what you wanted and I could have coped. I have been photographed before,' she pointed out.

'Pictures of clothes!' Stuhler protested. 'I focused on *you*.'

'It's the clothes they want to sell –'

'Oh, *them*. They'll sell those easily enough, vanity being the female actuation! Now, listen. The next time I ask for you, are you going to come?'

She couldn't find an excuse, didn't want to obtain one; she'd made her resistance.

'All right, Mr Stuhler,' she conceded. 'But bear in mind you are paid to photograph fashion, not me. Explain what you want. I can probably give it.'

'I'm sure you can,' he said, and rang off.

Bloody man, she thought. Complications, emotionalism. She was afraid of him and afraid of herself . . . For the fluttering in her stomach and weaknesses in words, even her raging, were symptoms, she knew, of interest in him; she should have squashed him within ten minutes of meeting and to hell with all that stuff about Africa and the primitives. A yawn or a devastating 'Oh, really?' would have humiliated him. Instead, she had to have pride, be offended, childish. He wasn't what she wanted. He was too powerful, selfish, cruel. Perhaps after all she was ordinary, needed no more than the boy next door. You're a fool, she told herself. He only *talks*.

Three days later she was asked to go to his studio. Audrey apologized, 'I'm sorry, Sheila, but he was very rude about Elizabeth. Either you go or we lose business.'

The tall, ascetic receptionist greeted her with calm, sad scrutiny: 'Miss Haward, isn't it? Good morning.'

Sheila couldn't resist asking, 'Have you worked long for Mr Stuhler?'

The answer was slightly evasive: 'I'm only nineteen.'

'Oh, I see.'

In the model's changing room she said, 'I'll turn on the electric fire.'

'I'm not really cold.'

And then *he* was there – a different shirt, but stained as usual; it was as if he must prove masculinity, even by olfactory offensiveness. Nothing must dominate him, not even clothes.

He smiled very slightly and there was something generous in it – an acknowledgement. Sheila decided that he was, after all, likable. You just had to be rude back. He had the most enormous box with him.

'Tilda,' he said, 'go to fetch the hat by Otto Ungerer. Well, Miss Haward, you're going to have a woman's day. This little parcel is insured for four thousand pounds. I want charcoal eyelids, not those green, and an overlay of Paraguayan Gold patted on.'

For a man who insisted on masculinity he seemed to understand women's technicalities all too well.

It was a coat of chestnut-coloured wild mink. Sheila, never satiated despite an endless procession of clothes feminine, gasped with delight.

'We're due in the foyer of the Babylon Tower Hotel in half an hour,' Stuhler said. 'We're also booked there for lunch. I hope you don't mind.'

She did not tell him whether she minded or not.

The hat by Otto Ungerer was a tall, crazy thing, absolutely right, the correct size, too.

It was an amusing morning. Other people had to endure or contest Stuhler's rudeness; it was laid on for *her*. At times, instead of being brusque, he could turn on a charm or, at least, a persuasiveness that was irresistible. One old taxi driver with a miserable face and a red-veined, enormous nose – poor little man, his very skin and eyes seemed wet, frozen – was surly and indifferent, in a hurry, but Stuhler talked him and his taxi into the camera's eye. Sheila herself was photographed by the taxi, by a Rolls-Royce (its occupant was ready to be indignant until Sheila used *her* charm); she stood by tables of inexplicable shape, examined cacti of dubious beauty and obvious penetration; bought a *New York Times*; sniffed at a tropical flower; entered a lift; stood in vague sophistication to be greeted by top-hatted doormen outside immense glass and gilt doors; and all the time Stuhler talked, inveigled, persuaded, urged, harassed – not her (who was a technician, in no need of instruction), but others; and it was amusing to see and hear his various techniques.

'I enjoyed that,' he said at midday. 'The human kind. Did you notice a sort of pattern, a flow, in the manner each was ready to puff and blow until they saw you?'

'I think that, for once, you underestimate yourself,' she told him, but smiling, complimented.

At lunch there were people at one of the tables whom he recognized, had photographed. He described them as they'd sat before the camera – pitilessly, but with humour that could not be denied.

'I've taken enough photographs,' he said. 'Let's take the afternoon off.'

'Wouldn't that be dishonest?' Sheila said, at once nervous.

'I don't see why,' Stuhler said. 'I'm paying for you by the hour, and I've booked you for the day.'

She said nothing, for she appreciated that by making one objection which he had been able to dismiss she had been manoeuvred into agreement.

'What about this coat?' she inquired.

He smiled in sudden enjoyment. 'Let's sell it! Let's go along to somewhere like Camberwell and see what they think of us and the coat!'

They found a shop of suitable shabbiness belonging to a Mr Lippiatt. A girl fetched him reluctantly at Stuhler's request.

'Wha's a matter?' he asked.

He was a man whose life would be full of things going and staying wrong.

'We want to sell this coat.'

'This thing?' Mr Lippiatt said contemptuously. He had the extraordinary capacity of not seeing Sheila, only the coat. 'How much y'give for it?'

Stuhler said, 'Three hundred.'

Mr Lippiatt laughed. 'It's amazing, isn't it?' he asked someone to his left, not there. 'You'd swear it was a real one.'

Stuhler had an expression of artificial conspiracy. Sheila's urge was to laugh. Now Stuhler managed to express surprise and criminal intention in the same astonishing facial manoeuvre.

'You mean it *isn't*?'

Mr Lippiatt pitied them.

'You in films or something?'

'The lady is.'

'Made in West Bromwich, I shouldn't wonder,' said Mr Lippiatt. 'What did they tell you it was?'

'Wild mink.'

'Wild mink,' mimicked Mr Lippiatt. 'It's the wrong colour, for a start. God knows what animal this was, if it was animal at all. Where d'you get it?'

Sheila said with a straight face, 'An American gentleman gave it to me.'

'A bloke said he'd give me four hundred,' Stuhler said.

'Take it!' urged Mr Lippiatt. 'My God, boy, you were on to something. Amazing, absolutely amazing, what they can do in a laboratory.'

He was so earnest that they almost began to believe him.

'You don't want to buy it?' Stuhler asked.

'I don't know. It's a risk. It means I got to sell it crooked, swear it's a real one. Three fifty I'll give you, and, my God, I'll sweat. I'll sweat until it's gone.'

'I'm not happy,' Stuhler said. 'You give me three fifty. Maybe someone who's not an expert will give me five hundred.'

'Never,' disputed Mr Lippiatt. 'You know what? I'll put that in my window for not more than three seventy-five and I won't dare insure it. I'll sweat until it's gone and then I'll worry nights in case the tart – excuse me, lady – the purchaser comes back, offended.'

'You know what I'm going to do?' Sheila said. 'I'm going to take it and throw it back in his face –'

'Mustn't be hasty,' observed Mr Lippiatt. 'What do hurt feelings matter? Three fifty in the bank is more to the point. A lady's safe with money in the bank.'

'Are you suggesting the lady's pride is not worth three hundred and fifty pounds?' demanded Stuhler. 'Listen, Mr Lippiatt, I was told this coat was worth at least two thousand. The only difficulty is that it was stolen –'

'My God, I'm not touching it then,' protested Mr Lippiatt.
'You better get out of here –'

'You put me in a difficult position –'

'I'll give you three hundred.'

'Good afternoon, Mr Lippiatt,' Stuhler bid gravely. 'I'm
sorry we can't do business.'

This was Max, the way he enjoyed himself in the limited territory of urban society. He was terribly unusual, amusing, nor did
he fail in the obvious excitements . . .

He took her in a Ferrari up the M.1. at over a hundred miles
an hour the whole way, at one point touching 143. This was the
difference, she saw : David touched the ton, which was exciting;
Max maintained it for an entire journey, irrespective of traffic
density or weather.

They went gliding at night. This might have been unintentional, although she thought not. It started in daylight, and a
strong updraft underneath heavy, rather thundery, bulbous rain
clouds carried the glider silently to six thousand feet. Stuhler
followed the weather, entered cloud, allowed the frail structure
to be sucked by powerful, capricious air currents. It rained, was
cold; Sheila got very wet, thought he'd turn back. The sun was
descending in wet, pink collapse behind strips of cloud that had
spent themselves, saturated elsewhere. A landscape without
brightness, pearl-grey, smoky; night climbed, did not descend.
Sheila felt the nibble of panic but defied it. That was what Max
would want – a howling, terrified girl would amuse him no end,
and he'd be merciless; it would have to be hysterics before he
turned back. Turned back to *what*? For there was no illuminated
aerodrome – the gliding school was merely turf on a hill,
scattered huts, a bungalow. Night finally floated up past them
and they were gliding in black silence. She was frozen stiff, wet,
anxious, but defiant. To hell with him, she'd die first. They were
lucky to get away with it, for visibility was bad; very lucky, for
the sliding glider missed trees by feet and it was not due to
Stuhler's skill. They ended in a hedge, scratched and wet, with a
two-mile walk to a pub and a telephone. Forty miles from anywhere. This worried Max not at all, for he had no sense of place.
That was perhaps his secret : he had no home despite the studio
in Belgrave Hill. The world was his home.

They did the round of night clubs and went to parties given by his friends and by hers. They went to several theatres, cinemas, a ballet, horse races, a motor race (two people were killed; he was fascinated, took photographs of exploding petrol). They travelled in a barge from the Port of London half-way to Birmingham with a man who hit his wife and used the choicest language on her and two urchins. They went fishing in a small vessel in a rough sea (the camera was his infallible introduction) and in a helicopter to a lighthouse which ships could not reach. She accompanied him, although with protests this time, to be 'amused' by two of his 'friends' who were to rob a warehouse, her heart thumping as they all sat in a stolen vehicle. It had a theatrical unreality, something done to amuse her, but it was real all right and she knew the police wouldn't excuse her if they were caught.

Stuhler was uninterested this time. 'Too boring,' he complained. 'You either get caught or not. There's no feeling of terror.'

'I feel slightly sick,' Sheila admitted.

'You're doing fine.'

She never mentioned him in letters to her parents. She saw him as a man of brilliance not canalized, with an unfortunate contempt of too many people. He was quick and accurate in his identification of vanity and weakness in others but failed to recognize it in himself. He was very witty about aldermen and bishops and other models he had photographed, but had long since forgotten the ordinary of the world, his roots in earth . . . For he was the son of a farmer in the Austrian Tyrol. It was incredible, proved something, for he had a mind like a computer, almost infallible, and his English had scarcely a Continental touch. He sought out danger and exhaustion in a bored hatred of the normal. She presumed sex would be his other outlet, but even in a photographer's world of beautiful women he was contemptuous of their vanity. Sheila knew that if she surrendered to him he must realize that she was aware of submitting to destruction. This, she believed, had some kind of illogical inevitability; it made sense. He would then continue to respect her, wouldn't dismiss her. But she must never cry, plead, even talk about love, and that would be the most difficult thing of all.

Inevitably he wanted to take photographs of her, not just for the glossy magazines, but for exhibitions, in the purity of creation. Some of these, she had to admit, were extraordinary, almost a mystique, extracted from her more than she'd known she could give. In all their time together Max never touched her, although there was no hesitation between them, not even any awareness of hesitation. He never attempted to make love to her, and she didn't know what she would do if he did. For it wouldn't be tickling in a car, or sensual pleasure on a bed, something known as temporary even as committed; it would have the brute stamp of his total personality and hers; it would be a permanent thing or, at least, leave a permanent scar ... He continued to be rude, although it became acceptable, part of a relationship (themselves and the fools, other people).

One day he asked her if she'd done nude photography.

'No. I'm too skinny. And it's not my kind of modelling.'

'Would you let me try?'

'I'm not sure. What for?'

'An exhibition in Zurich.'

'It wouldn't be syndicated, circularized in magazines?'

'If it was they'd not recognize Sheila Haward, fashion model.'

She had the weak, distressing feeling that it didn't matter. So long as nothing appeared in *Country Life*, which was practically all her parents read ... Her mind hoped that her eyes did not convey to him her wish. She could not deny now what the wish was, the longing to surrender, have that immense body and personality overwhelm her.

'If you really feel I would be suitable, I suppose ...'

Her accelerating heart and languid anticipating flesh sent the remnants of the past meal halfway up her throat. Ridiculous, she thought bitterly. I've been loved before. Would it be so different if *he* possessed me? The feeling of foolishness, weakness, answered her.

'You know the technique?'

'Nothing about it at all.'

'Simply that for some hours before you arrive you must not wear tight things that would make an indentation in the skin.'

It was ridiculous.

She was a clothes prop, not a sex-appeal model.

She felt rather a fool and told no one. There was on his side, too, something secretive, not related to work, for he arranged it for a Sunday morning in his studio when she would be fresh, supple, when her skin wouldn't be marked by brassières and suspender belts and panties.

He softened any embarrassment she felt by commencing in near darkness, with soft lighting and a black background. He was in darkness, a voice instructing. His treatment was two-dimensional, atmospheric. He then proceeded to obtain a rim effect to a profile, a rather twisted profile, by far-side lighting, a single-tone pattern in a moderate, low key.

He increased the light, using a spotlight as the main source, standing her against white Venetian blinds to produce a horizontal counter effect. An hour went by; it became warm. She began to feel other things – hunger, sleepiness, disappointment. He wasn't going to make love to her. He was simply going to take photographs for an exhibition in Zurich. Like all artists he was selfish. By the time he was working in full illumination she was angry and didn't care about the presence of her body.

Max said, 'Put your head slightly on one side,' and then criticized, 'No. Not like that.'

He walked over to her for the tenth, fortieth time in that hour or so and held her head in his enormous hands. He moved the head and it was unbearable – she must sigh, plead with the merest breath. He kissed her hard on the unpainted mouth and she felt her face going scarlet like a silly school-girl's. She said nothing, but he must surely hear her hurrying heart, know that her limbs had tired, turned to liquid. When his hand touched her breast she jumped at the touch, was instantly lost with him in passion. Her one hand made a gesture of protest, a technical slap, but he held her wrist, twisted it slightly (as if he believed the opposition was real, had to be overcome), and moved her toward the sofa on which she'd already been photographed. Neither of them said a word. He had no fear of her at all, had in fact a brutal polish, moving her like a pliable thing, a machine that he was qualified to use. He was technical, assured, opened a little drawer somewhere and extracted something even as he pushed her, so that she knew it was nothing new; he didn't even give her the pleasure of thinking so.

'Don't hurt me,' she pleaded, with at least three implications.

'Don't misunderstand me,' Max reassured her. 'I've never wanted anything so much in my life.'

Whether lie or truth, it pleased her, removed shame and embarrassment to the last stitch, so that she writhed under the ferocious glare of lamps (Coro on a sofa), so bright their warmth could be felt on her flesh, and in their eclipse she moved her head from side to side, groaned with pleasure. It was hopeless, she was doomed: whatever he intended, she'd be there; there'd be nothing easy, like marriage, no result, like children; it would end with the brute force and insults with which it began, but she was unable to alter it.

'I love you,' she said, feverish, breathless. 'You're vain and arrogant and you'll despise me for loving you, but I want you to know –'

'No, no,' Max pleaded, quite gently. 'I shall be unkind to you but never despise you.' He seemed to have something else on his mind ... 'The next time you see me you'll hate me very much –'

'Ridiculous, Max. Nothing could make me –'

'Don't tempt me,' he half defied her. 'I could make anyone hate me.'

'Then don't do it to me,' Sheila pleaded.

'I shall do it the next time I see you,' Max said with curious insistence, 'and I ask you now not to hate me.'

'I won't hate you, Max.'

'I hope not,' he said and for the first time seemed anxious, 'because you'll find it very difficult not to.' He was stroking her hair and doing tender things which proved to Sheila he was hers, permanent, total.

She went through the motions of being alive for other people, the affectation that they mattered, and the days and nights crawled by; the telephone rang in her flat, and every time it did she felt faint. She stood in front of cameras with a face that seemed without properties, concern; the eyes regarded the cameras as requested, but behind the eyes the mind was in ecstasy, turmoil, scarcely in charge of the body. And then one afternoon the telephone, and his voice, nothing changed, for he began, 'Sheila –' a word, an endearment, he had not used before. 'Can you come now?' She only paused before the mirror, wanting to be beautiful for him.

He was wandering about the studio in shirt sleeves, had evidently only just finished his day. She was hesitant for only a moment; beyond it she was an animal, waiting to be loved.

Max said, 'I'll show you the photographs.'

They were large photographs, obscene, nothing to do with the poses he had taken. She was a little astonished that he should indulge in pornography.

'Max, these are the wrong photographs.'

'No. Those are the ones you have to see. Look again.'

Sheila sat down, aware of something monstrous about to happen. The photographs were all large, had a brutal clarity; there was no mistaking her; she recognized the obscene animal as herself, in passion . . .

'I said you would hate me.'

'I see.'

'Automatic camera, of course.'

She was stunned, felt sick, but not afraid, for the implications were not yet clear. The most sordid humiliation of all was that she didn't care. Whatever coercion or trick he intended didn't matter, but the self-loving, body-consuming disease that wanted *him* and felt that he might not need her worried in case the trick might be entirely a trick, the seduction, so successful, only a seduction. She was shaky and weak in the impact but said in a plea from hell, the depths of personal degradation of which she'd never have believed herself capable, 'Did you think you needed photographs? I'll do anything you expect. All I want is –' And she told him with ferocious crudeness what she desired.

'I had no intention of using them,' Max admitted. 'They just exist. I was told to take them and to remind you of your – carelessness.'

'Carelessness? I don't care if you collect pictures of your own successes –'

'I was told they could be sent to your parents.'

She remembered that first afternoon; he had asked her about her loyalties, what she valued.

'It would kill them.'

'But then we are not proposing to send them. We have your loyalty without that.'

'I would have done anything for you without these.'

'I'm sure and I'm glad. But *they* have to have proof of pressure. Their little minds can't imagine love or loyalty.'

She looked up in hope at the word 'love'.

'You mean others have seen these?'

'It means nothing.'

'Max, I wish you hadn't –'

'Ah, no tears,' Max said quickly. 'You're through the worst of it.'

'I don't hate you yet. I don't care if you show other people pictures of the aloof women you've seduced –'

Max said slowly, 'I am not worthy of this. But listen, Sheila. What's required from you is relatively easy. And there's a limit to it. Once they – No. How can I express it?'

'What on earth can I give anyone that's of the slightest value?' she asked, genuinely puzzled. 'Max,' she said in comic realization, 'you're teasing, trying to frighten me. It's just one of those tricks of yours to terrify me –'

He dared to stand by the table, touch her hands. 'Let me explain. I began it for fun, you see. I had to carry things to a logical conclusion, and if you really despise the society in which you live –'

'I'm not understanding any of this –'

'It's political,' he said, but she just stared like a fool.

'But I have no politics.'

'Of course not,' Max agreed. 'Neither have I. What does it all matter? Let the fools arm and kill each other. What has it to do with *us*? You cannot tell me you're involved. Would you fight a war for the Conservative Party? It's not worth a war. For the Labour Party? It is too ridiculous to be taken seriously. Politics, my darling, are always in a condition of crisis. Politicians and idealists with guns in their hands will always tell you it is necessary for you to sacrifice – your money, your courage, your integrity, your health, your children, your life. . . .'

Feeling and hope were beginning to return. She crushed his hand against her face. 'But, Max, darling, if it's nothing to do with us, what's the fuss?'

'I got involved for fun and danger,' Max repeated. 'Now I can't stop.'

'Involved with whom?'

'Call them what you like. The other side. The enemy. The Reds.'

She was now frightened on his behalf.

'Max, what a fool –'

'It's nothing alarming,' he said. 'I do occasional photographic jobs for them. That's a bore. And then the other jobs, which are dangerous. Jobs like this one.'

She stared at him in bewilderment. 'You mean *I* am in this nonsense?'

He hesitated. 'Yes.'

'But it's ridiculous,' she said. 'I've nothing on my political conscience, nor have I information of the slightest value. If I go now to a police station they'd come here and you'd be in trouble, not me.'

'Possibly,' Max agreed. 'But my Red friends would send copies of those photographs today to your parents. But more likely your policemen wouldn't come back with you. They'd have me followed for months to find my contacts.'

'You wouldn't know that I was going to a police station,' Sheila pointed out. 'You'll *never* know. We'll both have something to worry about, won't we?'

Max said, 'I was enjoying it, you see, Sheila. What do little pompous soldiers and politicians mean to me? I had them in the studio and picked their brains and sent their pictures to my associates who use them as they see fit. Great fun! Twenty-two of them in various places are doing exactly what they're told.'

'I can see the attraction for you,' Sheila said. 'You love cruelty.'

'I saw you as a woman of vanity and arrogance whose spirit could be broken quite quickly. I didn't realize my own feelings would become involved.'

'Max, it's all so *unreal*. It doesn't frighten me at all.'

'Good. I'm glad. There are two ways of looking at it,' Max affirmed. 'You can be scared to death or you can enjoy the excitement of it.'

'Of *what*?'

'Of living a lie. Of being in a room full of people who don't *know*. Of meeting a contact unknown to you. You carry a copy of *The Times*, and he has some silly little code sentence, "The train has left Platform Seven two minutes early." Oh, terribly droll, and the spice is that *they* take it all so damn seriously. And, of course, there's that terror of the hand on the shoulder and a solid gentleman saying, "I am a police officer." It's amusing, Sheila, so long as you're not *involved*.'

'Suppose I refuse?'

'They'd send the photographs. You could phone your parents, I suppose, tell them not to –'

'Max, what do I have to do?'

'Does the name Alexei Antonov mean anything to you?'

'Not a damn thing.'

'This is his photograph.'

'Not one of your best, Max.'

'It's not one of mine.'

'He's got big ears, Max, and he looks scared to death.'

'He's a little man. You won't be frightened of him.'

'Why? Am I going to meet him?'

'You're going to marry him.'

It was too ridiculous. Sheila just laughed hysterically.

'Why have I got to marry him?'

'It will be easy. He's a colourless little man; he'll be staggered by your beauty –'

'I don't mean that. *Why?*'

'We want to know what he's doing.'

'I'm not going to do it,' Sheila said. 'I'd feel such a *fool*.'

She saw that Max was at last worried, frightened. 'My God, Sheila, I beg you to change your mind.'

'Why, Max, you're really frightened. Don't you see how silly I'd feel? If it was *you* ... But what will my friends say, my parents? I've had eleven proposals. To marry him would be downright absurd.'

'He's escaped from Russia,' Max said. 'Don't you recognize him now?'

'Ah, of course! A few months ago –'

'Why shouldn't a beautiful girl marry a hero?'

'Will I see *you*?' she asked, inferring her condition imposed. 'I might do it for you.'

'You are doing it for me,' Max told her. 'I wouldn't ask you to do a thing for them. And that will be part of the fun, too – deceiving him, meeting me. Then in six months, less perhaps, you just walk out, come here.'

'Then we'll get out, go to America?'

'If that's what you want?'

'What will I have to look for?'

'I'll explain it some other time. Papers, mostly. Notes. What's the project he's working on? Do you know how to use this?'

It was a miniature camera.

'More or less.'

'Have it now. Get used to it. Let people see it, be accustomed to it.'

'Max, I'm shaken, but I don't hate you.'

'Would you like a drink?'

She accepted it with trembling hands.

'Will it be safe, Max?'

'Why not?'

'It won't make me a Soviet citizen or anything?'

'Goodness, no. Oh, and Sheila, this little man's gone religious. Bear it in mind.'

'He's such an insignificant-looking man. Not like you.'

Max smiled, approached, responded. 'He'll worship you. Not like me. My love is carnal.'

Sheila whispered hotly, the frenetic urge consuming her, 'No photographs this time; this is something private,' as his hands touched, began with tenderness.

Upstairs, above the studio, was a bedroom. Max closed the window, shut out the sounds of the morning – church bells and vehicles, a Boy Scouts' band in the distance, someone's wireless – and turned to find her waiting, the blue eyes and the wide, thin mouth in supplication, an eager conspirator awaiting her reward.

It was evening when she left him, about eight o'clock at night, people walking about, leaving church, entering cinemas, holding hands, controlling dogs. Other people. She was exhausted. It would, of course, be different from this moment – the glamour, the friends, every meal she ate, every camera she stood in front of, every joke, every newspaper; every encounter would be touched with terror, but a terror she shared with Max. Sheila wasn't worried on behalf of conscience. It was all too remote for her to feel personally responsible, like a traitor. It was just dear Max, beloved Max, who loved to carry danger to its logical conclusion, to be really confronted with potential disaster and each day defy it, thrill to it, not be afraid although all of life was staked on a fraud. . . . She hoped she wouldn't have to give up work for this funny little man – what was his name? Antonov. Five years she'd been in the model profession; she'd reached the top in two.

She sat in her flat, tired, for once, bereft of emotion, put some milk on the little electric stove. It boiled over while she was deep in thought. She picked up letters she hadn't answered. 'Daddy and I are so proud of you. We never say anything, but we think a lot . . .' It was like the ones from Ian, George, Mr Harley, Lord Duguid, quite meaningless, unreal, not in the same world as Max. She struggled hard to overcome *him*, love them, some of them, but couldn't. Nothing was the same. She had to go to work tomorrow, be lively, beautiful, intelligent, responsive, but thought she'd be exhausted. She decided to go to sleep, felt ridiculous as she undressed. The phone rang. David.

'Can I come around? I'm bored.'

'No, David. I feel awful and I'm just going to bed.'

'I'll tuck you in, give you an aspirin.'

Couldn't he think of anything but what he desired?

'For God's sake,' she protested angrily, 'don't you know when you're not wanted?' and rang off. That would be the end of David. Two years, or was it three? It didn't mean a thing. No sense of loss or pain. Only Max could hurt now. And he would, of course; he would, often, brutally. There'd be tears, even, squeezed out of the eyes which hadn't wept since childhood. She knew it but was beyond caring. If you loved Max it had to be total, absolute. She sat awhile, half expecting him to telephone because she longed for it. In bed she fell asleep almost instantly and dreamed of her mother, weeping, and Max's hands fidgeting in a locked drawer.

6

GEOFFREY SUMPSTER

SATURDAY afternoon. Geoff tried to concentrate on the poem; he stumbled over phrases but excused himself, he was tired. A long hard week – he'd worked until midnight for four of the seven days. His mind was sucked dry.

> Awaits the overdriven Christ
> On cylinders and detergent whites;
> Negligible fools
> Absurd,
> With votes and calculable rights.

No. It wasn't perfect. Calculable was too definite, and the relationship between Christ and overdriven wouldn't be comprehended by idiots who were concerned with stop watches, must have meaning explained at a glance.

The sun shone into his tiny room and the motes rose from books closed yesterday and sheets shaken today. Despite tiredness, he felt an excess of energy, beginning of boredom. They'd all gone to a football match. He had proposed to do higher things, the poem of damnation, and panic flooded inside him like a hot soup now, the hopelessness of everything. Or was it just that he was no good, defeated before he began because there was nothing there? No. Creation was difficult, awaited moods, then application. Balls! He was just restless, needed a fight or a girl. He surrendered, stopped the creation, turned for comfort to Deverson's book. But Saturday had a powerful grip, and he only read a few paragraphs before realizing that he wasn't absorbing. His urge was to wallow in *Sex Sense* and he picked it up, opened it at random. *It is essential that the female partner be sufficiently aroused or passion will be one-sided, frustration or even frigidity result, and an act of beauty become mere masturbation.* His body felt hotter with the words. To hell with that; it weakened a bloke. Fresh air, a walk around this dirty city, or he'd surrender to his own flesh. He almost fled the room.

Three o'clock. A bright afternoon, even warm. Geoff Sumpster walking the pavements in escape, loneliness, boredom, inevitability. He stood outside antique shops and examined strange green Oriental vases (but his body instructed his eyes to examine reflections in the plate glass, girls' legs across the road). He strolled by shabby buildings, motor showrooms, past people. (Indians, Negroes, white men and women, Continental students, fat women, children – interesting, his mind instructed; the fascination of living in London, you see everything. But the body inside the suit and shirt and raincoat didn't tire with distance, scrutinized the world superficially, unless and except it was feminine.)

A restaurant, too classy for a student perhaps, but Geoff went in (a face seen at a table within, eyes interested apparently, but when he sat down nearby becoming as cold as handcuffs). Not many people there in the wicker chairs among the Oriental paintings and wallpaper, the elegant plants in selected vases, the tropical, illuminated fish. He inspected the girl's legs under her table, but her face became so charged with annoyance that he had to look away, outward, to the street. A parked Mercedes, exhaust manifolds or whatever they were, a real beautiful bastard. Other vehicles went by, halted, lights winked at this, which was a junction. People passed, girls sometimes, but mostly drifting groups of toughs and Pakistanis, a few Chinese. This was a Chinese restaurant, but Geoff merely sipped coffee, didn't eat, watched the road as if it had significance, must be regarded. And after a while his young eyes saw a poster on the opposite building, which was a cinema. The poster beckoned the body and even, because it was supposedly an intellectual film, his mind. But it was a sexual poster – a vague picture in which much was blackness but what was revealed was that which shouldn't be. The mind became a hypocrite, pretended it didn't know the promptings of the body, suggested culture should be attended. Its only protest was about the weather: such a pity to spend a pretty afternoon in the communal air of a cinema.

He sat in the stalls, ate a chocolate bar, was stunned with the impact of noise, music, became acclimatized, interested in the film apart from its X-certificate content. It was nonsense. the mind knew, not believed by anyone concerned in the film's creation; just an excuse to earn money by showing breasts and lace panties in dark corners for lonely people like Geoff Sumpster. Presumably, the mind explained, it was a vicarious experience for the ugly and incapable who would never experience what it portrayed. The dialogue was rubbish, which his mind was able to translate from its Continental origin: 'The world despises us' – 'We are lonely, but love is ours', which was quite absurd, flew in the face of the decade, which in fact regarded the act of sex, out of marriage, as normal, civilized, acceptable; only the fools married, had children. His intellect rejected the theme of the film – it would have been weak if it had not: the message was merely a vehicle (the very star had had three husbands, many affairs, was hardly 'despised by the world'). But it was not the intellect which had come to the cinema. The body, which had, responded. The girl in the corner of the screen crawled about in absurdity but with purpose – a scattered trail of clothes, progressive excitement, the man in the bedroom bored, not bothered, talking normally, accustomed, supposedly, to this sort of thing, the black lace and stockings, the dropped brassière, the plea, 'If you don't care at least give me the money', screamingly funny if the blood was cold, but the blood was not cold, and the strength pumped out of Geoff Sumpster and he moved about in wretchedness and climax in his seat. And his mind became supreme, too late, of course, and heard voices and toffee papers and giggles from people whose bodies weren't interested or aroused, and the mind was angry with the body and said it had humiliated him, wasted money, too; he might as well have stayed in his room; now he was unutterably soiled; the very film became too stupid to watch. But the satiated body stayed for the remaining forty minutes, while the tortured mind wondered if it could write a poem about loneliness in its relation to sex. But the feeling of Saturday, nothingness, discipline gone, was too much, and when he came out of the artificial world into the real one he craved company, not girls any more, but fellows, his kind, who had things in common, the mind, work, Deverson.

They were in the bar – Sam, George, Tharp, Barton, and Martin – standing like a conference, with bended secret necks, whispered platitudes. The bar was crowded. Saturday night. The ultimate, the last stage in the great, dignified search for senselessness, stupor, tired wit, buggery, and fornication. He recognized the failure of Saturday night but wanted to join in himself, belong somewhere . . .

'Here's Geoff!'

'Who won?' he asked.

'Ha!' muttered Tharp. 'Thereby hangs a tale or possibly a tail.'

'You lost?'

'*Me*? I was a mere witness, a supporter, a mere bra.'

'Alec broke his leg –'

'Ah, but that was a mere gesture . . .'

'They lost three nil,' explained Barton.

'We're drowning our inferiority complexes in inferior ale.'

They all had pints. Barbara joined them for valuable, amusing moments, the time to consume a medium sherry, whatever that was. South African, anyway, bless her.

'Where've you been, Geoff?'

Thus George in prepared malice. The chorus joined in:

'You look a bit pale.'

'Done yourself an injury?'

'He wouldn't know how,' sneered Martin. 'He thinks it's a toy!'

They all roared with pleasure, the evening livening up a bit, and not necessarily against him, Geoff, but he was unable to stop the blush. It was necessary to lie, for to give the name of the film, seen in solitude, would lead to conclusions and his blush confirm his weakness.

'I've been working on a poem. Then I went for a walk to get it out of my system, or into it, I don't know.'

There was some winking and nudging, identifiable as the usual scorn.

'What's it about?'

'You may well ask. It's a little difficult. Damnation, I'd say –'

'Whacko! Let's hear it!'

He was still naïve enough, brash enough, to believe that they would be interested or that, even if they were not, the mere words would persuade them, overwhelm. He was aware of other faces turning as he read:

> Morning men, accepted hats,
> In lines along the station.
> The Telegraph
> Four across,
> Incapable of passion.

He was drowning the dialogue of the woman nearby. She didn't like it. She was large and brassy and popular and didn't intend to be deafened.

'If you ask me –'

'We didn't,' Geoff said. 'You wouldn't understand.'

She flushed, was furious, for her minions – two men like cadavers, tall, one in grey, the other navy-blue, faces like ferrets, but pale, everything indoors, in smoke and sweat – they laughed at the mere twist of Geoff's words. These college kids . . .

'Oh, so I'm stupid, am I?' she inquired in a voice louder than the entire room, so that Geoff heard a man say, 'Oh, Jesus, Maud's off!' and knew he'd said too much. She was a Cockney, of course, or would claim to be, the type that would be proud to belong to those square miles of rubbish. 'Seems to me you're talking the nonsense, not *me*.'

Geoff said, 'I was talking to my friends, not you.'

'I know the world,' the woman said in foolish pride. 'College kids can't teach me anything. Not even good manners,' she concluded.

'I'm twenty,' Geoff said angrily, 'and I've had poetry published.'

He didn't say where. The school magazine and the home-town journal.

'Poetry?' the woman laughed. 'Poetry? Is that what it is? When I was a kid poetry used to rhyme. Sounded to me more like summat off a toilet wall.'

This earned huge laughter from the entire room.

'You wouldn't know the first thing about poetry,' Geoff said. He was angry with her. (The brainless of the earth, who damned what they didn't comprehend.)

The woman pleaded in a theatrical aside to Barbara, anxious at this early row. Ten-thirty was the normal time for quarrels, vomiting, the police.

'What do you think, duckie? Was that poetry or something out the dustbin?'

Barbara said, 'Well, I don't know' – which was at least honest, as well as conciliatory, for she didn't know a thing about it. She'd been pouring a milk stout for a lady with cancer of the womb at the time.

Geoff shouted, 'You've never been anywhere but in this dirty town. You don't know what I'm talking about.'

'Ho, dearie me! What a temper! I had a day at Southend in June!'

Laughter – she loved it. All for her, Maud, a real wit. She was winning in trash terms, because nothing mattered to her except herself. She wasn't going to be told anything by some damn college kid still wet behind the ears. She was fifty-five and she had her pride and wasn't one to be humbled. Hatred was in the flushed face when it met Geoff's, but laughter and coarse wit for others. She had no nerves – it was her territory; they, from the college, were the intruders. Nothing was of value to her, not even real; it was all platitudes from TV or irresponsible newspapers, improperly digested at that. It was real and true for Geoff, an act of creation, a protest against the values of England; he cared and could be hurt, worried, even crucified. She was a big cow who could get a laugh, frightened of nothing because she valued nothing. She had to win. She would destroy him with a flick of the wrist rather than be humiliated even to the extent of losing an argument. It would lower her status. The world could be destroyed by such ignorance and pride: she would press the button if it helped to win a mere exchange of words. Anything rather than lose face. . . .

They, from the college, didn't support him, couldn't, because it was his poetry and, although not condemning it entirely, they didn't like it. To them it was naïve, therefore without value.

He sensed some sympathy mixed with a horrible, sadistic satisfaction – him, not them.

She followed up now with, 'If you don't like this town why don't y'get out of it? It's good enough for *me*,' which earned a rumble of 'Hear, hear!' 'Where are you from, anyway, Mr Know-all?'

'I'm from South Africa.'

'Oh, well, we all know about *you*,' she said, ending up quite mildly but conclusively, successfully. And he hadn't the heart to go on, for such arrogant stupidity was indefeasible. Afterward, as normality began again – other voices, noises of glass, matches, feet, laughter – his hand picking up his tankard was trembling slightly. He could hear her (was intended to), 'A kid of twenty telling *me* what's what! They know it all, don't they?'

And his own college mates, with averted, smiling eyes, comforting (in whispers, of course; no louder support), 'What an old bastard!'

She would always win, he decided, because she had no logic; she valued nothing and would destroy anything in her need for popularity. She was far too ignorant to appreciate that her kind of popularity was of no value; it went with the room. And, as with all females, she was safe from the violence of his fists and thus in no way held back by the restraints of fear, civility, possibilities.

The evening went on. He became slightly drunk, but nothing overrode those angry moments, and deep in his stomach was the more permanent pain; his mates had loved it, watched like Romans in the Colosseum. They had no love for him, no respect for the merits of his poetry.

Why?

The mind which could analyse itself and the motives of the body within which it was imprisoned (knew it had carried the body to failure this afternoon even while it hypocritically claimed escape, supremacy) couldn't analyse their common dislike. It recognized the form of dislike in individuals – how far their courage or prejudice or indifference would carry them – but not the total, the quality they must *all* dislike. He'd been psychoed; he'd read books; he shared games and labour, meals and music with them, but they, without effort, shared something else between themselves. Was it the mere fact of their being English? He felt the weak temptation to buy a book and try to be different, make friends and be popular. (But books hadn't made any difference with Joan. Page 107 hadn't seduced her.) And, of course, they'd know, find the book. There was no free-dom here, no privacy; they'd see it and laugh at him more, even feel the better for knowing that despite his size and successes and intelligence he was abject before them, needed the help of a book. Anyway, those sort of books were a load of crap.

In a way they were as smug and insular as the woman, Maud. The one thing they didn't know was that he hated them more. Their laughter and sneers, quiet jibes, and carefully manipu-lated insults were hoarded by the mind. It awaited opportunity.

That was Saturday. On Wednesday evening he happened to go in the pub again, on his own, in slight hope of finding Bar-bara alone. And, oddly enough, and tremendously exciting, she seemed anxious to say something as he entered the bar.

'Hello, Barbara,' Geoff greeted her, very slightly conscious of Saturday's humiliation.

Her eyes, as usual, were interested in everything; her glance was too fast, surely, to obtain a stationary impression. The brain must be confronted with and exhausted by a ceaseless proces-sion of images, all momentary – bottle labels, faces on coins, old eyes, young grins – a kaleidoscope that was too hasty to allow any permanent impression. It was as if she were always afraid of the wrong person hearing gossip. Her hand flicked quickly and the collection of gold things tinkled, alas, with the noise of tin.

'Pint, Geoff?' But she didn't wait for confirmation, proceeded; the eyes dropped to handle, to tankard, back to the window, red buses passing, then to Geoff, a smile, and a giggle. 'Honest, I don't know whether I'm coming or going.'

'Coming, I hope . . .'

But something more interesting had happened and she said quickly while memory instructed, 'Listen, Geoff. There was a man asking about you.'

A man asking.

It meant nothing.

The world turned round once a day, or, more accurately, the day was created by the earth turning once; galaxies moved millions of miles while the impact, interesting, unusual, hit Geoff: a man asking . . .

'Who was it?'

'I dunno.'

'Do I know him?'

'I shouldn't think so. He didn't actually know your name, just that he'd seen you in here. And he wants to meet you . . .'

The message almost delivered; dozens, she had, each week: Fred to Sid, Joe to Eliza, a horse, a bet, the wreath, two o'clock at Sid's, by the bus, if you remember, ta, Barbara, and don't forget, see, 'cause . . .

It was frustrating for Geoff. She didn't have enough.

'Well, what's it about?'

'Just that he'd like to meet you. A nice sort of man, been in here a few times, quiet, respectable. Walks with a slight limp. Foreigner, I think.'

'I don't know him.'

'I *know*. I told you.'

'Well, where?'

She said in astonishment, 'He's just come in.'

The man was of medium height, stocky, about forty-five, had a kind, friendly round face with sallow complexion and brown, sentimental eyes. Not a man to be afraid of. Geoff took to him at once; the mere appearance was without arrogance at all. He did indeed proceed with the slightest limp.

Barbara said with a rush, 'I was just saying to Geoff – and then you turn up.'

'Would you like a drink?' the man asked. 'Ah, I see I am too late. A sherry for me, miss.'

Geoff said with unexpected nervousness, 'You wanted to see me?'

'That is so. I've seen you once or twice here,' the man said. (Geoff hadn't noticed him before. Perhaps he had the capacity of being insignificant, visually, that is.) 'Your poetry interested me. And your conversation. I presume you come from a college?'

'St Hanover's.'

'I think I know it.'

'Shall we sit down?'

'Yes, why not?'

The man was a corner sitter; that was why he hadn't been observed before. Tharp and Company, with their bloody self-importance, liked a central stance, in everybody's way, overheard by the maximum possible audience.

'I thought the poem the other night was undeniably impressive.'

Geoff's mind was in a tumult, a flutter; like all angry young men, he was easily overwhelmed by friendly words.

'You didn't think it naïve?'

'Not at all, not at all. I don't wish to flatter you, but I am on the cultural staff of my embassy. We are overwhelmed, of course, by the Italians and French, but we are not without significance –'

'That woman made me feel I was no good ...'

'Oh, my dear young man! If you take notice of illiterates like that... !'

'You really felt it was okay?'

'Not only technically, but the ideas expressed, which are far more important for they involve the human *you*.'

'I get angry,' Geoff admitted. It was fascinating, a new, delightful experience, to talk about that remarkable, exceptional person, himself, and have someone (on the cultural staff, did he say? My God!), someone vitally interested. Obviously this was so, for the very questions suggested intelligent analysis, probing, reminding Geoff somewhat of the psychiatrist at the clinic.

'It is a case of your environment not being adjusted to you,' the man said rather cleverly (for in a more usual reverse form the comment would have suggested structural failure in Geoff).

'Well, yes, that's about it,' Geoff agreed. 'You see, people think because we don't have the tedium of tube journeys and the unpleasant food and so on at a boardinghouse that living here is a pleasure. But for one thing, there aren't any females.'

'You'd like some?'

'Oh, I think it's more natural, Mr –'

'My name is Gouseev. But go on, this is most enlightening.'

Geoff said hesitantly, 'And sheer numbers overwhelm you, You stare across the refectory and after two years see faces you've never seen before; it makes things sort of cold, institutional. Even the tutorials make you self-conscious, a stranger. Except Deverson's, of course. He's fine.'

'But to return to your creative work – do you write for the college magazine or anything of that sort?'

'Write for it ! I was editor for eight months.'

'Of course, of course.'

'Then they manoeuvred me out. Too much criticism. They can't take criticism,' said Geoff, red in the face, hands, and feet scuffing in nervousness. 'I suppose you find this terribly naïve, silly?'

'Politically incautious, but sincere,' said Mr Gouseev, 'and therefore worth bothering about. Don't you feel your work isn't published because they feel it exposes decadence? I presume Authority read your articles and poems, knew your mind?'

'I'd never thought of it!'

'Ah, you'd be surprised at the suppression that goes on! A word or two in the influential ear and out goes yourself, never aware of the real cause.'

'You really think that criticism would be resented?'

'You see,' explained Mr Gouseev, 'personal degradation they are willing to have analysed – sex and all that – but your stuff hurt because it attacked *them*, the basis of rule.'

'Yes,' agreed Geoff uncertainly. He supposed there were meanings in his work that he couldn't identify himself: the heart crying the inexplicable that the brain couldn't rationalize.

'Do you get to the West End at all?' asked Mr Gouseev.

'That's another thing,' Geoff told him. 'Some of them come here, not to study but to enjoy the capital. You know. It divides the attentions, distracts when you get some idler describing the latest pleasure. Of course,' he qualified, 'we get to all the significant stuff, plays and films and music.'

'Who has published your work so far?'

'Well, nobody important,' Geoff said truthfully. (Nobody at all, in fact, except at school, the home town and *here*, himself as editor.)

'Have you thought of publishing abroad?'

Mr Gouseev asked his questions as if Geoff had control over those matters; Geoff felt cold at the thought of his collection of rejection slips. 'No,' he said, again with truth.

'But we must help you,' said Mr Gouseev. 'Many English and American writers even go so far as to live abroad and publish abroad before their work is seen at home. This would be almost the same.'

'I don't know what you mean,' Geoff said, conscious of how ungrateful the words were by the side of the warm emotion he felt in his body, nothing to do with the beer; they hadn't even ordered a second drink.

'You've no objection to publication in the Soviet Union?'

'No, no, I'm broad-minded, politically, as you know – I think you know,' Geoff said in confusion.

'There would be some payment. I know that payment is not important, but it is relevant, proves worth.'

'This is marvellously kind of you –'

'Not at all, not at all. I am here to help with things cultural. Type out a few of the poems, Geoff. May I call you Geoff?'

'Of course.'

'What are you working on now?'

'It's called *Damnation*. You heard some of it on Saturday.'

'Send some of your work to me, Geoff. Have you a pencil?' Mr Gouseev spelled out his name and title and address. The words Soviet Embassy did not alarm Geoff but rather impressed him, especially when attached to the others: Cultural Section. 'Register them, Geoff. We'll meet again, in two weeks, if we may . . .'

'I'd love to.'

'By then I may have news for you. I can guarantee nothing, of course, but I am not without influence.'

(The mind had cursed influence, despised it a thousand times when it had seemed to operate on behalf of others. Now it made not a protest, not a murmur. This was different; this was on behalf of Geoff Sumpster.)

'This is most kind of you, Mr Gouseev.'

'It is a pleasure. Would you like another drink?'

Geoff was almost afraid to stay with such enjoyment. He

wanted now to get away, think about it, gloat in secrecy. Published abroad. He'd say not a word until he had a copy.

'St Hanover's, you said?'

'Beg pardon?'

'You're at St Hanover's?'

'Yes.'

'What an extraordinary thing! Isn't that where Alexei Antonov's working?'

'He's working in the science block.'

'Is he now? How interesting. What at, I wonder?'

'Most of my friends,' said Geoff with a touch of bitterness, 'are in the old block. We study English and history.'

'I see,' said Mr Gouseev. 'But this is nevertheless most remarkable. I'm in a difficult position. I was a great friend of Antonov's in Kiev. I'd love to talk to him. Could you, I wonder, obtain his telephone-extension number for me?'

'I never go in the science department.'

'But you know people there?'

'Yes, a few.'

'Perhaps one of them would tell you. I'd like to talk to him. Of course I can't do it officially, you understand, from the embassy. Naturally they're angry with him, but as an old friend I could have a chat over the phone . . . See what you can do, Geoff, will you?'

Geoff thought he saw Mr Gouseev's difficult position.

'I'll do what I can, Mr Gouseev,' he said, and was aware again of apparent ingratitude.

'Next time,' suggested Mr Gouseev, 'let's meet somewhere different, eh? Have dinner with me at the Excellence?'

Geoff qualified, 'My clothes . . .'

'Not important.' Mr Gouseev was certain. 'The poet can dress as he pleases!'

They separated gravely, with courtesy, handshake, felicitations, promises, on the spittle-littered pavement of the dirty suburb, in the anonymity of darkness. No one had seen them, except Barbara. Geoff was glad. *They* wouldn't be able to analyse, condemn. Besides, they mightn't be so broad-minded about publication in the Soviet Union.

See Blake, the mind suggested; he's the one science man we

know. We have known him for two years; we danced with him in that crazy New Year's thing. . . .

Blake, twenty, tall, languid, droll, with a voice penetrating and cultured, second-year chemistry . . .

Not easy to encounter Blake, talk to him, bring a conversation around to the point. And would Blake know or care or be prepared to find out a telephone extension number? Would he sit about saying what he thought Alexei Antonov, political refugee, might be doing?

The days crept by as the mind became full of anticipation and terror. The flesh walked along that other main road, parallel with the one where Mr Gouseev had shaken hands – and the mind became incredibly capable and complicated. Astonishing the permutations of which it was capable: if he has soup, he'll be later than I, who won't. If I go in the bar of The Cross Keys he'll turn up. If he's with a friend I'll say – If he's not I'll suggest a drink.

The mind and the body were rewarded. With shock, Geoff, at four o'clock in the afternoon, walking among dead leaves and hurrying mothers, saw Blake come out of the gate, alone, rather in a hurry. His heart seemed to rob him of capabilities.

'Hello, Sumpster.'

Having said that, Blake would have passed on, but Geoff's confused mind remembered what it must suggest: a drink.

'Hello, Blake. Care for a drink?'

Blake grinned and said, 'Tea, you mean?'

'I meant beer – I'd forgotten the time – but tea's a good idea.'

He now felt the other's surprise. Why all this interest in *me*? 'I was on my way to see Railton . . .'

'Some other time?'

Geoff was feeling too anxious. He suddenly didn't feel capable of dialogue; wasn't there a way he could just ask? What about the phone exchange or even the porter?

But now Blake had relaxed, dismissed apathy, astonishment, had really become interested in tea, cakes.

'Where shall we go?'

'I'm not really familiar with this road.'

He was proceeding very badly. In a minute Blake would ask, 'What were you doing?' and he'd have no reply. But Blake merely suggested, 'Try Mary's. Bourgeoisie, but nice cakes.'

Geoff was in retreat mentally and now found it difficult to readjust to the skilful extraction of information. He needed luck. If they met any other science blokes, his mind promised, that would excuse him.

'How's the poetry going?'

'Not bad,' Geoff said. For once he didn't want to discuss it. 'In fact quite well. I'm having some published abroad.' (*Fool!* the mind shouted.)

'Does it translate well?'

'Not a hundred per cent, of course, but adequately.'

A door, bell, the smells of buns and freshly baked bread, warmth, even stupefaction in the heated air. A few women at tables, eating seriously, all handbags and coats and hats that seemed cold. One with a very pretty schoolgirl. Legs in dull brown stockings, but sensual, electrifying. A pink, tender face. A man with heavy overcoat still on, and Homburg, perfectly respectable, steamed glasses, but gross, eating chips.

'Chocolate cakes,' Blake said to the waitress. He never seemed to put on weight, despite cakes. 'Tea, of course.'

The schoolgirl said for him to hear, 'Honestly, it's so *awful*,' but the mother shushed her. 'Darling, you are untidy. Crumbs everywhere.'

'She means crumpet.' Blake grinned. 'How's that girl? What was her name?'

'Joan? Oh, that's over.'

'Never mind. Lovely while it lasted, I bet.'

'Yes,' Geoff said meaninglessly. He'd never thought he could hear about Joan with indifference, but it was happening.

'How's the science racket?'

'Chemistry, you know, not science. Science these days means physics and All That. Chemistry is becoming something for car batteries and soap.'

Geoff laughed with effort.

'You've got that little Russian genius there, haven't you?'

'Oh, *him*.'

'What does he *do*?'

'Damned if I know.'

'He must do something.'

'Not lecture, anyway.'

'Well, whereabouts does he do whatever it is?'

'He's been given some kind of sinecure, I imagine.'

'Why *here?*'

'Well, we do rather specialize in advanced mathematics, you know. Simpson's capacity is extraordinary.'

'He's working with Simpson?'

'Oh, I don't know about working. He lives with him and his wife.'

'Where does he go each day then?'

'I think they've given him a room on the first floor.'

If he didn't know the room he would hardly be able to give the number of the telephone inside it . . .

The hand that poured tea into his face trembled, and the mind was flooded with terror, the acknowledgement that the body must go into the science block and find out for itself.

'They tell me you've a marvellous common room and laboratories.'

'Out of date before built, Geoff, I'm told. Certainly we've no room to breathe.'

'I'd like to see them.'

'I'll show you around some time.'

'I'd like that.'

The schoolgirl spoiled any hope of arrangement. She was scratching herself, and she was saying in the same to-be-overheard voice (perhaps she talked her mother into things by sheer embarrassment): 'Can't I go on my bicycle?' and the mother said, 'Do make less noise, Rowena.' The girl, who looked like a Rowena as far as people do look like names, sighed heavily, plump chest lifting, and, eyes aware of Geoff and Blake, commented, 'Honestly, you'd think I was a *child.*'

Blake whispered hotly, 'Just about ready to cook, that one.'

Not committed, Geoff's mind said in pride. Not bad – you found out quite a bit, and he has no suspicions at all! But then, he'd always known Blake was a fool . . .

'I'll pay,' he said.

'Oh, thanks.'

'What have you got to see Railton about?'

'We're putting on *The Barber* –'

'Oh no, not *again*!'

'It's the only thing he sings!'

Go now, the mind urged the fluttering body. He'll be away for ages. I'm looking for Blake. You see, he won't be there. Quite safe. Legitimate. Leaves blowing and smoke beginning to lean from chimneys in an increasing wind. Perhaps the L.C.C. was changing the air. Once a century. Ha.

He felt a fool, incompetent, fearful, approaching the main science block. Rooms illuminated here and there as dusk penetrated. Young men, one smoking a pipe, tripped lightly down entrance steps, the day over. Stares, arrogant, and a question asked ten yards behind, 'Who's that?' And the comforting reply, 'Damned if I know.'

A porter grabbed him as he went in; it startled him, reduced initiative.

'Where are you going?'

'What the hell's it got to do with you?'

The right attitude – I belong here; to hell with you – although the flesh was weak in fright.

'You don't belong here.'

It was an accusation.

'So what?'

'You have to account for yourself. New regulation.'

'Holy God! What next? To *you*?'

The porter flushed, stung, became officious. 'I can't let you in otherwise.'

'I'm looking for Blake.'

'He went out.'

'I don't think so.'

'I saw him.'

'Then he must have come back,' Geoff said in apparent exasperation.

'Where will he be?'

Incredibly, the porter had a printed paper gummed to a piece of cardboard. Phone numbers. Geoff tried to look over his shoulder, but the print was too small; his eyes couldn't quite grasp the letters and numbers.

'The common room, I expect.'

'One-o-four,' the porter said into a telephone.

Geoff said, 'I thought 104 was the chaplain.'

'What,' asked the porter surlily, 'd'you ask me for if you know better than I do?'

'You're not logical.'

There was an alteration to one number on that list of telephone extensions, made in red ink. It would be the one. Geoff tried to press near the porter's bulk and see properly over his stomach, hands.

The porter admitted now, 'They don't know where he is.'

'Can I go and look?'

The porter tired of the game. 'All right. Half an hour, that's all.'

Stupid bastard, Geoff thought. They ought to have a nigger doing that sort of thing. He sniggered at this familiar thought. Even now, after three years here, he was still capable of seeing a man sweeping the road and feeling indignation : that's a nigger's job.

He went up stone stairs, met four of them, who stared, asked, 'Are you looking for someone?'

'Blake. I'm looking for Blake.'

'He may be in 31.'

'Thank you,' said Geoff, conscious of his own breathlessness, weakened voice.

He didn't go to 31. Additional excuses now available : try 32, 33, 34; they said 32, I'm sure. Blake – not here – sorry – withdraw.

He went into Room 32, but it was empty, except for a skeleton, small, female probably. Something squeaking. Mice or rats. A tap dripping at a specified rate. Horrible smell. Sweat was rolling down Geoff's ribs now, the terror, not of treason (he was technically free of that except in intention), but embarrassment, questions, Blake's return : 'But I have seen him. We had tea in a café.'

Room 33 was in darkness. He tried 34, but it was locked. He was angry as well as frightened. Where did the bloody little man hide himself? Why the hell did Blake say the first floor when – and then a door, no number at all, opened and the little man, Antonov, came out with Mr Simpson, engrossed in something. They just looked at the openmouthed, hesitant Geoff as if he was not there, continued to talk, and Geoff turned a corner, went in a lavatory, waited, came out. His heart was too large now for his frame; it pounded like a vast cylinder – explode, move, explode, up, explode, up, blood in the ears, nose, face, neck, he was almost floating in fear. If anyone saw him *now* . . .

His hands on the unnumbered door could scarcely turn the knob, they were so hot and wet with nervousness. Suppose one person was beyond that door. The hand hesitated, dropped. His body bent, he examined the keyhole – darkness, no light on. He entered, feet crashed into a stool. His sweaty palm rubbed the wall, searched in darkness for switches, found them, pressed one; light accused him from a corner. The telephone. The bloody whoring telephone. There it was, on a bright new desk. He looked at the white cardboard disc for the extension number. There wasn't one.

He was terrified. His whole being was drawn towards flight, the other side of the door. His hands dared to touch the thing, but his mind was perturbed, fingerprints, proof (of *what?* Sanity tried to calm him).

A voice said, 'Are you calling?' and whole seconds passed while his mind struggled for dialogue.

'Get me an outside line, will you? Elex 3330.'

If *he* forgot his cigarettes, a piece of paper, anything – 'Call me back, will you?' – and returned, there was nothing to say. 'I was looking for Blake,' or, 'I wanted to use your phone – you don't mind?' would be useless, insane, four hundred yards away, in the wrong building, room, seen in a pub, a man, foreign, Mr Gouseev, do you know the man? – and you believed, you actually *believed* his intentions toward Mr Antonov would be friendly?

A great shriek of noise as the telephone rang . . .

He'd forgotten the bloody thing would call back in mechanical terms.

He grabbed it, aware of a shattering headache as he did.

The voice said, 'Your outside call.'

'What outside call?' he said like a fool.

And was, in madness, rewarded. 'That is three twenty-seven, isn't it?'

'I've changed my mind,' he said, and dropped the receiver, fled, smashed the light switch upward with a passing fist, was in the corridor, exhausted. Three twenty-seven, for God's sake, don't forget it – and his feet were tireless despite the burden of collapse they carried; they moved him along the linoleum – 34, 33, 32, 31 – down the wide steps, another corridor, and the porter said from behind the folded race-horse results, 'Did you find him?'

'Who?' he asked, startled, guilty.

'Drake or Blake.'

'No,' said Geoff, and hurried into the air, now dark, breathed it, drank it, stood in the assembled darkness until the heart was calm, the mind adjusted. That was damn clever, he told himself, and grinned, living with secrets and success *they'd* never know about. He was an adult, a responsible adult in the world, able to alter its destiny. It occurred to him that he had achieved something that would hurt the England that so constantly wounded him. Funny, though, not to know what it was or would be.

People were arriving at the Excellence in taxis and five-litre saloons; they were received by top-hatted men and accorded their proportionate servility. It seemed absurd to approach on foot, shoes dirtied by rain and the spots from arrogant umbrellas in the Strand. The eyes in the weather-beaten faces under the peaked and top hats regarded him: his proportion of welcome was scrutiny, caution. It was a hotel that catered for people who knew what they were doing, moved in the world of hotels – actresses and minor politicians and important criminals.

Beyond the glass doors were warmth, people in slow motion moving like goldfish in a superior tank. A man passing another said in apparent desperation, 'See to the iced water. Mr De Haan is extrovert tonight.' Two women came from one of the gilded lifts, cruised through tropical plants, interested eyes, a line of charcoal sketches by Daubrie, picked up a *Harper's Bazaar* and *Herald Tribune* from the shop near the stairs. A phone rang and a man turned but refused to move – the two women were so exceptional. They were so flamboyant, yet fragile, delicate. They were so beautiful it hurt; the mind inevitably hardened. What, one wondered, was God doing, making these and in the same breath of divinity observing, allowing, pain, starvation, refugees, massacre, rape. The one had just that little more of whatever it was than her companion, and the man who should have answered the telephone smiled, ran to the acres of glass, opened part, said, 'Good evening, Miss Schwartzholf,' and clearly counted himself lucky to receive the creases in her face, the crescent of the mouth before it opened to say in a transatlantic drawl, 'Why, thank you.' The man answered the still-insistent telephone, and in a long five seconds the pleasure went out of his face, normality returned.

A scattering of people, plants, and on one of the vast white leather settees Mr Gouseev, relaxed, assured, apparently belonging, reading – with absorption, one would have sworn – *Time*; but the eyes must have observed Geoff wandering nervously, for Mr Gouseev stood up, greeted him with what seemed like affection, 'Why, Geoff, there you are!' a welcome so English that the face or two that turned presumed it was a father-and-son or uncle-and-nephew relationship – worth two to three seconds of their more interesting lives.

But the quiet dialogue on the settee between the two ordinary faces was altering the world faster than any impression Miss Schwartzholf would ever contribute.

'I had a bit of a job.'

'Tell me.'

'It's three twenty-seven. You dial the college number and –'

'No. I mean what happened?'

And later:

'That was extremely intelligent and courageous of you, Geoff. I didn't realize there would be actual difficulty about it.'

'I thought the less people who knew the better.'

'There's a lot in what you say. The matter is, I suppose, political. Would you like a drink? Then we'll have dinner. What time do you have to be back?'

'Oh, any old time.'

'That's great, because I've a lot to tell you.'

'You mean about the poems?'

'Yes.'

'You liked them?'

'Not only myself. Both *Damnation* and *Solitude* are to be published.'

'Mr Gouseev, you don't know how –'

'No credit due to me, Geoff. I merely put them where they could be regarded in their right perspective.'

And later, with Geoff's face red, not pride or modesty, but simply the warmth of food, wine, liqueur, Mr Gouseev asked quite easily, 'Look, Geoff, can you obtain some academic information for me?'

'Of course, Mr Gouseev.'

'I'd like the names of Antonov's associates, what they do, that sort of thing, which one he's friendly with.'

'Simpson, I know. He lives with Simpson and his wife.'

'Could you spare an hour or two, to see if he goes out in the evening? Perhaps where ... We'd refund any taxi expenses you might incur ... Then I could meet him in the most natural of circumstances should he be denied telephone conversation with me.'

'I'll do what I can, Mr Gouseev.'

'I know you will, Geoff. Don't think I've forgotten those girls.'

'What girls?' Geoff asked, but his blush confirmed the desire: *any* girl, so long as pretty, interested in Geoff Sumpster, and if you could explain that Geoff Sumpster is a poet, with the poet's need of liberty in flesh and spirit ...

'You'll see.'

And outside, on the pavement of the Strand by an illuminated camera shop, people passing in the darkened, mysterious, exciting air of ten o'clock – girls with green, heavy, sensuous eyelids, Negroes, a well-dressed man anxious to find a taxi, a crowd around a theatre, with the wash of voices drifting over the road – the air holding pleasure, anticipation, the night has other surprises – Mr Gouseev passed the notes into his hand. 'Twenty-five, Geoff. Don't hesitate to ask for more if you need them' – which surely didn't make sense if this was a payment for poetry to be published. And Mr Gouseev, too, was anxious now for a taxi, and they walked towards Charing Cross with their necks turned, and their separation was quick, decisive, the cab not shared, Mr Gouseev merely saying, 'Kensington,' and his last instruction to Geoff, whispered above the taxi's motor: 'Be careful, Geoff. And phone any night at exactly nine o'clock, from a public box. Reverse the charges if you feel it's going to be lengthy.' Almost as an afterthought he concluded, 'I may have your published work for you the next time.'

Geoff was restless, a pleasurable feeling of things happening, accomplished. He walked up the Strand, stared idly in the illuminated dress shops, travel agencies; regarded the assured as they came out of the Excellence; moved on into the tide of people, and they all seemed to be walking the other way, against him, which made him smile: it was the way he had chosen.

7

MAGGIE PRESTON

MAGGIE PRESTON, nineteen, five foot four, blue eyes, red hair, slender and attractive, a telephone operator at World Mechanical's offices in London, opened her eyes in response to the touch of the hand as it shook her shoulder. Her brain began working straightaway, recognized the fragile respect of the heavy, calloused paw. Eggy asked little. If you were fifty-four, with chronic illness, saturated in booze, and had a paunch, you asked – or, at any rate, expected – little from a nineteen-year-old with red hair and a long, beautiful, reckless face. But was it really beautiful? It had the attraction of asymmetry. People who disliked Maggie Preston said, if they were feminine, 'Her face is too long,' and, if they were masculine, they commented, with slight breathlessness that acknowledged hurt, 'She's a bit bandy,' or, 'She's too fey. She'll get into trouble one day.' But day after day passed and Maggie didn't get into trouble, and they who had wanted her retired, fulminated at the ease with which she surrounded herself with admirers eager to accept any terms. It was as if she gave a little of herself to everyone rather than all to one. She was separated from her husband (had walked out on him for reasons not explained), and this had the fascination of sin. It indicated to male minds that she was not a virgin and that he who had married her hadn't given her the pleasure they could. As well, she was known to be slightly mad, and this should have made her easy . . . But the days passed and she survived without 'trouble'.

Saturday, the awakening mind informed, and she protested, 'Eggy, what's the matter?'

Mr Eggerton was confidential, even conspiratorial. He sat on the bed, put the cup of tea on a dirty chair, eyed with a dull pain of pleasures not for him the disarray of scanties, stockings, shoes. Still, they (whoever *they* were – and there were many) didn't live in the same house, didn't see her in bed in the morning, didn't eat with her, have a drink, discuss day-to-day things, eat the food she cooked, give her the last and first fag of the day. The warmth of her seemed to ooze out of the bed now to disturb him. She didn't mind his presence. She didn't care that he saw her in panties in the little bathroom. He didn't know what it was – broadmindedness, indifference, tantalization, his proportion of luck, tit-bits. She was Maggie, slightly crazy; it explained everything. She was, however, not so wild or foolish as to let Vera, his wife, see his little gifts, pleasures.

'Eggy, what's the time?'

'Half past nine.'

Maggie sat up, and Eggy saw her smooth throat, the pale valley of her small breasts. (It was curious that she was sexually exciting, for it was true about the slight bandiness, and her waistline was slender, hips negligible; it proved that all of sex starts with the human face, the wildness in the eyes.)

'What! Mick's coming at ten.'

'Give us a kiss.'

'God, you old men are the worst.'

Maggie accepted a kiss – she knew, presumably, that it would be unbearable for him not to have something. He would go sour, and she hated to be disliked. A bit for everyone. Her life was full of explaining to men (or women, sometimes) that the portion surrendered on Friday had nothing to do with that of Monday.

Eggy's face was large, the skin yellow and dirty-textured,

but, because she was crazy, Maggie didn't object. She liked him.
All her relationships were enjoyed. She couldn't have enough
of them. Presumably therein was the end of her marriage, if it
had ended. She didn't say. Even Vera hadn't found that out.

When Eggy's fat, nicotined hands started to explore Maggie
rejected him, but easily, with compliments : 'You're a dirty old
man.'

'She's gone out.'

'What's that you keep waving about?'

'A letter.'

'For me?'

'Yes. From Germany.'

'Eggy, stop pawing me. Pass me my bag. Have a fag?'

'Your tea'll be cold.'

Maggie drank it, reading with excitement. 'It's from Dieter.'

Eggy, too, suffered : enthusiasm for her many relationships
was hard. Only when one had ended was it easy to talk,
analyse endlessly, explain what had gone wrong, and take her
side.

'Who's Dieter?'

'I've never met him. It started in school when I was twelve.
A pen friend.'

Eggy said, 'You don't want anything to do with Germans.
Listen, Maggie, when I was in the Army –'

'This is different. Eggy,' Maggie asked, excitement growing,
'what's the fare to Germany?'

'God knows. Twenty quid by air.'

'How much by sea?'

'I dunno. Ten.'

'He wants me to go for a holiday.'

Eggy was hurt, kept silent. Her capacity for enjoying life
was so high. She'd come back and tell him stories of pleasures
and events and crazy relationships and it would sting because
it would compare favourably with this – the shabby flat and
Vera's criticisms, stockings on the string across the kitchen, the
beer bottles and his mouth, touched with boiled egg, seeking
its consolation, payment for board and lodging while she made
her crazy mind up about her marriage. He couldn't imagine
how they'd lived before she came. Dull, bloody, unbearable

dullness: the fiddles and scrapes for money, the occasional row when found out; the queue in the doctor's dingy room, the pain of needles, the harsh condemnation of the doctor, 'You again, Eggerton. Well, how are you?' and Vera's sharp tongue and constant reminders that for two years she had been the breadwinner. Beer was the only consolation. And then this scatterbrained, delightful, exciting young thing, married at seventeen, had burst upon them, two suitcases and a pale face, but lively, even that first evening, happy even on the day she left her husband. She loved excitement and this was one that was fascinating. A bell ringing and the sweet smell of her perfumes, hair and body, and the voice asking in the hall: 'Vera, can you put me up? I've left Frank.' Germany, why Germany, why a pen friend at all? Why bother to even write when so many friendships were here, available at the drop of the eyes, the twist of her scarlet mouth?

'You wanna watch those things. Pen friends can be dangerous.'

'I've never been abroad.'

'There's nothing special –'

'I've got to see for myself, haven't I?'

'Give us a kiss, Maggie. I've got to go and see the quack.'

She kissed him. Vera no longer had much sympathy with his dirty illness – the messy suppuration, changes of pyjamas – but Maggie, without hypocrisy, consoled him softly, 'Poor old Eggy. Is it nasty?' so that he felt braver, answered, old soldier that he was, 'Nothing to it. I can keep going.'

'Pass me those things before you go.'

And he, Eggy, fifty-four, dying with dirty slowness, had the privilege accorded no one, of touching the weightless things that she wore. 'I dunno how you keep warm,' he said.

'Doesn't Vera wear them?'

'Not quite like this.'

She drove him from the bedroom by stepping out of bed, pushing him, 'You gay old dog,' so that he felt a victory, and then she read the letter from Germany again. 'I was so interested to hear about your job ... If you haven't had your holiday wouldn't it be nice to meet at last? If you came here we would show you ...'

She dressed and washed, thinking of it: a romantic picture of the Rhine, people singing in beer gardens, forests and barges, pine trees for hundreds of miles, blond, handsome men acknowledging her in guttural compliments. Twenty quid. Once she got there it would be all right; he'd pay, see to things.

A young man came in as she was eating her late breakfast. His eyes were interested to find that no one was about; he had her alone for once.

'Mick, have you been to Germany?'

'I did six months in the Army.'

'What was it like?'

'Pretty awful.'

'Germany, I mean, not the Army.'

'Oh yes, great.'

'Can you lend me twenty quid?'

'Hey, come off it!'

'Well, I only asked. If you can run a Midget I thought –'

Mick dropped the subject. 'Have you been out? It's boiling.'

'We'll go swimming. Is Reg coming tonight?'

'I don't know. Why?'

She had stood up, moved quickly, as always, with the crocks to the tiny kitchen which had once, in the original days of that house, been a dressing room.

Mick stood behind her, put his arms around her. He was torn between worry and infatuation, her stomach and his mind.

Maggie resisted. 'Let me wash up.'

'Maggie, you know if I could –' He kissed her hair and neck to prove it.

'All right. Now let me wash up. I wish there was some way to make a lot of money.'

'Who doesn't?'

'Yes, but it's not fair. You want it when you're young, not later when you're crocked up.'

'How's Eggy?' Mick asked.

'Oh, you know. He keeps going.'

'If he laid off the booze –'

'Why shouldn't he drink? It's a pain killer, isn't it? He's not nasty with it.'

She had finished, was moving around the room, adjusting things, acutely conscious of his thoughts. 'I've got to wash a pair of stockings.' He followed her about hopelessly, with hurt mind, itching hands; she was the most elusive of insects, couldn't be pinned. Eventually he just stood in her way and she collided. An allowable accident, of course, and at once Mick was breathless, infatuated. 'Maggie, don't you know?'

'Yes,' she admitted, serious for a mere instant.

'I can't help it. I know I shouldn't.'

'I can't fall in love with anyone,' Maggie said. It was an excuse that could lever her out of any situation. 'I'm not free yet.'

'But you left him.'

'Yes, but I don't hate him.'

'I wish I could help,' he said, meaning, Let me be involved.

'Well, you've said you can't.'

'You mean you *need* twenty pounds?'

Among other things she had the minor ability of being able to look straight into an infatuated face and tell untruths with such conviction that, because the need felt genuine, she almost believed them herself. 'I shouldn't have mentioned it.'

'I'll find it for you.'

Maggie turned her face away to hide astonishment; the result had been obtained too rapidly; it nearly embarrassed her. 'Oh, Mick, would you? I'll pay you back.'

But the fever of Maggie Preston was riotous in his blood, and as she conceded a little ground, took a pace backward, so that she felt the hard, cold edge of the sink behind her, Mick, allowed by the circumstance of the sink and stove to pin the insect, pleaded, 'Oh, Maggie, you're kind to me,' which was ridiculous but became true for moments, the portion for Saturday morning: wet, foolish kisses that meant little to her but excited him, convinced him that it would be the same on Monday, Tuesday. The touch of her arms and blouse and firm skin that was warm through the skirt – he was lost and insisted, 'No need for a loan. I'll give you twenty quid. I'll sell my camera.'

And as soon as the fool had committed himself in words the elusive slender body wriggled sideways, but, not wishing to wound, excused itself, 'Honestly, all this passion in the morning! It's ten o'clock. Let's go into town first.'

'Just one more, Maggie.'

'No. I must clean my shoes.'

'One, please, one.'

Mick advanced to obtain it, but she was too elusive, had bent down, was fetching the polish out of a low cupboard. He knelt, too, but the posture was too difficult, romance impossible on the lino. She fell over; it became giggles and a brief, Saturday's-luck view of her thighs and the weightless things that kept her private.

As with Eggy, she didn't mind or reprimand; there was even a childish innocence as if she didn't know. His hands, eager to touch, encountered sticky shoe polish and were defeated.

Maggie said lightly, 'If we're going into town we'll get your camera and take it in' – as if it was a good idea, she had beaten him to it by seconds, but no matter, she had conceived the idea; now he could have the pleasure of executing it, making it real.

And before the morning had ended Mick had sold his camera, Maggie was twenty pounds richer; they'd been to see the man in Cook's, and Mick found himself discussing and remembering Germany, like Eggy, rather chilled by her anticipation of what was not himself.

But still, the twenty pounds earned a long, if elusive, portion of luck: hours of chatter, shops, a fast ride in the Midget, a swim and sun bath in a country pool, and the remainder of her phrenetic energy at the Saturday-night dance. His luck began to end, become Sunday's portion, as others greeted and claimed her, and he could not dispute (and he dare not sulk), for her high happiness was always like this: uniform, never diverted, available for anyone. She had a capacity for enjoyment that was absurd in the middle of the twentieth century.

Mick brought her home – one o'clock – hoping for last pleasures, twenty quids' worth, but she was far too cunning, brought him in the flat (which was, on the face of it, a maximum, as much as he could hope for), and from then on she was in the dubious custody of the beer-saturated, dull Eggy, full of bonhomie (Sunday's portion might be his; a percentage of it was bound to be breakfast, fag, the kitchen chores), and small, cynical Vera, pleased to see Mick, even at one in the morning, was nevertheless there, present, like a figure in the statistics of gratification, pleasures obtainable or not.

'Have a beer, Mick?'

'Isn't it hot, Mick?'

'Where've you been, Mick?'

He was so infatuated she burned like a fever in him, and like a man in a fever he found it difficult to answer beyond 'Thank you,' 'Yes,' and 'No.'

Vera said with her usual air of contempt, above it all, 'What d'you think of Maggie going to Germany?'

Maggie interrupted quickly, 'He's lent me the money.'

'And how,' asked Vera, 'are you going to pay him back?'

'What's it got to do with you?'

'Well, how are you going to?'

It was much more difficult to defeat Vera than the infatuated males.

'I'll do it.'

'What's Frank going to say?'

'For heaven's sake!' Maggie pleaded. 'I work for my living. Can't I go to Germany for a holiday?'

'You don't even know the man.'

'I know him better than I know you . . .'

Vera was hurt. 'Oh well, if you're going to be stupid.'

'Well, I do.'

Eggy said, 'She'll be all right.'

'Of course I will.'

Vera said acidly to her husband, 'What do you know about it?'

'I've been to Germany.'

'In the bloody cookhouse.'

Mick said uncomfortably, 'I'd better be off.'

Maggie was in favour of this; in minutes she might be asked for that twenty pounds back. She stood in the porch of the dirty old house, submitted to Mick's consolatory pinching and pawing; he knew there'd been some kind of swindle, but what can a man with fever do?

'When'll I see you again?'

'I'm on late all next week.'

'On Saturday then?'

'Why don't you shave properly?'

'Maggie, Christ, Maggie, you're driving me mad.'

'And you can stop that.'

'What about Saturday?'

'I don't know. I'll see.'

'I'll phone.'

'Yes' – with relief – 'you do that.'

He was gone, rewarded and cheated, and she forgot him like the flick of a switch. He was just Mick, today's portion. A few hours' sleep and it would be time to turn on a different switch. Life was fascinating, but there was not enough time, and money – what she could do if she had money. She went back into the grimy flat, a careful smile and rehearsed romantic lies to please Vera; for if Vera was not on her side she'd never get to Germany.

'World Mechanical ...'

'Regarding XZ73 –'

'Our Explosives Department, just a minute.'

'Can I speak to your Mr Raffety?'

'Integrated Plastics. Give me Experimental Ballistics.'

'Will you take a call from Dublin?'

'World Mechanical. Good morning, can I help you?'

And then a tap on her shoulder, because the earphones cut out sounds that were not mechanical.

'Maggie, someone to see you.'

'Who? Did he say?'

She had no doubt it would be male.

'He didn't say, except that it was urgent.'

'What's he like?'

'About twenty, blond, rather tall.'

'Oh hell,' said Maggie. 'Where've you put him?'

'In reception, of course.'

And there he was among crippling furniture and mustard wall paper, copies of *Science* and *Punch*, and a model of a very complicated detonator mechanism, Frank, her husband. He was, like the others, nervous. He meant almost nothing to

Maggie. She'd soon seen that marriage was a mistake, for older people who'd tired of the fun. Frank was a radio technician. He had been possessive and jealous and drank like a mad thing, to be clever. She hadn't the slightest idea why she'd married him. Presumably, at seventeen, she'd believed in romance, permanence. He'd been very drunk, nasty drunk, when he'd opened her legs the first time; romance had died with pain. She'd stuck it for a year, because she didn't know one could do otherwise and be less than miserable. Then she'd walked out. Vera had been magnificent. Marriage to Frank had been disaster. Money was what won; even a girl had to have it. Or they could wipe their feet on you. She looked at Frank now, a dirty-skinned, blond youth of nineteen. He'd been drinking, he already, at nineteen, had ulcers. It was shameful to think of the things that had happened with Frank – dirty, vicious things in which she had, in innocence, participated, until she found she couldn't stomach them any longer. Now he stood there and in his eyes was the desire for resumption, continuation. A tiny, tender part of her admitted he had the fever too. But he had no proprietary rights now. Three days after leaving him she'd felt as free as air, zany. He came bothering her now and again, always uselessly. It was the same plea every time : I didn't value you enough; I was only a kid; I won't drink again; I'll see you're all right, only love me, love me, come back. And somewhere in the hurt eyes and sullen face was the acknowledgement, exciting and satisfying to Maggie : I didn't realize what a beautiful girl I'd got; I'll never be able to find another; they're not interested in me . . .

'Hello, Maggie.'

'You shouldn't come here. It's not allowed.'

'You're going to Germany with some man?' he asked like an accusation.

'Who told you?'

'Don't you have any consideration for me? I haven't –'

'Somebody did tell you?'

'Vera. She thought I ought to know.'

'She would. Well, I'm *not* going with some man.'

'But she said –'

'I'm going for a holiday.'

'But there is a –'

'There is nothing. I work for my living, don't I? Have I ever asked you for support? I'm entitled to a holiday.'

'Oh, Maggie,' Frank said wretchedly, 'please come back.'

She knew now the complaint about going to Germany was nothing, a mere justification for coming to see her.

'I'm not coming back.'

'But we're married ...'

'We settled all that a year ago ...'

'We could try.'

'No, Frank, I don't want to.'

'I'd be good. I don't drink now ...'

'I can smell it,' she said with contempt.

'I was scared –'

'Scared of *me?* Don't be ridiculous!'

'Vera said you were out with this bloke Mick on Saturday ...'

Frank was crucifying himself.

'Yes, I was.'

'And one called Ray on Tuesday ...'

'Frank, we're busy. I can't stand here anyway.'

'Meet me. Listen. Come home for a day, talk it over.'

She could see with shame the dirty, incompetent planning proceeding in his stunned mind.

'I must go back to work.'

He shouted now, 'You never did have any feelings,' reminding her of pain as if it had been some failure on her part.

'Frank, don't make such a noise.'

'You're just a whore,' he cried, near to tears. 'You go with anyone, I've heard.'

Maggie said coldly, 'That's the way out when you get tired of it. Goodbye, Frank.' She walked away, aware of how this apparent calm indifference left him standing there, silenced, with fists clenched and mouth twitching.

Ostend, a sky line like broken teeth, in the perfect August day. There was an hour to wait, and Maggie ventured outside the station, walked on sand, examined shops. A waiter's race was in progress and traffic at a standstill. It couldn't possibly happen in England – limousines having to wait while the sweating, rather grubby young men walked furiously with wiggling bottoms and trays of sand-filled glasses. Some of them cheated.

In the compartment of the express she sat and watched the Belgian countryside. There were two students talking in English among the passengers and they, believing she was foreign, eyed her when her face was turned to the soil, the pollarded trees, whitewashed houses – she saw them reflected in the window. It amused her to continue the performance and she stared them in the face gravely, smiled very slightly with politeness, looked blank when the one asked the other, 'D'you think she's French or Belgian?'

Brussels came and went, and still they hadn't used their language abilities on her, although they were, she knew, eager to try. The one, she could see, had the beginnings of fever – flushed face, his eyes could scarcely leave her.

It was this one who said eventually, 'God, it's hot in here.'

Maggie smiled and said, 'Why don't you open the window?'

They stared at her, remembering things said, opinions voiced, and began to laugh. 'We thought you were French!'

At once they forgot about the window, and the plain countryside was ignored. Where are you going? Where do you come from? All the elementary questions, and her replies fascinated them. They were both at Cambridge, were on their way to Italy. The one who was clearly infatuated was Trevor, his friend Vivian. They talked their way through timetables, college, music, holidays; shared food, coffee.

'Are you married?' Trevor asked, mountains outside, night coming in magnificence, but this was more important – seven hours out of England, and his desires and intentions were altered, forever, he was certain.

Maggie said, 'Separated,' and he was fascinated, eyes intrigued, the relationship different, the fever worse. Statistics leaped into his mind, articles in the Sundays, sex, love, always the most interesting subjects.

'You look so young,' he pointed out, like a complaint, the statistics disproved.

'Nineteen,' she told him, meaning quite old, years beyond *you.*

'Why?' he asked. He had to know the details. Each one had an effect, worsening the fever; no matter what she said his condition was deteriorating. He examined her as if she were a new type of girl; they were pretty far advanced at Cambridge, but not as far as separations. He'd heard of the type, and here, bewildering, disturbing, was one, pretty, normal apparently, wishing to talk, confess.

'Not suited. He drank, too ...' She told him, a stranger, what Vera hadn't learned.

'I'll never get married,' he said earnestly, like all eighteen-year-olds, but his eyes were delirious – another five hundred miles and he'd be pleading for it. ...

Ten o'clock at night now, and they took her to dinner. Foreign faces, foods, and wine, the air greasy and hot. A middle-aged Dutchman shared their table, a kind face – 'You are students?' – and giggles over the foreign menus, everything left for Vivian to deal with. 'I like England,' the Dutchman said into Maggie's face. She felt shock creeping like a blush as Trevor's hand found hers under the table. 'I have a British car. A Consul. Very good. Where are you going? Germany?' 'Germany,' Maggie confirmed. A girl was facing her some way off, a woman so beautiful even Maggie stared. Slender and slightly sunburned, pale-brown hair, wide foolish eyes. The man with her – not her husband, Vivian said – was furious about something. Like a fool he had placed her so that she met everyone's eye; she was so beautiful every time she lifted her blue eyes from her food someone was staring. She did not seem to mind the awareness, but the tall, angry dark man with her turned often to glare. 'Half a crown, see?' the Dutchman said. 'I always carry it. Here,' he said shyly (not infatuated, just remembering: war and empires lost, what they had in common, the Java Sea and the Battle of Arnhem), 'you buy a British beer, remember me, when you get back.'

Maggie was moved, excited. This was the way she wanted life – fun, mystery, foreign places, excitement, no harm done; the dozing Trevor sitting by her in the compartment, high fever now, whispering, 'Go to sleep if you like. Lean on me,' he urged, desired, and then his hands behind her, around her. 'We must meet again. I'm at Cambridge but I could come.'

And a blank face opposite, watching, not comprehending the English, and Maggie gay, giggling, sleepy on the unfamiliar wine, food. 'I'd like that.' Another giggle. 'Where are we?' It didn't matter. She wasn't a girl who worried. If she went five hundred miles beyond her station, found herself in Italy with them, she wasn't the kind who'd be frightened. Someone'd straighten it out, see her safely back, and she'd survive, no 'trouble'.

She was almost asleep. Something had stopped, rhythm, the train – it was stationary. She saw an illuminated word – Mannheim – couldn't believe it. Trevor couldn't grasp that she would really leave. 'I shall see you?' he begged, and she ran along the corridor, breathless for once, leaving behind an intriguing 'If you want to.'

It was nearly midnight when she reached Kaiserslautern. Not many people about, foreign words to worry her slightly, but outside the station she saw a Volkswagen. Two Yanks, slightly drunk, said, 'You lost or something?' But she walked on, was identifying the number of the VW, when Dieter, recognized faintly in the meagre illumination from a photograph of three years before, greeted her, shook her hand, took the case, spoke in fascinating, almost perfect English.

'Maggie, of course. You found your way? You are not tired? Will you have a cigarette?'

Phrases from a textbook.

She could see that he was slender, had a good-shaped head, was from a textbook himself: a handsome German, not blond though. He loaded her case, opened a door for her. His courtesy was absolutely perfect, not based on infatuation, need, conceit. Of course he had not seen her yet in proper illumination. There was a quite pleasing odour of some lotion from him, but it meant nothing to her, being merely a pleasant contrast from memories of Frank.

He drove through the town with fury, as if he had to prove something. It was not just fast driving but frenzied, skilled recklessness, and once clear of the town, she had a blurred impression in the headlights of trees, timber yards. He overtook other vehicles, driving the VW as hard as it would go, delighting in mechanical success. The speedometer read 130, but that

would be k.p.h. His hands on the wheel were pale, long, delicate, more beautiful than hers. All the while he was at ease,
talked without effort, question and answer, opinion and
prejudice.

'It's a souped-up Volks. I adore speed. Here, I am alone
with 1172 c.cs. I make them work for me, sing . . .'

'How many operators? Only six? That puts you in a position of responsibility. Oh, but it does! If you sold the information you overheard. . . . !'

'I am a telephone operator too. I speak two languages, you
see. I do translation work for the Americans. Where? Oh, in
the Yank base. No, we have twenty operators. Ah, but do not
forget – some of us have to be on duty all night to take messages from the Pentagon, girl friends!'

'You like Plymouth? I have been to Plymouth. I went in
1959. Lots of speedboats, battleships. So dramatic.'

'Tomorrow we go to Heidelberg. You like that? It is quite
boring, but my friend has a speedboat. Friday I've got tickets
for opera at Koblenz. No dressing up. You can go in summer
clothes. It's on the riverbank. They set the river on fire at the
end. So amusing.'

It sounded promising, as hoped for. But something was
wrong, odd; he was not infatuated; there was no fever, not the
slightest male-female interest. If his temperature was high it
was because of other things, those which caused the frenzied
driving. Why, then, if love was not his intention, had he asked
her to Germany?

'Jdar-Lauterecken is a small town, quite pretty and dull,' he
said like an apology. 'Glass and jewellery. The Amis have
livened it up, introducing hate, fighting. It's so gay now.'

He had already made it clear that he hated Americans. Yet
he worked for them. Why?

The car was climbing, turn after turn, pine trees seen in
each sweep of the headlights. They came into a small town,
darkened, with narrow streets, zigzagged, climbed again, and
at last stopped. Maggie was now anxious. Infatuation, fever,
love, she could deal with them, but courtesy, deep, acid prejudices, these were not of her world, inclination.

Dieter said carelessly, as if it was boring but necessary, 'My parents threw me out.' No explanation of this. 'Herr and Frau Wolff are nice, simple people. A bit deaf,' he concluded oddly.

It was a small stone house, and Herr and Frau Wolff were waiting, more nervous than she, like guests at a momentous occasion. Frau Wolff was in black – shoes, dress, stockings, the lot – but was inclined to giggle. They spoke no English, and Dieter had to translate politeness both ways. They were quite old, tired people, with the marks of war and tragedy on their faces, things past, sons lost, money defeats, property destroyed, jobs taken, position lost.

They insisted on wine; there was much coming and going, her case taken away. The phone rang. Dieter answered it quickly, and Maggie caught the word *Engländerin*. Special glasses of extreme fragility were fetched, two bottles of white wine. 'Notice,' Dieter pointed out, 'that they give you and I the 1955, which is good, and keep the 1958, very poor, for themselves.'

There seemed to be no sense of time. One o'clock or later and she was eating ham, cheese, eggs on bread, sliced onions, and was still sipping the 1955 wine. Afterwards Dieter returned with her to the intercommunicating lounge. She offered to help with the washing up, but he assured her, 'They would be offended. You are our guest.'

Dieter was completely at ease, sat on the floor.

'You like speed? Exciting things?'

'Yes,' Maggie said.

She stared at him, examined him face to face, but he was that rare male, the one who could look her in the eye, continue conversation. In the electric light she saw how good-looking he was. It was almost absurd, theatrical; perfect head, face, eyes, dark-brown hair, an appearance that suggested agility, recklessness, excitement, yet his curious dialogue went on :

'Ordinary people, they bore me. So dull. I like excitement. You like excitement?'

And even in her acknowledged 'Yes, I love it,' she knew he did not mean love, even sex. She did not in fact really know what he meant.

'And music? So lovely. Ivor Novello, I remember.' He was

putting on gramophone records while Frau Wolff, still shy, giggly, had brought coffee, was now in retreat. 'He was English, yes? I like it loud, very loud. You like music loud?'

It was indeed very loud, and Maggie said in perplexity, 'The neighbours?'

'Oh, gone away. A month in Austria. So unimaginative. Very rich, stupid. Do you like poetry, too?'

'Some of it.'

'Dylan Thomas, he's very good. So amusing, vulgar. I like vulgarity – so honest, you agree?'

'Sometimes,' qualified Maggie.

'You mustn't say you do if you don't,' Dieter insisted. 'I don't mean nasty vulgarity, of course. American. You should see the Amis – well, you will. They're nasty vulgar. I like Dylan Thomas, that's what I meant. And Truman Capote. You've read him?'

'No.'

'American, unfortunately . . . Are you tired? It is two o'clock. I never tire. Sometimes I stay awake all night, watch the street, the stars, listen to Schumann. Not Wagner. You mustn't presume all Germans like Wagner.'

It was confusing, more crazy than she, and meaningless. Her world was telephones, the bus, Frank's marriage, a drab education, Mick, Ray, John, Polly Sue, some cinema, coffee bars, dance halls, a few pubs, World Mechanical socials, Vera and Eggy; she was only nineteen, hadn't collected many memories yet. There had been no time, no place, in her world, her ordinary world, for music, poetry. The men she met – those that dull circumstance allowed her to meet – seemed only to talk of cars, football, television, cinemas, and their every remark was conditioned by infatuation, the fever in the skin. . . .

At three o'clock she went to bed – a small, charming room, pretty pictures and a crucifix and, alone on a table, a photograph – dead, of course, killed by the English or Americans or Russians. There was a key in the door, but it seemed pointless to lock herself in. She was in no sexual danger from Dieter, she felt certain. She fell asleep at once, dreamed of the train, Trevor's hand under the table, the speedometer at 130, and the kind Dutch face, the photograph on the table, the same war –

she'd been a baby, knew nothing of that. Her world was simpler: you lived until the bomb came and the world ended.

In the morning a feeling of having woken late, a glare of light, a church bell ringing, and the sound of a waterfall. Maggie looked out of the window and saw a small town in a valley – she was on the one slope of wooded hills; the church was on the other. The town followed the S-curve of a river; a pretty town, but too grey: slates, weather tiles, stone, all grey, in a day of utmost brilliance.

At breakfast the same odd dialogue, the three-way shouted translations, Frau Wolff's giggles and hurrying feet, obedient, fetching more coffee . . .

'You like Germany, yes?'

Maggie had only seen it out of a window but replied with truth, 'It is beautiful.'

'I like the English,' Dieter said, as one explaining a weakness, an absurdity. 'But sometimes I am ashamed for them. I see them in their coach parties and they are ridiculous. The waitresses snigger and I am embarrassed.'

Maggie objected, 'You mustn't judge a country by its tourists,' and that, for the moment, ended his trend of dialogue.

Dieter drove the Volkswagen with the same skilled rage, and now Maggie saw the forests, timber stacks. They went through a village in the trees, a secret small town, acres and acres of concrete buildings, large cars parked outside every door. It took five minutes to drive through this 'village'. There were schools and hospitals, uniformed men walking about, bored sentries here and there.

'Our saviours,' sneered Dieter. 'The Amis. *Das ist kein Volk, das ist eine Mischung.*'

'What does that mean?'

'Just something we say. That is no people, that is a mixture.'

'Do you think it matters?' she asked, but he didn't answer, preferred to describe the wine-garden countryside through which they were passing: who owned it, how it was worked.

It took an hour to reach Heidelberg. Outside the station were scores of taxis, American vehicles.

'It is the same as everywhere else in the world,' Dieter said. He was angry about something, nothing to do with her though. 'Dirt is overwhelming it from the edges. Soon they will say the most splendid thing is this railway station.'

'I think it is all beautiful,' she said with the innocence of one who can still see beauty, ignore what the uninstructed mind had not received.

'Here's Horst,' Dieter said.

A young man in the August heat, slacks and a pale-green zipped jacket, blond, tired face, twenty-two or -three. He had a smile for Maggie, but it was technical, courtesy, not fever, interest. At once he was in earnest conversation with Dieter.

'Horst does not have much English.'

'A little,' said Horst. 'How do you enjoy your holiday, Miss Preston?'

'It is most interesting,' she answered, but already it was wrong, peculiar.

'My boat is near the Friedrichs Brücke,' Horst said. 'We walk along the river bank, yes?'

Crowds of people, foreigners, Germans in their Sunday best, Yanks in uniform, beautiful girls, young men who stared, were interested. Large, impressive houses along the banks of the Neckar, pretty bridges across it, little wooden summer houses high up in the hills. Dieter was right: industry and office blocks were overwhelming Heidelberg from the edges.

Dieter held her arm suddenly.

'Watch this! It will be amusing.'

Four Yanks – recognizable as such, despite civilian clothes, by haircuts, immature, spotted faces – were running, eyes bulging, knocking people out of their way. People turned heads, cars braked; it wasn't going to be amusing, Maggie guessed.

'They will fight or be sick,' Dieter explained with glee.

Maggie saw that they were pursued by a middle-aged woman, one of the neuter of the earth, and now she had caught one. A second hesitated, returned; the other two vanished.

An argument began, all three absolutely heedless of the smiles, curiosity, embarrassment. The Yanks were very drunk, gross, unaware of shock and shame spreading.

Dieter had stopped, clearly with no intention of moving on.

'What is it all about?' Maggie asked.

'So amusing,' Dieter commented with biting anger. 'Sometimes it is sex, sometimes money. Sometimes it is fugging Krauts,' he said so that Maggie flinched. 'Today it is beer.'

'Have they no money?'

'Plenty of money. No. You are not looking at the lady with sufficient care. You will see they have poured beer over her.'

'But why?'

'Because it is amusing, or perhaps she asked them the time or suggested they be quiet. How do I know? Such gay children, up to little tricks all the time.'

One of the Yanks began to run for it, and a few girls screamed as the middle-aged woman grabbed him, was dragged, fell, exposed her old legs, underwear. Nobody did anything. Dieter watched in satisfaction, something proved for Maggie. A taxi driver headed off the Yank and he returned, shameless even now, grinning, to continue the argument with the recovering woman. People tittered nervously, kept distant; no one helped the woman – she was not pretty enough. Now the two Yanks were arguing with each other – 'You promised me' – 'Listen, whad'ya think?' – and they began to hit each other with wild fury. The woman got in the way, was struck also, and now a green Volkswagen arrived, two policemen emerged, new argument began. The Yanks were not the slightest bit intimidated by the policemen, disputed furiously, struck one. They smiled suddenly at the woman – today's big fun – and were handcuffed and taken away in the car, laughing.

'It won't make any difference,' said Dieter bitterly. 'Two days in the cooler, a great joke. Then along comes their provost marshal, fetches them out. Pigs. In Karlsruhe two of them stripped a prostitute and forced her to a window for their friends to see.'

It had marred the day.

'Shall we lunch now?' Dieter asked, but Maggie was sickened, didn't want to eat yet.

Her lighter mood revived in Horst's speedboat. They followed barges and steamers and turned at high speed, so that she screamed with excitement, and in an hour she, Yanks forgotten, said, 'This is wonderful! I wish I had a lot of money and could buy a speedboat!'

Dieter and Horst looked at each other as if something had been established.

'Suppose,' said Dieter with a new kind of care, courtesy, 'I said it was possible for you to make a lot of money very easily. What would you say?'

Maggie giggled, because she didn't really know how to answer. 'Do I sell my body?' And they, taking her seriously, shook their heads.

'It is a matter of trade,' said Dieter. 'But we will talk of it later.'

They were at ease, very happy, something difficult accomplished, at any rate proposed and not rejected. But she was baffled. Both were in their early twenties. What influence on any sort of trade could either possibly have?

'I don't understand,' she said. 'You are not in trade.'

'It is trade in ideas,' Dieter told her.

They were overtaking barges; someone waved, was ignored. On the hill, becoming visible as they moved, was an enormous *schloss*. Dieter commented, 'It is hideous, you agree?' but it was merely his own discomfort.

Horst explained – in perfectly good English, 'You listen to the telephone at World Mechanical in London. You hear things. You tell someone what has been ordered, by whom, how many . . .'

'We have a contact in London,' supplemented Dieter. 'There would be no risk, no letters.'

'It is worth money here in Germany,' Horst added into her silence.

'You are not angry?'

'Do you owe World Mechanical so much? It is a cartel, is it not?'

Maggie laughed nervously. 'They couldn't care less about little me, so long as I answer the phones.'

'Well, it is without importance, you agree? They are worth millions. Why should you not have money, a speedboat, dresses, jewellery?'

Dieter was pleading, but she wasn't listening. The word

'contact' worried her. World Mechanical meant nothing to her – the chemicals, ballistics, metals, aircraft, rocket components, refrigerators – she was just a girl who was paid seven pounds fifteen a week for being polite. It was pure accident that her switchboard was in World Mechanical and not some other company. You couldn't feel much loyalty to the company despite its pension scheme, cheap meals, free medical attention. Friendships with others were the only claims World Mechanical had on her. But the word 'contact' was an espionage word, and Dieter's hatred of things American was an indication of something.

She was never afraid of complicated infatuations, married men who wanted to be foolish and pleaded in long-winded madness how they loved her, younger men who had the fever badly, but she felt fear now. Too many newspapers glanced at, films seen. If she refused, she might drown – an unfortunate accident to a tourist. It would be wiser to hear more, refuse at the London end.

'What could I tell you of value?'

'There is no danger,' Dieter insisted. 'You must not do anything dangerous – that is the last thing desired.'

'It would hurt no one,' Horst said. 'Just occasional notes, in your mind if you can, of who talked to whom, what was ordered,'

'In particular that in relation to a thing, a proposition called Billiards,' said Dieter, and Horst was shocked, angry, as if now too much had been said.

'Would I really have some money?'

'A lot of money.'

'A hundred pounds now and then,' Horst reassured her.

Maggie smiled like a conspirator. 'Not much in values of millions,' she commented.

'It would depend on the information,' Dieter said carefully.

'And now,' suggested Horst, smiling, a host again, 'a drink and lunch before it is too late, so?'

'It could be exciting,' Dieter said. 'You like excitement, yes?'

The speedboat bubbled its way to the riverbank. The sun was warm; people were on holiday; she was. It was hard to believe her life had just been altered, her status. Sitting in a garden while Dieter fetched drinks and an old, attentive waiter suggested what to eat, it seemed easy, unreal. She did not think in terms of treason, police, prison, but what could go wrong. For if nothing could go wrong, then why not the odd few hundred pounds? Frank didn't contribute to her welfare, and Vera asked four pounds a week, which meant she had less than four for everything else, from fags to dress, from cinema to fish and chips. One day she'd marry again, and if she could put money in the bank for that day ...

Horst whispered, 'Don't look worried, Miss Preston. You are too beautiful for that. We understand. It is a little frightening at first. You will become confident when you see it is easy.'

Dieter, approaching silently, said, 'You are my old friend, Maggie, and so I thought of you first. But if you wish to refuse you are at liberty to do so.'

But she, doubting that, answered, 'I was a bit scared, that's all.'

'It is foolproof,' said Dieter. 'You listen to the telephone when it is possible. You have dinner with a London friend of your German pen friend, and who is to know what you talk about?'

'Tonight,' suggested Horst, 'we go dancing. You like dancing?'

'Indeed, yes.'

'And tomorrow,' said Dieter, 'we go to Munich or Karlsruhe and do some shopping. Pretty things. You like nice coats?'

Maggie smiled at such outright bribery.

She danced in the light of lanterns in the warm night with young Germans who wore their trilby hats. She became slightly drunk, zany, herself again. They all talked English, whispered feverishly, their own girls forgotten in the romance of her red hair and foreignness and obvious madness. And she began to accumulate recklessness. These were her kind of people – romantic, musical, courteous. She justified herself; it's just trade, business, and all business is a fraud, dishonest. Little people like me have the right to cash in on it when they are able ...

Pleasure froze when a Yank soldier, very drunk, began to be a nuisance. The German boys were baffled, didn't want trouble, but he shouted above the music and she, who understood what he meant, was sickened again. The Yank was insulting the girls, and when even this provocation failed he just hit someone in the face. Some young men threw him out, but he came back, fought others, was knocked to ground, lifted bodily, again hurled into the street. He returned, clothes torn, foaming oaths, and again fought until he was knocked down, and this time he was kicked and blood poured from his mouth. All the time the accordions played. 'It is always like this,' explained the young German who held Maggie. *'Das ist kein Volk, das ist eine Mischung.'* And when she asked, 'What about English soldiers?' the boy answered, *'Steife Engländer,'* and laughed. Thus the free half of the world was condemned in a few sentences, with emotional demonstrations by four or five drunken soldiers to prove something. But to partake in treason, even when a girl has no God or politics, is no light matter, and Maggie slept badly that night, heard the waterfall and the striking clock over the river in Jdar-Lauterecken.

There was no more unpleasantness. It was as if Dieter had wished to demonstrate how pointless it was to believe the American way of life had anything to recommend it. The Amis were just brash, coarse, uncultured people, not like the Germans. Perhaps there were insufficient English troops and tourists for him to make the same point about them. But it was impossible to avoid Americans in that area of Germany.

In Munich they walked around the vaulted arcades, listened to the clocks. Dieter was interested in shopping, translated for her. He had no qualms – underwear or jewellery, he smiled, conversed, translated. Her money went very quickly and then he began to buy things, not cheap items, not just the cakes, wine, cigarettes, postcards, but a leather suitcase. 'You throw yours away,' he said. 'Then you'll get this one past your customs easily enough.' He was quite without shyness about sizes in stockings and blouses, more fun to shop with, in fact, than any man she'd ever known. Beyond Munich he took her at speed to the beginning of the Alps, then back through tiny villages which had a clean white glitter and churches as slender as pointed pencils. At dinner that night the restaurant was packed, very masculine – hot soup, shouts, beer, smoke. Some Italians and Yugoslavs were celebrating at a long table, grossly ugly, full of themselves, eating with furious indifference, pig-like appetite. Two silly English youths appeared in Alpine hats, callow, effeminate. They stood about hopelessly, then left. Dieter smiled, said nothing. They were sharing a table with a quiet, pale girl and an American captain. The captain talked in a loud, nasal voice, quite without self-consciousness, but the girl squirmed, was aware of Dieter and Maggie. It was impossible for Maggie not to share something with Dieter – not his dislike, but certainly amusement as the dialogue went on . . .

'You got pretty teeth. Did they put a brace in when you were young?'

'I've always been dangerous, always.'

'You like to do that? Go dancing, champagne? You like that?'

The captain became aware of Maggie's giggles, but so far from being embarrassed, became interested in her. 'Animals,' said Dieter afterwards. 'If you'd said a word he'd have taken you to bed, left that constipated child behind.' He was cruel, but it was difficult not to be amused as he imitated: 'Where d'you stay when you were in Chicago? Dearborn Street? 1959? That's friendship for you . . .'

The days went by, hot and clean, fascinating. Swimming, dancing, strolling the foreign streets, sharing the electric tension as Dieter overtook with seconds to spare. Shops and meals and wines and happy people. Barges and electric trams and ferries and *autobahnen* and dusty lanes and mountain bends that caused the tyres to shriek. Munich, Karlsruhe, Cologne, Heidelberg, Ulm, Stuttgart, Mainz, Bonn, Koblenz. Big reconstructed cities of pink cubes and glittering glass. Forests and winding roads. Meals by the Rhine, to music. The endless procession of barges and steamers up and down the river. Castles at Marksburg, Pfalzgrafenstein, Ehrenbreitstein, Stolzenfels, Drachenfels. And as the days went by a new friendship grew between them – neither infatuation nor the old status of pen friend, nor even foreign visitor. It was just impossible not to like him. He enjoyed life, was courteous to her as no Englishman had ever been, and his interest in her was genuine, amounted to concern. Before the week was out she'd told him about Frank. Everywhere they went Dieter took the Leica camera he owned. Sometimes they both got drunk and he became affectionate. But there was no fever in it: she was safe. She understood now why Eggy and Vera had been concerned. If Dieter had been infatuated anything might have happened.

Friday came – anxiety, departure not far off – and now this was real, where she belonged, and London's grimy suburbs and World Mechanical and the occasional migraines were an unreality. The weather, sensing her mood, deteriorated, and in the evening it began to rain. Koblenz was full of cobbles on which she slipped. Dieter took her arm and hurried her uselessly from tree to tree along the riverbank. The rain had caught everybody. People strolled wretchedly; lovers hid behind trees. There were, nevertheless, hundreds of people at the operetta. The stage was on the Rhine, the set as fragile as an iced cake. Maggie did not understand the German but was impressed. It was pouring on the stage and some of the performers wore plastic macs over their vivid costumes. The rain in the glare of the electric lights had the odd appearance of snow, and the moving river confused her eye, made it seem as if Koblenz was floating away. The rain brought some leaves down and these fell in this atmosphere of fantasy. The only reality in the darkness was the occasional tonk-tonk of a passing barge, a train's hooter far off. The performers sang as if the weather was perfect; a brass band wandered to and fro; two horses pulled a cart; men rode penny-farthing bicycles.

A twenty-five minute interval was announced, and there was an orderly rush for the mobile toilets, the huts along the river, where barmaids began to work. There were many students, pretty girls with hair cut like medieval knights. A crowd of *Luftwäffe* men strolled about, very upright, quiet, well-behaved.

A man holding an umbrella whispered urgently, 'Dieter!' and started to walk out of the crowds.

Dieter followed, and Maggie guessed this was arranged; it was the operetta that was incidental.

He was a rounded, benign, middle-aged man, very wet despite the umbrella; he'd been in a cheaper seat presumably. They stood in the darkness by the Rhine; lanterns glittered, voices laughed, smoke of cigars drifted.

'This is Miss Preston.'

'How do you like Germany, Miss Preston?'

'I like it very much.'

'Dieter has said some kind things about you.'

'We are old friends,' said Dieter quickly. 'Old friends,' he repeated, as if this explanation was both necessary and urgent.

'And you work for World Mechanical? That is good. Now, we have your phone number. Is it safe to telephone you?'

'Yes,' said Maggie breathlessly. 'Our boy friends phone.'

'Boy friends. That also is good. Henry will contact you. Once a week. He will give you instructions as to how to meet. Is there any time of day which is most suitable?'

'Between one and two,' Maggie told them.

'One and two. And can you be overheard?'

'No.'

'It is perfect. But if it is supremely important, you must tell Henry and someone else will meet you. You know what I mean by important?'

'Yes,' Maggie said uncomfortably. 'Relative to Billiards.'

'You must have a drink,' the older man said. 'It has become very cold.'

A bell was ringing.

'I am sorry,' he concluded, and was gone.

That was at the beginning of August. By the middle of September the whole thing was beginning to seem unreal. When she looked in the morning mirror traces of sunburn were on her normally pale face, and her eyes had the clarity of a person who has been refreshed by leisure, but the holiday itself, unbelievably, was being drowned in memory, bludgeoned into perspective by normality: Eggy at the doctor, Mick in the sports car (although Mick for a while seemed immature, untouched by the world), the phone ringing at World Mechanical.

Then at half past one on a Friday afternoon she sang out

the usual 'World Mechanical, can I help you?' despite a mouth full of sandwich, and a male voice, ageless, asked, 'Is it permissible to speak to Miss Preston?'

Maggie felt a hot flush colouring her; food regurgitated; her limbs fluttered with fright.

'I am Miss Preston.'

'Ah, Maggie, this is Henry.'

'I have not heard from Dieter,' she complained.

'Is it possible for anyone to hear us?'

'No,' Maggie said.

Henry was not, presumably, interested in Dieter. He asked, 'What's the news? Has anything important happened?'

'Nothing important.'

'Anything at all?'

'It is impossible for me to judge.'

'But you have news?'

'Yes. I don't know what it means –'

'Never mind. We will judge that. It would be so pleasant to meet. Which day would suit you?'

'I don't know,' she said hopelessly. Her days were crowded with small events – Mick's arrival, Ray, Sue going shopping, Sunday's cooking shared with Vera – unimportant, but to explain her absence in acceptable lies wouldn't be easy or comfortable.

'Do you go home alone?'

'Usually.'

'Then let it be today. At six o'clock be strolling along Tottenham Court Road between Great Russell Street and Bayley Street. Is this convenient?'

'Yes.'

'I will approach you. I shall wear a brown trilby and will carry a copy of the American magazine *Esquire*, and I shall say, "Maggie, my dear."'

'How will you know me?'

'I have a photograph,' he said and rang off.

She knew now in mild distress that all those pictures taken with the Leica in Germany had been for a purpose. What her imagination could not know was that sixty-six prints had been made and were on file in buildings throughout the world, including Moscow, together with a description of her, her habits, weaknesses, abilities, potentialities.

She was late, breathless; men stared; people looked idly from buses crawling. It was ridiculous; the whole world could see. Men passed and their eyes winked, were startled to be under scrutiny by this slender, exciting redhead. They all seemed to be carrying papers of some sort . . .

'Maggie, my dear!'

She jumped in shock. He had materialized from nowhere. She was trembling. He was tall, middle-aged, professional – architect, minor solicitor, head clerk, bank cashier – the sexy cover of *Esquire* seemed slightly wrong, shocking.

They were in people's way, being jostled.

She said, with enormous difficulty, 'How are you, Henry?'

'But I'm fine, fine. And you look so well. The holiday did you good. Did you receive the photographs?'

'Not yet.'

'What a shame. So delightful! Dieter will be sending some, I know. He's on holiday, you know. Italy.'

'He has a lot of holiday,' she said, perplexed.

They were walking toward Euston.

'We'll get a taxi,' Henry said.

This took a few minutes. Maggie felt much less conspicuous inside the taxi.

'Victoria,' Henry said to the driver.

In the traffic's crawl he asked, 'What's this news you have?'

Maggie opened her handbag. 'I had to write it down.'

Henry reprimanded, worried on her behalf. 'I shouldn't do that.'

'There was such a lot. I couldn't keep it in my head. Shall I tell you? Will the driver hear?'

'He's not interested and won't hear unless you shout.'

She read it out: 'Two thousand seven hundred blast-recorded adapter tubes for Commercial Relays; that was on thirtieth August. Then on first September there was a call from Holland – Nijmegen – for Sir Charles and it was about the acid integrators for the turbo-alloy propellor dividers to be used at the chemical works there. They said the name, but it was incomprehensible. On eighth September the Air Ministry rang and asked about the delay on the focal-point gun sights for the Mark IV Skythrust fighters . . .'

They had reached Victoria before she'd finished.

'This is very good,' said Henry. 'Look, when this fellow's gone we'll get another taxi and take you somewhere convenient.'

In the second taxi Henry gave her twenty-five pounds for information which, when related to other facts, was worth about two million.

Thus began a series of meetings in various parts of London, usually transacted in taxis, for which Maggie was paid small sums. She never learned Henry's other name or anything about him, and he never asked anything about her, except if there were difficulties, if she was worried about anything. And as the weeks became months she had no worry at all. She had two hundred pounds in the bank, a fair but not conspicuous amount of new clothes, and she smoked a better brand of cigarettes. For this she was giving information, meaningless to herself, and she had a mental shutter that allowed her to believe it would be without significance to others. Dieter wrote, a letter which made no mention of anything but personal relationships, and enclosed ten photographs of herself which everyone admired. One was pinched by Mick.

Then, in November, she took a call from a London suburb from a company called Mayger Electric, and before she was interrupted by the midmorning tea trolley she had overheard two minutes of a conversation that would be regarded, she knew, as important.

Henry made his usual call four long days later.

'Hello, Maggie. What's the news?'

'Henry, I've got something important.'

'How important?'

'Very. You know.'

'I see. I will meet you, Maggie, and make arrangements.'

Four days beyond that Maggie stepped from a taxi in the brief cul-de-sac which gave access from the roar of London's traffic to the bronze-and-glass entrance to the Excellence. She arrived at precisely seven-thirty and was accepted as a minor film star or expensive tart by the doorman. She had never been in such a hotel before but, womanlike, was enjoying the experience. A scattering of people, chandeliers, a boy paging 'Mr Horlington', music somewhere and quiet laughter, the whirr of lifts, splendid arrangements of flowers on tables of absurd shape. She oriented herself as instructed and sat in the white leather chair, admired by one or two men, but overshadowed by at least one gleaming foreign beauty, very much at home, complaining.

A middle-aged man, dumpy, cheerful, strolled toward her, in no hurry, a slight limp, a likeable person, not stuffy.

He greeted her, as arranged, 'And how are things in Seattle?'

Maggie smiled, replied, 'Why Major, how extraordinary. Do sit down.'

'Are you in England long?'

By now inquisitive faces and heads lifted had lost interest. Major Gouseev inquired, 'Would you like a drink?' and she decided, 'Martini, Major, I'd love that.'

Great fun. Everybody fooled. She even spoke in a transatlantic drawl for the fun of it. The major was as charming as the situation allowed. He made the evening enjoyable, not just business. It was like a minor actress discussing terms with her agent, both happy to talk for a while of other things. But, inevitably, the questions came.

'It was a mention of Billiards?'

'Yes. I was interrupted –'

'Never mind. You were lucky. Describe the dialogue, will you?'

'It was a call from Mayger Electric, a girl said. Their Mr Bailey wanted to speak to our Mr Gascoigne ...'

'Who's Gascoigne?'

'Ballistics.'

'I see. Proceed.'

'Well, I got him through and this Mr Bailey said, "Look, Freddy, we can't put anything about this blasted Billiards thing into writing. Is it safe to phone?" And Mr Gascoigne said, "We were asked to calibrate to one ten-thousandth, but we find –" '

'What did they find?'

'That was all. The tea trolley came and it would have looked odd. Not that the trolley girl would know what I was doing, but –'

'Quite. This is very interesting. You were right to stop at the slightest possibility of suspicion. We can deduce ...' But Major Gouseev did not tell her what would be deduced or even who 'we' were.

At the end of the evening Maggie was flushed, warmed by food and drink. Like Dieter, the major did not become infatuated, but he was normal enough to stare, and it was clearly the situation which held him in check, not his inclinations. He was inoculated against fever by a position. He helped Maggie with her coat and she saw him put an envelope into one of the ridiculous pockets.

The major left her within yards of the hotel, and Maggie, burning with curiosity about that envelope, sought privacy in a toilet at Charing Cross Station. Inside the envelope were one hundred pound notes – all dirty, not in consecutive serial number. I'll buy a watch, Maggie Preston decided, hot with pleasure, while a mile and a half away Major Gouseev started with the elementary deductions that Billiards was a weapon of war; it had high priority and top secrecy; parts were made by World Mechanical – presumably at their ordnance works in Manchester – and parts, presumably radio, were manufactured by Mayger Electric in a London suburb. Not bad for a hundred pounds!

8

CHARLES FILMER

THE Communist headquarters was in a narrow, dirty shopping street: gramophones and barrows, louts selling rubbish, the smells of petrol and oranges, the pavements soiled by a hundred years of feet. An old woman was begging, sitting on a stool, glaring with unseeing eyes at the world she hated; on principle she never thanked them for their conscience coins. The other parts of the rat race passed by in eagerness to get somewhere else.

The headquarters was like a shop. It sold equality, presumably, mechanical love, proved by income and work.

Charles Filmer was nervous. Inside, a counter, two girls – so ordinary, pale, and dull that he flinched – and a phone ringing somewhere. Further up, a man of about thirty, pale face, pale-ginger hair, colourless until examined closer, when one saw he had some quality; it had torn his face into fanaticism. He was like a warehouse clerk with no hope of promotion, who has just been reprimanded unfairly by the boss and is consumed by it. He was talking to a man, counsel advising, all about rent tribunals and how to live your life in a condition of permanent anger until, finally, all the rents in the world were negligible. Then what? They'd think of something. There was plenty to hate.

The two girls were talking. They glanced at Filmer but dismissed him. He was nothing. The ginger-headed man could deal with him.

It was as stupid as a chain store. Filmer was waiting like a person in a cake shop for somebody to be polite, that is, unfair, but here there was equality, the dreariness of uniformity. Or should have been. But he was experienced in other people's indifference and arrogance and had been dismissed by the girls because – of all things – he did not look important! Anger grew in him and he said, 'Miss, would you mind?'

One sighed heavily, walked with infinite distaste to him.

'Did you want some help?'

'I have some information.'

'Information?'

She couldn't have cared less.

'My name is –'

'What sort of information?'

'Technical.'

The other girl sniggered because this one was baffled.

'Y'better see Mr Pratt.'

Take it or leave it was the implication of her heavy, undulating hips. I got things to attend to. Big-time.

Ten long minutes went by and then the pale-ginger man said, 'Don't pay it until you've heard,' and was about to enter a smaller room.

'Mr Pratt?' Filmer said.

The pale, pink-rimmed eyes full of hatred examined Filmer for a second. Nothing. He was nothing. But perhaps they identified some quality, for he hesitated, qualified the rejection on his lips, 'Just a minute, Comrade,' and went through into the room, which was apparently his office. Soon he returned, ready for the next belly-ache.

'I got information.'

The two girls stared in absolute disbelief.

'Who for?' Mr Pratt asked.

'The Party,' said Filmer.

'I don't remember you, Comrade.'

'I'm not a member.'

'I don't get it,' said Mr Pratt, relapsing into American.

Filmer began to explain his work, his motives, his convictions, and Mr Pratt's pale, prejudiced face began to be interested.

'Come in the office,' he said, a rare request evidently, for the girls had to move chairs, files. At last someone was taking notice of Filmer.

The office was a dirty, overcrowded room with green walls; there was a paler green space where a picture or photograph had been taken down. There were notices about rent tribunals, an International Social; there were photographs of strange towns and bridges and one of Chinese peasants, smiling. A few anti-American pictures, a cartoon from a newspaper, very faded now, of the Prime Minister holding England in chains.

'Just a minute,' said Mr Pratt, and he went to the door. 'Ingrid. Come here, Ingrid.'

The girl, who looked like a very plain Jane, said, rather worried, 'Yes, Mr Pratt.'

'Get some tea. No, go down to the co-op first – cakes. Ginger if they've got them.' Perhaps he fed nourishment to his hair, his long, infuriated eyelashes, with ginger cake. 'And you never fixed this table.'

'I'm sorry, Mr Pratt.'

'Yeah, all right. Tell Muriel to do it.'

He was demonstrating his power perhaps. It was faintly satisfying to Filmer to have the two girls humiliated. The girl called Muriel – fat and sullen – pushed the small table about, bent down; useless – it still wobbled.

'I can't find anything, Mr Pratt.'

'Use a book, Comrade. Use your brains.'

Mr Pratt winked one of his ginger-haloed prejudiced eyes at Filmer.

'There's only Lenin, that's big enough.'

'All right. Use Lenin.'

The volume of Lenin's work supported the table perfectly.

'I don't think,' said Mr Pratt in the girl's absence, 'that you ought to become a member, Mr Filmer. You're more use to the Party outside its normal activities.'

'Yes,' said Filmer vaguely.

'Tell you what I'll do,' Mr Pratt proceeded, coming to a decision. 'I'll get in touch with people. Is it safe to call on you?'

'No,' said Filmer, hot with panic instantly. Vi and Brenda, Ted and Marion – they would have plenty to say, too much; it would kill it instantly. You could bet Ted would be a 'patriot'. It was essential that the betrayal, the opinions canalized, in action, should have the benefit of secrecy. It was, after all, dangerous, what he was doing; there were those who'd say it was criminal, wrong. They wrote their leader columns; they sat in Trafalgar Square; they went on strike – but they hadn't his courage to go the final step: help to destroy the country despised.

'How about the International Social?' asked Mr Pratt, thinking aloud. 'We get some very important speakers.'

'I don't fancy it,' said Filmer. 'Dancing and all that. I'm against it.'

'Discussion,' qualified Mr Pratt. 'All sorts of nations represented. Coloured people, Germans, Irish – independent people with views, who care for the world. No teen-age whoring and dancing. Tea and coffee,' he concluded.

'I've never been to one,' said Filmer nervously.

'They'll make you welcome,' Mr Pratt reassured him. 'And someone'll make contact, that's the important point.'

'What do I say to my wife?'

'That's a point,' conceded Mr Pratt. 'You could bring her, of course. Quite safe.'

'She'd never come.'

'Wouldn't she?'

'She'd say it was daft.'

'Not politically minded,' suggested Mr Pratt politely. 'Well, you think of something, Mr Filmer. Billiards, the dogs, cinema, a drink with the lads – there must be some excuse.'

How inexperienced, his voice implied, you are in the necessity of untruths. We use them, as the British use hypocrisy, to keep everybody happy.

The International Social Party was, as might be expected, not altogether successful. It was held, ironically, in a church hall on a main road. In splendid unawareness of its motives the vicar helped to organize, loaned cups and saucers, projector, balloons, gramophone. The hall was a large ramshackle corrugated-iron building with faded, flaking green paint inside. One approached it through dogs' mess and the litter of Saturday-afternoon football five hundred yards away. It was a cold night. The party was due to begin at 7.30.

Filmer arrived just after this time and entered nervously. A youth stopped him at the door to claim one-and-sixpence entrance fee. Inside, things were brighter, but still cold. Six people were standing about and making heavy going of the evening. The vicar, whose presence was accidental and due entirely to good will, was holding things together. He grasped at subjects, examined them, discussed them to bits. Each arrival was welcomed by him – not by any of the comrades, who in fact stared just like Englishmen at any occasion – and greeted as if only he or she could make the evening complete.

Filmer was a little taken aback to find a clergyman at all, let alone one who rushed forward with eagerness.

'Ah, hello. Welcome. It's cold, isn't it? I've had the heating going since four o'clock, but never mind. Things'll liven up, eh, Mr –?'

'Filmer.'

'Let me introduce you.

Bosambo, a young man from Uganda, with large ears and a narrow head and wrists as fragile as twigs.

'You wanna know why they call me Bosambo?' he asked. 'It's because it's my name.'

Laughter, but difficult. Bosambo had said this little piece three times already.

'Mr Bean.'

Another coloured man, shy, a happy, round head and hair like wire wool and tiny fragile black ears. He was from Nigeria. He wore glasses, but they looked wrong, a decoration only.

Two girls, both not quite pretty, both in white dresses, as if going to be confirmed in their faith.

A Norwegian man who for reasons not explained spoke English with a Scottish accent. Mr Larsen. And a plump girl, heavily attractive, who sat in a corner and wasn't moving for anybody and roared with laughter when introductions were made. She was German.

The youth tired of being on duty, came inside, protested, 'Christ, it's cold. What about the gramophone?'

'Splendid,' said the vicar. He had been talking earnestly to the small group, lighting his pipe, puffing, warming the thousands of cold cubic feet with smoke. 'Can you manage, Cecil?'

Cecil managed, and an international mixture of music began to stun the air, very loud, drowning the long silences, very nearly convincing people outside that here was achieved what the United Nations had fallen down on: Charlie Kunz playing the piano, an unknown band scratching its way through 'Dancing with My Shadow', a hymn ('Not that, Cecil,' the vicar shouted. 'We're not on duty!'), a great blast of Wagner, and a similar concussive roar as the boy put the needle straight in the middle of the 'Eton Boating Song'.

A few others came, including Ingrid, the girl from the H.Q. The vicar had tired of introductions. In between records the boy went around with a tin box and asked people, 'Have I had your money?'

Four or five middle-aged people came in and gathered around, pushing a wheel chair. In the chair was a man of about fifty, middle-class, bulky, important once. A very beautiful, but cheeky, girl with red hair entered, hesitated – the wrong part – but, no, someone grabbed her. 'My dear Maggie, I didn't think you'd come ...' And her reply, frivolous: 'I'll try anything once.'

The organizer, it became apparent, was Bosambo. He was doing much hurrying about, checking loud-speakers, shaking hands like a diplomat. The vicar was still carrying on earnest conversations, and in a corner of the hall were scores of cups and saucers, plates, sandwiches, being dealt with by two horse-faced women who had been introduced to no one.

A young man, tough, intelligent, studentlike, said to Filmer, who was alone, unattended, and angry about it, 'Who's that gorgeous redhead?'

Filmer said, 'They called her Maggie.'

'What a wonderful name. I wish,' said the young man with sudden, shattering earnestness completely in opposition to the spirit of the party, 'they hadn't asked all these damn niggers. Still' – he grinned – 'they asked the girl!'

'Ladies and gentlemen,' said Bosambo suddenly. He was so ground in British institutions that he forgot to identify them as 'comrades', or perhaps he simply wanted to be courteous to the vicar, his rivals, Christianity.

'Silence in court!' some fool shouted.

'Ladies and gentlemen,' repeated Bosambo, his face shining like French furniture. 'Those who have not paid one and sixpence should do so to Cecil, who has the tin. We are getting to know each other now.' Bosambo smiled. 'There are not too many of us, so the difficulties of a film cocktail party are not probable here.' His voice had an angry edge when he said this, as if he spent many hours thinking of how shameful a film cocktail party was: the actresses revealing their white breasts, the producers valuing them like beasts at a cattle show ... 'We are going to have something to eat now. Help yourselves to plates, and may I say how grateful we all are to the vicar and Miss Wilkinson for their assistance.' Presumably, if he was in the agitation business, he was on the organization side, or distribution. Certainly he was no rabble rouser; his creative talents must lie in other aspects. Or perhaps, decided Filmer, baffled by the ordinariness of the whole evening, he is simply a coloured man at a suburban international social party.... 'Afterward,' suggested Bosambo humorously, 'we shall want to sit down, and so we're going to sing. Later we shall have a film show and games and finally dancing.'

Still no one was very interested in having international or any other relationship with Charles Filmer. They had all come with friends and the party was, if anything, a coalescence of four or five groups. Filmer stood and ate by the tough student, who was evidently very interested in the red-haired girl, and she, with no others in attendance, was cheerfully accepting the boy's attention.

Filmer heard the boy say, 'Actually, I'm a rich man's son – dirty rich, I mean, in South Africa – who's rejected his environment.' And the girl giggled and commented, 'I don't think I'd reject *that* environment.' If these two were Communists they were as politically improbable as a Socialist peer.

'All sit down,' shouted Bosambo. 'Please arrange the chairs.' He stood in front of the five rows of wooden chairs with an accordion. From somewhere he had obtained the improbable items: a blackboard and chalk. On the blackboard he was writing, 'It's a Long Way to Tipperary.' This was either the most peculiar or the most subtle Communist 'party' ever held, Filmer decided. It embarrassed him. He was forty-seven, soured in the blood, a long way beyond the days when he could partake in a singsong, and in his absurdest imagination he would never have anticipated singing 'Three Blind Mice' with twenty-five or thirty people, Negroes, Germans.

'You!' accused Bosambo. 'You are not singing!'

Filmer flushed, said nothing.

The girl called Maggie whispered, 'I don't blame you! Try la-ala-ing.' Her sympathy was most welcome, for Bosambo had spoken with menace.

'I will play,' said Bosambo. 'What you like I shall play, hey?'

It dragged on. Never again, Filmer decided. If they want the information the arrangements must be different.

The film show followed. There was no sound. 'I shall give commentary,' Bosambo said.

A very old film which commenced upside down. Bosambo didn't like the laughter. 'Wait a minute!' he said. 'A normal mistake. Lights, please.'

There was whispering going on by the side of Filmer: 'What's

your name?' – 'Geoff' – 'Do you work?' – 'I'm at college' –
'You look older than that' – 'Couldn't we meet again, somewhere else?' – 'You could phone me.' All the time the film
flickered – horses galloped, coloured men ran between buildings, a car arrived, men emerged, began to point, move in a
line. Filmer half expected to see Ronald Colman appear. But
Bosambo's commentary was assured: 'We acknowledge the
white man's contributions to our society' – this remark, quite
skilful, as the film showed violence in some tropical city,
coloured men hustled, one on the ground, batons wielded. It
was difficult to know who was fighting whom, when, or what
about, but the words flowed from Bosambo easily enough:
'Tyranny, lack of free expression,' and again his bitter social
condemnation: 'Here are the governor and his lady at the cocktail party, unaware of what is happening half a mile away.'

'I think,' said the vicar, rather taken aback, 'we ought to
show just one C.M.S. film, just to show our side of things.'

'Of course, of course,' agreed Bosambo. 'In the interval we
will have a game. Here are pieces of paper. Hand them around
in the dark. Each has an instruction, you see. I shall give you
all numbers, and when . . .'

The explanation went on.

'Lights, please.'

The balls of paper had been passed from hand to hand. The
small cool fingers of the girl Maggie had given Filmer his piece
of paper. 'You're twenty-two,' she said. Filmer was anxious,
did not want to be humiliated, unfolded his piece of paper,
read it. *Go out with Mr Keuscher at exactly ten o'clock.* Filmer
began to sweat, feel very alarmed. Was this part of the game or
an instruction in the larger game? Suppose Bosambo or the
vicar, in all ignorance, called his number? Wouldn't some innocent person – if anyone here was an innocent person –
wonder what was going on?

'Nineteen,' the vicar said.

'Me!' said the student called Geoff. 'It's me.'

'What does it say?'

'It says, "Make a speech on the subject of electric fires." '

'Well, go on!'

The boy rose to the occasion quite well. 'Unaccustomed as I

am to public speaking, I feel it my duty to draw your attention
to the desirability –'

'De da, de da,' said the girl.

'– when the climate is inclement and there are no power
cuts . . .'

Next it was the vicar's turn.

' "Explain the necessity of sin." Oh, I don't know about
that!' But he tried, with tedious good humour, to make a case
for white lies, laziness, hypocrisy.

The C.M.S. film was about lepers, blood, the colour bar, the
problems of big European cities. In complete contrast to
Bosambo's film, it showed cheering Africans, children's faces, a
white bishop talking to coloured priests . . .

Who was Mr Keuscher?

Filmer examined them in his mind – Mr Bean, Bosambo, the
girls in white, Mr Larsen, the student Geoff, the girl Maggie –
how was he to find out without making his curiosity obvious?
What was the time now? Would Mr Keuscher be white, Negro,
or one of the two Arabs who had turned up?

They were divided into teams to play some game with balloons and pins. Filmer dropped out, stood by the wheelchair,
the old handsome face staring, shouting vicarious sport, as girls
and youths crashed violently about, balloons popped.

'What's the time?'

'Quarter to ten,' the cripple said. 'Enjoying yourself, Mr
Filmer?'

'It's not bad.'

'I wonder, would you help with the chair? Mr Larsen and
Mr Ford will want to stay for the dancing.'

'I have to see someone.'

'I am Mr Keuscher,' the old fine face explained. 'Bosambo,
Bosambo!' he called. 'I am leaving.'

Bosambo was sweating, breathing heavily after violent exer-
cise.

'It is always a privilege to have your company,' he said with
breathless hypocrisy.

'This gentleman has offered to take me home.'

'You did not sing,' Bosambo said. It was all he would ever
know about Filmer. In three years' time perhaps he'd pass him

in the street, struggle to remember: voices, the sad face, he did not sing – to hell with him ...

'He has things on his mind,' Mr Keuscher said.

Filmer pushed the wheel chair. It squeaked, once per revolution of its wheels. 'Needs oil,' Mr Keuscher said; reading Filmer's mind.

Outside there were steps. Filmer tried to be careful, but inevitably the wheel chair dropped an inch or two for each step.

'I wish,' said Mr Keuscher with fury, 'that you were in as much pain as I am.'

'I'm sorry,' Filmer said, hot and bothered. 'I didn't know there was pain.'

He propelled the wheel chair over wet pavements, saturated newspapers, discarded leaves. This was the most peculiar evening of his life.

After a while Mr Keuscher said, 'I never apologize, but occasionally I regret a remark ... I read many books about cripples and I know they have an intense hatred of the normal, the healthy.'

'It does not matter,' Filmer said vaguely.

'On the contrary, it matters vitally. It is relevant. Turn left at the lights ... I analyse this animal, myself, search for motives. As far as I know my motives are political, genuine. I am a man of peace. I am surrounded by fools, Mr Filmer. I want something *done* about the condition of man. And I have made my small achievements.'

He was breathing badly, stopped, regained momentum.

'We are hunting down people to the ends of the earth. We kill them. We have prisons and brain washing. We steal ideas by hypocrisy, guile, and untruths. But we are *real*, we are in earnest. Is your England full of vitality, fanaticism like this? No. It is still the garden party, the polite appeal, the money talking, the decisions over dinner tables. They like to argue on a theoretical level. Then they go to play golf, for it does not really matter. But we argue and work with emotion, with fury, with reality. We shall win. They are too deep in pleasure. In China they flock to the public executions of enemies of the people. In England they read an article in a newspaper.'

Mr Keuscher stopped again to regain his breath.

'Turn left,' he said. 'And cross the road.'

Filmer said in the privacy of darkness, 'I hate the hypocrisy and the immorality and the stupidity and the dirt and bribes and their incapability of ever loving God.'

Mr Keuscher tittered in pleasure. 'You are a man after my own heart!' he said warmly. 'Come in and have a whisky.'

'I do not drink.'

'Ridiculous!' suggested Mr Keuscher. 'Why not? Are you ill?'

'It is against the rules of God –'

'Who says so?'

'I was in Christian Doorstep –'

'*Was?*'

'They were a crowd of fools, suburban fanatics.'

'Then damn them. Sample the first pleasure of whisky with me!'

Mr Keuscher was a hard man to refuse; his will was stronger than Filmer's.

'Ring the bell!' he said in the short, semicircular drive of the old Georgian house. 'Nelson will help you with the chair.'

Nelson turned out to be a stocky, middle-aged man. He grunted and laboured with Filmer.

'Any telephone calls?' Mr Keuscher demanded.

'No, Mr Keuscher.'

'Is there a fire in the library?'

'Yes, Mr Keuscher.'

'Take me there. No. See to Mr Filmer first. His coat.'

It was a small, warm room, magnificent with books.

'The mind wins,' said Mr Keuscher in explanation.

Filmer sipped whisky, pinkened. A few teaspoonfuls and his stomach, inexperienced in alcohol, sent delightful messages of absurdity and rash confidence to his brain.

'Is your wife one of us?' Mr Keuscher asked.

Filmer said contemptuously, 'No. She's just nothing. A fool.' He added in domestic treason: 'And my kid's just a teen-ager. A nice one,' he concluded, wallowing in sentiment for a moment. It would be a better world soon for Brenda. Little lamb of God, I will slaughter the ungodly so that you may live ... He tittered, commented, 'Very strong.' He had never felt so powerful, confident, or important in his life.

'You must be careful, then, about what you take in the house.'

'It wouldn't matter,' Filmer said grandly. 'I could be doing repairs, special work. Overtime,' he sniggered. 'They understand that, love it. They'd sell Christ again for money,' he said in sudden black rage.

'You are a man of peace, like myself,' Mr Keuscher opined, 'who sees beyond the frontiers of his own country. He sees the world, all those millions. Equality in weapons is essential so that nobody will start anything. You agree?'

Filmer smiled, a rarity. 'I agree,' he concurred, but his mind explained in the hot truth of whisky: the bloody arrogance of them all: Ted with his pork-butcher's camaraderie; Bull with his brute force; Mrs Farthingale and her educated quiet snarl and her money; the louts who wanted to soil Brenda and all things clean; the queue bellyaching about money; Dawson's pious snobbery, gradations, while he talked of God – all will be humbled.

'This thing called Billiards is enormously important,' Mr Keuscher told him. 'I do not worry about England's intention. But a weapon of absolute defence in America's hands – in invincibility she would become aggressive. You agree? More whisky?' Mr Keuscher offered. He glanced at his watch. Getting late. Never mind the persuasion. He is here, seething with hatred, and not fully aware of his own potential. He is willing. Let us deal with arrangements.

'Can you get me plans?'

'Good God, no! I'm a workman, a bloody nobody.'

'Don't shout, please. Nelson is a mere servant. What can you get?'

'Only little pieces, and then only one at a time.'

'But many pieces?'

'Not the heavy ones.'

'But many are miniaturized, light?'

'That is true.'

'The spatial impulse selector – can you get one?'

'I'll try.'

'You can describe the rocket?'

'Part of it.'

'Do drawings. Take your time. Now, about money . . .'

'I don't want money,' Filmer asserted quickly. 'I'm not a bloody worker like that. I'm an idealist.'

'Yes, but expenses. Train fares.'

'I'm not going anywhere.'

Mr Keuscher hesitated.

'Where's it taken when it's completed?'

'To the ordnance depot near Cricklewood.'

'In lorries?'

'Vans come to collect them.'

'How often do they come?'

'I don't stand about watching, you understand, but I think about once a week.'

'How many would each van take away?'

'Two or three. They're very carefully packed, of course. Straw and cases.'

'It is important,' said Mr Keuscher, 'that you see nobody again. The arrangement we have made is for you to meet your contact at three o'clock every other Saturday outside Canterbury Cathedral.'

'Why Canterbury?' Filmer asked in some alarm. 'My wife –'

'You live near the line from Victoria,' Mr Keuscher said. 'An hour each way, an hour in the city. Three hours. People go to football matches, theatres – it gives you a margin.'

'I don't like it,' admitted Filmer.

'You are a religious man. Why shouldn't you go to Canterbury?'

'Yes, but every fortnight!'

'Lies will not hurt your wife!' suggested Mr Keuscher. 'They are more merciful than truth. Canterbury is a nice city, full of earnest, pious people, people without suspicion, people on their way elsewhere. And it is near to Dover and Folkestone, from which you can sail on a day trip to Calais or Boulogne. You just put your photograph on a form and go for the day. Your real passport is neither taken nor examined. Or you could be gay, go with the Cockneys from Ramsgate – wear a paper hat, drink a lot of beer, sing, be sick on the way back . . .'

Mr Keuscher's voice was full of hatred – he was the cripple now who hated the healthy, the fools who abused the perfection they'd been given.

'Whom do I meet?' Filmer asked.

'You turn up on the Saturdays you are able,' explained Mr Keuscher. 'Don't worry about your contact if you can't go. It is his job to wait an hour, then leave.'

'How will I know him?'

'That is simple,' said Mr Keuscher. 'You will wear a badge of the Nuclear Disarmers – I'm afraid I stole it! – and you will be carrying your parcel. Your contact will say, 'The wind is blowing from the east,' and you will answer, 'It is warmer inside.' You will then enter the cathedral and somewhere within surrender your parcel.'

Not all of Mayger Electric's two thousand employees were working on Project Billiards. Many of them were not sufficiently skilled. Only two hundred and fifty men and women were diverted to it. There was a check that they were British, but scarcely more. They were sworn to secrecy under the Official Secrets Act, and each had signed agreement to the Random Selector. There was a Security man in fancy dress on the gate – a new gate, E, in fact, and a turnstile to get out. But the Security man was an ex-policeman who'd been retired for years; he was fat and pompous and no more than that. The mathematics of the Random Selector were to be feared very slightly. Filmer had found out, as the result of cautious inquiry and attention to others' conversations, that the Random Selector had four tumblers, each of which were numbered from one to nine. It made, he had noticed, only four mechanical checks a month. Four chances each month, he presumed, out of 9,999. A queue of two hundred and fifty, anxious to go to lunch once a day and home each evening: five hundred chances a day for the machine, 2,500 a week, 10,000 in a four-week month. He wasn't sure of the mathematics against his own safety; was it one in 9,999, or one in 9,999 divided by four, or some more complicated permutation? Two hundred and fifty thumbs pressing the button that gave the green light and allowed the turnstile to rotate once. But in reality a man was in a different position –

one of two hundred and fifty positions – for each exit and the permutation was swollen to an odds of tens of thousands by the difference in days – it wasn't always the same day each week. A mechanical spot check, to be feared only slightly. Minor tests had found nothing wrong with Charles Filmer. How could they? He would have passed any test devised. No test can examine the mind of a man for hatreds, private conscience, and beliefs . . .

The hemispheres were about a foot in diameter and stamped from sheet magnesium alloy. They were treated with the care of a very important human being. Each hemisphere was, after rough erection over a wooden jig on a lathe, placed on a lathe over a cast-iron spin block and reheated with an acetylene torch to 700° F. so that the flash could be trimmed off. Then a flat circular blank of magnesium was spun into shape for use as an inner ring in the hemisphere to form a pressure-tight chamber in the completed sphere. After this blank was welded to form the chamber the whole hemisphere, with its pressure-tight cavity welded in place, was heated briefly in an oven to relieve whatever stresses had been set up in welding and to eliminate future weld cracks. The pressure tightness of the chamber weld was tested, and then each hemisphere was placed over an extremely exact cast-iron machining block. The entire surface was then machined to 16/10,000s of an inch. In time each hemisphere would have instruments welded inside, become a sphere and, elsewhere, be welded into the framework of the rocket Billiards.

Each hemisphere was brought on a trolley to Charles Filmer and the other seventy-two people who were making and fixing the instruments which the assembled sphere would contain. So small were the instruments that a large template had had to be reduced photographically and etched on each insulated base. Instruments were fixed and checked through magnifiers and connected to their proper circuit for a full-scale test.

It was not, then, a mass-produced object, this sphere of miniaturized electronic equipment which was to be installed in the rocket above the second-stage fuel tank and below the spin mechanism and explosive. To steal just one of the tiny four-inch cylindrical spatial impulse selectors which had destroyed

Platform was not going to be easy. They did not lie about in scores. Each one represented several hundred hours of eye-straining work. Of the 1,750,000 components in each Billiard the spatial impulse selectors represented 2,087.

It was easy to steal one of the photographically reduced templates. It had a diameter about the same size as a cocoa-tin lid. Filmer slipped one into his pocket in the morning, regretted all day performing this deed at ten o'clock, for it was like a burning halo, hour after hour. He was extremely nervous, planned what to say if someone – 'Well, I'm damned!' – 'I always keep one in my pocket for luck.' But he knew this would be unacceptable; the magnitude of the theft and the acknowledgement in his face would convey everything.

The day passed normally, even pleasantly, for the seventy-two of them were rather special, skilled. There was no coarse humour to irritate Filmer; the work was too exacting. The siren blew its analysis and timetable for the district and the seventy-two merged with others, became two hundred and fifty, a queue, the right thumbs pressing the Random Selector button, and it was green, green, green, all the time. The two hundred and fifty went out through E Gate and merged, became part of two thousand going home. Filmer had the template. There were wardrobes and drawers, undisturbed, his, but even so he was anxious. Vi might have a fit of spring cleaning. There were old suits in his wardrobe, one used for gardening, one for the summer holiday each year. He slipped the template into one of its pockets.

It wasn't too difficult. Each day or every other day he put a tiny instrument into his sweating palm – it was fortunate that their very miniaturization made it easy – and put the hot hand into a pocket and released the tiny weight, felt it there like a diseased halfpenny. Each afternoon he went out through E Gate, alone usually, on his bike, sweating or freezing with terror until he was on the main road. Each arrival home was soon accomplished by a visit upstairs – to the toilet, to wash hands, to change clothes – and the disturbed hands operated by the anxious brain dropped the tiny instrument or part into a pocket and explored all the other pockets to see if everything else was there. But still he did not dare to steal one of the small four-inch spatial impulse selectors that would put Soviet defence on a par with Britain's. It would be missed. He explained to himself: it must be the last thing I take, for it will be missed. There would be inquiries. It must be taken on a Friday afternoon, handed to the contact on Saturday, and subsequently Charles Filmer must steal nothing from Mayger Electric, for eyes might be watching, aware that no one would be stealing an S.I.S. for fun, a home-made radio, toy for the kids; whoever was taking one should be followed, investigated, was part of a conspiracy. The last action, then, and assuredly the most important.

Saturday. He was angry with the anxiety. Stupid details tried to frustrate him.

'I've got to go out,' he claimed. 'I want dinner early.'

Vi said indifferently, 'One o'clock then?'

'No. Before that.'

'Where are you going?'

'Out.'

'Is it a secret or something?'

'Have I got to tell you every damn thing I do?'

The atmosphere was at once full of hostility between them, the characteristics of a quarrel. Nothing would stop it now. Days of silences, sniffing, accusations, then the apology, and still the self-pitiful whine: 'You don't care,' which left him wretched, nothing to say, wondering if it were true. He was weighted down at times with the knowledge that he was incapable of tenderness; only Brenda could reduce him to foolishness, sentimentality, decisions without logic.

'It's a meeting,' he explained.

'You've never been before.'

'What of it?'

'What about me? I'm just a skivvy, I suppose. On my feet all day, just so's you can go. And what will you do at this meeting? Talk!'

'It doesn't matter,' he said. 'I can do without dinner.'

'Oh no,' Vi said. 'I must do my duty. Half past twelve?'

They ate it in silence. He could hardly have tried harder to ensure curiosity about himself. But there could be no surrender, explanations, except in lies. The hatred would have to die in the air like a tired thunderstorm, die of its own volition.

He sat in the train, not happy, frightened. Chatham, Rochester came and went, stirred interest; he'd never been on this line before. In the summer people came to Margate and Ramsgate, but these were places he refused to visit; not even Brenda could talk him into it. 'Not respectable,' he'd said at least three times. 'Noisy and common.' Some small ships were in the harbour, a Polish boat unloading timber. That would be it: a Polish sailor would get on the train, visit Canterbury Cathedral; it seemed probable, became inevitable in his mind.

He saw the pale-beige stone of the cathedral miles before they reached the city; the pale autumn sun hurt the eye. It was quite easy to orientate himself in the narrow streets – a tiny city; you could drop it in Lewisham unnoticed. He was early, half an hour. Tired with nervous strain. A coffee. He wandered around, people jostled, vehicles, thousands of them; in the summer they must have colossal jams. The damp air sorted its way through the buildings and streets, clung to his face, his hands carrying the paper bag worth millions reddened. He changed over, right to left, the packet warming the guilty flesh.

The café was almost empty. Gentility, it worried him. He knew, despite the iron in his mind, that he was 'common' in appearance; old ladies in heavy coats, scent, gloves (he never wore gloves: it dated from youth, poverty, cricket in the alley, fights) would examine him. Not belonging. A man followed him in. Bulky, middle-class, a child with him. Was he following? Glasses on, and the child, but he had a carriage of physical toughness. 'Sit here,' to the boy. 'No,' angrily. 'Not over there. Do as Daddy says.' And that left him twenty feet from Filmer, but well positioned. Perhaps he was the contact. Both early. 'I want a cake,' the child said, in an accent of self-pity that started anger inside Filmer. I'd teach him.

Nobody came. He could have stolen coffee, scores of pale pottery teapots, walked out; the door didn't have a bell. An honest town? Did you have to take an oath to live here in sight and sound of the old cathedral?

A rush of people now – waitress, cashier, a scholarly-looking man of forty. 'The carrots have come.' It was interesting to see him (reduced in circumstances?) sweating through to the rear

of the café with bags of carrots, still himself, middle-class,
breathlessly pleading, 'Excuse me.'

'Would you mind?' the man said, so that he was served first,
and hate returned to Filmer like an old friend, inspiration. It
was easy to hate the old enemies, unfairness, selfishness, class
distinction. 'Coffee,' he said, and the waitress identified him with
apathy as they did each day in that hotel, tittering about his
demand for 'rice pudding' and glaring when he left no tip.

A woman was buying cakes, talking, time to waste, money to
spare. The faint odour of scent drifted over to Filmer. 'My husband hates driving. A bungalow by the sea. We go out in the
evening. He doesn't mind that. Everyone's in such a hurry.'

Filmer had been there a quarter of an hour. 'It is intolerable,'
he said aloud, so that they all turned. The cake buyer tittered,
whispered in the atmosphere of fresh coffee, 'Religious, d'you
think?'

The coffee, when it came, was too hot, scalding, and now the
clock was accelerating – ten minutes to go, nine, seven and a
half – and he hadn't more than sipped, burned his tongue. 'Not
another, Robin,' the man said, then weakened, 'Oh, all right, but
not the chocolate ones.' Waves of contempt seemed to flow from
Filmer, weakening him. England was full of these – charming,
weak people. There seemed no alternative – charm, money,
arrogance, or the louts, sex talk and money; you took your
choice. Filmer was tired. There was too much to do in the
world. It needed a God, patient, loving, forgiving the endless
weaknesses, squalid privacy, arrogance, dirt.

It was time to go, half the cup drunk. He felt too weak to
stand. No one came. He said to the cashier, 'Will you take it?
I'm in a hurry,' and she didn't believe him. If he was in a hurry,
why sit there twenty-five minutes or more? People. She said,
'Alice won't be a minute.' A fat woman came in to select cakes.
The waitress came, breathless, from the toilet perhaps. 'I'm
sorry, sir.' Now the cake selector had to be attended to before
Filmer; he was too angry to dispute, claim precedence. It was
good to be able to carry hate in the pocket. Fools! All the
insults of a lifetime, the sneers from indifferent people, would
be avenged, reduced to the cries of victims, in minutes. In a
stroke all the blasphemers and cultured whores and the whole

hierarchy of money would be rendered impotent by Charles Filmer. He was in charge of the world. His conscience was clear. They shouldn't have insulted him, wallowed in dirt and money and snobbery, despised God.

But outside he was frightened again, the timid man who fulminates impotently, is glad to see the mighty suffer, but unable to do more than think about it himself; to express an opinion was to have it laughed at by fools like Bull, Dawson, Ted.

He stood outside Christ Church Gate, a minute late, feeling silly. No one was there; no Christians flowed in under the *rebus*. By the war memorial a Daimler had stopped, indifferent to the queue of vehicles, and an old lady emerged. It couldn't happen in London; she'd be shouted at. A lorry was backing through the larger gate; presumably even a cathedral needed coke. People seemed to stare at Filmer from chemists' shops, dress shops. Two pretty girls in pale-blue slacks came along, eyed him carefully, went into the cathedral grounds. He turned to see what happened. An old man was viewing the books in the window of a shop inside the same quiet acres. Was he the contact?

People were passing along the pavement. Each one looked at Filmer. He became angry. Did they think he was dogsbody to stand about? He glared at a woman with a child and a bulldog. The woman was in her late fifties or early sixties, grizzled, pugnacious. No wonder she had a bulldog; she'd lived so long with it that she was beginning to resemble it. She wore a dirty raincoat and a black beret, and on both she had badges of bulldogs. She was tough and spirited and as British as Oxford Street.

She said, rubbing her hands, 'The wind is blowing from the east.'

Filmer couldn't believe it but had no option, for there was a southwest gale thrashing the trees, making people's eyes water. He answered, 'It's warmer inside.'

She had a shopping basket, half full. The bulldog panted, looked around. 'This is Marlene,' said the woman. Did she refer to the dog or the child? 'And this is my granddaughter, Polly.'

'Who's he?' asked Polly.

'Y'better hold Marlene while we go inside.'

'You said I could have sweets . . .'

'Y'got to *earn* them,' the woman said grimly.

'You said *now* –'

'Hold Marlene,' instructed the belligerent little grandmother. 'Sit, Marlene, sit.' The dog sat obediently, but the woman did not seem grateful. 'Idle bugger,' she commented. 'Lies in front of the fire, eats, slobbers on the furniture.' But Filmer could see the rough dialogue was love, one bulldog loving another.

She said to Filmer, equally impatient, 'Come on, then. I've got shopping to do. It tires me. Kids. They won't do a thing.' She examined the cathedral as if she had just noticed it for the first time : it had been specially built for her but wasn't quite what she wanted – take it down, start again. 'I'm a free thinker myself.' She was puffing as badly as the dog. 'They didn't oughta make 'em so big.'

There was no one on the porch, no one in the cathedral, it at first seemed. 'You haven't got a cigarette?'

Filmer said in horror, shaken by her blasphemous indifference, 'Not in here. It would draw attention to us.'

'Not in here. D'you think I'm mad. It is free, isn't it?'

She ignored the studded old doors of oak, the stupefying height of the nave, viewed the hundreds of cane chairs, the figures all prone, resting. 'These places make me tired,' she told Filmer, indifferent to the marble and stone, the scores of monuments; she was a Communist but thought herself better than these pious people. 'Hypocrites,' she said, fearless although, surely, not many years from death. 'It isn't right – all that labour and time. They could have built houses.' God did not inspire her; she wanted Him like a co-op manager, trade unionist. A thousand years' work by dedicated men meant nothing to her; they were fools or sweated serfs. She would, presumably, sign a petition to have the cathedral demolished, build a block of flats.

Filmer was afraid, awed in the silence and the odour of centuries. The vaulting, eighty feet above his head, crushed his selfish anger, hatred.

'Ridiculous,' the woman said. 'All these monuments and tatty flags.' She didn't like the Chartres-like stained-glass windows either. 'Make the place gloomy. My eyes hurt,' she complained.

'Do you want to sit down?' Filmer asked.

'Sit down? Me?'

She proceeded like a hurried tourist, up steps, down steps, searching for a deeper gloom.

Voices echoed from across the presbytery. There were others, twenty or so in fact, small groups, solitaries here and there, silent, anguished, in prayer. The two girls in pale-blue slacks were ten yards ahead. Filmer wished the woman wouldn't speak so loudly. Her contempt might draw attention, start an argument. One girl had turned: a rosy face, innocent, pure, hair like wheat in summer. Filmer felt old and tired, carrying the world in a pocket. Decades of hatred translated at last. You had to think of Mayger, Bull, Ted, the years of insults, remember the battle in the mind: the fools and the arrogant and the indifferent and the vile. Someone had to make a decision, end it, but it was here in the presence of God and with innocence staring from twenty feet away. What would happen to them when equality came? It wasn't easy to humble the world if it included the innocent. He felt the tired urge to give up, weep, go away – this woman with her margarine mind and bulldog made fanaticism difficult anyway. O, God, he prayed, let me do what is right, but even this faltered in his mind, for he knew God allowed *him* the choice.

They had proceeded around to the south aisle before the woman whispered, 'Put it in my bag, Mr Filmer,' and her personality was too much for him, too dominant. He wanted to plead, 'I'd like to think some more,' but he was too ingrained in obedience to argue here, too English, despite himself, to overcome the embarrassment of loud argument in a cathedral. He dropped the small parcel in the woman's shopping bag.

They went down steps into the fierce light of modern windows. An old man was sitting in a chair facing the stained glass. The woman said, 'Those are magnificent,' but whether truth or hypocrisy for the man Filmer didn't know.

'I'll be glad of a cup of tea,' she said. 'What about the impulse selector, Mr Filmer?'

'I couldn't manage one.'

'Never mind. Next time.'

He began to explain, 'It must be the last thing I take. It would be missed, you see.'

They were out in the watery sunshine. Grass and notices and a few parked cars and urgent clouds creating the illusion of the Central Tower moving slowly away.

'You do what you can, Mr Filmer,' the woman told him. 'Don't take any risks.' No bulldog spirit after all. 'They said about expenses – train fares and that.'

'It doesn't matter.'

'Here's a quid.'

'If you think it right.'

'You've had to come all that way . . .'

The girl with the bulldog pulling her approached.

'I'm tired. My wrists hurt.'

'I'll have her.'

'Can we go to the bingo?'

'I want a cup of tea first.'

'Oh, we'll be *ages*.'

'You can have a cake.'

'Is he coming?'

'No,' the woman said, and then, oddly, unnecessarily, disturbing, 'You leave him alone. He's got things on his mind.'

9

URSULA WALLACE

'HOLD these, there's a darling,' Mrs Wallace commanded.

'Shall I sit in the back?'

She smiled carelessly, thought about it. 'No. Why should you? This is not a taxi.'

Major Gouseev therefore sat by the side of Ursula Wallace in the Mini-Minor and held the box of cakes with delicate care.

Mrs Wallace looked at a fragile, expensive gold wrist watch, examined that enemy, time. 'Late.' She sighed. 'Why am I always late, Igor?'

'Because you never worry.'

'You mean I'm crazy,' she qualified. She liked to be crazy, although all she was was rather cunning and vain. But delightful, oh, absurdly. It was an electric shock to sit by her as she was rough with the gears and shot out into Bayswater Road without a glance in the mirror: mirrors were for the rearrangement and inspection of the small, full mouth, the oval, perfect face, and the large, wonderful eyes which saw nothing unless they wanted to. As she drove she talked, not looking ahead at the rat race of traffic, but turning her head (as taught in Paris fifteen years ago) to address him; and he, Igor, was sufficiently overcome to prefer this, to take the chance of her whacking into the saloon in front. He had the feeling she was too beautiful to have bad luck. She must always win; she was an ornament, valuable, ridiculous, to be handled with care.

'I do worry,' she told him, the head turned. It was impossible to imagine the face having content that included anxiety, not real, burning anxiety; her husband had left her, or something (he wasn't sure yet of the details), but she trotted around buying shoes and cakes and enjoying parties and she drove like a woman completely without worry. 'I mean, if Bill really shoves off with this girl, how can I cope? Angela's fees are fifty pounds a term.'

Only money could worry her, but Igor couldn't feel any political rage at such decadence; indeed, he saw Ursula's position all too well. But he had the certain optimistic intuition that she'd be all right. She was lucky, too beautiful to be without money. They didn't have people like Ursula Wallace in the Soviet Union. They'd killed them all in 1918. At times he thought it a pity.

'Did you ever work?' he asked.

It sounded like an insult but was not intended as such.

Ursula almost giggled; she choked for a moment, recovered. 'You think I'm just a decadent doll,' she accused.

'Not at all.'

'I did a little stage work.'

'Couldn't you go back to it?'

'I don't want to.'

'It's very difficult,' he agreed, in the tone of one who can, alas, do nothing about it.

She turned her head again; he said breathlessly, 'The lights!' and she braked fiercely, was glared at by pedestrians. 'Now you look worried,' Ursula scolded. 'You mustn't. I want you to cheer me.'

He put his right palm on her gloved small hand that was on the gear lever, thrilled absurdly to the tactile analysis beneath the material; fragile slender bones.

Ursula's mouth trembled, unbearably exciting. If she was brainless – she isn't, his mind qualified quickly, although he knew that in a report that would have to be his brief description: loyal, but scatterbrained, unreliable, without political comprehension at all – if she was brainless, she made up for it physically. Every functioning part of her was disturbing, eyes, lips, hair, hands. He wondered how long this could go on, where it would end. The thought of finality hurt, worried, although if he tried to think sensibly, plan, his thoughts couldn't proceed, for what could he do? You couldn't take Ursula Wallace to Moscow. To take her to the embassy would perhaps invite a caution, a reprimand. Marry her? Even presuming it was possible and she were willing . . . No. It was unbearable not to have these moments with Ursula. Let them proceed at will, see what happened.

There were other cars outside the school: Bristols and baby Fiats, Jaguars and Karman Ghias: it was that sort of school, those sort of parents. The children, young women almost, when they emerged were graceful, upright. It was impossible to deny that this type of English girl had qualities which didn't exist in – but he mustn't even think along those lines.

Angela was tall, shy, different, though, from her mother: serious-minded, intelligent, worried. She responded politely to the introduction: 'How do you do, Major?' and sat in the rear of the car, quiet, without interruption until the giggled comment, 'Mummy, you shouldn't have turned. You should have waited.'

Ursula accepted this quite calmly. 'Darling, you go by the book. Those silly little vans don't have the acceleration I have.'

The child said, again with humour, 'All the same, you were in the wrong. He swore at you.'

'Then his was the greater wrong!'

'Miss Featherstone says I need elocution.'

'Ridiculous! She just wants the extra fees.'

'She says I mumble.'

'Do you want to do elocution?'

'I don't know. If I need it . . .'

'Are you going on the stage?' Major Gouseev asked.

'Good God, no!' said Angela warmly, as if the stage was sinful or, perhaps, frivolous, part of her mother's world. 'I want to go in ballet.'

'Too tall, darling,' her mother told her.

'Tall girls do it these days,' Angela protested. 'It's ridiculous. Girls *are* taller nowadays. They don't want little dumplings any more.'

'All right, Angela, don't *lecture*.'

'Sorry, Mummy.'

'She gets carried away,' Ursula explained. 'What does Miss Featherstone say about ballet?'

'She says I'm only fit for the chorus.'

'I don't think I like Miss Featherstone any more,' Ursula chided. 'Take Major Gouseev inside, Angela, while I put the baby away.'

A tall block of flats, typical Kensington, small areas of grass, ferocious cars parked here and there, warm air as soon as they entered the ground floor, stupefying the senses.

'Are those cakes?'

'I think so.'

'Let me carry them.'

'It doesn't matter.'

'Well, let me have a look!'

The girl was child enough to be interested in cakes, to criticize: 'Oh, *those*. She never buys the ones I like.'

'Too fattening, perhaps?'

'I need fattening,' the girl said with terrible seriousness, as if it was a matter for politicians, artillery, troop movements, accusations. Major Gouseev had to smile.

'You should visit Russia to learn ballet,' he said, and for a moment his mind wallowed in secrecy, planned the careful conversation, years of it, until she became an excellent agent. But, no, she belonged to Ursula; he didn't want to, just this once he let the opportunity fade.

'I'd be frightened,' the girl said frankly.

'Frightened?' He was a little disconcerted.

'Of never coming back.'

'We are not as bad as all that!'

'I'm sorry. I was rude. I forgot for a moment you were –'

They were in the flat, fifth floor, silent, clean corridors, doors numbered, 512. 'Why five-twelve?' he asked.

'Oh, it's silly,' she said. 'It means twelve on the fifth floor. Do you like buns?' she asked doubtfully, then giggled. 'They're all you'll get! Mummy's rather the decorative type, as you may have noticed.'

She coloured crimson as she realized what she'd said but didn't apologize this time. How curious, he thought, that the child should be so different, untouched, yet living in the same rooms . . .

Ursula came in, excited, electrifying eyes, hair as black as coal, superb, a new idea, the latest craziness: 'I think we ought to have a dog. A Dalmatian.'

'Oh no, Mummy, you mustn't be so dotty,' Angela protested. 'It would be cruel *here*.'

'There's the park,' Ursula said vaguely. 'I just met Mr Phillips. *He's* got one. Never mind, never mind. Rather a bore. Is this all we have for the major?'

Angela laughed. 'Well, you did the shopping.'

'It gives me the excuse to sit by the fire, anyway.' She had pouffes for this, sat at once, silk legs revealed, then covered, her eyes meeting Igor's frankly, saying, well, what of it? You shouldn't look.

Somewhere a door clicked, feet trod, a male voice inquired, 'Are you there, poppet?' The major was uneasy at the alcoholic quality in the timbre.

Angela jumped up.

'Daddy.'

And Major Gouseev could see that this eagerness hurt, caused Ursula to flinch. But she remained elaborately casual, off-hand.

The man came into the room, tall, good-looking, a cruel, tough touch in the face, but a weakness, too, a despair. And he was drunk. Major Gouseev rose to his feet, fingers sticky with butter, crumbs.

'I didn't expect you,' Ursula said, like someone at the end of a second act.

'Just a few things I need. Can't find my Remington.'

'Typewriter or electric shaver?'

'I wouldn't mind a cuppa.'

'This is Major Gouseev. He's at the Soviet Embassy. This, of course, is Bill.'

'How do you do?' Igor said.

'It depends what I'm doing,' the other man said rudely.

'Are you going to be a nuisance?' Ursula asked.

'Depends,' said Bill, thinking, deciding. The presence of Angela prevented his thoughts moving too fast. 'Depends what you mean by nuisance.'

Angela said unhappily, 'How can you be drunk at five o'clock in the afternoon, Daddy?'

'Experience,' said Bill. 'I can be drunk at *any* hour of the day or night. Didn't know you'd be here.'

'Daddy, you know I'd be here,' the child said. 'I *live* here.'

Bill laughed, still standing, a cup of tea slopped.

'What do you do, Major?' he asked with an edge of rage.

'Communications,' Igor told him.

'What do you communicate and to whom?'

Bill had great difficulty with this question.

'We have to be in touch with Moscow.'

'I'll bet you bloody do, I'll bet.'

'Bill,' said Ursula, 'sit down or something.'

'I suppose,' Bill said to her, 'that it gives you particular pleasure that he's a Communist and I fought them – and won, Major, by the way – in Korea.'

'You're a bore,' said Ursula. 'I met Major Gouseev at a party. Anyway, why are you here? Why hasn't that travel agency sent you to Madeira or Trinidad?'

'Oh, nasty.' Bill smiled. 'Vicious, you know, Major, just like all the others. Don't be fooled by the inconsequential air. I say, that was rather good? Inconsequential air. Beethoven . . . She's just like all women, is poppet. Very practical.'

'I'd better go,' said Igor.

'Not at all. Just come for the Remington.'

'There's some bills,' said Ursula.

'Practical, see?'

'Including fifty guineas for Angela. Miss Featherstone insists on payment before term begins. I had to pretend you were in South Africa.'

'Fiddle Miss Featherstone!'

'Oh, Bill, don't be stupid.'

'Stupid? Christ, you can talk about — Oh, excuse us, Major. Private war. Quarrel within NATO.'

'I'll sell the car,' said Ursula.

'I'll send you a cheque,' Bill told her. 'How's school going, Angela?'

'All right, Daddy.'

'I never did like it myself. Listen, Ursula, I'll send you a cheque.'

'It'll bounce —'

'No. A beautiful cheque, non-bouncing ... Now, where's the blasted Remington. Very important dinner tonight. Sir Hugh something. Must shave.'

'You see,' Ursula said in his absence, 'it became impossible.'

But Igor could see the hurt in both of them. They were two people who had nothing in common except anger, love, and marriage. Presumably Bill paid a price for being married to a crazy extravagant, beautiful woman. He'd come back sooner or later. In fact, he had come back this very afternoon. If he, Igor, hadn't been there, reconciliation might have taken place. She wasn't the sort of woman who'd go sour over his infidelity with the travel-agency girl. Which implied that morality wasn't a large item in the philosophy of Mrs Ursula Wallace. Yet he, Igor, treated her with absolute courtesy, respect, awe. She was so beautiful that he could not imagine more than conversation, the touch of hands. He hadn't even kissed her. Yet he had the uncomfortable, sensual certainty that if he hadn't been there to prolong their quarrel, Bill wouldn't have gone to that dinner. Unshaven, still alcoholic in his breathing, he'd have become violent sooner or later this day, and she wanted it. The latter hurt but couldn't be denied. It was ridiculous to be jealous of a woman's husband, crazy if that husband had left her. He was being like a schoolboy in his relationship with Ursula — being extremely courteous, too cautious in his anxiety not to do or say something that would end it.

Bill came into the room again.

'Don't you want to eat something?' Ursula asked.

'No. Saving my appetite for the dinner.'

'Bill, listen, there really are a lot of accounts. Nothing extravagant, honestly. The car, school, rent, and so on.'

'I'll send you a cheque – two hundred?'

'Make it three, there's a darling.'

'Ouch! I wish I hadn't come,' protested Bill, but he was grinning, satisfied about something, the remnants of his marriage. ' 'Bye, poppet.' He hesitated, anxious, approached Angela. 'Take care of her.' A kiss for the daughter and the retreating feet and the door slammed and he'd gone.

'I hope he sends that cheque,' confided Ursula. 'And I hope the damn thing doesn't bounce. I'm sorry if he was rude.'

'I suppose he had the right to be.'

'I don't know what that means,' Ursula said, chilling him. 'I can ask friends in to eat, can't I?'

He couldn't claim to be more than a friend or explain his infatuation, with Angela's young, serious face there, her intelligent mind storing dialogue, making explanations.

He stayed another hour, long enough for Ursula to suggest drinks. All the time Angela was present like an accusation, although neither a word nor a glance conveyed any hostility.

Ursula followed him from the long pleasant sitting room to the hall, from the hall and coat hooks to the door. 'Goodbye, Angela,' he called, and her voice, distant, stationary, acknowledged, as trained by Miss Featherstone, 'Good night, Major.'

Ursula's hand touched his chest in restraint, caution, something, he wasn't sure. 'Igor, I'm sorry about that.' The apology was meaningless, the touch of hands electric, bare arm against him too much. He had to do more than worship her courteously, in awe. It was a little ridiculous, for she was taller, and in high heels, too. She wasn't surprised, of course; Ursula Wallace would never be surprised in this aspect of experience, life. She tottered slightly on her elegant legs, recovered from the first kiss, which was presumed to be a surprise, crushed against him for the second, while his hands pulled her harder, overcame, desiring more. He was hot in the face, shaken by his own emotion, overcome by the supple yielding softness under the frock. Her hair brushed across his face; her small full mouth was open, gasping as it kissed. Ursula whispered in sensual, collaborative conspiracy, 'Don't make a noise; don't mess my hair,' and ten yards from Angela, two doors away, they crushed and fought the first time, weeks of postponed love. The complications were there in his mind, the ramifications of the networks – the student standing in the darkness for hours watching for Alexei Antonov; the telephone operator listening for news of vital importance; Max's plans for the model nearing fruition; and the latest, magnificent, unexpected progress at Mayger Electric: a man working on the very sphere in which were the electronic devices that exploded Billiards – they were all neatly assembled in his mind; Moscow would be pleased, but it meant nothing in the presence of Ursula's large eyes, wild, entirely for him. 'I love you,' he said. 'It's not just foolishness,' and she smiled, a tremble on the lips, the firm stomach hard on his with promise. 'All the same, that's enough for tonight. We mustn't hurt Angela.'

He walked the dark pavements of Kensington thinking of her, wanting permanency. They'd have to hurt Angela sometime. Surely the child knew her mother would inevitably be loved by someone. She was too beautiful to be safe. He already felt concerned on her behalf – she was so foolish in a world of dangerous people.

There was reality on his desk, work, the world to carry, convert. He bit his lip, the weak, foolish, hopeless infatuation still like a fever in him. Ah, if only the world didn't need to be converted, what was not possible between Ursula and himself? The photograph on the desk reminded him that this was domestic madness as well as political.

To Gouseev. 3419.
Assignment.

1. World Mechanical. Your progress here is good and noted. It is, however, not entirely satisfactory that in this enormous concern we have only one contact in the London office. Maggie Preston's information is excellent but should be followed up at the various factories:

(a) More information requested on the blast-recorder adapter tubes. These may be used for military and not commercial purposes.

(b) Focal-point gun sight. Is this solely for Mark I Skythrust or all fighter aircraft? Could not one be obtained from an airfield?

(c) Obtain more details of transportation of parts of Billiards from World Mechanical ordnance depot in Manchester and, similarly, movement of electronic capsules for Billiards from Mayger Electric to Cricklewood.

(d) Is it possible for Maggie Preston to become friendly with this Mr Gascoigne? Check with her via Henry.

(e) The delay in obtaining miniaturized spatial impulse selectors is disturbing. Keuscher's opinion is that the man Filmer operates on an emotional, not political level. His emotions could backfire. He is concerned for his own safety, but sometimes a man will jettison even that if emotionally out of control. Accelerate arrangements if possible, but take care. Filmer can be disregarded once the selector is in our hands. He is a religious fanatic, therefore dangerous.

2. Photographs examined suggest that pictures of high clarity can be taken at night from aircraft (at present). Reid's information is that RAF Photographic Units have three cameras and they carry the name Tensen. This would refer to Tensen Lens Corporation in Belfast. Information is desired on these points:

(a) Maximum height of photographing at night.

(b) Type of lens, light power, and focal distance.

(c) Surface area illuminated by photo bomb.

(d) Composition and manufacturer of the bomb; its formula.

3. Veall Motor Bodies. Strike should be continued for at least another five weeks, irrespective of terms offered. Do not be concerned with unreasonableness. This is expected.

4. Alexei Antonov.

(a) Proceed with Max's arrangements to involve contact.

(b) Telephone Antonov, promote mild terror, but not sufficient for emotions to be too disturbed for (a). Simply remind him that we exist, haven't forgotten. Use student to find out his interests, movements.

DIRECTOR

He was an honest man, working in an atmosphere of lies, subversion, bribery, corruption, and fear because he believed it necessary, had done so since that day in 1942 when he'd ceased to be a mere infantry officer. But the scent of Mrs Wallace, the

breath of her, the animal magnetism, the absurdity, the weakness and the strength, no conviction about anything except
shoes and schools and cheques and crushed mouths and
passion ... Why was it so necessary to reduce her to the level
of the have-nots? She was an outrage, an insult to thousands,
millions of people in China and Russia, but was it so wrong to
be Ursula Wallace? She hadn't asked to be. Was anything going
to be improved if ... Oh, this was absurd. Love entering espionage and politics. Man must overcome his weaknesses; to participate in the life of Ursula Wallace was to go outside duty. Igor
Gouseev was honest. For one hideous moment he wallowed in
treason – the knowledge that it was all unnecessary. Britain's life
was being levelled off by elements within: trades unions and
Socialism and death duties and income tax and the end of
power. It was all happening quite sensibly, without pain or
blood; an occasional cry of anger, self-pity, a lot of apathy,
foolishness, no more. What business of his was it if ... ? He
struck the desk hard in rage, the knowledge that this was madness, led to nothing but death. She wouldn't ask that. There was
a shameful photograph of Sheila Haward, naked in body and
purpose, in a drawer of the desk. Igor looked at it. Was this what
he wanted from Ursula? No. Yes. He was in awe of her, infatuated. He wanted permanency, love, whatever she would give
for as long as she would give it. The sweat rolled down his face
and he was suddenly frightened and knew why. He pushed the
decision away, tried to be intelligent, cynical, tough, good-
humoured – all the qualities he'd had before that party at which
he'd met Ursula Wallace.

To the Director. 839.

1. Your 3419 noted.

Regarding 1(d). Henry had anticipated your suggestion. It is unlikely that Maggie Preston could become involved with Mr Gascoigne at World Mechanical. He is 62, married, far above her in
class status.

2. Attached is current list of arrivals in England of East Germans,
Ukrainians, Poles, Bulgarians, etc. In many cases information is
scanty, but in all cases home town or village is known and relatives
should be found, pressure applied.

Also attached is list of ship's passengers arrived Southampton in vessel *Port of Spain* to seek employment in UK. Usual procedure will be followed to ascertain weak or dissatisfied elements and exploit them.

3. Bosambo's Agitation Committee is now ready for demonstrations should events in Oogla Provinces prove successful.

4. Prosser has encountered a hothead, Dowell, who seems politically sympathetic. Should we cultivate him? He works in docks as clerk.

5. Re Filmer. His difficulties seem genuine. If he takes complete selector he risks investigations. He is not in position to take one piece by piece: it is assembled 500 feet away. He is willing to bring one providing it is his last action on our behalf. This, in view of your final remark, seems satisfactory, but expect to obtain information, as you suggest, re transportation of these spheres, so that in absolute necessity we could take one in transit.

6. Max's contact expects to meet Antonov within the next few days. This has taken weeks to arrange, for it is essential no suspicion is aroused.

GOUSEEV

PART THREE

*

Truth is so obscure in these times, and falsehood so established, that unless we love the truth we cannot know it.

PASCAL

1

FRANK PRESTON

ELEVEN o'clock and he had the bellyache, eleven in the morning, that is. It made him angry and sour, loaded him with self-pity. Whether or not one has the bellyache (the hour is irrelevant) surely decides whether one is important in this world or not. Frank Preston was not.

He felt tired and dirty, unwell, and a craving for drink, although fully aware that the amount he would consume would aggravate the ulcers. It was, he felt in great rolling self-pity, all Maggie's fault. The whore. The cheap (or was it expensive?) little whore. This was ridiculous both in logic and morality, for Frank Preston had been with whores in his time, had been proud of it. And the longing for Maggie was a warm contribution to the emotions that raged in his stomach. He wanted to prove something, win something, but failed to identify what it was.

He sat in the packed bus, refused to stand, was conscious of female stares, muttering, fat strong cows who wanted to rest their massive buttocks and felt entitled to. But sod them: he had the bellyache; he was ill, he'd sit. It ate at his conscience and ulcers for seven miles, so that he felt sick and faint at journey's end. In a coffee bar he stared with terrible longing at the lively young things, his own age, but without pain, loss. The sex urge stirred in him as they sat on stools, swung stockinged legs, giggled. He wasn't that ill: the urge of a nineteen-year-old without faith, restraint, charity, wisdom, still coursed his blood. He viewed them all as whores. Unpaid, of course – they were so stupid and hungry for it. His knowledge of the female kind, despite marriage, as that of almost complete ignorance, worse than ignorance, for it presupposed mistakenly.

The office was somewhere on the opposite side of the main road. Frank Preston blasphemed at the traffic as it ignored him. He walked along the pavement truculently, a young man without wisdom, the world on his padded shoulders.

He found the number, a score of brass plates, swung open the brass-and-glass doors; twenty or thirty steps confronted him. The bastards. No lift. It hurt, made him breathless; fury accumulated. Whore, whore, whore, being shagged by anyone – Germans, that fat pig Eggy, those slobs she worked with, anyone, anyone, oh, Jesus, how it hurt. He was in the absurd position of a twentieth-century made male who ignored morality and was now being crucified by immorality. Or was he? Well, that was up to this bastard to find out. He stood at the top of the thirty-two steps. Blood roared in his head; his heart pounded, frightening him. What's the matter with me? I'm scared. I've got a dose. The dirty whore's given me a dose. He didn't believe it. He was just angry with the steps that could slaughter his breathing and so poured foulness on them.

In the tiny outer office a coloured girl sat modestly, shyly, overcome, weeping quietly. Black cow, Preston thought; they'd better not attend to her before me. As if someone had read his thoughts a frosted-glass window slid to one side and a sharp, bespectacled girl, viewing him with interest (but not friendly interest), asked, 'Can I help you?'

'I'm Frank Preston. I gotta see Mr Evans.'

'Just a moment.' She turned to a telephone and said into it without the previous, heavy sweetness, 'There's a Mr Preston,' as if the Prestons of this world were its least important inhabitants.

But apparently not, for at once she reappeared at the window, ignored the girl.

'Just along the corridor. You'll see.'

And sure enough, along tatty linoleum was a door with a neat brass plate screwed in: HENRY EVANS, PRIVATE INVESTIGATOR. Preston knocked and walked in.

Evans was a solid, sallow, middle-aged Welshman. He was on the telephone; his eyes lifted in rage and impotence at Preston's entry.

Thirty-two steps below the red buses fought it out by a pedestrian island with the snarling saloons. People crowded the pavements helplessly: what to buy, what to desire, envy, long for. The four girls came out of the coffee bar, hot little sluts, art school probably; one had a red scarf, black stockings. He'd like to ... London was full of 'em, bold, superb, confident, sex bursting out at all points, but he was marked by something indefinable; they weren't interested. Bad breath, perhaps, maybe the ulcers had given him. And the jollity, of course, the rage to live, dance, scream with senseless laughter as they kicked their legs – ulcers knocked all that out of him. Oh, God, if only she'd come back.

A calendar, bright carpet, dirty curtains, cigarette ash, and now the telephone quiet, replaced, and Mr Evans interested, no, welcoming, 'Good morning, Mr Preston.'

'Yeah, it's nice, for once.'

'Who put you on to me?'

'A Mr Huntley. He got a divorce.'

'Huntley, Huntley? I can't remember.' So many people faithless, bored, not prepared to honour or obey, in sickness or in death, not inclined to stay once the conversation began to dry, the sex become boring. 'Ah, wait! A tall, dark man?'

'No.'

The crystal was wrong.

'You want a divorce?'

'I wanna know what's going on.'

Mr Evans identified the misery. These bloody teen-agers. He wanted her back.

'She's gone off with someone?'

'Not exactly.'

'Niggers?'

'She just left me. Now she's going around with several. I don't get it. She's on her back for someone,' Frank Preston said in rage. 'She's got good clothes all of a sudden. What's more, when I went to see her, she gave me five quid. She gave five quid to *me*!'

'Extraordinary,' agreed Mr Evans. It was quite outside his experience. Turned call girl presumably. Photographer's model, unusual poses, blonde, phone between 6 and 7 p.m., Sundays 12 until 2. Five guineas. Costumes extra.

'Does she go to work?'

'She's a telephone operator at World Mechanical.'

'Who's she living with?'

Frank Preston told him.

'What do you want me to do?' Mr Evans asked. 'You can be quite frank with me, Mr Preston. Nothing shocks me and everything is confidential. Do you want a divorce?'

'I wanna know what's going on,' Frank Preston said miserably. He had ulcers of the mind too.

'Suppose something is going on, adultery of some sort,' Mr Evans suggested. 'Do you want me to collect evidence?'

'If it's bad,' Preston said. 'I mean if she's really sleeping – It doesn't make sense,' he confessed suddenly, ' 'cause she wasn't keen on it.'

'I see,' said Mr Evans. 'Would you like a cup of tea?' he asked brightly, happily, in the certainty that here was a case, money. Two kids, happy for a while, but not suited; the one liked sex, the other didn't. It would be easy providing the girl also wanted a divorce. 'She's not a Catholic or anything?' he asked, and was relieved when Preston shook his head. These religious people were a bloody nuisance. Principles and all that rubbish.

'You realize it may cost a bit of money . . .'

'Can you give me any idea how much?'

'It's difficult,' said Mr Evans. 'Depends how much time, and if she's reasonable when found compromised. Thirty pounds or so.'

'I didn't realize –'

'You think about it,' Mr Evans requested. 'Hours and hours of waiting, all night perhaps. (It's *always* raining, too!) Time in court if we get to that. Thirty's a minimum,' he added. 'Ah, here's a pot of tea! Has Mrs Ali gone away?' he asked the bespectacled girl.

'No, Mr Evans. She just sits there, weeping.'

'She'll get tired before I do.'

'I've just had coffee,' Frank Preston pointed out. He'd wasted ninepence. Never mind. There'd been the dull painful pleasure, the swinging legs, the excited voices, eyes that regarded him, however briefly.

'Have a fag, then?' Mr Evans suggested. 'And let's get down to details.'

It took forty minutes, eased the jealousy in the glands. Frank Preston went down the thirty-two steps, on to the crowded pavements. If the world had been on his shoulders it wasn't now. Mr Evans was prepared to carry, identify, document, confirm, and prove all the dirt in it.

2

ALEXEI ANTONOV

SIMPSON explained, 'And the stresses. Tomorrow Cambridge will confirm – my God, I hope so! – the stresses. We'll go and see what these machines can do.'

Margaret Simpson pleaded, 'Hubert, please! A party, it's a party. Don't you ever tire of work?'

Simpson was rounded, jolly, like a schoolboy: life was fun. 'Never!' he confessed, and the aside, before forgotten, to Alexei Antonov: 'If the machines can confirm the stresses are negligible we can go on to skin temperatures and all that.'

An electric brain, a thing as big as a cinema: it did two years' mathematics in an hour, very useful. But Margaret was human, a woman, involved here and now, dress, hair style, arrival, who's there, laughter, relationships, gossip, food, furniture, dress.

'I can see Alexei would like to drop it for a few hours.'

Alexei was in fact nervous. A party. People staring. He was shy, preferred the loneliness of the room, the formulas, Simpson's eagerness, results. But even the party was relevant: Simpson knew Rice who was in the Marine Aircraft Establishment, and Rice was a personal friend of Stanhope, and Stanhope, of course, was very much at Cabinet level. But why a party should be necessary was beyond Alexei's comprehension. If Stanhope was actually involved, surely a party was the last place at which to shout information about Billiards or its successor, already planned, a mathematical possibility – well, they, he and Simpson, thought so; the machine at Cambridge could confirm them thus far . . .

He asked, 'Who will be at the party?'

Simpson answered, too quickly for Margaret, 'Stanhope, of course; Rice, I suppose; possibly Babbington; a few others, an artist or two, newspaper people, a few pretty girls.'

'I don't understand. No secrecy at all.'

'Oh, it's only to meet you. There'll be no talk.'

'But the very fact –'

'Alexei,' chided Margaret, pink in the face, 'this isn't Russia, you know. These are all responsible people.'

'I can't get used to this – freedom. It needs only one hostile brain in the room –'

'My gloves,' pleaded Margaret. 'I almost forgot ... We've known Norman for years and Stanhope is the brother-in-law of –'

'The Establishment,' giggled Simpson. 'Everything in the world settled over drinks, a meal. Much the best way.'

'Talking of drink,' Margaret scolded with heavy humour, 'four at most, Hubert.'

'Four,' echoed Simpson, his round fleshy face beaming. 'Four bottles, I trust?'

'You become silly if you don't stop,' she cautioned him. 'Red in the face and talkative. I feel a fool.'

'It's cold,' said Simpson, opening the front door. Lights were on in scores of the students' rooms; music issued like breath, and laughter, somewhere a cry, 'Oh, shut up, you clot.' Simpson identified 'Haydn', but Margaret corrected him, 'Hubert Beethoven, darling. The mathematics are quite different.'

They got into the car, cold leather and metal. Margaret always drove, Hubert complained, not always good-naturedly.

Margaret turned the headlights on unexpectedly and Alexei saw by the rhododendrons a student, alone, standing, blinded apparently, for he raised his hands in front of his face. Then he walked away – away from *what*? Alexei wondered oddly. The face and nervous stance had reminded him of something: a door opened, Simpson, huge with laughter, for it had been a good day, and in the corridor a boy student, tough but nervous, staring in terror, open-mouthed, feet hesitant, stationary, then back into motion. The shock of interruption, Alexei had decided at the time: deep in thought and a door and two people emerging. Nerves, he decided with bitter analysis, meaning his own; he had his fears despite the ordinariness, the routine, the apparent safety, Mr Bellamy's reassurances. Oh, God, would the day never come when he no longer expected to see Malinski on the opposite pavement?

Two or three miles, main roads, shops, quieter avenues, then the cul-de-sac, ten cars parked outside, seven in the circular drive: big ones, Alexei nervous now, intimidated by the size of cars. Ridiculous, his mind shouted.

'What time do we leave?' Simpson asked.

'I don't know.'

'Well, you give the signal. She's the boss,' he confided, although, living with them, Alexei was perfectly aware of their harmony.

The door answered by a woman who gave the impression of unfamiliarity with the house and the arriving faces. Staff shortage. Even Rice's money could only hire them for the evening, and transport home to be provided ...

Coats taken, 'Good evening,' and a wave of an arm. 'Will you proceed in there?' – the word 'proceed' having a funereal atmosphere at odds with the glare of lights, voices in pleasure, clink of glasses.

'We're late,' admitted Margaret.

'*We!*' said Simpson.

For a moment Alexei had the impression that they were nervous; it encouraged him.

A room about thirty-five feet long, packed, sixty people in it, all talking, a devastating roar of words – it must be important. He was intimidated at once. All so tall, sophisticated. Wasn't anyone small, shy, insignificant?

'Norman, *darling.*'

'Why, *Margaret.*'

A kiss from some tall, forty-fiveish, influential man, intelligent, sardonic.

'Hubert! How well you look.'

'We got as far as Jerusalem in September.'

'Good God!'

'Exactly. Oh, they've cornered the market in God there all right.'

'Incredible.'

'Norman, here's our dear friend, Alexei Antonov ... Norman Rice.'

'Well,' said Rice agreeably, 'I've heard wonderful things about you. Remarkable,' he qualified.

He was, perhaps, confused about names. This, surely, was the technique for actors, film starlets, artists, not spherical mathematicians. Ballet, perhaps, that would be it – Rice thought he was in ballet: a bit old and certainly frail ...

Alexei said dully, 'How do you do, Mr Rice?'

'A drink,' suggested Rice, as if he considered Alexei needed one. 'Gin or something?'

'Sherry for me,' said Margaret.

'Now, listen, Hubert,' Rice said conspiratorially, so that Alexei felt ignored, a puppet operated by others. 'Stanhope's coming about ten. He can't get here earlier. Don't go before, will you? The fat man over there by the bar is Marbrook. Do you know him?'

'I've heard of him, of course.'

'Have a word.'

'I see Bernard Ewing's here.'

'Your gin, sir,' the blank face said.

'Thank you.'

Alexei drank about half of it, was warmed; life became bearable.

Margaret took his hand. 'Let's meet Clara. Honestly, Hubert and Norman think they're running the world. I'm here for *fun*.'

People, all sophisticated, tall, still this unbearable tallness, so that he was making his way through a corridor of shoulders. Even the girls and women seemed tall. The younger ones were extraordinarily beautiful – tall, slim, with fine bones and simple hair styles which were, nevertheless, supremely effective. All wearing dresses that were not vulgar in any way but hid little; it only needed an inclined mind and imagination could scrutinize everything. They stood in careful, natural poses, tireless apparently, just beautiful, reasonably intelligent, pleasant to see. He was too overcome to even realize that he could just go up to one, talk, say pretty, absurd things; they would laugh; they had a sort of decorative kindness – the laughter would be genuine; they were there, yours for the moment, providing you observed the rules, which were that you just talked, amused them, didn't become too personal, didn't ask for more than this moment. To ask for tomorrow would cause them to drift away, stand elsewhere.

'Clara, darling, Alexei Antonov. You *remember*, escaped from Florence, the Russians.'

She was tall, of course, older, like a horse (strange the way Englishwomen grew into horses after forty-five), with a voice like a rasp. 'Margaret, my dear, how well you look. I feel so old.'

'Jerusalem . . .'

'Was it? Well, I think you're marvellous. Mr Antonov, forgive me. Old friends. I keep repeating that word! What do you think of Felicity's Miró?'

There was a painting on the wall behind her – vivid in yellows and odd red shapes, crazy but curiously acceptable.

'So absorbing, don't you think?' Clara prompted him. 'Vital.'

'Bloody awful,' a man said.

He was huge, fat, a gross body and face, glasses immense and right on his eyes – an unfortunate encounter between an owl and a pig. He was red with laughter, very drunk.

Alexei said, 'I like it.'

'There, you see, Mr Antonov approves.'

Clara helped herself to an oyster on a large mushroom, both on toast. 'Heavenly,' she recommended.

There was a girl yards away, surrounded, harassed almost; he had never seen anything like her, so beautiful it was unthinkable, the mind refused to accept – dark, mysterious, proud, arrogant, no, not arrogant . . . He was conscious of others admiring her from a distance, electricity in the males. She was hemmed in by laughter, success, admiration. At that moment her blue eyes, over some of the shoulders, met his, shyness entered; they flicked away, returned, dropped in modesty, but not offended. Alexei's whole being was warmed by the mere spectacle of her – not sexually, nothing like that, it was just stunned shock, almost an aesthetic experience, that such a beautiful thing could exist. Who could doubt God, having seen her? Nobody but a God could have created her.

'That's Sheila Haward,' Clara pointed out, frankly identifying his stare. 'She's a model. Do you know what a model is? *Bizarre* and all that. Very beautiful, isn't she? She may get to us if we stay until midnight.'

He liked Clara suddenly. Equine, yes, but human in a room full of conversations that were beyond him, excluded him; she was sympathetic, put him at ease. Alexei blushed a little at being caught but affirmed, 'I have never seen anyone quite like her.'

'Too thin,' said the gross man, his glass empty. 'No flesh. All right dolled up, but useless in bed, I should think.'

'I've no doubt you do,' Clara said tartly.

The girl/woman had moved slightly nearer when Alexei dared to look again.

'Modigliani,' Margaret was saying. 'Rather like his work, don't you think? A complete disruption of axis.'

She was here, radiating an atmosphere, a presence, an arrival, even a tension; everyone and everything was inferior, subdued before her, although not by her inclination; she spoke quietly, heeded others, did not tend to dominate. Others had drifted from her previous group, not willing to lose her mere presence; they accepted a new situation in which others must talk, but they might stare, admire. But their eagerness to be noticed overcame them and they interrupted – wittily, foolishly, irreverently, anything to be included. Alexei could scarcely bear to look upon her except in small, snatched glances. It was as if the light of her was too strong for his eyes; he was not yet conditioned to this kind of experience. Nobody spoke to him now, not even Clara. The others thought he was a clerk or something. But even if he'd been introduced to each of the surrounding seven or eight as 'the man who's working on the mathematics of an anti-rocket rocket or something' (which was the way he would have been introduced if anyone beyond Margaret had had that vital secret) they would have continued to regard him as unimportant, made a meaningless joke of it: 'Have some canapé marguery, whatever that is. Are you really one of those chaps who can blow us all up?' The implication being that he wouldn't – otherwise he wouldn't be *here*. The terrifying indifference, confidence, lack of seriousness, was, presumably, the secret of the English success. What an absurd people they were! And yet they had this superb sense of justice, were a people, he believed, who above all things believed in truth; they were even relentless in their frequent self-analysis. His mind, gaining confidence on the gin, drifted to other things: the orbital path, relative and progressive skin drag, with inconsistent heat. Why the variation in heat? Instrument failure? That would be proved, overcome. The astonishing thing was that already they had progressed from mere cur-vilinear movement to actual manoeuvrability. It had become electronically and, better, mechanically possible; that is to say, it was beyond theory, it could be done. . . .

She was staring at him in a small hush. Clara said quickly, 'How rude I am! But if you will talk clothes. Sheila, this is Alexei Antonov. He escaped from –'

'I know,' the girl interrupted, astonishing him. 'I remember your photograph in the newspapers.' It was delightful, worth the entire terror, change of life. Just to have the value of those words: she had seen his absurd face, remembered it five months anyway.

Alexei shook her hand; it was cool, small, and not reluctant. She did not touch and remove; she shook hands like a con-gratulation, the return from the South Pole, the winner of the Belgian Grand Prix, first man to eat corn flakes on the moon. He didn't know what to say, retreated to an English 'How do you do?'

'I thought it was most reckless,' the beautiful face said, a yard away. 'I remember I tried to imagine how terrifying it must be, because, I felt, you hadn't just got to overcome some-thing physical, you'd got to enter what would seem like a new planet, too.'

'I was frightened,' he admitted.

'Do you find us very different?' she inquired.

'More beautiful,' he ventured, the gin overcoming fright, shy-ness, the small audience which now laughed, encouraged him, admired him for saying it.

'No, I mean it,' the girl insisted. 'Did you have to overcome a kind of mental imprisonment?'

'I still haven't entirely escaped that,' he told her.

'I see,' she said, but he didn't believe she did; none of them in that room . . .

Clara said, 'Have some *pâté*, Sheila, darling. Not at all fattening. Or is it?'

The conversation altered slightly, returned, became general; others talked to her, but she hadn't moved – they all stood, bits of things to eat, a delicate way of holding glasses, a stance affected but also confident, poised. All the dialogue, at any rate male, was for her. He was unnoticed, nothing, a little thing she was being polite to. In a moment she would move on, reach the important people.

But she did not move on. A slight ebb of attention : there were other pretty women, more easily claimed, and a man or two drifted away, a splinter group was formed by the mere co-incidence of two subjects in the one conversation, and magnificently, too much to be hoped for, she was very nearly alone with him, standing, too tall, of course, like everybody else, but shoulder to shoulder, half facing him, and the long graceful neck and the superb face turned, strained even, if her movements could ever be called such, to continue. He moved his feet, the first time in nearly forty minutes, to ease their attitudes.

'I can see why you're a model.'

He could think of nothing subtle, amusing, to say, but it did not matter presumably. In a moment or two she would be gone, outside his life.

'You're too kind,' she answered, shyly, but realizing his implication. Her eyes dropped modestly, but she picked up confidence again immediately, whispered quite close to him, her fine skin texture within a foot, her magnificent eyes straight into his, focusing on his soul, burning it, her lips, wide, attractively thin, slightly open – a pale lipstick, just more than natural – and the quiet voice sympathetic, not at a party : 'You're the first person I know who's actually *done* something. I mean, not wishing to be unkind, but would these?'

The elegant sweep of one hand and arm condemned, however slightly, the entire room except *him*. The penetrating but impenetrable eyes, unflinchingly upon him, so that his whole being wilted in turmoil, suddenly became aware of a male per-

usal from elsewhere, froze, were worried, then became con-
versational, light, had returned to a party.

'I had reasons,' said Alexei, 'to make it necessary.'

The model said with quiet but intense conviction, 'You did
it because you believed in God. That was supremely exciting,
commands my admiration, because, you see, Mr Antonov, it
is not only heroic but unfashionable, and required extra
courage.'

He did not quite know what she was talking about and reassured her, 'I was afraid, not heroic. You must not believe for a
moment –'

'Modest,' she whispered, meek, conspiratorial, and he was
conscious of the flawless shoulders, fine young neck, the elegant
fit of the dress over the young hips. How beautiful she was!
A face so perfect could hold no evil; it was flawless because it
retained original content.

'You believe in God?' he asked doubtfully.

She looked around, apparently in embarrassment, but no one
overheard. 'I have my bad moments. I'm lazy . . .'

He was able to smile.

'I don't believe you have an unkind thought in your
head.'

She laughed, teeth perfect, throat sensual. 'Oh, I'm a woman,
Mr Antonov. Full of foolishness and awful spite!'

She was, he knew, identified, understanding faces, incapable
of spite; it would have marred the face if it had existed.

'It is interesting to meet someone so beautiful who does not
believe they are themselves God,' he said.

She blinked in shock, then laughed cautiously. 'Say that
again, only slowly!'

'Even some of the students are wiser, criticize Him . . .'

'You mean qualifications about behaviour, that sort of
thing?'

'Justifications,' he corrected. 'Things wanted, conditions
made with God. They will accept Him providing . . . You see?
It is a little absurd and immensely arrogant to presume . . . And
it would be more honest to admit wrong, say so; God would
understand, forgive.'

'Interesting,' she commented.

'I am boring you?'

He was aware that English people, except students, became bored or embarrassed very easily.

'Just the martinis,' Sheila Haward said quickly, a smile for him, more powerful than the gin. 'I can't take too much profundity. Oh, that makes me rude.'

'It was a party. I am too serious.'

'Won't you,' she asked, pleaded even, 'tell me about your life, your escape?'

'Here? The martinis –'

She qualified quickly, so that her aloof properties altered, he felt some female, sexual quality in her, something more than the charmed attention. 'Phone me tomorrow. We could arrange it. I'm home on Sundays. The number is . . .'

He was staggered, overcome, looked for the mistake; he couldn't identify his position: was he simply a 'hero' who was being lionized or a new friend about to share communication? There must be an error. Ah, it would be another party, lots of people there. For a moment he had, absurdly, anticipated a private conversation, the blue eyes regarding him, propelling the shyness, 'Go on! And when you left Rome –'

She was moving on; he did not exist, so changed was her face, impersonal, proud, her calm, assured movements and the hands swinging exactly as trained or required, the head and neck turned slightly, the eyes not seeing anyone, although instantly a new group welcomed her: 'Ah, Sheila, we were just talking about you!'

Mr Babbington's face appeared, materialized: the magician or the wicked uncle?

'Antonov,' he greeted. 'How pleasant to see you again. Stanhope's arrived. Will you join us?'

'Five seven two nine,' said Alexei aloud.

'I beg your pardon?'

'An idea,' explained Alexei. 'I must write it down.' He did so on a piece of paper. He always carried bits of paper; like a poet, he had inspirations.

'Ah, an idea!' Mr Babbington was full of congratulations. 'Wonderful they are, too!'

In the car Margaret, crashing the gears, complained, 'Because it's cold, Hubert. And these damn demisters don't work properly either.'

'Tra la la!' sang Simpson.

'Did you enjoy it, Alexei?' Margaret asked.

'Tra la bum tra la,' concluded Simpson. 'I say, you got on rather well with that gorgeous model thing. What did you talk about?'

'About God and life.'

'Holy cow!' shouted Simpson. 'You talked about God with *her*? What does she know about the subject?'

'Hubert, don't be blasphemous,' urged Margaret.

'She wants,' Alexei explained, not without pride, 'me to phone tomorrow, and we're to meet and talk.'

He did not understand their shocked silence. They could hardly tell him that he was small and insignificant. They liked him dearly; he was quiet and brilliant, occasionally funny, but this – this didn't make sense.

Margaret said, 'You're joking, Alexei.'

'Joking?'

Margaret didn't know how to put it. 'Isn't she married or anything? She must have dozens of men friends, surely?'

This, unaccountably, hurt Alexei. Not that he must have hopes, intentions. It would be very foolish. But if she believed in God would she be vain, conceited, selfish?

'I am not a friend,' he attempted to explain, but confused them further. 'It will be a political and religious discussion.'

Margaret could not entirely disguise her curiosity, disbelief. 'You probably made a mistake,' she said, dismissing it with the only logical explanation she could find.

'Is there some reason why we shouldn't have a conversation?' Alexei asked, but they were fortunately, by virtue of traffic density, not required to answer that question.

'Max,' she protested over the telephone, 'he's a funny little man, so serious, religious. He talks about justifications and being terrified. Do I have to go on with this?'

'You're not afraid of him?'

'Oh, God, no. He's *nothing*.'

'Does he admire you?'

'Oh yes, there's no difficulty about that.'

'When will you see him again?'

'He's to telephone in the morning.'

'See him tomorrow afternoon then. Have fun, Sheila. He doesn't matter; he can't hurt you. Quite unimportant. Enjoy yourself. Act coy, shy, pretend to be a virgin.'

'He said I was incapable of an unkind thought!'

'He's got an interesting future!'

'Max, darling, I will see you?'

'Tuesday. Not before.'

'Yes. And, Max –'

'What now?'

'Oh, never mind.'

'I know, I know. You want – Am I right?'

'Yes, Max, you're right.'

She answered at once, as if she had been prepared behind the door. In the light of Sunday afternoon she was still flawless, so beautiful that he felt privileged, nervous. She was dressed in slacks and sweater, and, seeing his examining eye, she said, 'You don't mind. I thought –' But she did not explain what was the content of her mind, the process inside the superb head which had made a relatively simple decision about clothes.

'Do you never look untidy?' he asked, a smile taking any harm out of the words.

'I expect so,' she replied vaguely.

'It was kind of you to –'

'Don't talk like that,' she cautioned him, 'as if it's a privilege to be here.'

'It is more than a pleasure –'

'Absurd,' Sheila Haward protested. 'The privilege and the pleasure are mine.' He made hopeless gestures with his hands, but she ignored them, suggested, 'Shall I take your coat?'

'It is charming here,' Alexei complimented, referring to the flat, the lamp shades and delicate colours, the water colours, the very atmosphere. 'I came in a taxi,' he confided conspiratorially, so that she frowned, puzzled – for her taxis were normal, 'without a word to Mr Bellamy.'

'Who's he?'

Alexei Antonov   245

'I shouldn't tell you, I suppose,' Alexei said, but there was no harm. 'He's in the Special Police.'

She turned away quickly. 'My cigarette case, have you seen it? Have one?' She had just found the case. 'You do smoke? You mean Special Branch?'

'I mean the spies, all that. They deal with people like me.'

She smoked slowly, with characteristic poise even in this small social action. 'Does this man – what was his name? Bellamy? – does he follow you about?'

'He likes to know where I am.'

'Whatever for? Why' – Sheila Haward's excellent mouth protested, a small splash flushed the face – 'I think it's monstrous.'

'He only protects me.'

'Do you need protection?'

'I don't really know, Miss Haward.'

'You mustn't call me that. It makes me nervous. Sheila.'

'It is a pretty name . . .'

'But, Alexei – can I call you Alexei? That's sweet of you – if you're safely in England why and who –'

'I am a political refugee,' he explained. 'A mathematician, too, with information. It is loss of face in the Cold War for someone like me to –'

'Yes, I see that, but surely following you about . . . Do they follow you about?'

'You are interested?'

'Why, yes, I find it a little frightening.'

'That I should be protected?'

'That you should report to a policeman that you're coming to see me.'

Alexei grinned slyly. 'I don't think they'd suspect *your* motives, Miss Haward. It is a question of necessity, when I feel it necessary, that's all. Long journeys, going abroad, political meetings.'

'Oh, I *see*,' Sheila Haward said. 'I thought you were followed about like – well, like a spy.'

'He would not be a very successful spy who was followed about!'

'Quite. Oh, I see that. Shall I make a cup of tea?'

'It is not too early?'

H.M.D. – 12

'It may be. Doesn't matter. We could have two – one early, one late.'

She seemed to wish at all costs to move about, arrange things, see him from a different perspective for each question. Now she said quickly, 'Excuse me,' so that he was left sitting, staring at the photograph of a woman whom he presumed to be her mother.

A telephone shrilled, startled him. Miss Haward rushed back almost as if it was important that *he* shouldn't answer, explain everything. Untidy, he thought; she was untidy for once, panic in her movements. It made her fallible, human, nearer to him.

'Darling' – breathlessly – 'quite impossible.' Her eyes turned despite herself, it seemed, to Alexei, an acoustic witness – well, half of one. 'I'm busy anyway. And you know I never work on Sundays.'

'The kettle,' she then said in one shocked exhalation, and rushed out in the same haste. He followed, commented, 'What a neat kitchen,' but the bedroom door was half open and that was prettier. Photographs on a mantelshelf, five or six, wounded, worried. He shrugged them aside with effort. Nothing to do with him – he had no claims; it was privilege despite her denial.

He sat on the fragile small sofa and she surprised him slightly by joining him, tea tray placed with graceful skill on a tiny table. The very faint excellent, careful scent of her reached him, almost the warmth of her; it was impossible not to be overwhelmed, emotionally involved. He realized that it was ridiculous and hid it in politeness, careful conversation. Not to see her again would depress, he decided, cause slight pain, wondering what she was doing, which photograph she had selected.

'What are you doing now?'

He was startled. 'Only thinking,' he said, scarlet, caught out. But the superb face didn't notice, merely qualified, 'Don't be absurd! I meant, are you working?'

'Of course.'

'Is it interesting?'

'It is exactly what I am capable of.'

'Mathematics. They decide everything in the end, don't they?

God, I can't even manage my expenses. I have to employ an accountant. Am I silly?'

'I do not yet understand your tax system . . .'

'Well, if *you* don't comprehend it shows – What do you do with yourself?' she asked abruptly. 'Theatres, films, night clubs?'

Alexei laughed. 'Certainly not night clubs! Not much,' he admitted rather wretchedly, as if it was failure. 'We are working on an enormous problem, you see. It is, frankly, exhausting at times.'

'Fascinating! What is it?'

'It is fascinating. The mathematics of deep space.'

'Deep space?'

'I shouldn't have said –'

'Oh, it won't matter. I don't understand a word. And I can keep secrets. I shan't tell Mr Bellamy,' she chided. 'What is deep space anyway? It sounds like a very expensive refrigerator!'

'You could say that deep space starts six thousand miles out.'

'Six thousand miles! It sounds terrifying. And you're going to work out rocket behaviour or something?'

'Or something,' he agreed, and added quickly, 'You mustn't say a word, Miss Haward. People do not know even the one problem's solved, never mind the next.'

'I wish,' she said, pouting in amusement, 'you'd stop calling me Miss Haward. I'm Sheila, Sheila, not a schoolmistress.'

'It is quite difficult.'

'I don't see any difficulty at all. Say it!' she commanded.

He said 'Sheila,' and the mysterious, aloof face, too beautiful for mortals, stared into his eyes, was for a moment weak, human, suggestive, had surrendered a little more than a name.

'You were going to tell me why and how you escaped,' Sheila pointed out. 'I think it was wonderful, Alexei. Please tell me. Start from Moscow. Was it Moscow?'

'No. Kuibyshev.'

'Spell it for me!'

He did this.

'I was sent,' he commenced nervously, 'to work on a problem. The nature of the problem crystallized doubts, beliefs, anxiety which had been worrying me for some time.'

'But what,' she asked, 'started the doubts in the first place?'

'My father,' he said unhappily.

'I'm sorry –'

'He was working on the mathematics of chemical warfare. You understand? The distribution of crop, animal, and human diseases – infinitely complicated problems of air currents and densities and the rotation of the earth and its differing temperatures. This thing, Platform, on which I had helped, could be used as an observation machine for the entire world – its cloud formations, oh, things beyond your comprehension. The authorities were delighted. But I had to stop, think about it. Humanity, you see, Communism embraces humanity. Yet here was a thing – There were others, too, and they were at odds with the professed Party line. I had information which was kept from the people, would always be kept from them. Our whole intended world was a lie. I didn't know if yours was better, but when we went to this hypocritical, ridiculous conference in Florence ... You see, there was a moment, in the Hall of the Five Hundred, following some Scandinavians about, so gay and innocent, lovely, were they, and Gourshkov stubbed his cigar in that superb place. It crystallized. I knew then that God is older, wiser, that things like evil exist irrespective of politics, which cannot supersede them or Him. Oh, my God, Sheila, I tell you, I was so frightened. The entire world, and it was up to me. I had to be fair to those Scandinavians, *everybody*.'

His voice was shaken with emotion. So silly, she thought, absurd, all this fuss about God and the world. Darling Max. But politely she didn't look into the shaken face, the emptying heart.

'You are a wonderful man,' she confided. (Max's hands on her breasts were the world; this little man was nothing, *nothing*.) 'Tell me what happened.'

He told her about the schoolteachers in the Ford car, the child in Naples. It quite interested her, was amusing, albeit pointless. She pressed his hand that was agitated. 'What a tremendous decision. And yet you are so shy, modest, like someone ashamed.' (Max's hands, shameless, pulling small sensual things downward. So ridiculous, all this nonsense, religion and politics, nothing to do with *life*. This was life, Max's face above her.)

'I am not a brave man; it has shaken me. I have no roots now.'

'Do you regret it?'

'No, no. There are some disappointments, so much arrogance, selfishness, indifference. I thought your England was a godly country ... And I am anxious. You see, we've solved the problem of near space, but what if they orbit in deep space? I can see no end as long as the intentions are there.'

'There is the terror of countermeasures,' Sheila Haward suggested. 'They ought to cancel out.' (End of the problem, now back to the real properties of living: the fused bodies on the bed, the camera's eye, the assembly in the fashion show, the turned eyes, examining, electrified, in the fashionable restaurant.) 'To think,' she continued softly, 'that I might have been in Florence at the same time. I'm often there. Very photogenic, Florence. Shall we have that second cup of tea?'

It was unintentionally brutal, almost winded him, as if he'd been talking about the weather.

'I've bored you –'

'I don't understand,' she assured him and, incredibly, had blushed, appeared shaken. 'What did I do to suggest that? Alexei, it's hard to comprehend, but no one admires you more for what you did than I do.'

'I must leave,' he said. He had bared his soul, now felt a fool who had done something unsophisticated, wrong by England's curious values. 'It is five o'clock.'

'I've offended you ...'

'No, no. It was kind of you to listen –'

'I'd like to see you again,' the superb mouth said unbelievably.

He hesitated, stopped walking toward the wrong door.

'You would? Why?'

'Have you a car?'

He was baffled. 'No.'

'We'll use mine. I'll take you out to dinner.'

It was not a request but a statement of fact.

'It would be delightful,' he asserted quickly, 'but I don't understand, Miss Haward.'

'I shall be offended. I am Sheila. Tuesday, then. No. Wednesday.' She urged in a rush of breath: 'Tell your Mr Bellamy it's not political. Definitely not political,' and her guarded smile made him flush with eager confusion.

'I shall not tell him anything.'

'Let's have secrets,' she pleaded, a sensual warm quality in her face, movements.

'I still don't comprehend . . .'

'Of course not!' She laughed.

She nevertheless, despite smiles, sensuality in the hands that smoothed the clothes, a toss of the head, wasn't detaining him, had fetched his coat.

He stood in the descending lift, walked the pavements, sat in the returning taxi, drunk with the only implications he could think of. She liked him. No more than that, and that only related to her romantic interpretation of what error had made him capable of, but it was enough for him. She'd never know, of course, that he was in love with her – he had, he was sure, hidden that from her quite skilfully. And he must not spoil their friendship by foolishly admitting it, claiming it. The pleasure of seeing her must be enough. Just a little, a week or two, a month, until the novelty wore off for her and she realized that he was human, no hero; she had created that quality in the generosity of her mind's eye. Her mind, like her tall, proud body, was too perfect, uncorrupted.

She stood at the foot of the four steps in the beam of illumination from the opened door. Simpson grinned; this was great fun. Simpson, fifty-six, was as frivolous as a student at times. She was, as usual, flawless, mysterious, impenetrable; if there was a *mystique* in being feminine Miss Haward certainly – But Simpson, and behind him Margaret, were doing their best to reduce her to warmth, absurdity, mortal condition.

'Bring him back alive!' Simpson half shouted, roaring with laughter. 'He's valuable.'

'Oh, I appreciate that,' Miss Haward assured them.

'Hubert's always rude,' Margaret apologized. 'He never quite recovered from Cambridge.'

'Where are you going?' Hubert asked impertinently.

'I thought Swallow Street.'

'Oh? Who's taking whom?' Hubert inquired, bellowed with mirth again.

Across the gravel someone began to walk away quickly, Alexei noticed. Someone standing by the rhododendrons had now moved. Fright, he analysed bitterly. I'm too nervous. I expect Pervukhin and Malinski. ... Oh,' God, he pleaded, enjoyment marred, don't let them, anyone, hurt *her* ...

'What a cute little car,' was Margaret's frank comment. 'What is it?'

'Fiat 600,' Sheila Haward answered. 'Engine's at the back. A great baby,' she enthused.

Hubert said with sly amusement, 'Not a lot of room, back or front.'

Alexei sat in the front passenger's seat, examined the figure walking ahead. The same student, he was sure. Did he meet some girl in the rhododendrons? Too cold, surely. And where was she?

'They like you,' Sheila said, turning out of the college grounds. 'Why do you keep looking behind?'

'That boy, he's always there.'

'I didn't see any boy.'

'He stands there, by the rhododendrons.'

'Astronomy,' suggested Sheila. 'It's a clear night.'

'Ah, yes,' accepted Alexei, but he immediately worried: had it been a clear night when they went to Rice's party? He couldn't remember; doubt remained. He could, of course, tell Simpson or Bellamy, have the boy questioned, but it would feel cowardly; there would be an explanation. It wasn't students who really worried him.

'Did you get on all right at Cambridge?' Sheila asked.

He was startled. 'Did I tell you about that? Sheila, I am becoming foolish.'

She, too, was shocked, the driving indicated for an instant. 'I don't think *you* said anything, but Margaret, just now, and I concluded –'

'Did she not mean Hubert's student days?'

'Oh, I *see*.'

'As a matter of fact, a coincidence, we did go to Cambridge the other day.'

'And when she said *recovered* – I thought you'd been having a high old time, drinking or something.'

It was a curious explanation, but she was, after all, a person he didn't know well, and confusion in language was to be expected. Besides, if he was going to see alarm in *her* as well as students . . . ! He shook with the absurdity.

'Did I say something funny?'

'It was rather funny. The one thing we didn't do in Cambridge was drink.'

'You mustn't tell me, explain it, if it's about your job.'

'Not very funny, anyway,' Alexei told her, and the incident of words was closed, forgotten.

'You drive well.'

'Thank you. I drive big cars, too.'

'You own several?'

'No,' she answered awkwardly. 'Just Daddy's and – friends'.'

He grinned at her discomfort and explained, overcoming shyness, 'You do not have to apologize for your boy friends. It would be absurd if anyone so beautiful did not have some, many, with others wishing.'

Sheila said, 'You're charming, you really are,' and he glowed in the pleasure of her generosity, impulsiveness.

'I don't know why you bother,' he confessed in the security of darkness.

'You don't seem,' she chided, as if it were wrong, a mistake, sweet, but definitely a mistake, 'to have any conceit at all.'

Alexei said nothing but thought, I am proud, conceited, dazed with the pleasure of being here. But in the too-sophisticated restaurant he was himself again, nervous, unfamiliar, in a world of tall, superb people, women as elegant as she – and he was relieved to be in a corner, observing, but not seen.

'Alexei,' she whispered over the caviar, 'no nonsense tonight about who pays. Understood?'

'I cannot be your guest,' he protested.

'You *are*,' Sheila claimed.

'But is it not wrong, not traditional?'

'Darling, you're sweet but absurd! Do you know how much money I make in a year?'

'I've no idea.'

'Five thousand,' she told him.

He was astonished, even alarmed. 'But that's more than twice what Simpson –'

'I know. But bear in mind I can only do this sort of work for ten or fifteen years. I mustn't drink,' she added, seeing wine bottles, 'or not much. It would be fatal for dissipation to show under my eyes!'

He did not care for this analysis of her as a technical thing. Her beauty was from God, for God, an end in itself, a perfection.

But soon, warmed by wine, he was amusing her, describing Rice's party as he had seen it. 'And this funny man, with a great big red face and spectacles like magnifying glasses over each eye – who was he?'

'I don't know. Go on, go on!'

'And this lady who was called Clara said, "What do you think of Felicity's Miro?" And to give me the answer she said it was vital, absorbing – what did that mean? – but this great big man said, "Bloody awful." Then she said, about another painting, "A complete disruption of axis." '

Sheila Haward laughed, said, 'You're too cruel. You must find us *crazy*.'

'Oh no,' he confessed. 'Terrifying!'

'Have they shown you much of London?'

'We've been very busy.'

'Oh, they'll work you to death. Listen, Alexei, an idea – I could show you, in the car though. Yes, why not? Perfect! I'll tell you a secret, Alexei. I'm starting my old age from the wrong end! My feet get tired. All that standing.'

'My brain . . .' he supplemented. 'Exhausted!'

They both laughed – something, he imagined, shared.

'That's what I meant,' Sheila proceeded quickly. 'We could go all over the place – so many beautiful things. Would you do that? Say no if –'

'I will say yes before you think of anything else, change your mind.'

'Why do you continue to talk like that? It is a custom in your ex-country? I'd love to take you about, enjoy things with you.'

Over the glasses, bottles, and cutlery, the serviettes and flowers she smiled guardedly, apprehensively – too much said, surrendered – but he didn't understand, presume too much. The gods had rewarded him too extravagantly for his bit of courage. In the opposite, carefully attended, magnificent face the blue eyes looked at him from above the mouth, wide and slightly awry in a nervous smile, and they were frank in something tender. It couldn't be love; he was too small, ugly, with big ears, without some quality, he wasn't sure what. Did she feel pity? In her purity – she was religious, too; 'I'm terribly lazy,' but she was – pity would be a content. How old was she? Was she young enough, foolish enough, charming enough to mistake her pity for love? Oh, it was absurd.

'How old are you?'

'Twenty-three. Why?'

'Old enough to know your mind.'

'I know my mind,' she reassured him. 'I don't make mistakes. Not serious ones.'

She had read his thoughts, must have done, for her answers fitted. But he still found it hard to believe; the mathematics were there, but the answer couldn't be true. Was there another way of proving it? Only by putting theory into practice. He was afraid of that. He was in love with her. That prejudiced the mathematics, made him examine every answer for the result desired.

It was hopeless odds, of course : a massacre. His understanding of mathematics was outstanding, but of humans, well, he *was* human, open to the same absurd behaviour of anyone susceptible to beauty. By the time they confronted the *crêpes suzette* he was prepared to swear qualities were in her, always had been. A massacre – she had been right to be so confident, boast to Max. If she had at this table admitted to Alexei, It's all a trick, and had explained the deception, but concluded, I love you, he would have believed her sincerity. It would have needed the details about Max to really convince, hurt. Knowing nothing, except that he'd encountered her at Rice's party, he was deceived by the face, the frank eyes. She was beautiful, therefore she had the other contents of beauty. He couldn't be expected, opposite a face so 'honest', to identify her thoughts.

In the Fiat Sheila said, 'I'll drive you back. It's not late, but if I don't get my quota of sleep . . . The camera's too truthful. You don't mind, Alexei?'

'I can get a taxi.'

'Ridiculous. I insist. I like driving at night.'

'You never told me the story of your life, Sheila.'

'It's not like yours.'

'You haven't led a dull life.'

'Exciting,' Sheila agreed, but qualified at once, 'but I'm ordinary, really. I can cook and sew. I like to read a book. I get fed up with being stared at.'

It was too easy: calm, not involved, with private information, she could say what would convince him. In a while, she supposed, he would become conceited, claim he had identified all these qualities in her: she was his type. At any rate, she had no need to be afraid of him. He would always be subservient, awed, under control. Fetch this, bring that, go here, go there – it might be amusing one day to test him to breaking point and, when it came, claim with monstrous confidence, 'You don't care! You talk about love, but –' She was able to smile – Max was right. It might be amusing, but she mustn't be too cruel.

In the college grounds she lost her way deliberately, stopped in darkness, silence, by trees and goal posts. 'I don't know where I am!' she lied, and laughed. A touch of hands. He said pitifully, 'Sheila!' and she, still thinking of Max, waiting to describe it to him, in the same bitter style – but this was more exquisite than anything told by Max – she sighed, 'Oh, God, dear Alexei,' and the little man was upon her, but so absurdly respectful, devoted, in awe. For amusement she sighed deeper, protested, 'No, no, Alexei,' meaninglessly, as if overcome, an unbearable, beautiful moment, not quite expected, not quite ready for it, but delicious, overwhelming, all the same, and please continue! His hands untidied her hair gently. She timed him. Eighteen seconds before he kissed, but once this was permitted he became quite ferocious, muttering some foreign nonsense, so overcome. It was quite meaningless, but she didn't actually despise him. He was just *nothing*. It worried her that the act would have to be carried on into marriage – or could she claim illness, frigidity, a serious operation when younger?

'Darling,' she boasted, the elegant arms and hands able to move him; he was so slight, weightless, perhaps not even as strong as she, 'this is the most beautiful moment of my life.' The urge to laugh, cry out, tell him, nearly overwhelmed her, but she remained silent while he translated carefully his endearments: 'I don't deserve this. I am only ordinary,' and for a bleak moment conscience worried her, heated her face. But then she remembered others, equally ridiculous in their pleading. All fools, all absurd, all insignificant beside Max. This little man was in love with a lie, with properties not there. How, then, could he really be in love at all? It was vanity and it was right that he should be humiliated.

When, three weeks later, they announced that they were to be married it surprised a number of people.

Geoff Sumpster saw it in the *Mirror*: a half-page picture of Sheila, no photograph of the man, but his name was there, and Geoff thought, That musta been the girl in the Fiat. I don't get it – she's too beautiful for *him*. And his thoughts, vain, absurd, wallowed for a few minutes. Sheila Haward, she was his type, tall, beautiful; if only he could get to know people like that. Still, there was this bird he'd met at the niggers' social. Maggie, my God, she was a hot one, or could be, elusive though. Married woman, he thought proudly. He was in the world of adults. Even Tharp hadn't been with a married woman.

Captain Dean felt a curious relief when he saw the photograph in the *Mail*. It pleased him to know that she wasn't going to marry that arrogant pansy airline pilot with the Jag. It also comforted him to know he himself didn't have to bother any more. He wasn't sure what he meant by that. She's marrying money, fame, he decided, not love. She'll be miserable; serve her right. Very satisfying.

Peter, in marine insurance, saw the photograph in a Continental *Daily Mail* and thought, Christ, the lucky bastard. But

it didn't matter very much now. Since Sheila had rejected him
on the telephone he had become involved again with Janine,
and it would be amusing, he thought, strolling in November
sunshine along the Quai de Gesvres to the morning's business,
to gossip about it with her.

The other Peter, Lord Duguid, heard about it from a woman
friend, and his comment was, 'The bloody fool!'

Frank Preston saw the beautiful face in his *Mirror*, identified
it vaguely from advertisements. Whore, he thought. Expensive
whore. It clarified his own position: Maggie was identified now
as a cheap whore. He was warmed by one sour moment of
envy, lust, and then returned mentally to his own troubles,
stomach-ache, and hatreds.

David was bringing in a Viscount from Düsseldorf, where
he'd made love to her for the first time. There was slight trouble
with the flaps and he came in rather fast, sweated a bit, braked
fiercely as buildings loomed in a larger perspective, taxied,
yawned, talked to the stewardess and wireless operator, waited
for the small procession of passengers to cross into the cover
of glass, authority, elsewhere. He strolled into the crew restaurant, and someone had left an *Express* lying amid dirty
crockery.

He saw the well-known, loved face – astonishing, it was in a
news item, not adverts. The caption hurt. She might have told
me, he thought. It was a lousy end to what had been a bad day.
He supposed he would have to send a telegram or something,
buy a wedding present, pretend to be concerned about her
happiness, although he felt the spoiled desire to wish her unhappiness. I'll phone her, he decided, but the prospect deterred
him. Who was this little man? Alexei Antonov. Never heard
of him. Well, David concluded, she would have been bloody
expensive to live with. He was able to smile grimly, in satisfaction, things remembered, warm, sordid memories, that
aloof face – ha, that little man didn't know what *he*, David,
had claimed first. It made him feel very masculine, confident.
If he could make the cover girl of *Bizarre* he must have qualities. He thought about others who interested him, but the cold
injury remained; the insult and depression left him angry. He
went to complain about the flaps, some instruments, and others

had to endure his temper, his converted passion. I'll be damned, David decided, if I'll give more than thirty bob for the wedding present.

Sheila was nervous, manoeuvred herself in the tiny office so that the light was behind her, expressions eclipsed, paled.

'Darlings,' she ventured, 'I'm getting married.'

They were delighted, thrilled. The girls behind the phones smiled, ignored the waiting world, summons of bells. Miss Grilli ran to kiss her, although her mind couldn't quite keep off business: a year and she'll be leaving us, having a baby, she decided. Elizabeth and Suzé were there, pencils and diaries in hand, elegant, poised, even here, but in their pleasure they became careless of stance. The questions were like an embarrassing barrage:

'Where will you live?'

'Where will you marry?'

'Will you continue working?'

'What does he do?'

'In white, Sheila, please. You'll look a dream thing.'

'We all knew,' Elizabeth confided, 'when he wouldn't photograph anyone else. I must say, Sheila, I feel pangs of envy.'

'I don't think you know him,' Sheila claimed.

But Elizabeth didn't detect the terror. 'Of course we do!' And even Audrey laughed. 'Darling, don't look so serious. You should thank me – I gave him the phone number.'

'All that rudeness,' Elizabeth was certain, 'doesn't *mean* anything. Terribly witty really. And brilliant, of course.'

'His name's Antonov and he's a scientist –'

'Oh!' They sighed, shaken. They'd seen her in restaurants with Max Stuhler, in a car, at night clubs, and there had been a stunned, involved expression on her face every time. 'We thought Max Stuhler –'

'I don't know why you should think that,' Sheila disputed with difficulty. 'Max is just a friend, your client.'

They were a little confused, anxious to discuss this in her absence, analyse. 'Why,' claimed Suzé when she was able to, 'I saw her with Max only two weeks ago. Arm in arm at one o'clock in the morning.'

Elizabeth said with acid, 'He called me a pallid scarecrow! Oversexed animal,' she concluded derisively.

'Well, has anyone *seen* this other man?' Suzé asked, but none of them had.

'Max,' Sheila informed him over the telephone, 'I've done it. We're to be married in a few weeks. It was frightfully amusing. He proposed in the Victoria and Albert Museum!'

'What about your parents?'

'They met him last weekend. They actually *liked* him.'

'They said they did.'

'No, they really did.'

'Don't be a fool. They were being kind, merciful.'

Sheila didn't try to convince him. It wasn't important. But her mother and father *had* liked Alexei. She had been in a condition, herself, of acute embarrassment, ashamed of the little man, and, to be sure, they had stared a bit at first. But less than a day had passed before her mother took her aside, confessed proudly, 'Sheila, we *do* like him. A dear kind man. He seemed so – foreign – when you arrived, but he's such a gentle person and so in love with you. . . .'

It was confusing, for it meant that the image of a kind Alexei would have to be destroyed when she left him for Max. And they wouldn't like Max, she was perfectly sure. Her mother disliked rude people. 'Too clever,' she called them. She hadn't even liked David.

Hubert and Margaret were so surprised that they very nearly admitted their shock, the improbability of the mathematics.

'I don't know how you caught her,' roared Hubert, shaking Alexei's hand, 'but you damn well did!' while Margaret, rather odd and English, presumably, explained, convincing herself perhaps, 'You can never tell what's in a woman's mind, can you?'

Major Igor Gouseev mentioned it in a message to Moscow.

It was all wrong, out of a hat. Mr Bellamy, whoever he was, would want details if they were abroad. She'd wanted to go to Paris, at least see friends. Instead they picked *this* out of a hat. Miles of shingle and hotels that looked – and were – frozen. Not that it mattered: she had no intention of bathing in the

cold washing-up-water sea of December. Sheila regarded everything with outright hostility, but it all had to be contained in
the privacy of the mind.

The hotel was monstrous, five stars supposedly, but in the
squared-off section of the dining room – a quarter of summer's
capacity – the old dears, scented, pensioned off, complaintive,
eating with surprising gluttony, viewed her with something akin
to hostility, resentment. She was a reminder of summer when
they were elbowed out of the way.

Nothing to do at night after the ghastly dinner. Oh, God,
it was so funny really. The town full of soldiers, pimply young
cadets who stared. A cheap dance hall or two, bingo (closed
for the day), three cinemas: they sat on the first evening of
their honeymoon through some incredibly stupid film about
Maryland. Alexei asked questions. People turned from their
toffee eating, love-making, to protest. Drunk, Sheila decided.
To hell with my complexion, eyes – I must get drunk tonight
or it will be unbearable. But in the bar was a selection of
Britain's finest bores. It was a conspiracy to drive them to bed.
The old women had eyed her with disdain. Now the bores
wouldn't leave her alone with their eyes. They'd never seen
anything quite like her down here. Except in the summer, of
course, when they lay in cracks in the sun like tortoises and
exuded feeble acid for four whole months. It kept them alive,
mutual detestation, fear of the noisy kids, dogs that misbe-
haved, young men of dubious integrity, scantily dressed girls
who stared them out contemptuously – the blood and filth of
Ypres and the Somme – it meant nothing to these, no gratitude
felt. Die, you old fools, die. Don't examine my freedom with
your staring, envious, critical rheumy eyes. . . .

The fondling hands, caressing words, things permitted, it
was awful; she'd never have believed her honeymoon could
be so bloody, so *English*. The very room was frozen, the window rattled, a train shunted outside somewhere near. Funny,
agreed – she'd be terribly witty about it to Max – but amusing
afterward, not while extant. Alexei was unfamiliar, had never
had a woman, was overwhelmed by this one. With difficulty
she refrained from explanations, guidance. Afterward he fell
asleep like a child, arms outstretched, within the warmth of

her, while she stayed awake hour after hour for no reason she could identify.

Morning dialogue, suitable only for Max's derision ...

'You are all right?'

'Of course I am all right.'

'Are you happy?'

'Yes, I am happy.'

'You are not in pain?'

'Why should I be in pain?'

Blushes, idiotic concern, shyness: it's a *man's* world and he's trying to break the news ...

'Well, I understood that the first time hurts a girl.'

Very, very frustrating to have to withhold from telling him about the first time, the twenty-first, the first time with David, with Max ... Oh, the vanity of this concern! Oh, to puncture his blasted sentimentality! Be witty, she instructed herself, before you do.

'I'll get used to it. Alexei, what do we do today?'

'Whatever you wish. Sheila,' he pleaded – joy, the ridiculous stupefaction – 'won't it be wonderful when we have a baby?'

The shock of that was sharper than the weather, the porridge, the freezing bedroom, the old eyes staring, criticizing.

'Alexei,' she countered breathlessly, 'not for a year. Not yet. Let's have *fun*.' But he wouldn't identify the scorn in the final word.

She dragged him, a willing spouse, along the Georgian High Street. His nose was cold; so was hers. The shops weren't bad. They raised a meagre enthusiasm, a technical interest. In a book shop he was wallowing with pleasure among the science books, papers, while Sheila selected magazines to overcome boredom.

Afternoon dialogue in the pale sun, the feeble warmth ...

'Stand still a minute!'

'What's that?'

'My camera. Please. Alexei, keep still.'

They could have a new portrait of him; that was a lousy one Max had shown her.

'Now let me look at it.'

'It's a miniature. Austrian, Japanese, or something. Christ, Alexei, I'm cold.'

'You mustn't blaspheme.'

'What must I do?'

The same possessive, tender, idiotic grin. 'Wear more suitable clothes!'

'Ha, ha. I want to make a call.'

'The telephone?'

'No, silly. The toilet.'

'We'll have to go in that café again.'

'Oh no, Alexei!' Laughter shared, almost genuine. 'Not the woman with the brown felt hat again!' (Fat and simple and smelling of fish, and mesmerized by Sheila's mere presence.)

'There's one on the pier.'

'Alexei, it's not clean.'

'Back to the hotel then.'

'No, I –' She nearly protested, 'I hate it.' 'No, I'll go on the pier. You can look at what the butler saw.'

The old woman's face, pink with cold behind the glass partition. Fourpence each. A few people fishing. All stared. She didn't belong. She was an enemy of ordinariness, ugliness. The sea like pewter, a tanker miles out, a black slender trail of smoke miles behind. Going somewhere hot.

She looked back at the small town, the miles of empty shingle, saw no beauty because it wasn't sophisticated. She was ashamed of England; no difficulty about betraying such a dull place, unimaginative people, for Max, who was ten times more *alive*. Seagulls wheeled about, bored stiff, as she was. Old posters from summer, faded blues, empty car parks, battered boats, paint cracked, holes in some. The smell of fish and a handful of people watching around the harbour wall as a small vessel came in.

Alexei, on the other hand, the fool, was moving in a trance, delighting in these absurd things. Everything was conditioned, she supposed, by this idiotic love, this tender infatuation for something not there, entirely in his persuaded head. Everything, he pointed out with tedious delight, like a child who hasn't seen things before, is marvellous (being related to you), and she enthused weakly while her eyes watered and nose moistened and she felt the useless compulsion to hurry, move on, to the next absurdity, excruciation. She was embarrassed by such unsophisticated gaucherie.

She sent postcards to sixty-seven people, and to most of them, not knowing what to say, she wrote with bitter humour, *It's only warm in bed,* but to Max she pleaded quickly, infidelity on her honeymoon, *Wish you were here.*

On the third day, soup at seven-thirty sharp, the chandeliers illuminating the mere thirty occupied tables, the old dears, bread – please, I love a bread roll with my soup – and pepper, hot – when my husband and I lived in the estate outside Rangoon ... The menu was in English. It pleased Alexei. He could identify himself with it: brown Windsor soup: made or grown, or whatever it was that happened to create soup, in Windsor, where the Queen lived sometimes. But the very language proved other things to Sheila.

A voice, miles away, outside the radius of light from the chandeliers, a child's voice, calling his name, 'Mr Antonov', approaching. There were only four men in the dining-room. Ninety-two people and only four of them male – it proved something about widowhood. It was wrong; surely a royal commission should be set up to save the old men? 'Mr Antonov?' the boy queried. The old lavender-scented bodies turned, eyes re-examined. Rumanian, or perhaps Hungarian. A film director presumably. Not married to *her*, of course. Disgusting. They permitted anything these days. Hard times, they'd claim; you had to take what came in the hotel business, not question personal integrity. There was no personal integrity these days. Complain to Mr Barrymore. Not frightened to move on: Brighton (no, not Brighton; too many Jews), Hove, then, or Eastbourne, Hastings, Folkstone.

'I am Mr Antonov.'

'Phone call for you,' the boy told him.

Sheila said, 'Who on earth can that be?'

The ninety-one faces watched for moments, while spoons descended. Don't wait; it'll go cold. Could we have some more bread? He looks worried, frightened. Not a film director after all. Nothing intimidates *them*, least of all ninety-one staring people.

'In there,' the boy pointed out by the desk, the tired flowers, lifts.

'Who is it?' Alexei asked.

'Comrade Antonov,' a male voice said in his ear along the miles – or was it yards? – of wire. The voice spoke in Russian. 'Comrade, we are watching you. We haven't forgotten you.'

Terror burst in his stomach, hotter than the pepper, soup.

'Who is that?' he asked, but no answer, a mechanical cessation.

The pure fright was calmed now by a feeling of relief. He was like a man who is very ill and frightened, but frightened mostly of the doctors, not the illness. And now a doctor had said there was no escape, no end to illness, and fear was crystallized, couldn't get worse. One could begin, however uselessly, to take a cure. I must be brave. Alexei thought, as she mistakenly believes I am. I must not tell *her*, but Mr Bellamy must know, protect us both, investigate. Think. A male voice, fluent, not a foreigner – I mean not an Englishman. Not young, not old. Remember that. How, he wondered in new shock, did he know I was at this place, in this hotel? Perhaps Mr Bellamy had a process to find that out. The time? Seven-forty.

He looked in the cracked, faded mirror and saw an opaque, green, terrified version of himself.

The boy was still somewhere about. A tip? Waiting for money? Such a long, difficult walk for him, a hundred feet at least.

'Was that a local call?'

'I dunno, sir.'

A very quick drink, and then back to the table and the cold soup, the first lies.

'Mr Simpson,' he explained.

'Oh no,' Sheila protested. 'Not some silly problem?'

'Just to ask if we were all right, happy.'

'You took a long time to tell him we are.'

The two faces stared at each other over the plates, the cruet, the sauces, smiled tentatively, two illusions.

3

SAM BELLAMY

SAM BELLAMY stood at a window on the seventh floor and looked down on the beginnings of the meeting. It was, he noted with pleasure, raining, but about three thousand people had so far turned up. He knew perfectly well what the organizers intended: they'd work the crowd into a frenzy, then the whole meeting would march to the Oogla Provinces Legation and smash as much of it as they could and dared. The sodden banners carried the mistaken, pessimistic messages, 'Long Live Tupoka' – 'Out with the Murderers' – 'Justice in the Oogla Provinces' – 'We Demand an Election' – 'Keep out UNO'. All rather fifth-form. But Bellamy was under no illusions: Bosambo's boys, Communist-trained – literally so, in the Soviet Union – knew their stuff. Already, despite the pouring rain, the crowd began to roar 'Tupoka!' The bulge of people swayed and billowed. In a few minutes it must take a direction. At least three thousand people, others arriving. Some coffee-bar intellectuals, many coloured people with private grievances, others out for excitement, the fun of the new-style metropolitan Sunday afternoon, a few there to prove they hated their own government (Britain always wrong). There were hundreds present with good intentions but thousands on fire with malice, anxious to inflame the afternoon, to show derision, to goad the police, to claim 'freedom' of opinion. All these knew better than God, considered themselves wiser than the laws moulded, incident by agonized, idealized incident, for a thousand years; these fell into every emotional trap the Communist and other agitators cared to contrive. It was their only emotional capability. For the rest they were deep in the apathy of what others thought on their behalf.

It was bitterly amusing. They did not know who had killed Tupoka or why. Thousands of people were killed every week in Russia and China. People who claimed the very small privilege of wanting privacy, to live in a room, to love their children – in

China they were killed or imprisoned by the million for the mere 'crime' of 'warm feelingism', 'parental love', or the 'repellent crime' of love itself; to hate the commune, the shed life, the crime of looking attractive, the weakness of wanting to stay at home, all commanded pain, humiliation, death. The intellectuals who shouted so hard down below had the freedom to do so. In China and Russia they disappeared, committed suicide, went insane, unmourned; it was too far away from Trafalgar Square. In Coventry that week seventeen thousand men were on strike because of a Communist-organized strike about laundries. (Bellamy had a copy of the distributed circular.) The eggheads who shouted all over London and marched to air and submarine bases and despised all things American had the freedom to do so precisely because of the existence of these and other bases. There was freedom in the street below only because Strategic Air Command existed. There was no other reason for its continuation.

All this Bellamy knew perfectly well, but he was a policeman and aware of the British 'chummy's' capabilities. England was not a country to be entirely proud of. The freedom to protest should be used. England had lost some kind of innocence: too much fabrication for consumer interests; a lost memory, like childhood, of earth, soil, sea, wisdom, affection, honesty, charity without the cheque-book. Overdrive and scampi, the ignorance behind four walls. The insulting stupidity, part identified, of things advertised: clean, expensive, better than others have; with sex thrown in to weaken resolve, prove it was a dirty world, only you and your neighbours were the fools not having fun. This was corruption from within, and with its parallels in art, in part justified the Communist cry of Decadent!

Bellamy was dedicated enough to care. He was without the tiredness, the sense of failure, and inevitable spoliation of the intellectual, the satirist, the newspaperman who'd seen too much. He had a kind of innocence in that he cared about things no longer mentioned. His dedication was overlaid by fifteen years' police work; prostitutes and violence and drunken sailors from ships in Southampton where he'd first moved into Special Branch. He knew degradation wasn't confined to concentration camps or the upheavals in Africa; it was here in London. Worse, it wasn't a product of violence or want; it was just an end in itself, a bored degradation – there was nothing 'better' to do.

Some of his men were down below, a part of the crowd, listening, watching, involved. Bellamy looked through binoculars to identify faces in all areas of the mass. The uniformed police were controlling the meeting. Two hundred of them to handle three thousand people. Twenty-five horses somewhere, ready to help. It was laughable, depended considerably on the rain, the fundamental fairness of chummy. Bellamy only wished to identify a face here and there. Who did the shouting, made the 'speech', who started the panic – if there was one – in which bystanders were hurt.

Some poor soul had arrived at the edges of the crowd in a small car with L plates. There was a hurried conference inside the saloon, a change of driver; the vehicle shot off backward. Bellamy smiled.

It was getting rough. Moving. Stones were being thrown; there were some screams, but the main cry was still the same hopeless one, 'Tupoka! Tupoka!' and a sudden surge toward the legation half a mile away.

Forty policemen stood in a line to stop three thousand. Sunday strollers, clearly shaken and alarmed, were swept into the crowd, which broke through the forty policemen, fighting. A constable went down, hit hard on the head (helmet fallen seconds earlier), and Bellamy worried, hot in the guts on behalf of the young man. The binoculars revealed that an excited coloured man had struck him with a banner. Bellamy identified the black face, worried further for that constable, but saw him being passed, unconscious, over heads, through the crowd. That was chummy, the British crowd. In Paris they'd have killed him, emasculated, smashed ribs.

They were booing and roaring, a few laughing, and there was panicky female screaming. A few fell, were lost, hurt. The forty policemen were joined at another edge of the crowd: flailing banners and fists, arrests, bodies taken to Black Maria vans. Peace in our time – all the symptoms. It was funny really, but Bellamy knew the potential: one 'martyr' and every paper in the land, especially the intellectuals', would hate the police; it would be a victory for Communism. Any hatred of law and order was a victory for Communism. It thrived on chaos, on carefully planned injustice.

Now the situation was beyond the two hundred, and the mounted police came out of side roads. Ten horses stood and moved against the wedge of thousands. It was possible, from Bellamy's high vantage point, to see thousands who didn't know about the horses pressing into the few hundred who did and were in retreat. These few were having a bad time of it and were in a panic. But the organizers had anticipated horses, and now thunder flashes exploded. One banged right under a horse's belly. The animal reared, but neither it nor its rider fell. A coloured man smashed a long banner across a horse's eyes, but it merely shook its head. A man stubbed a cigarette on a horse, and again, beautifully trained to overcome pain, it reared only a little. But now some animal expert poured marbles on the road, and a horse, treading on them, couldn't stand. It fell; the rider was pulled or fell. Bellamy, shaken, saw the beating he took, the faces and boos and jeers, the kick someone got in the chest from the animal. This was very rough, nasty. The other horses moved on; batons flailed, but inoffensively; people scattered. Hundreds of the three thousand had got through, but a small handful of policemen were waiting for them at the legation. There was some smashed glass, but they couldn't knock down the door.

It was ending, dispersing slowly, the propulsion fading, people scattering, perhaps ashamed, perhaps frightened, perhaps satisfied: their money's worth of freedom, their opinion expressed. Thirty-two had been arrested. Bellamy had identified five known faces, seen the agitation actions of three unknown.

He went home through the litter of broken banners, shoes, rain, hats, horse dung, posters, pamphlets, an ambulance or two, people still talking in small groups, red-faced policemen.

Simon was doing his homework, had been all this time. 'He should have done it yesterday,' Mary claimed angrily.

This was real, permanent, faintly astonishing, that Mary's anger should be genuine; her principles, confined to a household, were limited to Simon, Joan, and himself; so was her love. It was beautiful, moving, to think that there were millions like

Mary, only three thousand, this afternoon, of the others. It was up to him to keep it that way.

'There's a man rung. Three times.'

His telephone number was an unlisted one. Whoever had telephoned had the right to; it was relevant to work.

'Who was it?'

'Said his name was Antonov.'

A small man with a kind, frightened face, a political refugee – important, though, because of the spherical mathematics.

'About what?'

'He didn't tell me.'

'What's for tea?'

He hadn't seen the little man since his arrival in August. Threatening letters from some Communist organization, you could bet your life. There were twenty-seven thousand registered members of the Communist Party in Britain, but these were not regarded as so dangerous as those who had renounced Party membership or had never taken it up, or who swore or would swear they had no affinity with Communists. There were 400,000 foreigners of Slav origin resident in Britain, nearly all genuine refugees, but here and there, presumably, the dangerous hostile mind. This left out of account the Irish, bless 'em, and the coloured people who, Bellamy was aware, were sometimes approached, usually by vice gangs but occasionally by Communist organizations. Half a million foreigners, maybe more. A handful of genuine spies, from Russia, East Germany, Poland, Czechoslovakia. Seamen coming and going, tourists flying in and out. Two hundred or more people working at the Soviet Embassy – they couldn't all be followed to and from every party, dance, discussion, demonstration. Others in the Polish and Czech Embassies. There were two thousand people working for M.I.5, but the majority were office workers – screening people for Government work, nuclear physics, radar ... There were only a thousand Special Branch men and most of these at seaports and airports, checking the entry of undesirables. It needed at least eight men and women to follow someone about all day. There were thousands who might be legitimately followed. No. It was impossible, needed a police state.

The curious thing about counterespionage was that there was

no fixed point from which to start, no crime to investigate.
Sometimes there was a suspicion that a crime might be in progress, and its ramifications, if existing, had to be identified, individuals followed, suspicions not only confirmed but proved.
And the people who were the enemy had not the stupidity of the
average criminal; they were aware all the time of what might
be happening. A suspected person might have scores of in-
offensive contacts – butchers, doctors, librarians, friends who
knew nothing, neighbours who were neighbours in the accident
of place available. All had to be investigated carefully, without
their knowledge if possible, and a dossier gradually brought
into existence of who were guilty. It became like an epidemic.
As fast as one found a contact it was proof of the existence of
another, and you had to think and prove in terms of time and
place: on the 15th X was in Sheffield and on the 19th in
Birmingham; therefore he could have contacted Y who was
known to have been in Birmingham on the 19th. Watch, watch,
listen, see what happens, but do not let the wish to find guilt be
the cause; that would be to imitate the enemy . . .

Antonov phoned.

It was interesting.

Other things emerged.

The little man was married. To a model. Bellamy worried.
There were seven thousand models in London alone, and some
specialized in –

'She is famous,' the excited voice told him, overcoming the
fear of that other telephone call in Russian. 'Sheila Haward.
Bizarre and *Trend* and . . . You mustn't let her know. She
mustn't be frightened.'

A spy or traitor or double agent should never be conspicuous.
A woman as beautiful as Sheila Haward – Bellamy thought he
remembered the face – was least of all inconspicuous. Therefore it was quite certain the little man had merely been
lucky.

'Where are you speaking from?'

'We have half a house. The chaplain at the college, you see, is
not married –'

'You mean this is a party line?'

'Party line?'

'A shared telephone?'

'I do not know.'

Christ! thought Bellamy.

He saw the little man next morning. Ten o'clock, an empty café. Bellamy sat at a table with him. The man was frightened, he could see, but determined for all that. He played with brown sugar and a spoon, looked about anxiously, but answered question after question helpfully, truthfully, Bellamy was sure. What did the man say? How old do you think he was? Did he speak in perfect Russian? Was it a local call? Which hotel? The time? Who knew you'd be at that hotel? Everybody. Who was everybody? My wife had sent sixty cards two days before. And you? To whom did you send cards? Student, what student? Yes, it may be, but let's assume ... Have you seen him again? No? That telephone. Not party. Do you mind if we tap it? Another one? Oh, in the college. What extension? Anyone written threatening letters? Anybody phoned before? Any person, you feel, following you about? No, we won't listen to what your wife – or the chaplain! – says; straight out of one ear ... You can refuse if you ... That's most cooperative. I think, Mr Antonov, that they intend to frighten you. I think it may be possible that they want you to double on *us*. What do I mean? Well, that they may eventually threaten some kind of harm or may promise something conditionally ... I don't want to be brutal, but it may be relative to the safety of your parents. Have you heard from your parents? Not that angry, surely? Agreed, agreed, mail might be stopped. Well, now, bear it in mind and listen. If there's another phone call keep the man talking. We'll be on to it at once. We may even get a man around to the phone box – if it proves to be a phone box – in time to make an arrest. (Or follow, Bellamy thought: follow, follow, follow, just like the song.)

Nice little man, made you think what a pity the Cold War existed, for there must be others. Bellamy had the telephone call traced, and it had been made from a box at Victoria Station, which was not a thousand miles from the Soviet Embassy in Kensington. He had a very limited number of men to spare, but two of them tapped the telephone to the chaplain's pink-brick house in the college grounds. And on the third day they reported to Bellamy that Antonov's wife, married three weeks, was making passionate telephone calls to a man named Max Stuhler.

No fixed point. No crime committed. But it startled Bellamy, being out of character. It was not his business if the nice little man paid such an agonized price for having an exceptionally desirable wife. But it didn't really make sense. Three weeks was a bit too soon to be disillusioned, and the reported dialogue was odd: the woman spoke of her husband as if he was a fool, always had been of lesser value than this man called Max. In which case why had she married him at all? No money was involved. Then what was involved? Bellamy was conscious of the temptations of his work: how easy it was to interpret wrongly, become suspicious when one examined private lives, how very odd was human behaviour. Watch, watch, wait, listen. There was nevertheless something too hasty about Mrs Antonov's love affair, something brutal, sordid. Bellamy felt very sorry for the little man who would find out sooner or later. It was just possible that . . . If a woman entered espionage she was asked whether, in necessity and the line of duty, she would sacrifice her virginity. (It was assumed by British authority, for the most part correctly, that unmarried girls of middle and upper-middle class who entered the work still had their physical integrity.) It could perfectly well happen, then, that a girl in the enemy's ranks – Ridiculous. No, continue. That Sheila Haward was married to Alexei Antonov didn't necessarily mean – No. It *was* ridiculous. Time would explain. Watch, listen, follow. A surface investigation revealed only that Max Stuhler was a society photographer of high quality, and Sheila Antonov was a model of exceptional ability. She had the usual background of the type: father a colonel, schools in Cheltenham and Lausanne, no political ties at all; probably voted Conservative time after time without a thought, if she bothered at all. Bellamy left it at that, although the Russian-speaking sergeant and detective-constable still tapped Antonov's phone.

That was Sunday to Thursday. On Friday Bellamy was asked to go along to a suburban police station where a man had something rather curious to say.

There he met Mr Henry Evans, a stocky, irritated Welshman,

private investigator – a face that had the guilt of a thousand bedrooms, much unpleasantness.

'This is wasting a lot of my time ...'

'We regret that, Mr Evans. You could claim for expenses ...'

'The point is,' said Mr Evans, 'they ought to be able to make a note of it, my information –'

'The fact that I've been asked to talk to you indicates the value of your information,' claimed Bellamy not very modestly. 'Now, you say this girl –'

'It was for a client,' said Mr Evans. 'A kid of nineteen or twenty, nasty. His wife had walked out. He wanted her back, wouldn't admit it. Said she was with niggers. No. I said that. Call girl, I thought, being paid for fun. Don't suppose *he* paid her much. Want a divorce? I asked, but he wasn't sure. He wanted to know what the situation was, who was screwing her. Then he'd think about divorce. A masochist or something.'

'Would you like a cup of tea?'

'Yes, but no sugar.'

'And a cigar?'

'It ain't Christmas!'

'Not far off.'

'Very kind of you.'

'So you began to follow this girl?'

'It wasn't difficult. But it was bloody peculiar. She met a man, out of her class altogether, twenty years older, in the Tottenham Court Road. Hallo, I said, I was right. Call girl, extra pay and all that. They got in a taxi. I was lucky, found another, followed 'em to Victoria. They stood there a few minutes, got another, went as far as Clerkenwell Road. No kissing, nothing, just talking. She had a bit of paper in one hand, read from it. She got out, caught a bus, went home. Nuts! It happened again and again, once a week. Sometimes I couldn't get a taxi to follow. I got fed up with her, decided to follow him.'

The point emerged that the man went nowhere. He took a bus, a tube, another tube, the same journey backward. His behaviour, not conspicuous if you merely passed him, became very odd if you followed him. He was a hard man to follow. He'd get in a tube train and jump out, change his mind, catch a different tube train, and all the time he looked, at times literally, over his shoulder. Mr Evans still hadn't found out what was the man's final destination. His behaviour, the same every time, was not a change of mind; it was a technique.

Mr Evans was only a private investigator, but he had an idea what this technique indicated.

'Anything else?'

'I'll say there is,' Mr Evans boasted. 'Listen. This kid who's my client says she gave *him* a fiver. It was a shock to him, out of character. Then he was worried, very bothered, because she'd been for a holiday to Germany, to meet some bloke. Pen friend, she'd told him. The things they think of! Then there was the Excellence Hotel. Again, I said to myself, out of her class. Call-girl work, must be.'

'She went to the Excellence?'

'Yes. Well, in my work you've got to have cheek, so I sat in the lounge, had a drink. She met some man again, all wrong, not the vice type.'

Bellamy smiled at such a confident identification.

'I didn't go in to dinner with 'em,' continued Mr Evans. 'Wouldn't be fair to my client. But I saw them when they came out. They separated in the Strand. No kisses, not even a touch of hands.'

'Couldn't it be an arrangement, introduction? Does she live alone?'

'Lives with a couple.'

'Did you follow this man at all?'

'Of course I did. Got to get names and addresses for my client, solicitor, all that. And the other one had been too quick. I don't know what this one's name is either.'

'But you know his address?'

'The Soviet Embassy.'

'I see.' Bellamy had difficulty in remaining calm. 'And it was not the man – the Tottenham Court Road one?'

'No. Fat, dark little bugger. Walks with a limp.'

'Where does this girl work?'

'World Mechanical. She's a telephone operator.'

'Mr Evans,' said Bellamy carefully, 'you've certainly found something odd going on. We'll take it from there. It can be innocent, you understand – they can have friends at the Soviet Embassy – but that business about taxis and tubes is very disturbing.'

'What can I tell my client?'

'Just tell him the truth – that she's not committing adultery with anyone.'

'He'll never pay me. He probably won't anyway.'

'Doesn't she have any ordinary boy friends? Dancing, walks in the park, that sort of thing?'

'There's two or three.'

'Well, then . . .'

Mr Evans stayed another hour. Question followed question: times, places, his face, the Excellence, dialogue, were you seen, any photographs available of the girl? And the nice thing about Mr Evans, although you could hardly tell him so, was that he was small, gross, and looked like a man in a cheap boozer. The last thing he resembled was a Special Branch officer.

No starting point.

There had to be the possibility of a crime, not the result of one. It was all vague, but it was suspicious. World Mechanical, a journey to Germany, friends at the Soviet Embassy, a friend who talked only in a taxi and had the technique of a secret-service operator in throwing off anyone trying to follow, a girl with a sudden small abundance of money, enough to cause impulsiveness, carelessness. Bellamy was pleased, confident; this was the tentacle of something. Watch and follow, listen, ask questions here and there, collect evidence, times and places, a long list of coincidences; follow, follow, follow, contact after contact, eliminate some, suspect others, follow them, additional contacts. Not easy. They were careful. You were still a police officer, had not only to find evidence but to prove it. A nice-looking girl of nineteen, walked out on a vicious husband, answering the telephone, the whole nation, several nations, depending on her honesty. A small, parental part of Bellamy hoped she was innocent.

4

MAGGIE PRESTON

'WHAT I want to know,' reiterated Vera in the manner of one who merely desired confirmation, 'is where's she getting this money from?'

Eggy swilled tea into the gross, Sunday-unshaven face, pinkened its jaundiced colour with heat; he touched the fried egg gently. 'What money?' His expression was evasive. He didn't wish to be involved in an argument about Maggie. He didn't want Maggie to go; a little tenderness, some teasing, some lies to please him, a kiss or two, Sunday's portion was often his: the view of her in the bathroom in panties, in the bedroom pulling on a skirt, changing stockings in the kitchen – 'Now, Eggy, mustn't look,' but not caring if he did. The long, reckless face all his, the crazy, wonderful eyes staring without reserve into his, a hint of something : if you were twenty years younger I'd give you a whale of a time ... He was ill, tired, stale in the flesh; just the small, delicate proportion that was his, that was all he asked.

'Oh my God,' complained Vera loudly, 'you can be stupid. She's getting it from somewhere.'

'Who says so?' he asked dully.

'I do,' Vera told him, 'and if you weren't a bit silly in the head about her you'd see it, too.'

He hadn't known Vera was conscious of it. 'Stop yelling like a bloody barmaid. What if she has a bit extra? Who cares?'

'She's living here damn cheap, that's who cares. I'm just a skivvy. I work all day and then have to cook for her and her boy friends come barging in and out when they like. It's not good enough.'

Maggie walked in ...

A little pink – she'd heard; a silent approach because in her dressing gown and slippers.

Vera was clever, but Maggie had the effortless advantage of being in a dream world : lies didn't matter. If happiness was available she would plead, stare in the face; so intently would she desire that the lies became truth, and invariably she would begin, hope for conviction, with the word 'honestly'.

'Morning, Vera. Morning, Eggy,' she said meekly. 'Honestly, Vera, I did oversleep.'

'I don't mind,' said Vera in confusion.

'Honestly, Vera, I'm happy here, and I'm sorry if I'm doing something wrong.'

She had obviously overheard something.

'Sit down, love, before your bacon goes cold,' urged Eggy. He didn't want a row; whose side would he take? Vera paid the bills.

But Maggie stood by the cheap wooden mantelshelf. 'You're mad with me,' she accused softly, the sincerity of the voice and face not indicating any of the turmoil in the pretty head. What did they know?

'I'll be frank,' said Vera. She always was 'frank', which meant cruel, brutal. 'We don't want to pry into your affairs, but we know you're getting more money these days and you're not really contributing a lot *here*.'

'You want me to go?'

'No. We just feel ...' Maggie could see that Vera's 'we' meant nothing. Eggy sat there, hoping she'd stay, this would end amicably – nice old Eggy, she'd kiss him later. 'We just feel if your wages have improved you ought to help more. And you don't do much about the flat,' she got in quickly.

'Oh, Vera, that's not true. I often cook the meals. I'll do today's,' Maggie offered quickly. 'What is it?'

'Beef,' said Vera, 'but that's not the point.'

'But, Vera, darling, it's only a little flat and there's not all that much to do ...'

'All those boys who keep coming leave plenty of mess ...'

'You don't mind Mick and Ray? I thought you liked them. Honestly, I thought they cheered old Eggy up, a drink of beer ...'

She was difficult to defeat.

'There's still the money,' persisted Vera.

'Oh, *that*,' Maggie said lightly. 'Well, I sold an old ring of my mother's. I was never so surprised in my life, honestly. I laughed and laughed. They offered me a hundred pounds. *A hundred pounds!*'

'Your mother's ring?'

It was a criticism.

'Well, no, not really. Her sister's, but she gave it to Mum to give to me when I was twenty-one, but she died and Mum gave it to me when I was sixteen. Listen Vera,' Maggie pleaded, 'I'll pay an extra ten bob a week. I did get a small rise at World Mechanical, and you've been *so* good. Honestly, I don't know what I'd have done without you.'

She was very careful to keep her 'you' singular; she'd heard that bit about 'if you weren't a bit silly in the head about her'. Nasty, Vera was, a mean streak. If Eggy was affectionate did it mean he was unfaithful? As if she'd let old Eggy do anything. Why, he smelled very slightly. He was an old dear; she pitied him, especially married to that vinegar. Oh, Lord, Mick was coming at ten!

Vera couldn't think of any way to alter the situation. The anger inside her had confirmed that it wasn't, as she had almost believed, a question of money; it was all this flightiness, and Eggy like a great wallowing fool.

'All right,' she conceded. 'But keep your room tidy – that's what I can't stand.'

'I'll wash up,' Maggie contributed.

'You're in your dressing gown.'

'Vera, you're not mad any more?'

'No, no.'

'You must tell me if there's anything else.'

'There's nothing.'

'I'll go out later. We'll have a bottle of wine, celebrate.'

'Celebrate what?'

'I dunno! We're friends again.'

'You are a funny girl.'

'Vera, I think Mick's coming. Do you mind?'

'No, but I don't know what you see in him.'

'I don't either!' Maggie giggled. 'I can't get rid of him! But I've got a new friend. He's at college. He's rich – well, his father is – a South African. He takes me to concerts and theatres. He writes poetry.'

'He doesn't give you money?' Vera asked anxiously.

'Whatever do you mean?'

'All that stuff about a ring – you never showed it to me.'

'*Of course not*, because it was kept by solicitors. Vera, I'm hurt. You think I'm a cheap beatnik or something. Do you think after Frank I'd let anybody –'

She sniffed, turned away.

Vera was hot and bothered, believed her. 'Maggie, I'm sorry. I believe you. But you're so *crazy*. I worry about you. You've no mum and no husband ...'

'Let me do the dinner.'

'No. Don't be silly. If Mick's coming, you ought to be dressed.'

In the bathroom, dressing gown off, Eggy caught her, whispered, 'She was mean. You stay as long as you like. Stay forever,' and his eyes feasted on the long, slightly bandy legs in panties, the bare shoulders. If he hadn't been so ill she would have driven him crazy. He touched the bare shoulder – no resistance. It was cool, goose-pimples forming; the arms, they were without opposition. The long, reckless face, granting him Sunday's proportion, smiled, whispered, 'Are you mad, Eggy? She's only in the kitchen.' He was hot in the face – those legs, the indifferent eyes, the implication if she'd been further away than the kitchen ... His sweating hands ran along the silk; the body inside wriggled, threw him off lightly. 'A kiss,' he pleaded. 'A kiss, Maggie, love.' And his hand smacked her nylon bottom, stayed recklessly, while the wild mouth below the straight, fine, untruthful eyes kissed him. Sunday's portion. 'Be off, you naughty old man.' He lingered at the door, his heart pounding, his face red, a bit of a headache – he was in such a condition of tumult. A good kid, generous, no harm done, Sunday's bit of luck, keeps me alive. I felt ill, better now, hot with life for those seventy or a hundred seconds. If only I was young, those legs, the slight bandiness fascinated. By God, whoever had her was lucky; that Frank was a bloody fool.

'Lend us a quid, Maggie,' was his next plea. 'She's mean with me, too.'

'All right, but get out of here.'

Washing the slender neck, the white shoulders, the arms,

Maggie began to worry about money. Honestly, if the income tax didn't take it, someone else did. If only a second phone call would come, someone'd mention Billiards.

Why not? she thought.

Her desirable body felt colder in the shock of the idea. Why not? No. It was too dangerous. She remembered the small boat on the Neckar, the feeling of helplessness as Dieter and Horst talked of 'trade'. But that was Germany. England was different, safer. Besides, if these activities were ever investigated, uncovered – she didn't really believe they would be: how could you tell what two people talked about in a taxi? – she could claim, 'I was trapped, honestly, terrified, and so I gave them false information.'

The beauty of the situation fascinated her. It covered every single aspect of her world – the dream world and the remote world of actuality. She wouldn't do it often – once in three months. It had an irresistible perfection: whatever happened she would be right. If she mentioned the name of some big company Henry's organization would be lost in its ramifications, wouldn't be able to prove she was a liar. And some day, if a policeman asked, 'Why, then, did you accept the hundred pounds?' she would claim, 'I had to, didn't I, to be convincing?' Then he'd ask, 'What did you do with it?' and she could say, 'I'm awfully sorry, I spent it!' It was so funny she shook with amusement before the mirror. The nice thing about it was that she was paid for information, nothing more. It didn't have to be proved.

In her bedroom she decided to wear slacks: that would halt Mick's attempting hands. Out of the window she saw people strolling, standing about, entering church. The church bell began to plead, and in the rat race of traffic, ignoring the plea, she identified Mick's Midget. Maggie examined the face in the mirror. There was no vanity in it, just the wild impulse to be alive. Honestly, why they went crazy about it she didn't know. How much was a bottle of wine? Sixteen bob? Perhaps Mick would pay; he'd get a free dinner, Sunday afternoon's portion.

'Here's Mick.'

'I'm coming,' she called.

Her heart fluttered in impending pleasure. She didn't love him, but he was fun; he'd got it bad, too, poor thing. But he wasn't clever like Geoff. Did Geoff's father really have a lot of money, or was that one of the everlasting series of tricks they all tried to get her into 'trouble'?

She went back into the living room, all energy, haste, things needed, dropped, to be collected, decided: an impression, rendering Mick too dazed to do more than follow the day as she propelled it, an impression that there were many urgent things to do, but, as he was here, he could stay, be involved for a time, sneak a kiss or two if she wasn't too busy. His eyes, slaughtered by failure to capture her – time after time she failed to be pinned, although sometimes capture, experiment, was partially obtained – his eyes were disappointed to see the slacks. Opportunity was limited already, conditions arranged; the brief moments that would be his this day were restricted to what had been obtained before.

'We've got to get a bottle of wine,' she told him. 'You can stay to dinner. We're celebrating. It's beef. Red wine, that right, Eggy?'

'Claret,' said Eggy knowledgeably.

'What are we celebrating?' Mick asked.

'I dunno!'

A normal explanation from Maggie – no logic in it, but an explanation seized, like an unexpected invitation, a wild beckoning to be alive within the limiting factors: the flat, the money, the world, her strange, comparative faithfulness to that lousy husband. She would include him in her life if he'd accept her terms, and Mick accepted them, begged for new ones now and again, but would in fact accept any so long as he could participate in the life of her who was so exceptional, beautiful, mad.

'My gloves,' she now asked the world, 'where are my gloves?' as if the tiny flat were a palace of acres. 'Is it cold out?'

On the stairs Mick had to stop her, pull, seize; he felt clumsy and stupid (as she intended he should), like a man who grasps the wind. He kissed her ears, her neck, just missed her mouth. She wasn't involved, merely asked, 'What's all that about?' and was moving on all the time: brighter things were ahead; she must run to find them – the pace wasn't fast enough.

The crowd came out, still warm, talkative, bursts of laughter, smoke followed. An inexplicable play, significant, important, but the crowd wasn't fooled: brilliant dialogue, dirt, that was all. They moved on – brittle amusement, that was that.

Geoff took Maggie's arm.

'What did you think?'

She was not, like Joan, intimidated by sophistication, overcome by art. She was honest, straightforward, didn't give a damn. God, he thought, I've never met anyone like this, and he was proud, wanted to show her to others.

Maggie, answering, told him, 'I thought it was crazy. And so *rude*!' She didn't mind though.

Geoff abandoned the dialogue collected, rehearsed during Acts I and II. He could be honest, too – well, fairly honest.

'Yeah, he's a screwball all right. When Oakley said – and she pulled the chain. Laugh! You realize the significance of that? Brilliant, absolutely brilliant. I shall see it again.'

'Where are we going?' she asked, female, practical.

'Listen,' Geoff pleaded. 'We're not all that far from the college. Come and meet my pals. They'll be in the pub.'

'I'm hungry,' she objected, but added quickly, 'I'd like to.'

The bus was packed. She slipped on the dark pavement. Geoff lifted her bodily on to the bus platform. A few people stared; someone said 'Blimey!' Geoff wasn't concerned; Maggie didn't mind either. It was almost impossible to embarrass her – she was too fey, happy, in love with life.

'I'm strong,' Geoff told her. 'Too strong. And complicated. I get mixed up. I was psychoanalysed.'

Maggie was fascinated. 'What was it like?'

His hand went around her waist, steadied her, as the bus turned a corner, and the hand stayed. 'The usual stuff, Father and mother. Sex. I have to take a little red pill now and again to counteract mental strain. I often study until two in the morning.'

'Why?' she asked. 'Why, when your father's got money?' It was absurd! 'You could –'

'You've got to have freedom, personal freedom. Like Oakley in *Snooz* when he killed his mother. Agreed?'

'Well, I suppose so. But not to kill your mother!'

'I write, you know,' he told her. Maggie was subtle enough, experienced enough to recognize that this was all shyness, not arrogance; he wanted a high estimation; he had the fever badly. It was pitiful, lowered his status; college became meaningless. 'Poetry, mostly. A few essays. Not published here. I have to have it published abroad. I had dinner only the other evening at the Excellence with a cultural attaché . . .'

They stared at each other, hypnotized, fully aware in a charged atmosphere of something else in common, more than love, the beginnings and hopes of one-sided passion. People trod on their feet, bells rang, they were thrown about, seats became available, but they didn't take them.

She said, 'Geoff! I've been there, too.'

He was frightened, pale with it, and she was touched, for it was all on her behalf.

'Christ, Maggie, you don't know what you're doing.'

'It's all right, Geoff. Honestly, it's only about trade, things like that.'

He stared at her face, inches away, the splendour of the red hair, the burning, frenzied wonderful eyes that outstared his. She was unbelievable; how clever he was to find her! And she was excitable, pleased, humorous, not like Joan with that whining. She was so honest, confessed what she didn't understand. His bowels were hot in the rush of emotion : I love her; this is it.

'You mustn't. Listen. Let's get off, walk. It's not far.'

She found this acceptable despite high heels.

'Honestly, Geoff, nobody can find out. What do you do?' she asked with qualms, in the privacy of night, wet air, impending rain. People passed, yawned, spat in the gutters, laughed; louts and tarts, old fools, gleaming cars; nothing mattered, intimidated; he loved her. Yes, he decided, he'd loved Joan, but this was the real stuff; he was totally involved, personality, flesh, the lot. And they were fellow-conspirators against the world, its sneers and rejections; his was literary and mental, the hatred in the library and dining-hall; hers was – what was hers? 'I'm married,' she had told him in a cinema when he'd tried to feel her legs. She wasn't cheap, despite the electrifying sensuality.

'What about your husband?' he asked. 'Does he know?'

'I'm separated,' Maggie told him, eyes and head dropped in shyness, humiliation.

At once Geoff felt a surge of confidence. She was mortal, a failure. He'd make her. His face flushed in anticipation, the certainty. In the darkness she failed to detect the alteration in his eyes, the deterioration of awe, respect. Separated, therefore her private life was a mess. A mess meant you could take advantage. She's hot, his mind assured him, not very logically, and his body was already responding to this imaginary heat. In a few minutes, other things permitting, he would be trying to feel her thighs, make substantial claims. It was a heavy price that Maggie had to pay for private unhappiness – if she'd allowed unhappiness to gain control as Frank did. It had taken courage to walk out on Frank and his drunken viciousness. Now she was punished by dirty thoughts for trying to be decent, survive what Frank had done. Anyone less resilient would have given way, wallowed in dirty pleasure; but, slender and fragile and fey, she survived, enjoyed herself, kept all the sly intentions from becoming sordid reality. There was not much logic or morality in it; it was just personal female dignity.

'What do you do?' she repeated.

'Nothing,' he answered rather weakly. 'They've told me to stop for the time being.'

'What's South Africa like?' she inquired, a touch of something telling him the way her thoughts ran; he was on fire with the possibilities: she wanted him, to go to the Union. If she wanted *that* she'd be easy; the mind sweated.

'Beautiful,' he reassured her. 'Hot, magnificent. Like you,' he declared.

'I'm not a bowl of porridge,' she said.

'You're not inhibited?' he asked, a touch of snobbery; wiser, he knew, than she. 'The psycho boys told me all about that. People can go crazy because they stick to the rules.'

She was evasive, uninterested. 'I'm crazy already. What's the time?'

'I'll see you home in a taxi,' Geoff promised, planning a wild ride, something claimed at the other end. Where did she live? Alone? 'We won't stay long. A drink or two.'

'Some food,' she requested.

They were there – well, some of them – in the hot assembled atmosphere, among the old dears in black. Small bright lights, glitter of glass, faces reflected, bloodshot Negro eyes stared, stung by the smoke. Voices, voices, the privilege of uninformed opinion. And by the bar, eloquent, supreme, Sam, Tharp, George, that bastard Tom Inman, and Ritchie, one of the queers. Inman noticed; even before the door closed he'd peeled her clothes off with his eyes, attracted the attention of the others with some astonished aside: strewth, look what Geoff's brought in! God, what talent, what a face, hair on fire, and bandy but marvellous legs.

All except Ritchie were touched at once with the fever, and perhaps she caught it, too; perhaps she carried it with her all the time, incurable. She wasn't vain, not more than slightly conceited, but within her was some property that responded, effervesced, when masculine attention was aroused, brought out all the zany quality in her, and from there it was mad progress, a multitude, indeed a surplus of friendships. And then all the complicated evasive words and actions to cope with a timetable that must include all of them (she couldn't bear to leave anyone out, let him go away sour), and the childlike innocence that wished and managed to survive, enjoy, without 'trouble'.

They all talked like mad to her, showed off, laughed; admiration even ricocheted on to Geoff: if he could find this then he couldn't be such a clot, could he?

'*Snooz*? You went to see *Snooz*? Oh, God, isn't it crazy?' This was Tharp, never a hypocrite about culture. His eyes shone with excitement; his very beard was part of his parody, imitation. 'And what, Oakley, is the significance of significance? In the name of God – ah, no, they didn't say God, did they? I'm forgetting the whole point of the thing! In the name of Snooz, why have you cut your mother's head off? Honest, Maggie, did you ever see such a load of tripe?'

Ritchie qualified, 'It had its merits, I considered.'

Geoff sneered, 'You would!' which made Maggie flinch, for in her environment people didn't talk like that.

There was a barmaid there, all blonde and pulchritude and jangling bracelet. 'Well,' she said, arriving, 'I do feel I've been jilted.'

'One more all round,' Geoff ordered, generous, forgetting yesterday's barbed remarks, the herd, the very world he'd betrayed, in intention and no doubt in tiny contribution.

'Geoff, you said – I mean, I'm *hungry*,' Maggie reminded, giggled.

'Pork pie and onions,' Barbara explained. 'All we've got.'

They all bellowed, 'Not onions,' but Maggie put on her most naïve face and asked, 'Why not? I love onions.'

'Oh hell,' Geoff said later, outside. 'It's raining.'

They were all saying good-byes. 'We'll see you again, Maggie?' and someone suggested, 'At Geoff's twenty-first.' Half a mile's trot, breathless, to find somewhere where taxis flowed, could be captured. Puffed, she said, 'I like them,' wanting to please him, true nevertheless – they were likeable, funny, too clever for her, made her dizzy with jettisoned ideas.

'Some of 'em are okay.'

He found it unbearable to tell her *they* were why he had committed treason; better to maintain the illusion that he was popular, loved by all. (Girls took fright otherwise.) In the taxi, wet clothes, beer on his breath, the scent of onions, her sherry, he smothered her at once. 'Maggie Maggie, listen, be serious. Did anyone ever tell you –'

'I thought you were over twenty-one,' she said.

'I'm old enough,' he asserted, pulled her. His hands became wet, cold, on the rain spots of her coat. He kissed hard. 'That's for nothing. Now start something!' And he grinned, explained, 'I'm not drunk, just crazy, Maggie. It's serious,' he qualified. 'I've never met anyone like you. I love you.' He got it out at last.

'You shouldn't,' Maggie said, terrifying him. 'I haven't the freedom yet to love anyone,' and this, with its hint of possibilities, gave him confidence. 'But you will?' he asked vaguely, and he was strong, insistent, held her; his hand was between her legs.

'You bet!'

But she wasn't alarmed even then, just moved slightly, told him calmly, as if it was relative to the here and now (as, perhaps, it should have been): '*Honestly*,' she qualified, perfect face and large eyes seen in the meagre light from street lamps, cars, still-illuminated shops, 'you can't Geoff. I'm married, you see. If anyone saw, the driver – we're in a taxi,' she giggled. 'You'd be in trouble, divorce court. Your career would be in danger, think of that.'

He did not care a damn but slowed, aware that they were in a taxi. Wait. She'd invite him in.

'To hell with my career,' he said, stunned by the proximity of her, the weight of her softness in his strength; she accepted that. 'I shall go back to South Africa anyway. What will you do?' he asked abruptly.

'About what?'

'You can't go on with telephones forever. It's dangerous, the other part.'

'It depends,' she told him vaguely. That was next year, the year after; today was what she coped with: money, collect the money, avoid Frank, have fun, live, travel, dress, buy a watch . . .

It was a long ride, cost him twelve shillings. On the wet pavement she invited awkwardly, 'You want to come in?'

'You bet!'

She lived in a flat in a great ugly Victorian house that smelled slightly. There were scores of doors, numbered. A nigger put his face out of one, smiled. Maggie said, 'Good night, Mr Mohammed.'

'Okay,' the nigger said. 'Plenty of rain, sure.'

On the stairs – the structure of the banisters frail, trembling at his slightest pressure – Geoff pleaded, 'You don't speak to niggers, do you?'

'He lives here.'

'It's not right. If he tries anything I'll –'

'Don't be silly. His wife and kids –'

'You don't understand, Maggie. You haven't lived among them.'

This seemed contradictory, but she just said, 'It's different in England.'

They had arrived, door number six, and in disappointment Geoff saw a streak of light underneath it, heard voices behind the old wood. Inside, it was cheap, rubbishy furniture, no books, the paintings hopeless, so stupid. But theirs, presumably, not hers.

A big slob of a man in shirt sleeves, swilling booze, and a vicious small woman, quite well dressed, hair done like a tart. Common, Geoff analysed, and stupid like that woman, Maud or whatever her name was. He felt confidence in abundance. He was above them in money, brains, family: they were like niggers. Maggie looked too beautiful, out of place in the shabby room. He'd marry her, take her back to South Africa. She'd come – anyone would. He'd never find anyone like her again. Crazy and wonderful, she drove him mad, always would, but what an experience, when he caught her, obtained reciprocation.

'This is Geoff.'

'How do you do?'

'A drink, kid?' the fat slob invited. Geoff could have struck him for saying 'kid'.

He said, 'Yes, thanks,' in order to stay, see Maggie, to delight in the very movements of her, the turn of her head to a mirror, her moving body, hands picking up something. 'Oo!' she cried like a child in pleasure 'A letter from Germany.' Geoff caught the flicker of shock, guilt, in her eyes and was anxious; a man, a soldier presumably.

This slob Eggy and the small bitch Vera talked pretentious rubbish, asked questions, analysed his answers, proved themselves ridiculous. He felt fine, above them. He despised them, but there was safety here, he decided, for Maggie. How long did a divorce take?

Quite soon it was past midnight; he had ten miles to go, perhaps walk. 'I don't care; I keep fit.' She saw him to the door, beyond it, gave him his portion, not wanting him to leave too frustrated, angry. 'Maggie,' was his final plea of the night, 'when I go back to South Africa, come with me. We could say, if you weren't divorced – no one'd know, and if you were –'

It was, presumably, a roundabout proposal of marriage, caught even her off guard. 'I'll think about it,' she promised him, truthfully enough, amazed, flattered a little, but quite able behind door number six to laugh about him, agree with Vera's bitter analysis : 'He's a conceited bugger. He didn't think much of *us*!'

Six o'clock, dark, and pouring with rain. Henry couldn't get a taxi. People hurried along the pavement in the thousands, heads down, saturated; water ran off their hats and umbrellas. All the shops were still illuminated, some open. January sales. Maggie's attention drifted to the windows; senseless, charming things caught her eye, her mind, became relevant, necessary.

'Do we have to get a taxi?' she asked.

Henry was flustered : something slightly wrong, not proceeding correctly. 'It's safer. We could walk to –'

'Who do you think –?'

She wasn't frightened. It had become a habit, a game, a way to earn money, a recognized part of her income; soon she'd be careless.

'Who can see us in the dark?'

'You don't seem to care,' Henry chided.

'If we stood in a doorway – I don't want a cold,' she complained.

'I don't like it,' Henry said. 'Movement is the essential element.' But the rain and the crowds were too much for him. 'You shouldn't have picked Oxford Street,' Maggie reprimanded.

'I try to be helpful.'

'Henry, if we stood *here* –'

'All right, all right!'

They stood by a shop, wandered down an avenue of glass; on the other side were raincoats, travel rugs, suitcases, shoes. 'I'd like some like those,' Maggie told him, but Henry was a true Communist, protested, 'You talk rubbish,' and then, in a more serious aside, 'Well, quickly, what was it?'

'It was Strang Chemicals in Liverpool. They asked for instructions about content for Billiards.'

'Asked whom?'

'Ballistics, of course.'

'Why "of course"?'

'I don't know. It sounds right.'

'It sounds *wrong*,' Henry said, terrifying her. But his worries were elsewhere, technical. 'Surely, if they've fired one, that's fundamental . . . What else?'

'Mr Reynolds said a manual was in preparation.'

'At World Mechanical?'

'I don't know, Henry, *honestly*. You said be careful, and I had two more calls come through then.'

'If a manual was in preparation, who would prepare it?'

'How do I know? I'm a telephone operator. I wouldn't know *anything*.'

'Can you find out?'

'If I hear anything –'

'No. Find out. Get one.'

'Honestly, Henry, that's impossible. I'm in a little room. You talk about risks! Will I see the major again?'

'It's too risky. They probably keep an eye on the embassy. Haven't you got a boy friend there, someone clever?'

'I only see the representatives now and again.'

'Get to know one.'

'Honestly, Henry, they only sell *soap*.'

'We'd give a lot for that manual.'

'We don't really know if World Mechanical will do this manual. And if they do, the printing work's done in Glasgow,' she told him, anxious to be rid of this insoluble problem.

Other faces stared from behind opaque, wet glass; voices talked, criticized, and the roar of traffic never stopped. Two middle-aged women wandered around the corridor of glass, keeping dry, comparing values: 'Three guineas for *that*. I like these shoes though,' and the other one: 'They haven't got them in fives.'

Henry didn't like it; he was a worrier; espionage had tired his face, lined it like a road map. He crushed against her without passion, his breath slightly flavoured, distasteful, a bad lunch, confided in visible steam into her right ear: 'Here's the money. Thanks, Maggie. Get more detail about that manual. We'll see to Liverpool.'

'How much?' she asked. It felt thin, this envelope, and it was as if they'd read her mind.

'Fifty.' He said, 'I got to get a taxi, got to,' and his eyes searched in despair among the Fords and Wolseleys that threw mud.

'Only fifty?' she complained. 'It doesn't get easier.' All those lies, the risks, for fifty. It wasn't fair. 'Last time he gave me a hundred.'

'I was only authorized –'

'Honestly, I take such risks –'

'For the cause,' he insisted. He'd forgotten, or had never known, that she didn't give a damn for the cause; dialectic materialism, Maggie might have claimed ... 'You don't pay tax,' Henry pointed out like an accountant. 'There's a taxi!' he cried, a capitalist gesture of the hands, in a hurry to leave, as if her best friends and not his needed the courage to inform. He was ankle deep in the wet gutter, inside the taxi, a hundred yards away, before she could even voice an opinion. Silly thing, she thought moodily, like an employee about her employer; he takes it so seriously.

That was over. She was relieved. When a possibility had retreated a few streets away Maggie had the enviable ability to believe it nonexistent. She relaxed now – not that she'd been very frightened; Henry was poor material for intimidation. Besides, Strang's Chemicals *had* telephoned – about soap or something. She was calm now, the lies, as usual, confused with the truth, accepted; neither had the smallest reality; it was faintly surprising that Henry and the major existed, were real. The point was, money was found for Maggie Preston.

Her eyes and brain became interested in the shops. She wandered in the rain, found one open, feminine, glittering. There'd be something. Ah, yes, there was – beautiful, the right colour. Made somewhere in the world particularly for her: the conviction was so total that she could believe the desired object had been made in Italy with the specific thought in mind, 'This will suit Maggie Preston'. Therefore it was right, the lies and treason justified, ignored now, forgotten already; it was right to buy it. She opened the gilt door and entered.

MAX STUHLER

SHEILA walked, her carriage professional, graceful, along the specified catwalk, pivoted, smiled, strolled away. The announcer, facing a second camera, talked toward it. Fourteen technicians, shirt-sleeved, some with headphones, stood, watched critically for failure – theirs, not hers. The producer, also shirt-sleeved, was standing outside the fierce circle of illumination, a whispered conversation with a girl – his, presumably – who sat in a chair.

The air was stale, dirtied, hot, although the studio was nearly as big as a cinema – it had intimidated Sheila only slightly. Now Elizabeth paraded with slow grace across the arc of the camera, gyrated, turned, took off the jacket in the very rotation, proceeded toward Sheila. Sheila now showed the new coat. A little man was on his knees, rather alarming, as if something had gone wrong. He held a card, thrust it into the line of vision: 30. Thirty seconds to go.

The announcer was concluding: 'With this new material Britain can capture markets all over the world. And with pretty English girls like these to model them, who can doubt that we shall do so?'

I do, Sheila thought; the blasted stuff tears like tissue paper. And Elizabeth's Welsh, not English. Not to worry. Three hours they'd pithered about, talking, rehearsing. Five minutes live and a ridiculous little fee. Now there was some canned nonsense on and the fourteen technicians were beginning to relax. Sheila tiptoed toward the producer. 'Darling, you were marvellous,' he whispered. The all-in wrestler, who had been the other third of this weekly series, was standing about nearby, waiting to go home. The woman being interviewed in the street in the canned third was saying, in complete contrast to the poise and sophistication which Sheila and Elizabeth had shown, 'What? Me go in an airyplane? Whaja think I am? A seagull?' And that was that, all over. Start again.

The fourteen technicians yawned, took off headphones. One, more cheeky than the others, came over and pleaded, 'Can I have your autograph?' and Sheila, ready to smile, acquiesce, giggled, for the youth wanted the signature of the all-in wrestler. Didn't know the poor man could write, Sheila thought.

The producer and the girl in the chair and a man called Mr Maclean and two others began to move somewhere; Elizabeth and Sheila followed.

'Mr Morris,' said the producer to the all-in wrestler, 'we'll be in the bar.'

'I don't drink,' said the all-in wrestler.

'Well, thank you, thank you anyway ... You'll have one, just one?' he half pleaded to Sheila.

'Only one,' Sheila committed herself. 'Mustn't get bleary-eyed.'

'I suppose not. Wasn't she marvellous? She went on five minutes after that stuff about the sea gull, you know. When you get them natural like that, TV's a marvellous medium. It's not easy, you know.'

They were ascending steps, treading over cables, past lights; the air was still stale, hot, the light artificial, forever.

'No, I suppose not.'

'It's a fortnight's hard work,' the producer said. 'We all get ulcers. One mistake and –' He made a gesture of cutting his throat.

They were in the bar now. The all-in wrestler had decided to come. 'I can't find my way out,' he said, and they all laughed – really funny, all those corridors, steel, girders, glass, but in fact Mr Morris meant what he said. He began to drink rather heavily and became involved in earnest conversation with two men who urged him on, 'Oh, really?' and, 'Another?' It looked as if the drinking would go on as long as the rehearsing. The producer, still in shirt sleeves – sweat rolled to a visible stop on his face, stained his arms – looked tired, a man heading for ulcers, who never saw the light of day, would lose oxygen entirely, given enough time, and simply die from engine failure. Meanwhile, here and now, he was very much alive. The girl who'd sat in the chair was here somewhere – the small bar was packed – but the producer, who perhaps preferred Sheila to

Elizabeth, now had an arm around her waist, not with actual familiarity, but in what he presumed was a permissible gesture of camaraderie; we're all artists; this is fun; you were great.

Sheila stood it for as long as the drink. It didn't matter. He'd be turned off like a TV switch, forever, as soon as they'd finished the gin, or he'd tired of talking about himself, or the girl who'd been in the chair did something about him. Then she requested, 'Be a darling and find me another gin. But only a small one.' She wasn't going anywhere tomorrow. Her functioning, not responding heart fluttered for moments in pure terror as she thought of tomorrow and what she must do. There was no need for fear, but it was a condition, inescapable, a property, like stuttering or inexplicable, unnecessary shyness. Now the producer returned with the gins – four of them, not one – and when he reached her it was to a different arrangement of stances, bodies, voices. The girl who'd sat in the chair was with him now, a tall, rather beautiful thing who seemed to say nothing, just follow him about. Secretary perhaps.

'No,' Mr Morris was saying, hefty, red in the face. 'Nothing phony. If I try to hurt a bloke I ain't doing it to amuse the crowd. I'm trying to kill the bugger. There was a Mexican . . .'

'Our friend's getting a bit steamed up,' commented the producer.

'I must go,' Sheila said, inspecting her watch.

'The make-up, darling. Do you want to take it off? Rather heavy.'

Outside the air was black and cold, like hatred. 'Give you a lift?' she offered, but Elizabeth was going elsewhere. Sheila drove the tiny Fiat through London, wanting to be left alone, go to bed; she was tired. The thought of going to dinner across the college grounds, Margaret Simpson, Hubert's bellowed idiocy, was tiresome, appalling. Couldn't she simply claim illness, tiredness, the TV? – they went on for hours, did you see it?

There were scores of lights on in the college buildings. Music, as usual, drifted; someone pulled a chain. She could smell cooking, cheese; surely they didn't cook cheese in their beastly little rooms? She sat in the car, engine off, afraid, not wanting to go on with it. For one long breathless moment she wallowed in what had been: David and the Jag, New York, committed to nothing, no one, but self; the dresses and the diaphragm discipline, the controllable contours; the superb face in the mirror, unmarked, not involved in the stupidities of the world; the restaurants and the camera's eye; frantic expenditure of energy, not mattering if there was excess; day after unfaltering day, year after year, scarcely a headache, never a failure – it was like looking back at a perfect childhood. But she was adult, beyond that, the reciprocal, brutal passion, the claims made, payment demanded. Life was Max, entirely, all else a parody of what had been. It didn't matter. Before Max she was naked, flesh and mind, could give no more, take no more; fitting the rest of the world in was what tired. Not to worry. He was worth it. There must be an end – an end, she hoped, insisted, of the parody, not of Max.

Alexei was there in the cold hall, as expected, an obedient, faithful dog, devoted, in awe, as usual. Pain awaited him some day, the damaged vanity, the shattered self-deception.

'Did you see it?'

And, of course, he had seen it, said so, visual perfection, it had delighted; he'd seen her in a new element, the camera's mind, fraudulent, for she wasn't really sophisticated; she was pure, innocent, his wife, he knew . . . Did she enjoy it? Was she nervous? Tired? Did she mind going to Simpson's? They liked her, Hubert had said. Lucky, he was lucky, and Margaret thought she was beautiful, a dream, out of this world, she'd said.

'Terribly clever,' Margaret greeted her. 'I don't know how you do it. Even Hubert watched this time.'

'A drink?' suggested Hubert.

'A sherry,' said Alexei. He'd taken to sherry, which proved something dreary.

They stood talking, sipping, for a quarter of an hour, then sat and ate. Sheila was tired, glad to be at table. The food was quite interesting, but English, of course; one could commit treason simply on the grounds of English food.

'We're going to Malvern on Friday,' Hubert said. 'You'll like that. Discrimination radar have a problem, relative to our work.'

Margaret complained, 'If you're going to talk about work –'

but Sheila's mind made shorthand notes. Discrimination radar – what on earth was that?

Alexei asked, 'Where is Malvern?'

'Oh, very pretty,' Margaret said. 'Worcestershire, isn't it, Hubert?'

Hubert explained, 'It's a question of hesitation in the reverse trajectory, then identification of decoys, followed by warm-up and Bob's your uncle.'

'Bob's my uncle?'

This clearly baffled Alexei.

They all laughed kindly; words moved away of their own volition; there'd be no further mention. It was awfully hard to hold that tiny piece of dialogue in the mind. She'd have to write it down as soon as they went or slip into the toilet here, find a pencil first.

A woman was serving, had obviously assisted with the cooking. Now she was anxious, clock watching, and at the coffee stage she asked in a ridiculous, deafening whisper, 'Will that be all, Mrs Simpson?'

'Yes, all, and thank you, Mrs Benson.'

'See you in the morning, mum.'

Margaret said in her absence, 'A treasure, but worried all the time.'

Ten minutes beyond this Sheila volunteered to clear the table and, despite protests, did so. In time she found herself washing up with Margaret, a job she hadn't done on this scale for five years. It was quite ridiculous, embarrassing almost.

'We do like him, you know,' Margaret confided. 'He's such a dear little man. Oh, I shouldn't have said that. Still, you understand.'

'No one could pretend Alexei is enormous . . .'

'He's been with us for months and always kind, gentle, considerate . . .'

It sounded like a reference for his next employer.

Margaret rushed on, 'I can perfectly understand why anyone even so beautiful as you –'

'I'm not beautiful.'

Sheila was red in the face, almost in the rare condition of being hot and bothered.

'Oh, come, don't deny *that*. You could have married anyone, but I think, well, that you were right to pick Alexei –'

'He's a dear,' said Sheila, hoping to close the subject. How far was Malvern? Would they be away for the night? Max, Max ... The possibilities were hot, disturbing. She went to the toilet, wrote frantically – discrimination, hesitation in reverse trajectory, identification of decoys – and squashed the piece of paper in her handbag.

She slept that night as one stunned and in the morning was still tired. Exhaustion was accumulating, terror tiring the nerves despite her not being involved.

It was the first time since their marriage that she'd been alone in their home. It was not a home easy to love. Belonging to the college and furnished for the chaplain, it was completely without sophistication. The rooms were quite large and light, but everything in them dull, unimaginative, by her standards.

Their own rooms were limited to four : two bedrooms (one of which was empty), a living-room, and a kitchen. Sheila began with the bedroom. Alexei's possessions were few, pitiful. She went through pockets, found only pencils, ball pens, money, stamps, elastic bands, a length of string. It was ridiculous, like spying on a Boy Scout. He was supposed to be a supreme brain but carried bits of string, a penknife. Nothing. She emptied the dressing-table drawers, but they contained nothing except clothes.

In his wardrobe were a few shelves. The top one was empty except for collar studs, but the two lower had letters, papers, and there was a very large envelope packed with material. She withdrew this, examined it. It was addressed to him, posted in London. That meant nothing. An envelope large enough, useful enough, to keep, use. Inside her fingers contacted the sharp edges of papers. Scores of pieces of paper, the quality and texture of each being different. She did not know what to expect – material for Max, the price she was paying – but certainly she did not anticipate what she saw. There were photographs, hundreds of them, some in black and white, some in colour. They were all pictures of herself.

It was impossible not to be involved, touched, however slightly. If one drank a wine which one did not wish to drink, one was nevertheless warmed, the face reddened. A little man, nothing to do with her, but always kind, always gentle, in love with the photograph. Not her. He didn't know her. She was a girl at a party. But day after ridiculous day she lived with him, and it was impossible when you lived in the same rooms to be completely unaware of him. There had to be a choice: do you like him or do you hate him? And she liked him.

That was all, of course, absolutely all. A nice little man, but she said that about several people. She wasn't in love with anyone, anything, except Max. Her hand nevertheless trembled. Fear, presumably. She didn't have Max's ruthless capacity for truth. Sheila selected photographs at random, stared at herself, two years younger. She flushed with the weight of betrayal, was humiliated at such intense, private devotion to her beauty.

In another drawer were a few letters, a notebook, with endless scribble in Russian. She took them to a clearer light, tried to photograph them with the miniature camera, but her hand was not yet steady enough. She went into the kitchen, found a mincing machine, and used it to grip the tiny camera. She had nearly finished when the telephone rang, causing her to dither, panic. She went out of the room, locked it, ran down the stairs, breathless, headache coming.

'Who is it? Sheila?'

'Yes. Max, is it you?'

'Who else?'

'I'm just taking photographs.'

'There was something?'

'I don't know. It's in Russian.'

'Any numerals?'

'Yes, I think so.'

'Splendid. You're as clever as you are beautiful. Well, now, Sheila –'

'And, Max, listen. There was mention last night of – wait a minute, I'll read it – discrimination, hesitation in reverse trajectory, identification of decoys. Does it mean anything?'

'Of course it does! Sheila, come to North Africa with me.'

It wasn't a request, it was a plea. Her frightened fibre now shook to the heartbeats of pleasure, ecstasy.

'Max, oh, darling, how can I? You mean it's over? I can leave?'

'Not yet. I've got two tickets. Will you come? For four days.'

'If I can –'

'The usual excuse,' instructed Max, 'is a sick mother. Calling for you.'

'That's too dangerous. He'd phone up every evening.'

'An aunt in the Hebrides. Not on the phone.'

'Oh, Max, darling, I'll come. Think of something. I'll come. Where is it?'

'Tripoli. I have to photograph some oil refineries not far away.'

Two hours later Sam Bellamy listened to a tape recording of this dialogue and realized its implications. Within a fortnight he had had the good luck to find the beginnings of two conspiracies. He did not yet appreciate that Maggie Preston's traitorous ears in World Mechanical's telephone exchange were part of the same conspiracy as Sheila Haward's unfaithful body. And he knew nothing of Charles Filmer.

They were in a bar on the Avenue 24 December with this American couple, Arnold and Judy Gertz. Outside, beyond the mosaics, over the glasses and tables, in the Italian-style boulevard, the afternoon was too brilliant, tired the eyes. The sunshine, not of tropical intensity, nevertheless warmed the face. Arnold was an oil expert, a nice man, although corny, of course – photograph after photograph of his kids, sentimental little jokes with Judy about them and the dog, pronounced dawg; not like Max, but large, generous, likeable. His hospitality, and that of other oil experts, had been overwhelming, very nearly exhausting. He was talking oil now, options and leases and yields. He made it interesting, although it meant nothing, was just words in a bar, a minor claim on Max's attention.

Max had taken photographs of the oil derricks, machinery, people; he'd alarmed her, walking about high in the air on steel. For commercial use he had also photographed the town wall, buildings, the ruins of Sabratha; boring, he'd complained, magazine stuff.

There was only another night – Sheila contemplated it with sensuous skin, wilting body, the mind's eye of previous nights – and part of a day, the dull stuff, packing, paying (the hotel, Max said, not making any claim, just amused, cost £8 a day; prices inflated by oil, he presumed cynically). Judy Gertz was rather sweet, overwhelmingly full of female compliments paid in an honest, American voice, beautifully dressed out here in the middle of an American nowhere. They'd done the shops together; it had been fun. Neither Judy nor Arnold asked about relationships; they'd called her 'Sheila' from arrival.

'You know something,' Judy said. 'You haven't shown these folk the native quarter.'

'Relax,' suggested Arnold Gertz. 'You can't do everything in two, three days. It stinks anyway. We're gonna show you a belly-dance girl tonight. Very primitive stuff.'

'Max is in love with the primitive,' Sheila informed them without meaning.

'Yeah, we guessed that.' Arnold grinned.

There was an acute silence, but comparatively harmless.

'Did I say something?' Gertz asked.

'Sure, you said something all right,' Judy criticized. 'You're great with oil. Got big feet though.'

'Yeah, well, as I was saying, we got this exploratory concession and then the actual concession, and that's on a fifty-per-cent basis, so all we got to do now –'

'Arnold, they don't wanna hear about oil –'

'Sorry!' Arnold Gertz apologized. 'But someone did ask. Didn't ought to ask if you don't want to – I'm just an oilman. Another drink? We're not going any place, are we?'

'What about this native quarter?' Max inquired. 'The light's good.'

'You can't take photographs,' Judy Gertz said with finality. 'They don't like it.'

'Should be fun then,' Max asserted.

'No, I mean that,' Judy cautioned. 'Positively, you can't.'

Max was going to be rude. Sheila knew it, didn't want it to happen. Max didn't like people to tell him what he couldn't do or what he had to do.

She said, 'I could use a drink. Never mind going anywhere.'

'I'll get it,' Gertz said. 'Another gin?'

But Max was not diverted; he looked at her, the smallest, cruel smile. He would be unpleasant now, Sheila presumed, was sure, to embarrass her. He'd explain it later: you're so Puritan, really, despite this (*this* being what he'd be doing), so English; you belong to horses and drawing-rooms, not the real world. You wanted me to be charming, didn't you? And he'd make 'charming' sound like a dirty word in the accepted values of dirty words. He was impossible to criticize. To make moral judgements would be to invite goodness knows what obscene unfaithfulness, to prove independence, his own values, something she'd never cure. She just had to accept him as he was, violently individual, indifferent to anyone's feelings in the preservation of self.

And sure enough he began, but with apparent reasonableness, politeness to Judy: 'I realize it's blasphemous by their standards, but they should be acclimatized by now to the camera. Lots of Americans here.'

'Yeah, and all ordered not to take cameras into the native quarter.'

Max began to be rude.

'I hear many of them never leave the air base at all. They live there for two or three years, then go home.'

This was true and did not for long moments penetrate as rudeness. Judy even boasted quite proudly, 'It's fantastic. They've got everything there.'

'In cans,' suggested Max, and Judy blinked in shock, flushed a little, but still was not certain of the impoliteness. Two whole days she'd been around and they'd been very pleasant, no trouble at all. Think nothing of it. We liked London; we stayed at the Savoy and the kids went to the Tower and all that. My feet – Jesus, my feet on those pavements. Paris was better, I think – on the feet, I mean. They say you never get tired in Paris, not the first time anyway ...

'They're getting rid of Europeans here,' Gertz supplemented. 'They're doing it the slow way – bringing trade to a standstill, making them uncomfortable, so on. Especially the Italians.'

'Would you like to see the native area?' Max asked, an edge in his voice.

Sheila had to take his side; there was an instruction in his tone. 'I don't mind.'

'You two feel like coming?'

He made it an insult, not a request. He was going to prove something. Sheila felt the flurry of civilized distaste for unpleasantness in her stomach.

'I'll show you around,' Gertz said coldly. 'No cameras though.'

'No need to bring yours.'

There was now not even a pretence of politeness.

'Max, you don't have to be so rude –'

'You frightened, too?'

Gertz rose from his wicker chair. 'Now, wait a minute. I was just telling you. I've been here for three years.' Sheila was very sorry to see his face pink, irritated, goaded into whatever Max intended. Judy, too, was flushed, angry, alarmed.

'Then sit down,' suggested Max brutally. 'No need to move if you've seen it before. Sheila and I can –'

'If you think I'm chicken –'

'Arnold, don't be stupid,' Judy protested. 'If they wanna go –'

She pronounced 'stupid' as 'stoopid', which Sheila found infinitely amusing.

'I'm coming with you,' Gertz said. 'Three's better than two, safer. Judy, you stay.'

'I think you ought to have more concern for your *friend*,' Judy said with dislike, moral condemnation. She made the word 'friend' sound like 'prostitute'.

'Max,' Sheila said, despite this, 'you are being a bit bloody.' She was sorry it would never be the same again with Arnold and Judy Gertz. She'd wished to return to England without a sour moment, anyone insulted.

'He doesn't have to come,' Max repeated, but, of course, Gertz did.

Outside in the warm sun the incident seemed unreal, unnecessary. The shops were normal, civilized, full of European things. The buildings in Italian style made parts of London seem a slum. Max was, of course, right; it was absurd to be afraid of part of this town. The streets were wide and splendid, the traffic heavy; Italians, Jews, Arabs, and American airmen strolled about, talked, no trace of anxiety. There were cameras in the shops; what would they be there for if ...?

It took half an hour on foot to reach the native quarter. Ramshackle, walled off from the European, it was certainly different, like a criticism of the more European quarter. Shacks and dust and animal dung and dark, inexplicable faces. It was packed, people moving. What did they do? Sheila wondered, in terms of factories, nine-to-five offices, the clock, for here everyone was about, selling fruits, silverware, jugs, baskets, leather. Her clean, fine, exceptional clothes rubbed against mules' ribs, rather to her distaste, and her dainty shoes trod in piddle and dung without option. There was a smell of crowds, foreign sweat, animals, something untouched by time. There was also an absence of other white people, rather worrying to her, and a sensation of hostility in the people who stared, jostled, besought, but this was, she presumed, in her mind, caused by the minor quarrel in the bar.

'This is tame,' said Max. '*National Geographic* stuff, but it'll do.'

He stood still and adjusted his camera, focused, wound on. A man waved a fist and two veiled women turned away in quick protest.

'We told you,' Gertz said. 'They don't like it.'

Max said harshly, 'For Christ's sake! A man waves his fist.'

They walked onward, Sheila uncomfortable, stared at too hard by faces she couldn't read. Certainly there was no compliment in them; they weren't interested in the *Bizarre* type of perfection. She was just white, feminine, worth the value of the things she wore. Gertz was saying to her, 'He's asking for trouble. I hope you can run in those high heels.' Sheila was now aware in increasing fright that Max would continue until they did have to run. It would amuse him to have *her* screaming as well as Gertz alarmed, panicking. Nothing frightens me, he'd complained. I get bored. He was trying now to become frightened. He was a masochist of some sort. Well, it was one way to spend an afternoon. These people were only traders, after all, but it was hard to counter the emotional feeling that Gertz had been correct to warn them, try to dissuade them. He said. 'Things are different in Africa now, all of it. The white man's afraid, on his way out, and they know it.'

There was a crowd of Arabs arguing outside a ramshackle building. Dust rose very slowly from below their feet, hovered in the sunlight. Max said, 'That's quite good. Humanity in the raw.'

One of them saw Max taking his photograph, spoke in angry objection to others, who turned – a crowd movement, hostile opinion.

'That's enough,' insisted Gertz. 'Let's go. You've made your point.'

'One more,' Max sneered, 'as they come to smash the camera.'

Sheila was retreating, her desirable skin electric with shock, pure animal fright, what *he* sought, presumably – a hundred-per-cent involvement in the moment; not a single extraneous thought about elsewhere, other things, what we do tonight, tomorrow, how much . . .

They threw stones as they came.

'Max, you fool!'

The stones hurt, were real, were intended to damage.

'*Run!*' Max shouted.

He'd been hit by a score of stones, was at last frightened sufficiently, involved in today, tomorrow.

Her shoe fell off the right foot. Oh, my God, she pleaded, hesitant, sweat streaming, the civilized urge, need for that shoe. Gertz ran back for it, was hit by stones, threw the shoe, was hit by a larger stone. It burst the skin on his face, like a tomato. It split; blood poured down his neck. He couldn't get up, was bleeding, stunned. She was dry inside with terror, couldn't speak, ran as hard as life would take her. Max was insane. He'd stopped, turned to take a picture. She went past him, screaming now; instinct told her what was happening. She turned, too. The beautiful eyes were involved, had to witness. The crowd had reached Gertz; it delayed them. Gertz was down, easy, so they were on him. White. It wasn't a question of their religion – the blasphemy, humiliated souls; she recognized that. It was part of the twentieth century, the down-fall of the arrogant, the rich, the mighty, the enemy. They were killing him; here was no screaming, only theirs, just a raised hand and arm, legs in convulsions. Sheila ran and ran, aware that it could happen to her if she didn't. Death wouldn't be quite enough, as the satisfied shouts behind proved: they were battering beyond death; Gertz was a bloody pulp.

She ran until she could run no longer; she reeled about in the more fashionable sun, comparative safety. Then she was violently sick. Arabs and Jews stared, angry, contemptuous. Drunk, they presumed. All the same. American, of course. Wrist watches and cameras and haircuts and loud talk and the vomiting. The hatred deteriorated the atmosphere; it was hard to breathe. She thought hysterically: he died for my shoe. A thought for my elegant feet, not used to earth, the dainty featherweight shoe, purchased in – oh, where was it? Milan, Lucerne, no, I do believe New York – oh, my God, and the mind's eye remembered the shops and windows and traffic *he'd* never see again. She was too frightened, even now, to weep. People were staring at them. They were walking now, she and her lover, Max, rather more than a stroll, but presumably they looked as people look who've just seen violent death, missed it themselves by a shoe.

'I'm cold,' she said in the sun.

'A drink,' suggested Max. 'You'll feel a bit better.'

They sought the safety – that was how she felt it: retreat, shame – of a European-style bar, collapsed into chairs, stared meaninglessly over plants and foreign heads at the sea of traffic, the perfect sky. Something had come very quickly.

'Whiskies,' Max said to the barman. He stared, too. Did she look so very pale? Or was she, even after Gertz, still beautiful? Did it show when you'd seen a man beaten to death for your shoe?

'Max, oh, God, Max, what will she say?'

Max said angrily (he wasn't pale, only worried in terms of something else), 'He was only an American.'

She stared at him, not understanding, pale in the mind, too. 'He was a friend. He saved my life. Didn't you see? He went back for my shoe.'

'I didn't know that.'

'No. You were very busy with your camera.'

'You talk as if I did something.'

'I wish to God you hadn't made a thing of it.'

'It'll be a hell of a photograph. Racial love, all that.'

'Max, don't try to be tough. We know you're tough. Don't go on proving it. Throw that film away.'

'I can't do that. It's got oil-refinery shots on it.'

'You know what I mean.'

'I wish you'd stop this sentimental accusation.'

'I don't know what you mean.'

'I didn't want him to be hurt. He just irritated me.'

'What are we going to do?'

'He's dead, isn't he? What is there to do?'

Sheila was stunned. Max was too realistic; one had to do something. 'I mean, the police, his wife, I don't know. My God, Max, you can't just leave it at that.'

'You think this is the time for a fuss, attending inquests, Mrs Antonov?'

'Max, I don't care about that. I can't feel clean until something's done.'

Max examined her with new, cold, unsentimental eyes. 'You want to feel good again? You want to feel *clean*? What's the matter with you? We live in a primitive world. Haven't you seen anyone killed before?'

'Is that all you're going to say?'

'I was frightened,' Max said in pleasure. 'At last a moment of pure feeling. I identified myself.'

'I feel sick. I want to go back to the hotel.'

'No, no, you don't mean that,' Max insisted brutally. People were staring now at a quarrel: drunk, of course, dirty English or Americans, as usual, spewing their feelings about, anyone's property. No dignity. 'You mean you want to go home, to England, where they all talk, no one throws stones except children.'

'Someone's got to have the guts to go and kill his wife,' Sheila said with hatred.

'Mind what you say to that doll,' Max ordered, gripping her wrist, twisting it so that colour ebbed from her face, she became a death-mask parody. 'Don't go slobbing emotional crap. We have to be on that plane tomorrow. No newspapers must know about us, name us. Bigger things are involved than Sheila Haward's lachrymatory glands or the pleasures of her –'

She had to walk out on what he named, or she was nothing, just a vehicle for his moods and flesh. 'You're dirtier than those who killed him,' she said with fury. 'I hate your brutal existentialism or whatever it is. You didn't run back for my shoe. Gertz did.' It gave her hard pleasure to see the insult sting. It would crucify Max to be thought or called a coward, and equally, he'd find it unbearable to have to explain anything: I didn't know about your shoe, if this, if that ... It satisfied her, eased the guilt felt in her bowels, to see Max flinch, to walk out on him. But in the foreign street she knew it was temporary: part of pain, shame, an adjustment being made before they returned to the reality of loving each other. She couldn't lie naked under that face until the adjustment had been made, he'd conceded something.

Judy was no longer in the bar. Sheila was weak with relief, decided to telephone. She rang the oil company. Judy wasn't there. She lived, Sheila was informed, in a hotel. Which hotel? The operator told her. The hotel was a hundred yards away. Too far to walk. She phoned, the sour smell of vomit in her breath and nostrils, her body weak in shame and fear, the dirty anxiety to be on that plane tomorrow, not involved in the agonies of Judy Gertz. Bigger things are involved, he'd said. Meaning picking the brains and mind and heart of Alexei Antonov. Christ, how dirty she felt this afternoon.

'Why, hello,' the American voice said. 'That you, Arnold? Where the hell d'you get?'

'Judy, this is Sheila.'

'Well! I'm glad you got back.'

'Judy, we lost Arnold.'

'Hell, Arnold's a big thing to lose. How d'you do it?'

She was amused, relieved – the afternoon was over. Sheila could almost taste the breath of relief along the wire.

'He left us, wouldn't come.'

If there was a hell, she'd go there for these lies.

'You mean Arnold didn't go in the native area?'

'Yes, he did, but when Max took photographs Arnold got mad and left us.'

'I don't get it.'

Sheila was not surprised.

Judy commented, 'You sound all shook up.'

'⸱ ⸱y threw stones.'

'I told you they would.'

'I'm sorry.'

She didn't say what she was sorry about or how much.

'Arnold may be looking for you.'

'I'm not happy about it, Judy.'

'I'm not either.'

Judy pronounced 'either' as if it was 'ether', but it was no longer possible to feel infinitely superior. Sheila would never again feel superior to Judy Gertz.

'What do you think I ought to do?'

'I wish I knew, Judy. I'm sorry about this. I'm sorry Max was so bloody. I'm sorry –'

'That's an awful lot of sorry. Relax. Arnold's quite a man. He'll turn up.'

'Call me when he's with you,' Sheila said with appalling cunning. 'We'll have a last drink. No hard feelings?'

'Okay, I'll call you back. Your Max is a bit of a rough character. Still, never mind, honey, he's quite a proposition, too. I get sick of this place,' Judy concluded unexpectedly. 'I'd like to go back to the States.'

She would go, of course. Life's little joke. Life, or God, or something, or somebody, always gave you what you wanted hard enough, and you wished you'd never been born. What she'd wanted most in the world was Max.

There was nothing to do now but sit around and wait for him to come and prove how wrong, how painfully wrong, she had been to want him so much. Presumably Alexei Antonov was going to wish he'd never been born either. Presumably there were people somewhere who lived without this sort of love; they had kids and stayed in bed late on Sundays and scrubbed floors and talked over the fence and watched the little blue box in the corner of the room and thought Sheila Haward too beautiful to be real – she belonged inside the box.

The smell of the afternoon was in her nostrils. She looked in the mirror and the hour or two had altered her. She couldn't ignore it: she was feminine, emotional, found that a pulped acquaintance from Texas involved her. It would hide in the mind's eye forever. She'd be eating or making love or changing gear or facing a camera and into the mind would come that incident from the world of TV and newspapers: the rabble at work, beating a man to death for no reason at all. Only an American. No, she couldn't stomach that, let it go at that. Arnold was nice, had a wife, kids ('I took this one on the porch; that's Betty on the left'), was modest; he was real.

Max came into the bedroom, eyes unkind, no capitulation; she did the surrendering (the bed was there; the indentations proved it). He threw his camera on the bed.

'Did you phone her?'

'I did.'

'I knew you'd phone. Easy.'

'I phoned because she wasn't in the bar. I'll go and see her if you think I haven't the guts. But if I see her I *talk*, Max, and to hell with your bigger, dirtier things.'

Max twisted her arm behind her like a bully at school. It proved nothing, only strength. He pushed her on the bed as if to confirm conditions.

'All right. So it was unpleasant, not suitable for *Bizarre*. But essentially it was the fools of the world killing another fool.'

She questioned breathlessly, shaken, 'Suppose it had been *me*? Or you? Are we the fools of the world, too?'

'We'd have been fools if we hadn't run.'

Sheila waited, said nothing, stared at his tough face, saw no uncertainty. Oh, my God, she thought, sick in the heart. It's going to end. I can see an end. He's flesh and blood; he can't think his way out of this one with contempt, so he's going to smash me to prove something. The first time we go primitive and he talks like a conscientious objector or intellectual or something.

'You think I was scared?'

So it was that. Gertz didn't matter, only the masculinity of Max Stuhler.

'I didn't say that, I don't care anyway.'

'Did you think it?'

'Not really. It was just the way something worked out.'

'What do you mean, it?'

'Max, I don't know. Don't try to prove something. Or disprove. I'm just shaken, that's all. He was a nice man.'

'Yes, but American. Americans are expendable.'

'I wish you wouldn't talk like this.'

'Can't you take a thing to its conclusion? For Christ's sake he was *nothing*, just something we found in a bar. Straight from the wheat fields. A dead American. Oil expert. Too many of them are oil experts. You realize, Sheila Antonov, that your work of recent weeks may kill Americans, may have done so already? You think it's different if you don't see them dead?'

She was white-faced.

'I do what I do for you, not the Cold War or lukewarm or whatever it is.'

Max was at his most cruel; he wasn't going to stop. She was going to be hurt, humbled, caused to weep. It was months since he'd slashed her with words; she'd forgotten his capability, the day in the studio.

'You'd like to stop? Be a housewife perhaps? God, you make me laugh. *You* wanting to be a faithful little housewife . . You've never told me. What's he like? Is he good at it?'

'Max, don't quarrel. It's a bad time to quarrel. We just saw a man killed. We're upset. Even you are.'

'Is he as good at it as I am? As big?'

'Don't be vile. Don't try to spoil it.'

'What do you really think I ought to have done about your oil expert?'

'I don't know. Nothing, really. It's just this callous – I don't know. For God's sake, stop this.'

'How much do you bet me I can't seduce the oil widow? We've only a day left. I really need two. Do widows wear black pants, d'you think?'

'Shut up, Max. There's a limit.'

'No. Honestly. It's amusing. Consider it. I mean, we both know that it doesn't mean anything – this absurd business of physical faithfulness I mean, you wouldn't *mind*, would you? So long as I wasn't involved –'

'I'm going to bed,' Sheila said.

'Are you tired? We could go dancing. Time for a hand at bridge with some nice Americans.'

'I'm bored. Bloody bored, Max, with your theatre. Max –' She hesitated. 'I love you, but I can't stand this. I'm not saying you could have saved the man or even that you should have tried –'

'Why don't you cry?' Max sneered. 'I've never seen Sheila Haward cry. You arrogant, self-satisfied slut, *weep*!'

She struggled and he let her go. She went out of the bedroom into a corridor, a toilet, the lift, anywhere, so that he didn't see the silly tears. She couldn't eat, and by midnight it was impossible to hang about; she had to go to bed, she was too tired. Perhaps he'd have gone. She went back to the bedroom, very frightened, not of the world any more, Judy Gertz, the newspapers, the treason, but frightened of him. He had to win – that was his trouble. He was perfectly capable of finding another woman, quite quickly, and taking her to that bedroom for Sheila to come and find; whatever insult hurt the most, he could think of it. He'd taunted her, mocked her, insulted her, because she'd witnessed an afternoon when he didn't win. There was more to come, she didn't doubt; it was unbearable, made her tremble. She was sick of the day, the journey. There was a fantastic unreality: they were due in London thirty-six hours from now, and here they were, burning with inexplicable hatred, all based on shame; love, their love, in misery because of the afternoon. He felt responsible, she supposed, because he had mocked Gertz, caused him to come, to die.

He wasn't in the bedroom. Sheila undressed, washed and put on night cream and fiddled with her hair and waited in fear and self-pity for him to come. For if it went on they'd end, and she didn't want it to end.

His hand on the door and his beloved, ruthless face flushed, drunk, here to continue ...

'Are you all right?' she asked absurdly, to show concern, surrender, anything, only don't resume what went before.

'Sheila, you know damn well why I'm like this. Because I'm *human*. I was frightened, but this time it was different. This was beyond my control.'

'No, Max, no. Your first impulse was to save me. Run, you said, because I had to, couldn't fight.'

'I didn't know about your shoe –'

'I'm glad you didn't because it would have been you, wouldn't it?'

They were sharing the death of Gertz now: it was a property with value; it had spared *him*.

'I never say I'm sorry, but – I've brought this bottle. We'd better get drunk.'

The relief was overwhelming, merged into the bottle, stupor, went beyond that, some tears, shame; moved on to ecstasy, the burning hands and mouths, the impulses and submissions, not a word said. He never apologized, surrendered, but he had feelings, must have, suffered for Gertz. It was enough that he did, not how. Never mind, never mind, it was over. A man dead. An American. It couldn't have been prevented or it would have been. It wasn't going to matter.

She lay awake all night, because if the telephone rang the affair with Max was over and there was even the danger that minds could interpret the marriage to Alexei Antonov. She felt now like a professional spy – dirtied by blood, living from lie to lie, her body sold and her conscience valued at the price of a french letter and a pair of shoes. But the telephone stayed quiet, didn't condemn.

They woke late, different. It was possible now to view Gertz from the colder perspective of twenty hours; possible to feel hungry, to eat, to rush from the hotel to the airport, to pulse with the energy of escape, renewal. In the air she acknowledged the probability: there's nothing she can do now.

An hour over the Mediterranean, calmed, European again. She was able to analyse, decide: whether Max was responsible for anything. She decided not. They did not have to kill Gertz. It was their decision, not Max's. You might make something of it intellectually, morally, but emotionally it now became acceptable.

The pilot was walking along toward the tail, a smile here and there, both hands in pockets to prove his confidence in the aircraft's stability perhaps. He walked like someone she'd known.

It was David.

His eyes were shocked to see her; he identified Max, not as a husband or photographer, but as a lover, and her averted face confirmed analysis.

'Hello, Sheila.'

'David! Well. How are you?'

'Oh, fine, fine.'

'This is Max Stuhler, the photographer.'

'I hope you had a successful journey.'

She didn't answer that one. 'Thank you for the cake dish. Are we on time, David?'

'Yes, we're on time. Excuse me.'

And that was David. Rather amusing, she decided.

'What was all that about?' Max asked.

'Nothing. Just a boy I knew.'

'You're too old to play with boys,' Max said.

She smiled, a touch of shame, fellow conspirator; how insipid David seemed after Max. She was in love with Max, could bear anything. He had betrayed all values and it meant nothing, was acceptable; nothing could shatter except the betrayal of herself.

'Sheila, my dear.'

Alexei held both her hands, examined her with love, saw the slightly sunburned face and neck and knew that she'd betrayed him somehow. And yet, and yet, she had the stunned eyes of the bereaved, the appearance of one who has slept little, travelled the long journey from Scotland. He'd had two letters from her, in what he knew to be her writing, the second to say the grandmother had died and she must stay for the funeral.

'Thank you for your sweet letter,' she was saying, which surely meant she had been to Scotland to receive it. There couldn't, could there, be a conspiracy of persons to prove his beloved Sheila had been to Scotland and not ...? But where else? Not for a thousand miles would there be sunshine. How could she travel two thousand miles in four and a half days? For what purpose? It was absurd, yet his heart, thumping with sick distress, and his brain, with its immense capabilities, assured him that it was sunburn on the neck, not one of the creams she used.

'I will make a cup of tea.'

He had learned how to do that!

'Was the weather bad?'

'Terrible,' she said, just as the man had said on television, in the newspaper. 'Beautiful, really – I've never seen such snow. Except abroad, of course. And you,' she asked, 'have you been all right?'

'Hubert and Margaret were very kind.'

'They like you.'

'Let me take your case upstairs.'

'It's not heavy.'

'You look so tired.'

'Do I?' Sheila asked, and her eyes were alarmed, concerned. Did she worry about illness?

'You're not ill, are you?'

'Do I look so bad?'

'No, my dear, just tired. You looked frightened for a moment.'

She now had the curious appearance of guilt: it was wrong to be frightened.

'Is something the matter?' he asked.

'Nothing, Alexei, darling.'

'You would tell me?'

'I would tell you anything you asked,' she declared boldly.

But he didn't dare ask about the sun marks. He preferred not to know, to believe they were properties from some kind of health lamp. It would also account for the fear, the tiredness, the anxiety: worry about health.

'Then tell me if you're ill.'

'No, I'm not. At least, I presume not. Make the tea, Alexei, darling, because I'm frozen.'

He took the case first, saw a slight alteration in her again, a flicker of limbs unable to stop a gesture of protest. It didn't make sense. On the case, he saw as he put it on their bedroom floor, was a label, peeled off sufficiently to prevent identification of place, hotel. He had the unhappy certainty that the label had not been there when he'd carried the case to a taxi nearly five days before. How had he carried it? Like that? Or like that? He wasn't sure, dismissed the matter from his mind.

She was reading the letters which had come for her.

'Anyone phoned?'

'Oh yes. Your agent, Audrey Grilli.'

'I forgot to tell her.'

'Did you come across the Forth Bridge? They said –'

'No, the other way.'

'The other way's closed by snow,' Alexei said in cold, terrified certainty.

'I meant going,' she said, definitely flustered.

He was now too worried to make conversation at all in case something else emerged. There was certainly something wrong. Her letter had been tender, had repeated the word 'love' again and again. He had read it ten, fifteen times. It meant something. It had to or he was living in a mad world, a huge fraud. And how could there be a trick? What would be its purpose? He had met her at a party. She was a fashion model, had been (the magazines confirmed it) for five years. It was impossible that she could also be a mathematician of his calibre, or a Communist – much as he loved her he saw that she enjoyed, expected the world's goods, had no knowledge or interest in poverty, politics – or a spy. She would be such a very incompetent spy! It was laughable. He could think of no reason for her to deceive him, except a lover, and that, too, was absurd: if she loved someone else why marry *him*? He had no money, no properties of value. Except his mind, but she could not understand his mathematical mind, never tried to, never asked about his work except in terms of food, tiredness, are we going out tonight? And yet she was slightly sunburned after four days in Scotland where they'd had heavy snow, and she had made a tiny slip of the tongue about the trains over the Forth Bridge. He was in a foreign country (it still felt foreign) and his understanding of foreign minds, psychology, especially in so beautiful a woman, must, he supposed, be limited. Yet he was afraid, in terms of Malinski and Pervukhin, the people he had 'betrayed', the two toughs who could trace him without effort from Florence to a table outside Rome. He knew their capabilities. He loved Sheila, but it was possible, just possible, that she was part of a counter-conspiracy in which things like 'truth' and 'love' and 'God' would be manipulated as desired, without reference to meaning, without original values. Money it would be in her case, nothing else, just a foolish love of cars and clothes. But she made £5,000 a year. No. It, thank goodness, still didn't make sense. Some of her behaviour since marriage had been slightly strange. She had been embarrassed when other models had been introduced to him. They'd had a party, had been to others, and the curious, more frank eyes of these other girls had been, he felt, perplexed, even astonished, and the men who had come with them had all been tall, young, of a type.

Naked, washed, she was still slightly brown on the skin of her face and neck. But he dared not ask, preferred to let it go. In the warmth of bed he touched the desirable flesh, proceeded slowly with passion, the mouth and hair and nipples and thighs. She didn't stop him, but reciprocated, sighed, moved her body about, sobbed slightly, crushed him at the end, shared climax.

'You see that I missed you.'

'I love you,' she answered breathlessly. 'I do love you, Alexei. I do, you know. You mustn't think –' But she didn't explain what he must not think. 'Nobody could help loving you a bit.'

There was something in this curious dialogue that was oddly sincere, more fervent than anything preceding it, and his being was warmed, suspicions eliminated.

'I prayed every day,' he told her.

'I never pray,' she said, astonishing him. 'I daren't. I never bother. You don't know me. You don't know what you've married.'

He was surprised – not only at the burning truth in this outburst, but in its content. She had shared belief. It had been a special claim, something in common: at the party, that party, they'd met, the talk, chatter about pictures, and these eyes, different, sober, had been frank: 'Nobody does anything like that now for God . . .'

'But you said – It was why –'

'It was the wish to be thought sincere,' she confessed.

He did not stop to analyse – how easy to deceive me, how easy to carry conviction – or take it a stage further – how easy to find me at a party, overwhelm me . . .

He just questioned in marital astonishment, 'I cannot understand why you married me.'

She laughed, brittle, uneasy, frivolous. 'Can't you?' Meaning the bedclothes, the shared nakedness – weren't they reason enough? 'It was because I wanted to.'

'But if our views –'

'Oh, Alexei, don't be stupid. I didn't give a damn what your views were. No woman ever does. It was because you were different. You were modest, shy, I don't know, different. Even the way you loved me was different –'

'Different from *what*?'

'Just different – not selfish, vain, dirty.'

'I am a long way from understanding you,' he admitted, baffled, but content.

They fell asleep in each other's arms, and she woke him hours later, shouting, struggling. 'My shoe,' she called, and she was sweating. It poured over the sunburn. Her legs kicked, *ran*. 'I've lost my shoe.' And then he was comforting her. She had awoken, was admitting, 'I had a nightmare. What did I say? Did I say anything? Oh, my shoe! How peculiar. Anything else? No, I'm not ill. Just tired.'

Morning, the light in the room, the miracle of another day; his mind, working in the mathematics of orbits, relationships of movements in the sky, recognized the daily miracle . . .

She lay as one stunned. He regarded her in tenderness, love, so beautiful, the hair, the moulding of the face, the fragility of the ears, grace of the neck. She lay on her stomach, like a casualty.

An hour later he re-entered the bedroom and she was awake, cautious, skill in the eyes, motives, guilt.

'I had a nightmare, didn't I?'

'Do you feel tired?'

'About your shoes.'

'I must get up.'

'Not to work?'

'No, but I'd better see what Audrey has lined up.'

Work – for him – the confines of knowledge, the behaviour of a piece of metal at given, accelerating, proportionate speeds, within the content of an envelope surrounding a sphere; the content had varying degrees of electrical and other behaviour. . . .

The telephone and Simpson, sure to be for him, three slow, indifferent paces . . . 'Yes . . . Just a minute. For you.'

Fright weakened his stomach, took the movement out of his legs. The mind lost its impartiality and capabilities, became a fool, began, in the four, five paces, to recover, to remember. Talk, accept, go on and on. Mr Bellamy will be listening, tracing. It'll be Sheila, he realized, and relief began to strengthen him. But Simpson would have said it was Sheila, have smiled.

'Comrade Antonov?'

'It is I.'

Simpson staring; Alexei moved his body slightly so that Simpson couldn't see his frightened eyes. Out of a window, through grey streaks of dirt (or was it soap?), a few students strolled, stopped, talked, changed direction. On the main road an ambulance tore through the traffic. Two thrushes down below approached each other absurdly, puffed, in love perhaps.

He had answered in Russian so that Simpson wouldn't understand.

'Comrade, it is time for you to help us.'

The urge was to say, No, no, why do you think, but instead he inquired, 'Why should I help you?'

'You are in a position to do so.'

'What is this help you desire?'

'First, we must meet.'

'That is impossible.'

The sweat rolled down his neck, but it wasn't a nightmare: it was real, happening. They would kill him, presumably.

'You have some freedom?'

'I have complete freedom,' he exclaimed.

'Then it is not impossible.'

'It would need explanation to others.'

'To whom?'

'My wife, friends.'

'You will receive instructions.'

'I can't carry them out.'

'Your father is well.'

'How do I know that?'

'We will bring you a letter. He asks –'

'All lies,' Alexei shouted. 'Do you think anything you say has any value of truth? Truth would be coincidental.'

He hated them.

'We won't hurt anybody,' the middle-aged voice said fluently, with neither conviction nor hesitation. 'But we can. Today your beautiful wife will go to work. When she returns examine her coat. It will have a chalk mark on it. This could be a bloodstain.'

'I will do nothing if you harm her. *Nothing*.'

'The instructions will come soon. Look at the coat, Comrade.'

There was the metallic click. What to do? He was terrified, knowing their capabilities, indifference. Sheila's desirable perfection meant nothing to them. Down below the thrushes still puffed their absurd, spotted chests and the students still had the same stances. Had so little time passed?

'I say, was all that in Russian?' Simpson asked.

'Excuse me,' Alexei pleaded.

'Everything all right?'

He telephoned the chaplain's house; the receiver was shaking and his skin wet.

'The number's engaged,' the voice said from nowhere.

He had to stop her, think, wait for Mr Bellamy.

'Excuse me,' he repeated, and rushed out of the room, along the stale warm corridors, the spiral of steps. The face behind the sports page was startled, caught, by such speed, but was left behind. Alexei was running in the cold air. The students, indifferent to February's temperature, stared, stopped, recommenced, 'And then she said . . .'

The chaplain was just going out. 'Ah, Mr Antonov, life is urgent, I see.' A brittle, comfortable laugh, hesitation, astonishment as Alexei jostled, went past, kicked at doors that wouldn't respond quickly enough.

She was there, safe, calm, superbly dressed; it stunned the mind. His brain fought its way, as out of breath as the body, through the permutation of words, probabilities. He had, absurdly, to be at ease, indifferent, casual. He couldn't quite do it, was too out of breath.

'Don't go to work today,' he begged, suggested. 'You look tired.'

'Darling, I am, but Audrey won't mind.'

'Couldn't you phone?'

'Darling, I get bored.'

'Who was on the phone?'

'Alexei, what is all this?'

'Who was it?'

'Nobody was on the phone,' she claimed, but there was too much care. The capabilities drained from his mind; suspicion made its claims; he didn't know what to do.

'The phone rang,' he said absurdly. 'She said it was engaged.'

'The chaplain,' Sheila suggested. 'Did you ring me? Is that what you mean?'

'Yes.'

'It must have been him. Why did you ring?' she asked.

He couldn't stop her. 'I just wondered if you were all right,' he said truthfully, and she was, obviously: the elegant hands pulled on fashionable gloves; 'Is it cold?' and she was going. They, he, whoever, wouldn't hurt her. He could ask. She might help. It was so-and-so, and Mr Bellamy would arrest him, they, whoever it was. He had no doubt, though, that they would make the chalk mark. And if they could make the mark they could cause the injury. 'Take care,' he begged, but she was assured: 'Don't fuss. I'm all right.' It was, she thought, her world, safe, sophisticated, ran smoothly on wheels, money conversation.

Hours later, mid-afternoon, she returned. He was there, tired, work abandoned – 'I don't feel well' – Simpson sympathetic, but curious, aware of the relationship; it must be that, between the telephone call, the sweating face, alarmed eyes, and the claim.

He met her at the door, before she removed the coat, and there it was, a chalked X, between her shoulder blades. He admitted now in his mind that he, they, would win. He must deceive Mr Bellamy, compromise with them. I'll do what I can, only spare *her*. It was foreboding, that cross of chalk. Mr Bellamy hadn't spotted it.

'There's a mark on your coat.'

'So there is. How peculiar. Chalk.'

'Didn't you know? Didn't you see? Didn't you feel it being made?'

'No, darling. Glad it was only chalk! This thing cost forty guineas.'

'Where did you go today?'

'Nowhere special. Audrey's and then a restaurant and to the *Bizarre* offices. I came home early.'

He didn't want to press her with questions. She was unaware of who had made that chalk mark anyway. He mustn't frighten her, involve her. It was alarming that Mr Bellamy had done nothing. What would he/they want him to do? Was it possible to compromise? Was it possible to defeat them – lies, false information, lay a trap? He knew it was not. If he wished to spare Sheila, he had to surrender the world.

6

SAM BELLAMY

THE laundry van braked rather fiercely, stopped in the roar of Victoria Street's traffic. The tall slender girl jumped out, waved a hand, hurried, dodged the vehicles in Vauxhall Bridge Road and a taxi in Wilton Road, and went into Victoria Station through a side entrance. It was ten o'clock in the morning, not too busy, ferociously cold, and dirty, a tired building, everything used for too long, the dirt ingrained. There were people here and there; not many, it might seem, but in fact they totalled three hundred and four. The tall girl in the drab coat was not stared at much; she had deliberately dulled all her attractiveness, even to her characteristic walk, and now had the pale appearance of a typist in a warehouse.

She looked at the telephone kiosks as she had been instructed.

Oh hell, she cursed mentally, he's gone. She was a hundred yards away but could see this. She felt the panicky, warm sensation of failure: they were depending on her. The little man had talked and talked so that she might be here. Too late. Hell, she thought, but the timid, warehouse eyes were looking in last hope for anyone moving away, a man's glance over his shoulder. Nothing. The telephone box was empty and it had to be faced: they'd missed him.

The young woman was not a warehouse typist but a Special Branch policewoman, and she approached the box rapidly now, entered it. There was the smell of his breath, smoke, almost his hands and body. They had taken less than four minutes. It was impossible, almost, that anyone else could have used the telephone. The girl checked the number; yes, indeed, it was the one. Someone had doodled a flower. Had it any significance? A daisy. No. Names and slobbed cigarette ash and someone's spittle and the windows grey with dirt – this was the society she was trying to save.

The girl was aware of the limitations set by that society and accepted them. Any fool could sit at a desk and comment on the world, explain how things could and should have been done better. It was an irritation, but it was the fool's privilege. The girl had no wish to take away the privilege of opinion, whether formed without experience and courage behind a desk or otherwise. What irked her were the limitations which this free society placed upon her. Rightly, of course, but in the middle of the twentieth century what an advantage it gave to people such as the Communists. They could take a man from the street and question him for a month, and if he was, incredibly, innocent, let him go, not a word of protest from anyone. They not only had the advantage of indifference to truth and meaning but also this further advantage of being unquestioned. Here in England you had to be able to prove a man was guilty before you even spoke to him.

The minds so intent on preserving freedom from behind desks placed these severe limitations upon you. You had exactly the same powers as a constable on his first day on the beat. It was right, just, fair, but laughable. For counterespionage was different from anti-crime and anti-vice work. In them you could question a suspected man's friends, employer, fellow criminals about him, deduce whether the answers were relevant and truthful. But in counterespionage it was, under the limitations imposed, scarcely safe to question anyone, for any person could be a further contact. Therefore, to begin with, you could only ask people at the very edges for information; the expectation of proof was restricted.

Thus, evidence was hard to obtain, valuable, and the girl in the dirty atmosphere of the telephone box considered the few cubic feet around her and wondered what evidence they could prove in a court of law. Then, doubtfully, she picked up the receiver delicately by the earphone with two fingers – so that her hand did not contact the normally held part of the instrument – and dialled a number. In the quarter of an hour she now had to wait two people summoned up the impatience to open the door and ask what she was doing, but she simply told them, 'Out of order', with an authoritative edge to her voice that didn't belong inside a warehouse. Then the post-office van came and the telephone was very carefully replaced with another, and the girl walked back toward Victoria Embankment with the stale, dirty piece of bakelite wrapped in her scarf.

Eight fingerprints were found. None corresponded to any in Criminal Records Office. Every Western European police force was sent copies of those eight prints. They were also examined in Australia, Canada, New Zealand, and the United States. Seven days later the Royal Canadian Mounted Police in Ottawa sent the encouraging message that one print belonged to Henry Derber, ex-printer, who was forty-four, unmarried, and wanted for 'suspected espionage activities'. A very poor photograph, no doubt taken through a restaurant window with a telescopic lens, showed Henry Derber standing outside a building, talking to a girl. It had been taken in 1958.

The small restaurant was packed – one o'clock. Hot steam, laughter, voices, 'Excuse me, sir', the hurrying feet and the smiles, glass and cutlery made their contributory noises. French, this was, and here and there literary folk were talking their way recklessly through the menu in that language. A well-known ballet dancer was perhaps the most distinguished person present.

A few people turned to have a look, but she was used to that, didn't see their rudeness.

It was a little expensive for students, but these two were obviously in love, wanted the comparative privacy, and he perhaps to prove values in terms of food, wine, exclusiveness.

The girl was dressed in costume, black net stockings, crazy shoes, a vivid scarf; she had squared spectacles, was, it seemed, a mixture of beatnik and intellectual. Her friend was, despite February's temperature, the flurry of snow outside, in sandals, summer slacks, pullover; perhaps his beard kept him warm.

They were a little shy, hesitant. 'No, John, by the radiators,' the girl requested, and they smiled as they pulled out chairs, 'Excuse me' to the two who were in such earnest conversation, and then sat back to back to these two, silent, overawed, waiting for soup.

The man had looked at the two students in one brief examination, then dismissed them. Nothing, not relevant. Now he continued talking to the extremely beautiful woman who was across the small table: 'And so it was all right?'

'Not exactly, but safe enough.'

They talked like lovers. It was fascinating. It was life, this absorbing, seventy-year experience that takes twenty years to get into top gear and is back again into second within another twenty-five. Perhaps that was why the two students didn't talk much, preferred to listen.

'Before you leave the studio,' the man was saying oddly, 'I have to make a chalk mark on your coat.'

'He is frightened already.'

'He was alarmed today?'

'I don't like it, Max.'

'I am aware of your squeamishness.'

A silence, too long, the wrong thing said. Then the beautiful woman pleaded, 'How long, Max? I can't stand a lot more.'

'You've done very well.'

'I feel dirtied.'

'It has no reality.'

'The trouble is, it has.'

'He is nothing, *nothing*.'

'He's human, kind, done nothing wrong.'

'Don't be so sentimental. He's the means to an end.'

'I don't want coffee.'

'Remember the photographs. *They* wouldn't release you from your contract.'

The couple stood up, paid, fussed with coats. The woman's marvellous face outstared coldly the inquisitive admiration, the male minds which acknowledged that she was better in the eyes' experience than the ballet dancer, who had a poor skin, hairy legs.

The two students relaxed as people do when a restaurant thins. The girl said, conversationally, 'John, I've thought of a way to design the entrance,' and she brought out a small notebook. It was not a drawing that she made but words written, remembered. 'Let me have a look,' the boy asked, and he added details, descriptions that indicated he was no student in whatever it was he was doing.

Oxford Street, six o'clock, pouring rain; reflected shop windows on the glistening roadway, voices, thousands of wet shoes, umbrellas slashing rudely at other eyes in the darkness, cars, the protest of rubber, music from somewhere; crowds, crowds, people. How many? Thirty thousand? One hundred thousand?

Fifteen people followed Maggie Preston, or, more accurately, two or three followed her, despite the difficulties of darkness, and the others followed each other, ready to take over if a face followed Maggie for too long, became familiar, on successive buses, twice on the tube. The procession of fifteen was in fact quite lengthy, enough to be sure *they* were not being 'coat-tailed', that is, followed themselves. (For espionage is aware of counterespionage and, if identified, stops at once.)

One of the two very near to Maggie was Mary Bellamy. She was not a Special Branch officer, but so short of 'ordinary' persons were they for this work of following about that wives had been asked or had volunteered to help. Mrs Bellamy had the particular advantage that she looked what she in fact was – a middle-aged, middle-class housewife. She kept Maggie within twenty yards, so crowded was Oxford Street, and then, when Henry met the suspect, dropped distance, noticed that this man, unlike the indifferent or inexperienced girl, did in fact stare at faces, stopped, twisted, looked over his shoulder. Mary Bellamy watched him step into the flooded gutter twice to hail a taxi uselessly and saw his angry breath blast at the girl. He was worried. Within minutes the girl made a gesture to a shop doorway; they entered.

It was a square corridor of glass. Mary hesitated, waited for the second policeman's wife. 'Let's go shop gazing.' Others were doing it. They progressed around the illuminated corridor, from the other end, as the man and Maggie Preston approached from this. Only the girl window-gazed in genuine absorption; the man looked around, talked.

Mary Bellamy and her associate did not inspect Maggie Preston or the man at all; others would do that, follow further. But in the moments of approach Mary commented, 'Three guineas for *that*. I like these shoes though.' Please God, let me hear something, serve Sam, my husband. The other housewife answered complainingly, 'They haven't got them in fives though,' and within yards, seconds moved; nothing, they'd have to pass, move on, leave; there must be no suspicion at all – Sam would prefer nothing to that. And then the girl said, 'Will I see the major again?' and the man replied sourly, 'No. It's too risky. They may keep an eye on the embassy. Haven't you got a boy friend there, someone clever?' And that – meagre, meaningless – was that, although, to be sure, they'd mentioned in two breaths an embassy, risks, and a major. Move on, out into the rain, drink tea somewhere with the other, then home on a bus, wet, nearly seven o'clock, normality, complaints. 'Oh, Simon!' (doing homework). 'You've let the fire out.' 'Sorry, Mum.'

The third was a man and he saw Henry rush out into the street, the swinging taxi door, 'Liverpool Street', and the vehicle was on its way. The third moved back, said, 'Liverpool Street,' as he saw number four, and there were three of them in the second taxi, but whole minutes behind. Each went to different platforms. Number five saw Henry, stood near him for three stops, got out with him, followed. Henry doubled back on another line. Number five, middle-aged, 'ordinary', was likely to be noticed. He identified the technique, evasion, and identification, that Henry used to see if counterespionage was here but held Henry in sight, two hundred feet away, on three trains.

Henry went into a hotel, but number five knew this trick, too, doubled around to the parallel street, saw him crossing it. He was an enemy agent all right. Henry was followed, in thinner crowds, to a car park. Number five, the surviving eyes of all fifteen, walked to a phone box, pleaded for a vehicle, his eyes on the car-park exit, a red Morris Oxford saloon, but just too far for the eye to read the number.

The grocery van squealed around the corner. Number five, a detective-sergeant, jumped in, urged, 'Morris Oxford. You're half a mile behind. He turned left at the lights.' The driver of the van said, 'Blast!' and drove with a speed that would have perplexed the manufacturers of that van.

'There he is!' said the detective-sergeant in satisfaction.

They kept behind the Morris Oxford a hundred yards, a few other vehicles between. This was easy until they reached a long main road. Then the road behaviour of the Morris Oxford became odd. It was driven at sixty to seventy miles an hour, then, for no normal reason at all, dropped to thirty. But the two Special Branch men identified this technique, too. It was a method of finding out if a vehicle was following; if it displayed the same odd behaviour then it was. The police officers couldn't afford to be identified. 'All right,' acknowledged the sergeant. 'Let's get past him and get his number.' They did this, then left the Oxford alone.

The car was identified as belonging to Henry Stenning who lived in a semi-detached house in the suburbs. Bellamy was not surprised to learn that Henry owned a small printing works. A major at an embassy taking risks. Well, there was a plenitude of majors at the Soviet, Polish, Czechoslovakian, and Bulgarian Embassies, and some very strange chauffeurs and clerks, and doormen. Bellamy increased the watch on and near these embassies. They were on the edges of a conspiracy all right. An operations room was set up to deal with it.

The behaviour of the Morris Oxford was watched day after day. Its journeys were regular – to the printing works, to a bank, to the suburban house. Day after day for three weeks. Then on a Saturday night Henry Stenning's driving became erratic again. He was followed, despite a zigzag course and violent alterations of speed, through half of London but lost in a suburb owing to this extraordinary routine. Half a dozen vehicles – the laundry van, the grocery van, an ambulance among them – went to the suburb, quartered it, in an hour found the Oxford. It was parked in an avenue and was watched. When Stenning came out for it, it was from a house fifty yards away. This house was found to belong to a Mr Keuscher.

Who was Mr Keuscher?

Whoever he was, he had some remarkable visitors : Mr Bean, Bosambo, Stenning … He was, Bellamy learned, a cripple who earned his living buying and selling foreign stamps. Despite his incapacities he went abroad several times a year – to Holland, Germany, for certain, and probably elsewhere. Mr Keuscher was watched day after day with extreme care by a small army of 'tradesmen' – plumbers, men on bicycles, even a woman pushing a pram.

Bellamy felt himself now to be in a position to do more than watch, follow. He and his junior officers began to question people. The landlord of Stenning's house. The terms of the lease. How long had Stenning been there? Four years. Where did he come from? He said Australia; he'd been a printer there. Who introduced him to you? An estate agent. Who are his bankers? They in turn were consulted. How much has he? Eight thousand pounds. Any in foreign currency? Yes. How long has he had the printing works? Three years. How many employees? Only ten or a dozen. Has he anything deposited here? Just a moment, I'll find out. A deed box. No key. I think I can open it without Mr Stenning's key! A thousand pounds in French currency, two hundred in Belgian. A passport, with Stenning's photograph, but a new name and citizenship! New Zealand. All photographed, replaced.

The neighbours. Bellamy began rather cautiously with the neighbours of the neighbours. Mr Stenning. Yes, with the red Oxford saloon. Visitors? Well, yes, I think so, now and again. Usually men. Coloured people? Don't think so. Do you know anyone on the opposite side of the road who would let us borrow an upper room for a few weeks, months? I'd suggest Mr Cartwright.

Within a few days Mrs Cartwright was putting up net curtains in her front bedroom.

It was the same with Keuscher. He was wheeled each day through a local park by the man Nelson. He made regular journeys to a bank and occasional ones to a reputable stamp dealer in the city. Neither Mr Stenning nor Mr Keuscher had wives, children, animals; they were devoted to something else. Mr Keuscher had been in his district longer than Stenning had been in his. His neighbours did not like him. Arrogant, rude, didn't speak to anyone. But cripples were sensitive, inclined to snarl sometimes. And Mr Keuscher did engage in occasional social activity. Every fourth Saturday he went to an international club, drank coffee, watched feeble films, talked earnestly to coloured people, Germans, workingmen of sullen disposition. His bank account, like Stenning's, was substantial – seven thousand pounds, most of it deposited since 1957. It seemed there was a good living in making two bob on packets of stamps from Mexico, Liberia, Occupied France. He, too, had things deposited in his bank; the confidence of these Communist spies in the English banking system was flattering. Mr Keuscher had deposited no documents, no birth certificate, marriage certificate, discharge from the Army, deeds of house, nothing like that. Just some Swiss currency, some American dollars, and a passport, ready for use, in another name.

Mr Keuscher's history, being local for twenty years, was more easily ascertained than Stenning's. He had been a Communist, someone said (it couldn't be confirmed, though, was merely hearsay from wherever Keuscher had been before). He had been arrested in 1938 for fighting the Fascists in Trafalgar Square. His political history went blank in 1947. That was the year in which he'd had the accident. No one knew what sort of accident; they'd all presumed a vehicle collision.

All this was routine questioning, dull but necessary. Bellamy did not expect surprise information, although the false passports were sufficient to ensure participation in a crime of some sort. But after four slow weeks of watching diagonally across the road (for opposite Mr Keuscher's house was an allotment) one of Bellamy's men reported a different visitor. This one had been followed by two men who were dealing, not with this conspiracy, but with the threat to Alexei Antonov. The name of the visitor was Max Stuhler.

Bellamy began to feel very hopeful. When the contacts began to overlap you had grounds for believing you'd found the extent of the 'cell'. Maggie Preston, Henry Stenning, Sheila Haward, Max Stuhler, an unknown major from an embassy, Mr Keuscher, possibly an unidentified student – all these were members of a conspiracy. The conspiracy might have ramifications here. Certainly Stenning, Keuscher, and the unknown major would be more politically involved than Sheila Haward and the zany Maggie Preston; in fact, Keuscher had contact with Bosambo and his agitators. It might also have foreign aspects. And almost certainly it would overlap with other conspiracies. This was why it was more important at the moment that it should be watched than that it should be taken into custody.

A week after Stuhler's visit Keuscher, as a stamp dealer, went to Amsterdam. He visited one stamp dealer for thirty-five minutes; the rest of his behaviour was odd. Its oddity had aspects. The aspects were watched, other contacts followed to Koblenz and on to Jdar-Lauterecken. And then, on a Friday afternoon, a Mrs Ursula Wallace had an accident in her Mini-Minor in Kensington.

7

URSULA WALLACE

As they came in from the street, wallowed in the pleasure of the heated air that drifted along corridors, from the restaurant, the porter looked up from his glass-partitioned small office, acknowledged her with a sour 'Good afternoon, Mrs Wallace.' It was as far as he dare criticize, the lack of something the only indication, nothing positive, no outright rudeness, but she flushed, identified. Cow, the porter thought, rich cow. He turned back to his newspaper, the stimulus of the photograph: Miss Miriam Macvie, this year's Texture Queen, has had an offer, will go places – the flesh, legs, there for people like the porter. Comparative morality. Very amusing. He was wrong to assume

Mrs Ursula Wallace had committed adultery with her companion but right in assuming she expected to.

'Horrible man,' Ursula said, waiting for the lift.

Major Gouseev shrugged. 'Why?'

'He leers. Thinks I'm a tramp, but a tramp out of his reach, therefore condemned.'

'You imagine things,' suggested Igor.

He wasn't displeased. That her thoughts worked on these lines, in this area at all, indicated disturbance, traces of conscience being overcome. She had stared over the lunch table at him shyly, embarrassed, creating an atmosphere of electricity. It was impossible to doubt why. They would, must, be lovers; he was concerned because she was creating the opportunity, lunching elsewhere, bringing him back to the flat at two-thirty in the afternoon. The very dress she wore, he could see in increasing heat, had zips that made partial promiscuity all too possible, could be refastened at the ring of a bell, the door opening.

He was helpless when with Ursula, could do nothing but drift, wherever she wished; she did all the arranging – times, places – a good deal of the talking, too, absurd, most of it – cheques, Angela's dancing, Bill's illness, the contents of shops – only stopping when the possibilities were there, taken. Then she, too, was helpless: 'Oh hell, Igor, what do we do? It's absolutely dotty, hopeless,' surrendering to it nevertheless, crushing, sighing, all the time.

A woman now by the lift, middle-aged, arrogant, a hard, foul rich voice, easy to despise. Carrying an absurd little dog, Pekinese.

'How do you do, Mrs Ross-Harrington? How's Beeky-Boo?'

The woman drooled. What, Igor wondered, did it signify? A weakness? An outlet for sympathy, love? Some form of sex, insecurity? Or just a fool?

'He's cold, so cold. Don't you think the winters are getting worse? Damper, I believe. Say hello to Mrs Wallace, Beeky-Boo?'

The dog sniffed.

'This is Major Gouseev.'

A malicious stare, careful insult. 'I've seen you before,'

meaning – what did it mean? The same conclusions as the porter? 'Ah, here it is!' The gate opened. Three people came out of the lift; one stared at Ursula, interested. Mrs Ross-Harrington pleaded, insecure, old, frightened of the twentieth century, 'Would you mind? The third floor. I'm always doubtful . . .'

It had an effect. There were still people – despite the endless plays, novels, discussions, the empty churches – who despised you if you talked to a man who was not your husband, who concluded . . . Well, they were right – damn them – this time. Love? Was it love? She didn't know. She hoped it was but hadn't decided. At any rate, it left her dazed, more absurd than usual. Even Angela remarked on her behaviour, 'Mummy, I do wish you'd *listen*,' or 'Mummy, you left it in the bathroom,' or, 'Mummy, please watch where you're driving.'

The unspoken criticism left them, even in privacy, slightly wounded, worried by the world's opinion.

'I'll make a cup of tea.'

She had to walk about, do something, feign necessities, an itinerary, something. But he valued time; it belonged to the Soviet Government. 'We've only just had coffee.' And he dared to touch, to hold the slender thing that was so restless. 'Oh, Igor, I hate these damn people who spoil things, make you feel dirty.'

They were standing, she too tall, now bending, responding, forgetting the porter; this was what they'd come for, the only privacy they had. And not a lot of time: once in ten days, two hours at most, and no letters at all – they weren't safe for either party – and phone calls were rare, had the wrong possibilities – the occasional visit by Bill, Angela home with mumps or something.

'We'd better sit,' Ursula said, flushed, eyes evasive. 'I'll just see . . .' She went out – he was trembling – came back, the door locked, latched – even Bill would have to wait – sly, both of them now, hot in the face.

She curled on the dainty, absurd sofa thing. No room for him. He had to kneel, bring his face down to the proximity of the dark, vain, absurd, decorative beauty of hers. He kissed, within the dark hair, expensive perfumes; his face was smudged

y the fire of her. She was soft, voluptuous, beckoning. Her
eck and throat, and hands and mouth, around the eyes. Time
ed. 'Oh, Igor, what can we do?' He had intended to be sane,
emember his position, the spider's web of conspiracies, be
alm, remain within limited intentions. But electrified time, her
oft body that edged slightly nearer to make things (what
hings?) easier, her shudders and sighs, kisses became insuf-
cient. The first zip, by the shoulder, and her shoulders and no
rotests, or, if there were, meaningless, civilized, polite man-
ers, the technique of being seduced, loved, or whatever it was
hey'd know soon), took him beyond politics, caution; he
ecame human, foolish. The tactile touch of silk, straps, flesh,
nd nothing but the sighs, softness, absurd talk even now, 'Igor,
didn't intend ... You're a very naughty man, but, but I can't
top you.' His intentions to be 'good' had fought with the
nowledge that it was ridiculous to see her at all, no point in it,
ut he hadn't been able to control the weak compromise, Well,
I just see her ... The legs curled on the frail furniture were
lender, revealed; the cool touch of nylon, firmer flesh, was too
uch; to hell with circumstance, sanity, time.

A bell rang, rang; they – he, she, whoever it was – knew
omeone was here, would persist until answered. Ursula pro-
sted, 'Oh, damn, damn, no, not now,' but she was a creature
f habit: she answered doors, bells, telephones; it was her
eminine curiosity perhaps; she had to know. She was zipped
p, in control, in seconds, pleaded breathlessly, 'I'll have to
nswer. Wait, my darling, more fun. We'll do it later. They'll
o if they see you're here.'

He stood, shaken, while she rushed, heard her answering,
Darling, I thought it was you,' and a woman's voice, young,
legant, if voices can be elegant, 'I just popped in because I've
ound the most heavenly –' And then the voice stopped, the
ll, Ursula-type friend saw Igor, considered him, identified the
reathless stance; perhaps she'd committed hurried afternoon
dultery herself, appreciated the difficulties.

'Major Gouseev. Call him Igor. Joanna ...'

'Hello, Igor. I say, I'm sorry if I came when you –'

'Don't be silly. Have a cup of tea?'

'Yum. Yes. How's Angela?'

'Such a darling child, but so serious.'

'I *know*. Polly is just the same. Talks about theoretical apti-
tudes, the significance of this and that, and watches all thos
dreary hospital things on TV. She says I'm disillusioned.'

'Aren't we all?'

'But I must show you this dream of a dress I found.'

They examined it, very technical. Igor commented, 'Beautiful,' which it was. They were both similar – tall, elegant; long
fine legs; superb faces, clothed by extravagance : delightful
fashionable, useless, but he loved the one. What use was
woman but to be beautiful, loved?

Joanna stayed twenty-five minutes. She followed Ursula into
the kitchen 'to help', but he could hear the agitated flurry of
voices, a sympathetic laugh. And as soon as she'd drunk the tea
made a few remarks, she consulted a watch, had gone,
guarded smile and an encouraging, impertinent eye on Igor a
she left the room.

He felt weakened, curiously frustrated despite the departure
but Ursula returned, the door again latched, warm, eager for
continuation. 'She's a darling, really. I told her to buzz. Ar
you cross or something?'

'No. Just – I don't know. Interrupted!'

She pleaded – no reserves at all now, in a hurry to catch u
with time, opportunity, 'Darling, don't be put off. Joanna won'
breathe a word.' And she curled on the frail fabric again, leg
shining, eyes frank. And he resumed, regained momentum
the hard firm legs, warmer now, no longer cold from the stree
and her breasts, purity of skin. Hot as fire, she qualified, 'No
here,' and took him to the one room in the house not seen be
fore, the bedroom.

Afterward he was glad. He considered her, like a man please
to have this fever. She was far more beautiful than anythin
ever known, imagined. He could not regret his unfaithfulnes
to the face that stared from the frame in the steel-shuttere
room. It had been an experience too unbearable to regret. H
touched the splendid slim white body, smacked it lightly, an
Ursula smiled ruefully.

Then she cried abruptly, 'The time! My God, Igor, what'
the time?' And, knowing it was late – time had been burned up

fiercely, once, twice – she was on her feet, practical, the bed tidied, the zips fastened.

'Half past three.'

'Angela will be out.'

'I'd forgotten . . .'

'So had I.' She was thinking. 'You wait here.'

'No. I'd like to come.'

'Darling, how nice of you to say that.' She smiled shyly. 'Not had enough of me today?' And he flushed with recent memories, expectation of repetition.

'Everything all right?'

A brief visual check – of themselves, switches, stove – then into the warm corridor, hesitation because the lift was somewhere below, 'We'd better go down the stairs,' and his calmer reassurance, 'No, here it is.' And her anxiety, nearly amounting to terror – as if, should Ursula not be there to collect her, Angela would be seized by someone, a child missing, last seen wearing, ponds dragged, frogmen – all the potential deaths to worry the mother, this mother, who'd committed a different sin; it was as if Ursula believed God would punish her. She pleaded, 'Oh, Igor, I hope she's all right.'

Along the ground-floor corridor, even warmer, a few people bumped – 'Excuse me' – and the porter's re-examining eyes, sensual scrutiny, vicarious molestation : why, the seams of her stockings aren't straight; they were when she came in; the dirty bitch; a shock despite the earlier analysis, condemnation – he hadn't really believed his own dirty mind.

Breathless, the car doors slammed, off violently in first gear. A few cinders flew backward; people stared because of engine rasp. 'What's the time now?' she asked, and looked right, waiting, cursed like a man, 'Come on, you bloody little Ford, put your foot down,' and, as the Ford went past, she shot out to make the right-hand turn, shrieked when she had identified her error, but had completed the right-hand turn when the other car hit. An almighty smack of steel, glass everywhere. Ursula Wallace, dazed, a slight cut on her face, got out. People gathered. The other driver wasn't interested in her glamour, only himself, his own car; he was right for once, in the clear, wanted justice – well, not exactly justice, but money, her fault.

'You stupid bugger, what y'think you're doing?' A gentleman of the new school. And the small crowd made its analysis: woman driver, not looking, she came out, bloody actress or something.

Igor Gouseev was not involved, was going colder and colder. A police constable had witnessed, took his time, peeling gloves, grinned.

They all had plenty to say, witnesses by the score, and Ursula still concerned about Angela, said, 'A hundred yards off – he must have been doing sixty. Well, I mean, *look* at what he's done.' Then, when the constable didn't reject this instantly, she added, 'Surely the onus is always on the car behind.' She was regaining momentum, normality; in a while insurance companies would be exchanging tedious typewritten lies. It would be amusing to see who won the typewritten battle.

'My friend will bear me out, won't you, Igor?'

'And your name, madam?'

'Wallace, Mrs Ursula Wallace.'

'And yours, sir?'

It was betrayal, the end.

They were going nowhere; nothing permanent was involved: they'd reached the only climax possible forty minutes ago. She was beautiful but useless; he couldn't be involved. He was in a battle – they must understand that – and had had a moment of weakness. Now was the time for strength, betrayal, ending. It had been a tender, sensual experience, but he couldn't be involved with fools, witnesses, husbands, publicity, policemen. . .

'I cannot be involved,' he said with scarcely a qualm. He nevertheless couldn't look at her again. 'I must claim diplomatic immunity.'

Ursula was perhaps beginning to suffer from shock – the collision, no doubt. The trickle of blood ran down her face which was as white now as her body.

'You saw, darling,' she urged, not understanding his implications. 'Igor, he only wants to know what you saw.'

'I'm sorry,' Igor said. 'You must understand I cannot be involved.'

The constable said woodenly, 'It's up to you,' but had dropped the 'sir'.

'There are plenty of other witnesses,' Igor said to Ursula.

She saw the shame and fear in his eyes, was unaware of the spionage, identification.

'You damn swine!' she shouted, a little colour returning.

He began to walk away. Not far to the embassy. No need for a taxi. The small crowd stared at him, let him pass, did nothing. They didn't know. By the time he'd turned two corners he was contemptuous; he had to be to survive, continue. Fools, they all were. Decadent and dirty. Selfish, without a thought beyond money and motor-cars and the vanity of sex.

It was easy to hate because it was duty, part of intention, political creed. A drunken husband whoring around with some travel-agency girl, and Ursula – It was no good. He sat behind his desk and wallowed in misery, loss; there'd been some tender property which was unbearable to be without. She was a fool who allowed sensual pleasure, but he'd loved her and was ashamed of his betrayal.

Two days later Ursula, also in pain, missing him, hating him for what he'd obtained, jettisoned so easily – *why?* she'd asked herself a hundred times – had a visitor.

'My name's Bellamy and I'm a policeman.'

'How amusing,' she told him. 'Is it about the car?'

It was not.

She didn't quite know what it was about. Who was this man? Where did you meet him? Whose party? The names of the guests? All of them. Where did you go? What did he say? The times. The places. Whom did he mention? Did he walk with a limp? Why had she called him a damn swine? Why would he not give his name to the constable? Did she go to work? Did he know people of importance? Well, people who might have information of value to the nation.

It lasted half an hour and she found it very satisfying and absurd. She hoped he got into trouble. Serve him damn well right. It could have been quite an affair!

To GOUSEEV. 4019.

Assignment

1. Alexei Antonov. It is our information that Antonov will *not* cooperate and has every intention of continuing to work for the British authorities. It is suspected that the telephone conversation

reported in your 977 was deliberately prolonged in order that it coul be traced. Do not, therefore, communicate by telephone with Antonov again. Use the student Sumpster to deliver letter, or, i emergency, give verbal message. (Student is useless, expendable.)

2. Spatial Impulse Selector.

Filmer must now take one of these instruments irrespective of risk He is in an excellent position to cooperate. Other contacts repor that the lorries which deliver the spheres are accompanied by arme military personnel and/or vehicles. Filmer therefore is the only person who can obtain a spatial impulse selector for us. He mus do so.

3. The following are the arrangements, subject to your qualifica tions, being made in regard to Alexei Antonov and Filmer.

4. The Polish MV *Grajawow*, 2100 tons, will dock at Rochester Thursday, 18 March, and will unload timber. The *Grajawow* is du to sail Monday, 22 March, in ballast, but will be made ready t leave Sunday, 21 March, if our arrangements make it necessary. Sh will carry three extra 'officers' who speak English.

5. Filmer should take the spatial impulse selector on Friday, 1 March, and deliver to contact in normal manner in Canterbury or Saturday, 20 March. Contact should proceed to Rochester on Sunday with spatial impulse selector. One of officers will meet her outside Marks and Spencer's stores at 3 p.m. He will be there, if need be, a 4 p.m. and 7 p.m.

6. Henry must arrange to take Antonov by car on the A2 t Rochester on Saturday, 20 March, arriving after dark. After 6.30 p.m two of the officers will be outside the railway station. Each wil carry peaked hat in left hand irrespective of weather. They shoul be contacted and Antonov handed over.

7. It is hoped that both these assignments will be successful, but th risks are realized. If necessary the Antonov assignment can be aban doned. Certainly it should in no way jeopardize the more importan task which Filmer must be persuaded to set in motion. I welcome your comments.

DIRECTOR

8

SHEILA HAWARD

Saturday, twentieth March. At ten o'clock Sheila Antonov, née Haward, took the dress out of the box, considered it – a sensual contemplation, her blue eyes shameless in privacy, aware of her intentions. The other half, in the mirror, smiled, the thin, ravenous mouth hungry for today.

Five hundred yards away, inside an anonymous window, Geoff Sumpster began his day, opened the envelopes, thirty-seven of them. Twenty-one – he'd made it, was a man, could vote. Christ, this was going to be a hell of a party. An array of bottles confirmed it, and the cards from Maggie, Joan, Barbara, and others continued conceit, pleasurable anticipation: he could pick and choose. He'd select Maggie, of course, but if she wouldn't, well, there was Joan; hell, they'd fight for him! It was good to contemplate the day: there was nothing the matter with it at all. He felt happy, powerful, full of love; his guilty fingers examined the french letters – what peculiar things they were. His mind considered Maggie Preston, inch by inch remembering.

Seven miles away she awoke late – Eggy in the bedroom, his mouth yellowed, as eggy as his nickname, pleading, 'Give us a kiss, Maggie. She's gone for some fish.' And Maggie thought, Saturday, stretched the limbs Geoff desired, and analysed the day in terms of laziness, then remembered, Oo, Geoff's party! What shall I wear? And the first stab of anxiety: I hope he doesn't try anything.

The dress was weightless, narrow, skin-tight; there was no intention of sensuality – it was priced far above vulgarity – but with the back slit widely, moulded to the beginnings of Sheila's small buttocks, it was breath-taking. Her eyes delighted in it, mere ownership. Black organza, the skirt ruffled with curled organza petals. For a thing so light it was a complicated structure. Because her spine would be bare the bra was built in. It would give the elegant impression of being unattended by other things – wool, straps, zips, buttons; it had in fact the purity of creation. Naked, she stepped very carefully into it, paused long before the tall mirror, alone, surrendering to the Sheila she loved. Her twenty-three-year-old face would never again, she decided, be so perfectly what it was: a woman young enough to be beautiful, old enough to be wise, ageless, and illuminated by the appetite of passion. It wasn't just a superb dress worn by a model at the peak of her profession; it was worn by a woman who was a model who desired above all things to be faultless today for the man she loved.

It was to be her first public appearance with Max. Harmless, a collection of photographs, some his – she could perfectly well be there without it mattering to any kind of morality, opinion, that she had a husband. She was a model who was photographed thousands of times each year; it was reasonable that she should be interested in an exhibition of photographs by the men who photographed things like her.

The shoes had four-inch heels, were from Italy, fabulous. The gloves, in white, up to her elbows, were clean, elegant, and the hat, a small, absurd thing, exactly right. She hoped there would be time and opportunity and occasion for sensuality; it would be so pleasurable and easy to step out of this creation for Max. The thought of nakedness in the small bedroom above the studio, she was amused to see in the mirror, could cause the proud, mysterious face to blush. She was human; the flesh was more than a thousand photographs. Like Geoff Sumpster, she was a healthy, amoral animal that contemplated the day with physical anticipation.

She went in a taxi, forgot to say farewell to her husband. He was somewhere around. Nice little man, but nothing. Becoming very English, a creature of habit. He made love every fifth day, at about 10.30 p.m., irrespective of weather. Very English, like winding the grandfather clock. She wanted someone who'd make love in a telephone kiosk if the urge was strong enough. He'd tried to stop her going at breakfast; something had upset him. She was glad he hadn't seen the dress. She couldn't hide her guilt, intentions, in that; it touched her pale, smooth skin, aroused it slowly for Max. She'd assured the little man that she'd return for lunch. She didn't expect to. Like Ursula Wallace, she planned for afternoon adultery. . . .

In a second taxi Max was with her. There were people walking about wretchedly, becoming saturated in the heavy rain. They were nothing, didn't matter. Let them walk, become tired, get wet. It was warmer today; spring had begun within the confines of wet streets.

'Sheila, it's nearly over. It's all arranged. Don't go back today.'

Her heart pounded inside the organza. A faint flicker of something: she was human, English, a hypocrite, must compromise. 'He won't be hurt or anything?'

'He'll just be taken away.'

'I wouldn't like him hurt.'

'You're not involved. Just stay away until evening. I shall tell you nothing more. Your ignorance and anxiety must seem genuine.'

'When do I come to you?'

'As soon as it's socially permissible.'

'Today – it must be today. You haven't seen the dress, Max. I bought it for you.'

They were there, a small crowd drifting in. A tiny door, typical of London: it appeared small, insignificant, leading to nowhere, nothing important, as seen from the street. But inside the building had dimensions on the scale of palaces, an immense stairway, people ascending slowly, reduced to dignity, a quiet hum of conversation. Her coat removed, almost without thought, taken away by someone, somewhere.

In this place of elegance she was supreme. People stared; dialogue withered. She was tall and arrogant, in love, a magnificent female animal, none better at this moment. She heard someone say, 'What a wonderful woman,' and it was a compliment without intention, desire, simply an aesthetic truth, God the superb artist; man had made the clothes; time and food and health and experience had moulded the degree of expression, intelligence, sensuality, perfection.

Upstairs, in a room of vast dimensions, people in groups, bearded men, fussy little committeemen, grey men like elder statesmen. Waiters with trays, the chink of glasses, smoke drifting, propelled in the still air by the movements of doors, shoulders. A few women there, hard, ruthless faces, intellectual, now like her. Journalists, perhaps, or female photographers. She didn't know any of them. They looked at her, faces turned.

'*Darling!*'

Elizabeth's voice.

Elizabeth with Richard. He liked photographing Elizabeth did it extremely well; nothing emotional, sensual, a question of work; some models were able to express themselves better with certain photographers.

'You know Max Stuhler?'

'Of course, by reputation!'

Polite laughter, pleasure in association, and it didn't matter if Elizabeth's eyes were malicious, full of questions, gossip. Soon the whole world would know she loved Max Stuhler.

They strolled very slowly together, picture after picture, immense photographs, things of beauty – very few of fashion – most of them foreign, or taken abroad.

'Here's one of yours,' announced Richard.

Sheila didn't care about the photographs, only the dress, the flesh inside, the end; the end of this absurd espionage drama was near; Max, he was what she loved.

She stared with unseeing eyes, then spilled the drink, and the gloves, one of the gloves, and if one then both, of course, stained, ruined. Never mind.

It was the photograph of Arnold Gertz being battered to death.

'My God!' said Richard. 'You must have taken risks to get that one.'

Max explained, 'It was the accident of time and place.'

Elizabeth was distressed.

'Your glove, darling. What a pity. I adore that dress. A dream thing.'

'Sheila didn't like it,' said Max. 'She's squeamish.'

'Didn't like what?' Sheila asked quickly. 'Max, what are you talking about?'

'That American we saw killed.'

Elizabeth was now open-mouthed.

'You saw it, too?'

'No,' Sheila disputed, a flush beginning. 'Max's humour.' She saw that Max was irritated by her civilized denial; his eyes gleamed with something: malice, scorn. Not today, she pleaded in her mind. Not again. It would be unthinkable today.

They moved on – a second sherry, other people, introductions – minutes passed; alarm remained. They admired two of Richard's photographs: one of Venice and a second of wrought iron, incredibly complicated, a gate behind a gate behind . . .

'Some more of yours, Max,' Elizabeth said.

'Congratulations!' Richard was offering Max. 'I didn't know.'

'Know what?' Elizabeth's beautiful mouth asked.

'Zurich,' Richard explained. 'The award. Max won it.'

'It looks,' Elizabeth claimed with malice, 'like Sheila.'

Sheila had only to admit it: yes, my nakedness; Elizabeth wouldn't care. But she was confused and in confusion mistook the pattern of words, presumed condemnation, completed uneasiness by retreat to civilized fashion. She couldn't admit it; admit was a silly word, acknowledged guilt of some kind. She was ashamed, remembering, not the immense, technical creation of the photograph, but the longing of that nakedness, what followed. It was as if Elizabeth might read the mind on bromide paper. It didn't matter; it needn't matter even then, but she was confused, even embarrassed, therefore, for the second time, hesitated, disputed . . .

'Don't be ridiculous.'

Max's face was cruel; she became nothing; he had to win.

'You recognize the face?' he suggested.

'It doesn't *matter*,' Elizabeth hastened to contribute, alarmed now.

'Of course it matters,' Max insisted. 'The truth,' he said with madness, 'always matters. Tell them the truth, Sheila.'

She refused the humiliation. 'Don't be stupid,' she said angrily.

'You have doubts about the face?' Max inquired.

Sheila identified the process. He had to win, irrespective of her. Instinct leaped over the next exchange of words, identified disaster, but the mind and heart refused to believe.

'If you don't recognize the face, then surely the breasts?' Max asked. 'Quite small, Sheila's breasts; couldn't be mistaken.'

'I don't think I'm very concerned either way,' Richard said coldly.

'But you haven't seen Sheila's breasts, of course . . .'

His hands, beloved, sensual, were too quick; what he did was in any case too improbable in that civilized room.

People were talking, standing on one leg, sipping sherry and gin, throwing canapés into open mouths; laughter here and there, interest, everybody passing the morning pleasantly. Seventy-one persons in the room, sixteen of them in a position to see Sheila.

Max knew about the structure of the dress, the fitted bra . . .

He tore the beautiful organza vertically in one shattering insult. There was nothing to hide her, nothing. It was the worst moment of her life, everything ended in one foul moment of rage. Sixteen people saw Sheila's body naked to the waist, a few bits of organza and her flailing hands all between her and the astounded eyes.

He had to win.

'The same, you agree?'

It was too sudden to cause normal distress. She was humiliated, everything ended – her career, her joy, her love – so that Max could win an exchange of words.

Nobody did anything.

Elizabeth cried faintly, 'Oh, my God!' and Richard was incapable in horror.

Everyone in the room saw her – the instant silence confirmed that. It was the most unforgivable act any man could have committed; and Max had done it to prove –

She fled from the vast room, long moments, hugging the humiliated body, floated, graceless, down the wide stairs, found by chance, the cloakroom, covered the insulted flesh with her larger, heavier coat, ran into the street. Physical escape was a first condition, a necessity.

Nobody followed.

She walked in crowds, the warm rain, zebra crossings. People stared, stared because she was, for them, Sheila Haward, beautiful, unbelievable. Cars, taxis, people's eyes from buses, this tall superbly dressed woman with the unseeing face. They looked while opportunity allowed; she was with them. I'm cold, she thought; the humiliated breasts and shoulders were cold under the coat. Oh, my God, I *hate* him. Her mind was numb, pain scarcely beginning. It was only conscious now of the insult, the quality of it; if he'd planned for months to humble her he couldn't have obtained a more successful fruition.

The rain ruined the Italian shoes, muddied her stockings, saturated the absurd little hat, her hair, but it didn't matter, would never matter again. Her career had been ended by the tearing hands. She bumped into old women, men, 'Excuse me', and, 'So sorry', and any irritation they felt melted at the sight of the marvellous face, distressed. She walked and walked, tireless, districts changing, from fashionable to middle-class, from Georgian stone to Victorian slum. Lamp-posts and dogs and old women; kids outside a shop; margarine and corridors of tins; the smells of bacon, fish, cheese; a man, unbelievably ugly, without hope at all, selling papers, saturated; tired women in a bus queue, couldn't afford a taxi. *Fools!* She began to cry, hurried in case anyone saw her. War and rockets and the out-patients' department. They'd never know. They hadn't been finished in Switzerland, Paris, made love in Dusseldorf, Tripoli. It was unbearable. They were real. She had betrayed all of them, without a thought. It hadn't mattered. It was more important and beautiful that the delicate pale breasts (now defeated) should be fondled by Max Stuhler, the long legs widen ... All of them betrayed, quite willingly, because they didn't matter, were fools, weren't beautiful, couldn't hold a knife and fork properly, do their hair, dress, enter a restaurant, theatre ... She'd jettisoned the lot of them.

For what? For this passionate illusion. *Love.* She'd been fooled. She was as weak and absurd as Alexei Antonov. Worse, for he had at least, in his illusion, been convinced by real properties. Her beauty was undeniable; he couldn't be expected to identify the lies in the mind. But *she* – she'd almost been told by Max that it was deceit. . . .

Two old fools in a Morris Minor or something. Panicked, of course. (The glass like spilled sugar, terribly amusing about the string vests.) And I rather wanted to know, did Mrs Harrington-Smythe, Smythe-Harrington, to ask, to stutter, what do you do about facials? Did you notice that they were all naked? Simply that they'd never heard of Manchester. I'd like to get that pride on bromide paper, humiliate it. Or God. Are you afraid of Him when you decide to sleep with someone? To what do you owe loyalty? Anybody? Anything? My parents, I think. Not the fools in the buses, in the rain, on the unfashionable beaches, with the squawking kids, the everlasting tiredness, pain. Funny how hospitals and pain were for these; it was right, proper, nothing to do with Sheila Haward. Little people buying bolts in Woolworths, kids pleading with sticky mouths for more chocolate, women standing by vegetables in misery, analysing their own deaths, children, tiredness. Don't misunderstand me; I've never wanted anything so much in my life. (The competent hands find the familiar drawer to prove otherwise. Sheila Haward dismisses the world for a french letter.) He's got big ears, Max, and he looks scared to death.

You could say that deep space starts six thousand miles out. I had to stop, think about it. Humanity, you see. The entire world – it was up to me. I had to be fair to those Scandinavians, everybody.

You ought to have more concern for your *friend*, pronounced whore.

Yes, but American. Americans are expendable. For Christ's sake, he was *nothing*, just something we found in a bar. Straight from the wheat fields. You think it's different if you don't see them dead?

She entered a telephone box, stared at her own eyes. The surrounding skin was the same, a little pale perhaps, cold, and tired. Nothing revealed the contents of the mind behind the charcoal-patted eyes. She was conscious of being slightly tired, a proportion of mental fatigue in the inexhaustible machine of perfection. She consulted her gold watch. Quarter to three. She'd been walking about for hours. She was hungry, thirsty, still existed.

I love him, she thought.

She went in a coffee bar, sat on a tall stool, ignored the louts who stared. The atmosphere was warm; her hair and shoes began to dry. I love him, she acknowledged again. She had to face the problem. It was impossible to pretend the brutal humiliation had altered that. Love. She didn't want to love him any more but couldn't deny that she did. What was this love that went on in the skin, the mind, the heart, despite insult after insult? Was it a beautiful thing? No. Profound? No. Moving? Oh no. He's finished me, she thought. All that was Sheila Haward had been torn beyond repair by Max Stuhler and the dirty conspiracy in which he was involved.

If only, she thought, I could destroy *him*.

The idea filled her with warmth, was hotter than the coffee, the stupefying air. They'd jettisoned the rules of society long ago. She thought about the other people he had coerced into his dirty enjoyment. She remembered in shame that her father had been a colonel. If she could get rid of Max Stuhler the world would be a bit cleaner, safer . . .

There were properties she had which Max didn't know about. One of them was courage. He was far stronger, of course. She needed a gun. She sipped coffee and realized how hopeless it would be to find a gun on a Saturday afternoon in London. A sword, she qualified absurdly, even sniggered in tiny hysteria. Then she sat bolt upright. It was frightening but, once thought about, was inevitable.

She walked slowly back to the telephone box, planning it. The glass of the box was dirty. It had stopped raining. Cars and people moved; doors opened; a man went out, a woman and kids in. A dog looked at her through the glass of the box. Nothing meant anything. She was hot with purpose; her heart smashed about like an almighty cylinder. She would kill him. It didn't matter what was beyond that. Go through the drill.

His voice.

'Yes?'

'Is that you, Max?'

'Who is that?'

There was a trace of something, fright even, in his voice; he recognized hers.

'Sheila. Max, I want –'

'Where are you?'

'It doesn't matter. Max, I want those photographs.'

'Don't be absurd. The gallery –'

'I don't mean those. The others. And the negatives.'

'Are you threatening me, Sheila?'

'I have information, Max. I can give it to you.'

'You will, my darling.'

'No, Max. We're finished. I'm opting out of your conspiracy. But I'll sell you this information – it's good; you'll love it – for those photographs and negatives.'

'Where are you?'

'Or I go to a police station and I *talk*. I shall enjoy talking, Max.'

Silence, his bloody cruel mind working, plotting new filth. Then he agreed, 'All right. It had better be good, that information.'

'Where will you be?'

'The studio.'

'Forty minutes,' she instructed, and slammed down the receiver. She smiled, wondering what anxiety would be in his mind. She emerged from the telephone box and, like a good omen, found a cab to hire.

Captain Dean was startled by her arrival but soon warmed, explored possibilities. Eighteen boys, some sweating with exertion, stared at her.

'For a prop,' Sheila explained. 'Terribly urgent. I'm on my way to the studio now.'

She followed him about; he was nothing, something in a dream, would do exactly as she desired. The boys were silent in admiration.

'An epée,' Captain Dean suggested.

'A sabre would be better from the photographic point of view.'

'I really ought not to lend you one,' the captain said doubtfully. 'It's not my club really,' he explained in minor humiliation. 'It belongs to Mrs Worthington-Elliott. She's a terror,' he confided.

Sheila used her eyes, pleaded. The captain pinkened, overcome at once.

'There's a beauty in here,' he told her. 'My own.'

In the small office he kissed her. It excited him, but Sheila qualified, still in the dream; it was easy, absurd: 'Another time, Captain.'

'Call me Paul.'

'I'm late as it is.'

'Is that your cab?'

'It is.'

'I'll take you in my car,' Captain Dean offered recklessly. 'A Rapier,' he punned, but Sheila didn't notice. 'No trouble,' he assured her. 'No trouble at all.'

She stood there holding the sabre when Captain Dean went to pay the cab driver. It cost him twelve shillings, which, he considered, was worth those things in prospect. I must drive carefully, he cautioned himself, drunk on the single kiss.

The sabre was an exact replica of a cavalry sabre, a very light reproduction. It weighed sixteen ounces and its total length was $41\frac{1}{8}$ inches. The blade was triangular. He would be standing there, in his shirt sleeves. The sabre, without the *pointe*, would penetrate the shirt and the vest and the skin, kill him. An accident, she could claim, but didn't really care whether she would be able to make claims or not.

Presumably Captain Dean made conversation, but she never heard it. She stood at the corner of Belgrave Hill, very quiet on a Saturday afternoon, and was aware of having accepted Captain Dean's invitation to dinner somewhere, some time. Call me Paul. Never mind. She had been equally foolish, and far more vain, than Captain Dean.

She trod on the sabre and after a while snapped off the *pointe*. The weapon was now dangerous, could kill.

The door was open and she went in. The place was cold, the heating, she presumed, turned off for the week-end. Her humiliated breasts felt the loss of temperature.

He was in the studio, a small electric heater going, but the majority of the air cool. Because the air was cool Max wore a jacket. She did not think the sabre would penetrate the jacket. Oh God, she analysed in terror, don't let him win. The throat then, her courage instructed, or his eyes.

'What's that thing?'

She could smile.

'For my protection.'

'What's this information?'

'Max, you're a bastard. You know that, don't you?'

'I have been told that.'

'Why did you do that this morning? I loved you.'

She was moving with infinite patience, inch by inch; all must be natural, no hysteria, talk, talk, anything, but make no mistake.

'Loved?' he jeered. 'You still do!'

'Did you ever love me?' she asked.

She hoped with all her heart he would say 'Yes'. She would still kill him but wanted him to say it.

Instead he became tiresome, political, angry in a new, unexpected way.

'Do you think you were the first?' he asked in sour rage. 'I hate all of you. I am a Communist, and I despise your dirty elegance. Woman after woman I've photographed, all vain, selfish, stupid in their love of self. I seduced them all, insulted them afterward. It was hard to insult them. I couldn't get low enough.'

'And you?' she inquired. 'What do you love apart from yourself?'

'Nothing,' he admitted.

'And do you feel good, fine, clean, superior to us all?'

'I look outward,' he claimed with fury, 'not inward.'

'And what do you see?'

'I see vanity, greed, obsession with self. I see rubbish, money, lovers, fools.'

'And your eye that sees,' Sheila asked with hate, 'is it not dirty?'

There were another two paces to take. Did he know she had taken fencing instruction?

'You were easy,' Max told her. 'Your pride was so almighty! Did you really think I wanted your skinny body?'

She flushed, lunged.

Max flicked his head; the sabre pierced his left ear; blood poured. He grunted with animal fright. A hand, once beloved, struck her across the face. She reeled, was recovering, would lunge again, but he saw the intention. His hands were quicker than the sixteen ounces of the sabre and, of course, Max had no qualms about striking a woman.

He struck her as he would have struck a man with the same weapon in his hand. The blow half stunned her, sent her slender nine stone flying. She had not fallen down since she was a child.

t hurt. Her head had knocked over the small electric heater. A mall electric fan, throwing warm air through a mesh. Quite safe n a room full of children because if it was knocked over it went ff automatically. It went off now, but tiny wires remained red ot, and the fan, although slowing rapidly, was turning still at hree thousand revolutions a minute. The brown hair on her tunned, dazed head, not quite fine but certainly not coarse, ried by the coffee-warm air of the bar, the dry sky outside, and he heater in Captain Dean's Rapier . . . If only it had still been vet. But it wasn't. About eight thousand hairs went through the vider rear mesh, were gripped, twisted by the fan, pulled tighter nd tighter; a few thousand touched the still-red wires: the mell of singeing, a sizzle, a flash of flame, a terrible halo . . .

She screamed and screamed, leaped about, lifted the weight f the electric heater with her hair. The thousands of hairs urned, the fire broke away; Sheila rushed about with agony ropelling her, smashed her head against the wall to ease the ain.

Even Max paled in horror, was overcome for moments, help-ess.

Someone came rushing in – 'Max!' – caring more about Max's torn ear than this screaming, once beautiful thing that vrithed on the floor. It was Tilda, the sad receptionist.

Max put the flames out, but too late: the hair and half the uperb face were burned, would never be photographed again xcept by hospital staff.

Max said, 'I can't think.'

Tilda was satisfied apparently. 'It's all over then?'

'Over? It never began.'

He knelt by the groaning Sheila. 'I'm sorry, my darling,' he onceded. 'Really sorry.'

She whispered from somewhere in the pain previously re-erved for the others of the world, not her – she belonged to hem now, was one with the hospital queues, the neutered of the arth; she put all her remaining strength into what she must say o him:

'*Why don't you take a photograph of it?*'

The ambulance came in three minutes.

Two other men.

'Who the hell are you?' Max Stuhler asked, knowing.

The one who answered smiled grimly. 'We're police officers. You're under arrest.'

'Stupid fools!' the dark girl shouted. 'It was an accident. I saw it.'

'What,' questioned Max, 'are you proposing to charge me with?'

'Let's start with grievous bodily harm to Sheila Antonov. Then we can proceed to blackmail, the official secrets, and other matters, eh?'

Max said with finality, 'I shall not answer any questions.'

'Shall I cancel Monday's appointments?' the girl asked.

The police officer qualified, 'You're coming, too.'

Max lost his temper, it seemed, shouted in panic, 'Don't be so dim. She doesn't know anything. She's just a receptionist.'

The policeman permitted himself a smile. 'Our information,' he told Max, 'is that she is your wife.'

In the studio and the flat above it was enough evidence to prove ten times over that Max Stuhler and his wife were giving information to a foreign power. It took Bellamy's men several hours to even list it.

His hands reached for the telephone, rehearsed, assembled words. Mr Bellamy, a letter, lunch. She must return for lunch, she *said* she would.

The exact words.

'Darling.'

And all that.

The frightened hand dropped, couldn't take the chance. They had made the chalk mark; Bellamy hadn't stopped them. The letter had come through the box, had been found this morning, 'A drink of tea?' 'Darling, how sweet you are to me,' and the pale limbs stretching inside the exclusive fluffiness. Eighteen stairs down, the rectangular white thing that was someone's death, his or hers.

Alexei prayed with desperate intensity, O God, I have sinned, sinned, have participated in the mathematics of evil, unutterable destruction.

Therefore do not spare me, but spare her, be gentle; she, with ou, is the receptacle of that portion of love of which I am apable . . .

The sweat rolled, an exhausting tiredness, cowardice defeated im, the flailing of nerves inside the body.

It was a trick, of course, all deceit and evasion. Anything they aid must inevitably be part of a plan for his overthrow, destruc- on. There was no question of them ever forgiving him as he orgave them that trespassed against –

Unstamped rectangular commonplace linen stationery. There- ore delivered by hand, Mr Bellamy and the postman avoided. here was an enemy in the grounds. No. Simpler than that. It ould be the milkman or the paper boy . . . He could not doubt ney were everywhere.

'Darling, tea, how lovely.'

The shaking hands.

'Angel, you look pale.'

He would follow their instructions, die. But they must prove, ne condition must be met, *she* must live. They wanted his nind; all right, they could have it, but that was his condition. therwise he reserved the right to die. They could extract con- essions, but a man had to have a degree of willingness to exert ne capabilities of spherical mathematics.

'I do have a headache.'

You will take a bus, then a train, a tube, return, go via, then ross, follow, turn right, wait. A man in a red Morris Oxford aloon will –

'You'll be back for lunch from this exhibition?'

'I don't know.'

'*Please.*'

'All right Alexei, angel.'

Obey instructions. Otherwise your wife, mother – remember ne chalk. You will say nothing to Mr Bellamy.

She went out of the house without good-bye. It proved the alue of the day in her eyes, its ordinariness, her expectation of eturn. From a hundred yards away he saw the coat that hid the rganza dress that hid the body not yet humiliated. He sighed in uiet esteem at the characteristic swing of the long, elegant legs, ne gloved arms . . . Christ, how beautiful. If they hurt her they ould wound God.

He waited, did nothing, sweated the morning away, twice walked to the telephone, once prayed that Mr Bellamy would ring: is everything all right?

She was, of course, going with others, tickets for five. Other models presumably: it had a slight value of protection. . . .

Sheila didn't return at twelve, or one, and he knew she would never return. Or, more accurately, he wouldn't see her again. Five minutes to two came. He hadn't eaten, felt tired, was without initiative; he had a headache, something aspirin couldn't cure.

He caught the bus, train, tube, went via, doubled back, and after an hour waited. It was raining.

The red Morris Oxford saloon approached, slowed, stopped, the rain drummed on its twenty-gauge steel. The window was lowered and the unknown masculine forty-five-ish, respectable, solicitor-surveyor-banker face was mildly surprised.

'Why, Antonov, you're getting wet.'

'I want to know –'

'Get in, Comrade. You cannot make conditions.'

Alexei said absurdly, 'I can walk away.'

'Then why have you come?'

'My wife. It must be guaranteed, proved –'

'We can guarantee her safety if –'

He climbed in the car, sat on the maroon leather. Movement, perspective, quite meaningless, altered; traffic lights, other cars, buildings, bright advertisements: You Can Be Sure of, brassières, biscuits, middle-cut salmon, puddles, a crowd of youth with coloured scarves, rattles, shouts.

'If you can prove she's safe I'll come whatever –'

'I can prove that.'

The driver was sniggering, a huge, private joke. Against *him* of course.

The behaviour of the Morris Oxford was peculiar. Fast, slow, turn left, right, left, double back; a quarter of an hour of this mechanical nonsense and even then the driver was not satisfied, eyes in the mirror all the time. And suddenly a swerve, into a garage, not just on to the concrete but straight in, under cover.

'I'm having a little trouble.'

'Mr Green is out. He has Sat'days off.'

'There is no hurry, but if I could hire –'

'No Oxfords, sir. Got a Cambridge or a Zodiac.'

'It is irrelevant.'

'What?'

'I don't mind.'

In the Zodiac, a repetition of the zigzags for a few minutes, then a glance at a watch, then a definite course, and finally a main road, crowded at first, then opened out, the countryside, rolling land, attractive farms, a windmill.

Not a word the whole way.

It was dusk when they reached Rochester. In the station yard the driver parked; a silence ensued, wait, his eyes examining, a train shunting; the quietness was beautiful.

'Outside, Comrade.'

The air, too, better than London's.

He felt tired, half asleep, out of control, capable of nothing.

Of all things, a naval officer!

Rapid dialogue in Russian.

Hope diminished, was dying.

He felt it would be useless, lies, a waste of time to even ask about Sheila. She was not really involved; they wouldn't bother.

'This way,' said the naval officer. 'No trouble or I'll kick your face in.'

'I must ask –'

The driver sniggered in private pleasure, sadism.

'Wait! He wants to know –'

'Just about my wife –'

'We must tell him! There was never any danger,' the driver asserted. 'She is one of *us*.'

It hurt; there was truth in it. He remembered the small things does Mr Bellamy follow you about, know about *me*? Cambridge. The sunburn. That she should marry him at all was peculiar. But he recalled her cry in the night, saturation, 'My toes!' She lived with terror, too, was under pressure. That sudden rush of words: 'I never pray. I daren't. You don't know me. You don't know what you've married.' He wouldn't stop loving her for these rats.

'If, therefore, you can guarantee her safety –'

'Oh, sure. Of course! Absolutely!'

He walked by the side of the naval officer; no trouble, he had nothing to live for. Well, he'd done something. Simpson and Mr Babbington and the others would take it from there, already had.

It was dark now, quiet among cranes and timber and silent ships. Street lights reflected on peaceful water. Up the gang plank on to the little ship. Polish, he saw from the bows. They wanted him alive, then.

He was handled with respect, as a dangerous cargo, always in sight. A cabin, with miniature proportions, and there was Pervukhin, in fancy naval dress, grinning, satisfied.

'Close the door,' he instructed someone, while Alexei paled in anticipation.

Pervukhin hit Alexei hard a few times, kicked. 'Just for fun,' he explained. 'They want you alive and well, but a rough sea causes bruises, eh?'

... While in London the telephone rang and rang and the chaplain finally answered.

'How dreadful. How very distressing. I don't know what to say. He isn't here. I don't *know* where, but I'll tell him when he returns. Such a beautiful girl,' the mouth said, but the pious mind had qualifications, had to admit to a little satisfaction. Very wrong of me, but she was too much of the world, that one, had need of pain to alter her perspective, enlarge it.

9

GEOFFREY SUMPSTER

It was late when Maggie arrived. Things were hotting up; several of them were well away, but the supply of booze was endless and could always be reinforced. The lights were on in the two rooms in use; music blasted along the corridors – it was how she found her way. People came and went, shook his hand, 'Fine, Geoff, fine. Congratulations' – 'Have a drink?' – 'I don't want to dry up the party' – 'Rubbish, there's plenty' – 'Cheers, then, Geoff!' The warden had broken his leg – no

ountaineering in Wales, but returning from mountaineering
ere; he'd fallen out of a train at Chester. Priceless!

They'd played a few games, scattered along the corridor.
an had been good to him – 'I really mean it, Geoff. I wish you
ts of luck,' and a willing, prolonged kiss in front of every-
dy. He was intoxicated on that, but more was to come. They'd
ought presents. Barbara came, and a cute dish called Susan
10 was ready for anything, but anything.

He was slightly drunk, very hot – a change in the weather,
e stifling atmosphere of the crowded small room – it didn't
atter.

'Christ, it's hot.'

He took his jacket off.

'Listen!'

He wasn't drunk, God, no; he could take gin. Funny, that,
cause beer bloated him out; usually he was sick after six or
ven pints.

'Geoff's going to make a speech.'

'Like hell I am. Not yet,' he qualified. 'I just wanna show
u –'

Two chairs, his little party piece, brilliant if it came off,
rn clothes and bruises if it didn't.

It was successful. He landed on his feet.

Applause for him, they hooted with laughter, admired him.
e was happy, hot, drenched with affection. His pals. All that
ap, solitude, Mr Gouseev . . .

Maggie walked in, green, a green dress, the flaming hair,
xy stockings, high heels. Holy God, how beautiful!

'Maggie!'

'Many happy returns of the day, Geoff.'

Introductions, pride, satisfaction.

A male voice, sober.

'Oh, Keith. Hello.'

'Best wishes, Geoff.'

'What's this?'

'Oh, that translation thing.'

His heart thumped. He was involved; the mind, saturated,
ppy, at ease, acknowledged now some uneasiness, new plea-
re. Anticipation always frightened one a little. . . .

'Oh, thanks, Keith. How did it come out?'

'Not too good. Not to worry. They paid you, eh?'

'They sure did.'

'Tomorrow, then, with the hang-over.'

'Stay for a drink?'

'Sure thing.'

'And this gorgeous thing is Maggie.'

Others claimed him. 'Geoff, hey, Geoff, time for a speech.'

'I'm not drunk enough. I must be uninhibited.'

'Five-syllable words! You're stone-cold sober!'

'I sure am. More gin, Sam.'

Sam was barman.

'Let's dance.'

The music floated, or was it his head? And he danced wi
Maggie in the rooms, the corridors; she was pliant, willing, r
sponding, smiling at him. 'You're enjoying yourself, Geoff?'

'Geoff!' voices insisted along the corridor, from the ligh
he was drifting away to darkness with Maggie. 'Geoff! Speec
Speech!'

'Oh, sod the speech!'

He couldn't care less what they wanted, thought; he w
with Maggie.

They came to fetch him.

'Must make a speech.'

'All right, you buggers.'

Back into the glare of illumination, stifling hot air.

'Christ, it's hot.'

'Take your shirt off, Geoff.'

'Not yet, gentlemen. Not yet.'

The confident lover. Trained by the psycho boys, paperbac
Stand on the chairs, one foot on each.

'I feel dizzy.'

'They're moving the building, Geoff.'

'Oh, is that what it is?'

'Speech!'

'Gentlemen. Oh sorry. Ladies *and* gentlemen. I am now,
the grace of *Snooz* and the strength of my parents, twenty-o
fit for anything. You, who are my fellows, will understa
that, standing here tonight ... Am I still standing?'

'Rhubarb,' said someone.

They took it up, a cry from the intellectual heart, the necessary madness; it was quite beyond Maggie's comprehension: Rhubarb! Rhubarb!

> 'Rhubarb keeps you fairly fit
> Because it tends to make you sit . . .'

'What about my speech?'
'You just made it.'

> 'Rhubarb can be very sour,
> Keep you upstairs half an hour,
> Rhubarb!
> Rhubarb!'

'Let's eat, gentlemen.'

They ate rapidly, standing, conversing, a few sitting; the gramophone flat out, people coming and going, not invited but dropped in to wish Geoff well, have a drink, view the talent, identify the quality of the party. Not bad. Geoff Sumpster's twenty-first going on over there, hence the lights and noise and music. (Good job the warden's broken his bloody leg or he'd have something to say, eh?) Any good? Not bad. Some splendid talent. I'll walk over, I think, and wish the poet well. Rhubarb.

His stamina, and theirs, was tremendous; two hours later the party was still going strong, only a few casualties. No one had looked at the clock, but if they had it would have told them: quarter to midnight. A party was identified in terms of success by the hour it ended – it proved maturity. Geoff had every intention of going on until four o'clock or unconsciousness, whichever was the sooner. How the hell he'd ever take Maggie home he didn't know. Taxi, presumably. Or stay the night. That was a disturbing thought.

She wasn't as drunk as himself, nowhere near, but was enjoying it, he could see that. Like himself, she was tireless, had an endless capacity for life, enjoyment.

Joan and Susan had vanished. So had Inman and George. And two bottles of gin. The lights were off in the room over the corridor. Someone was giggling. Noisy love-making. Nothing serious. Slap and tickle.

'Come on, Maggie,' he urged, excitement, prospects, sober
ing him a fraction, his heart thumping the gin, cheese, pies.

She was interested. Scared, but interested.

'Where? What is this?'

'I'll show you the college.'

A broad wink to the assembled drinkers, flushed, coopera
tive. The confident lover.

'Show her the laundry room, Geoff. Lovely and warm in
there.'

'Rhubarb, gentlemen.'

In the cooler darkness and silence of the corridors he held her
arm. 'My God, I'm stinking. I've had nine or ten. How many
did you have?'

'Two or three,' Maggie answered.

'Well, I suppose one of us had better be under control.'

Down an iron spiral of steps, cold air blowing from some
where. 'Hell, it's cold,' Geoff protested. She could smell the
sweat of him, but it wasn't that she minded. A bit of fun, yes
a fondle, perhaps, if necessary, even a few things removed, but
not what he wanted. He was too strange; she didn't love him
She was crazy, but light of heart, essentially innocent, wanted
tenderness, the quality Frank had been incapable of; she
thought Geoff might, in his curious solitude and fears, which
she identified, be glad of love, her kind.

The air belched out of the laundry room, hot, stupefying
Naked, Geoff thought, out of control, we could do it naked
But someone was there, two people. The meagre illumination
identified Tom Inman and Joan. Joan was sitting on Inman
chest, all legs and wild hair and clothes unfastened. They were
laughing and fighting, but, incredibly, proof of maturity, Geoff
found it didn't hurt, he didn't give a damn. Only get them out of
here; he had heat to generate, Maggie to taste.

They didn't even care that the door had been opened.

'Hey, sod off,' Geoff said crudely, in a hurry. 'Our turn now.'

'We haven't started,' giggled Inman. Joan was silent, still
for a moment, contained embarrassment. 'Go in the cupboard,'
urged Inman. 'It's large enough.'

Geoff compromised.

Maggie was pulled in – a confined space, but adequate.

as boiling hot; her skin felt the touch of heated air. There was click, some laughter.

'They've locked us in!'

Outside, Inman's voice corrected, 'Locked us *out* would be ore correct, Geoff.'

'Hey, come on!'

But they outside had hastened back to their giggles and easure; Joan's hissed protests and pleas, a chink of glass; a dy bumped against the locked door, silence; the flesh crawled. In the cupboard the smells of sheets, blankets. Pitch dark-ss. Pity. He wanted to see her. There was the reek of his eath and sweat. His hand found hers, a bottle of something. Have a swallow. Let's get hot.'

'I can't breathe, Geoff,' she said in fright. 'I don't like it.'

'Sit down,' he suggested. 'It's better.'

He had found a blanket. Everything arranged. Good for oody Inman.

She was not so drunk and was alarmed. When she sat down e was only too aware of his seeking hands.

'Don't talk loud,' he whispered.

He was kissing, all over the place, the pitch darkness, a ggle – 'I can't see what I'm doing.'

She didn't mind the kisses, was at a party, three sherries, and e had – or would have – money, would marry her, a factory – s dad owned a factory – oranges, sunshine; the only chance e'd ever have of marrying money, big money, so things had be permitted, a degree of pleasure . . .

But the things allowed urged him on, claimed more. He nsed there was some resistance, qualification. 'What the hell,' e pleaded. 'I'm twenty-one. You're gonna marry me, aren't ou?' And his fingers were, for her, vicious, impertinent. 'I feel bit sick,' she excused herself. His breath pounded in her face, rs, gin and cheese, and his hands were pulling down the eightless things that kept her private. Pain and degradation ere ahead. He wasn't tender; he was the same as Frank, raw, ude, in seach of himself. 'This is good,' he whispered, sweat lling, as if it could be compared with other, lesser occasions. Vonderful. I'm big tonight, Maggie. Twenty-one. Come on, by.'

'You can't,' she shouted, so that the silence outside was alter▪ in intensity: they were listening.

'For Christ's sake!' he insisted. 'Be *quiet*.'

Above all things he didn't want Inman, of all young men, a▪ Joan, of all young women, to overhear the progress of ▮ seduction or whatever ...

'Don't be frightened,' he whispered. 'I'm good at it. I wo▪ hurt.'

She was crying, the insect pinned. 'I feel sick. You've got ▮ stop. *Open the door!*' she demanded.

'What's a matter?'

Inman's sniggering voice.

Some quality of terror, beyond a party, joke, alcohol, m▪ have been identified by Joan or Inman. One of them open▪ the door. Light flooded in, shameful.

'Christ!' said Inman, getting an eyeful. 'What's going on?'

'Isn't Geoff behaving himself?' Joan asked, smirking.

Maggie told them wildly, 'He's just like – just like ▮ nigger.'

Just a reference, an association of ideas: the darkness, blac▪ ness, raw crudity, nothing more intended. She'd forgotten t▮ South African context, his racial hatred.

He was confused, feeling ill now, angry, hurt, stunned, w▪ his dulled mind realizing scores of implications: Joan h▪ heard, seen; they'd all know soon – like a nigger – it would ▮ tittered around the college – Geoff tried to rape her or son▪ thing; Geoff never made that ginger talent at the party. ▮ didn't get her coked up enough.

Geoff ran after her.

'Maggie, I was drunk.'

'Geoff, it's one o'clock.'

'I'm sorry.'

'All *right*, Geoff, but it's still one o'clock.'

'You won't say anything ...'

It was his plea: don't smash my status, my masculinity.

'I won't,' she agreed, 'but will they?'

He knew he was defeated again; there was some prope▪ he had which attracted hurt, defeat. And he felt ill now – was going to be sick.

'I feel ill,' he admitted.

'I'm not surprised,' Maggie said.

The headache was shattering, decisive. Party over. One 'clock. Not bad, could have been better. There was no strength left in him, no pride, even, in all the drinking, for it had been useless, led to nothing.

He had to go back eventually to his room. She'd gone, of course; so had Joan and Susan. The other faces welcomed him without pity. He was utterly humiliated and they knew every inch of it, found it hard not to tease, snigger, smile.

'God, Geoff, you looked shagged.'

'But he ain't,' said Ritchie with acid, things remembered.

'I spewed my guts up.'

'Musta been the cheese.'

'We'd better pack up, call it a day.'

He was alone in the bitter smell of cigarette smoke, surrounded by bottles, birthday cards. His head hurt badly; he couldn't think at all. When they'd all gone he shut the door, conscious of the silence, the whole world at sleep, the middle of the night. He began to weep. He'd never been so unhappy in his life or so wretched, so physically defeated. Nothing could save him. Not a day would pass by now without some small reference to it, a mere facial expression. He didn't know what to do. Nothing stared him in the face, an insulting nothing that would embarrass, wound, and humiliate him for the next year or two.

It was too much even to contemplate. He searched for the box of red pills, but there weren't any left. He remembered that he'd been so confident of Maggie – joy, sensual success – that he'd thrown the last few pills away. Troubles over, he'd thought. You never escaped. His disappointed blood flushed his face as he thought about Joan and Inman opening the door.

What would Maggie be doing, thinking? She'd threatened him, hadn't she? Geoff couldn't recall the exact words, but surely . . . No, he had threatened her. Terror shook him, aggravated the headache, as he considered what he had done. They could send him to prison. Espionage They'd paid him money. You could bet your life they'd got proof of his participation.

That doe-eyed Mr Gouseev would, via some bloody hirelin
make him carry out tasks more and more dangerous. He'd
paid, but sooner or later the thing would be found out. N
Gouseev would scuttle back to the safety of his embassy ar
everybody else would go to prison.

He had put the envelope in the letter box late last nigh
Perhaps he'd been seen. The thing would carry his fingerprin

His heart thumped in panic.

All this. For what?

His art, his poetry, his cry from the beleaguered heart, pu
lished in a foreign country.

He was worried about that. Something Keith had said. Kee
it for the hang-over.

Don't look, he instructed himself.

But the mind inside the shattering headache was curiou
even a little proud. Keith had translated the article that su
rounded Geoff's poem in the Soviet magazine. They'd pro
ably put down the biographical details incorrectly. As if th
mattered.

He had to know how it translated backward, what they sa
about him.

Keith had written an explanatory note about literal transl
tion, alternative words.

Geoff wasn't interested in any of that. His bloodshot ey
wanted to know about *himself*.

... as an example of sordid English poetry, symptomatic (
current decadence, a proof, if proof were needed, a pitif
revelation of the degradation into which English colle
life ...

He couldn't believe it.

They'd used him as a political pawn. He and his cry-from
the-heart were just so much rubbish to indicate the conditio
of English society.

Wait a minute! Don't panic! That, supposedly, was th
point of the bloody thing, to condemn these nigger lovers.
was just the manipulation of words; it looked funny seeing it
print like that.

... hopeless, immature, brash texture ... inadequate grasp (
political meaning, reality, just a secondary justification of se

*typical moaning of one unable to support life even in a
*-called 'free society'. The constant reference to sexual
ilues .....*

Geoff was stunned. He couldn't stand, his legs fluttered so
adly.

Just like a nigger ...

One unable to support life ...

This, too, would be all over the college.

He wept silently, wallowed in misery; the hours went by –
was nearly three o'clock.

He was doomed – fated to humiliation, scorn, sniggers, and
• justice, courts of law, prison. He was finished. He was, the
eeping mind knew, nice, kind, brave, a good sport, quite hand-
•me, very strong; he could dance, box, debate, play tennis,
icket, swim, make love ...

All uselessly. In their bloody pick-nosed English arrogance
ey knew better, defeated him before he began. Not interested.
igger lovers.

He could defeat them all. One gigantic demonstration to
ow they were unworthy of *him*.

They'd be sorry then. It would shake them out of their sel-
shness and meanness. They'd carry the guilt of it all their
ves. It would change every one of them. And she (meaning
an, not Maggie) would read about it and be sorry, too, know-
g what a little maturity, passion conceded, would have done,
evented. Every time she pulled her cheap pants down she'd
 conscious of his death.

It had the attraction of an important work of art, carried out
 pain, exhausting the artist, killing him, but carrying the abso-
te conviction of truth.

He couldn't find rope and knew it had to be a razor blade.
e had been very fussy about cleanliness, skin condition, bad
eath, and stood in front of the mirror for forty minutes con-
dering it, courage coming and going. Then courage flooded,
came conviction, necessity, and his left-hand fingers obtained
e throat to the satisfaction of the right.

They found him in the morning. Sam came in for an aspirin,
eing the light still on.

Half an hour later the police arrived.

No one knew why he'd done it. Opinion was collected inste
of evidence.

He was popular!

He was a success with the girls!

His work was excellent!

He was good at sport!

He was everybody's pal, one of the chaps!

Deverson said, 'He would have made a good historian,
cause he was without prejudice.'

It was the epitaph Geoff would have wished for.

The faces meant nothing now; she did not have to be po
to them any longer. They were shrieking at each other, cra
with enjoyment. Geoff was their excuse, their permission. Th
meant absolutely nothing. She would never see them ag
She found her coat and went along the corridor into
safety of darkness, conscious of mild distress, a residue
something that, despite Geoff's bestial behaviour, felt
guilt.

Down spiral stone steps without turning on any light switch
for she didn't want to have to make explanations, even acce
able lies. She nearly fell once in the darkness. A door. It v
locked, but the old key was on the inside. She opened
door, went outside – cooler air, the stars, the infinity of G
The trivial rubbish that had been this Saturday night cau,
her emotionally by the throat for a moment; what on ea
was she doing? All the world, the complicated, fantastic bea
ful world, all the elements, things ignored, rain, sky, earth,
sea – she was humbled for a second, troubled by these m
important things, the pitiable foolish perspective that one we
human being is capable of. Ah, God, I am sorry ... All
world there, available, and she, Maggie Preston, had to ansv
the telephone, reject dirty hands in a cupboard, sell informat
to people for the possible destruction of the earth, all so t
she could buy a dress, stockings, a gold watch to examine
time that was useless.

I'm sorry, I'm sorry, she acknowledged in the private m
of Maggie Preston, the reality below the 'Honestly' and va
absurdities, the dancing and lies and conceit and the possess

urge for more friends, additional admiration. I'm sorry. I can't promise anything. It's the way the world is. But I'll try.

She crashed into a dustbin. The noise terrified her, and she rod, ran, on gritty coke. She was lost; the college grounds onfused her, unfamiliar paths, a new building under construction, scaffolding and wheelbarrows and mud ...

Things have got to be different. I must stop.

He threatened me.

No one has evidence.

So stop. *Now*. This moment. When they phone again ignore them: 'I'm sorry, Henry, I don't know what you're talking bout.' The absurd, dream quality that motivated her and yet aved her, time after time, couldn't really believe it had to ontinue. Nothing had happened, only Geoff's party, but her maginative, zany mind played in courtrooms, was questioned, ut, as usual, was evasive; television scenes went along the etina: 'If you shoot me they will open the letter and read bout Dieter, Major Gouseev, everything.'

A gate, an unfamiliar street, dirty air, a cat bellyaching. What's a matter, Tom?' Was he Tom? 'Haven't you got a girl riend?' A taxi, she decided. I've got the money.

She knew, despite her featherweight heart, that it would lways be the same. She had just rejected the only opportunity o make it different. It would always be Eggy and Vera, or omeone like them, World Mechanical, hard work and headches for each Friday's pay packet. Sunday's portion, the dirty ity streets, a fortnight at Butlins, a bit of jewellery, some new tockings. You couldn't defeat the world if you hadn't been orn in the right place and if you were a girl. She didn't carry esentment, but the long emptiness of the rest of her life conronted her, questioned her under the stars. She had to stop; here was no future in espionage. She had £575 in the bank, olly good for a girl of nineteen. It would straighten out sooner r later, her light optimistic mind assured her. She'd marry, et rid of Frank.

Two drunk men on the pavement. Huge, rough – they could mash her like a twig. But she was unafraid, still Maggie, evaive, good humoured, not frightened of men (despite Geoff), ven drunken ones, at two in the morning. 'Be off, you wicked

old man. I'm a policewoman,' she said to the one who want‹
to get fresh. 'I'll have the lot of you in jail.' They laughe‹
rolled about with the humour of it, moved on. 'A policewoma‹
A fornicating policewoman!' They couldn't get over it.

She found a taxi, which proved luck still existed, was on h‹
side.

The light was still on in the flat. They were pretty decen‹
waited up for her, the gossip, a cup of tea, laughter and subu‹
ban life shared.

Vera's voice said from up the stairs, 'That'll be her now.'

Mick, she thought, and was filled with love, joy. He was ‹
good kid, straight, kind, never tried anything nasty, and ‹
had the fever badly.

No voice cried out; no one rushed on to the landing to gre‹
her. Not Mick then. But someone despite two o'clock, and s‹
forgot the anxiety under the stars. Voices, people, laughter; s‹
was *alive* . . .

Light was strong in the room, startling after the hour's dar‹
ness.

Oh, my God, she thought.

Two men sitting, now rising, but not politeness; duty, n‹
conversation. Not her class, her world.

Her leg muscles fluttered, her stomach was in protest, se‹
sherry up her throat. Too late. She'd never marry Mick or Ra‹
never meet another Trevor, Vivian, or Geoff. It was a battl‹
ground and there had to be casualties.

Eggy and Vera stiff and alarmed, but fascinated, the inse‹
pinned, to be destroyed. She swallowed; entire conversatio‹
timetables, and rehearsed lies passed through her mind in t‹
time it took for her eyes to revolve half an arc, smile.

'Mrs Maggie Preston?'

There were things on the table – photographs, letters fro‹
Dieter; they'd been here hours. They, too, curiously enoug‹
seemed tense, ready for something terrible.

'That's little me. Got a cup of tea, Vera? The party w‹
ghastly.'

'The party,' punned the less humorous of the two men, ‹
over. We're police officers.'

'*Honestly,* I'd never have known.'

They smiled feebly at her tiny, useless courage.

'Where's Antonov?'

She could afford to grin; the name meant nothing to her.

'Is it a place or a name?'

'Take that damn stupid smile off your face,' the one said
arshly. 'Antonov's gone. I'll see you get fifteen years, Mrs
reston, but if you talk and talk I might get it down to five.'

'What on earth is all this?'

'Your friend Henry has gone off with Antonov. *Where?*'

'I've never heard of Antonov.'

'Then where's Henry?'

She confessed quickly, her mouth stiff in fear as though
aaesthetized, 'I did it for you. I didn't mean ... You see, they
apped me, and so I *had* to do it, and so the only way, honestly,
as to give them false information.'

This outburst, so unlike her normal control, was crazy talk
or Vera and Eggy, but it seemed to make tiny sense to the
olicemen.

'Who enlisted you?'

She told them.

'Do you know a Major Gouseev?'

She admitted that she did.

'And you met this man Henry each Friday?'

'Yes. Like I said.'

'And you gave him information about World Mechanical's
ading position?'

'I was frightened. I thought it was big business, honestly,
othing to do with me. They said it was a cartel. They could
ave drowned me in Heidelberg. And then they had photo-
aphs ...'

'And you were asked particularly to supply news if you over-
eard any about a thing called Billiards?'

'Yes.'

'Which you did?'

'Yes.'

'Did you know what this Billiards was?'

'Not for a long time. Then I was frightened, told them un-
uths.'

'Everything you told them was untrue, or just some of it?'

'I'm sorry, sir, a bit was true. I had to be convincing . . .'

'What did you tell them that was untrue?'

'I said, one thing I remember, honestly, I told them th
Strang's Chemicals in Liverpool was manufacturing chemic‑
for this rocket.'

'Anything else?'

'Oh yes, lots, honestly, but I can't remember *now*. I've be
to this party and I feel awful and you've surprised me. I ca
think . . .'

They allowed themselves to grin, knowing this, at any ra
was honest.

'But you did tell them that Strang's was producing stuff ‑
this Billiards.'

'Oh yes.'

'Mrs Preston, you should have gone on the stage.'

She smiled. It was true, now considered; she'd just nev
thought of it. 'You really think I might have succeeded?'

'Of course. You tell lies with such conviction. As I think y
know very well, Mrs Preston, Strang's Chemicals supplies t
propellant fuel for Billiards.'

There was no answer to that one; not even her imaginati
could wriggle out of this situation. It was as if truth its
wanted a private joke.

10

CHARLES FILMER

'WHAT made you take part?' Filmer asked carefully, fasc‑
ated, paralysed.

The dog panted, rain fell, cars went past, doors opened, sm
children stared, Easter was nearly here, buns, chocolate eg
Time to mourn, but it was quiet inside the cathedral. No r‑
of desperate feet, no hands grasping at the torn cloth, Ch
forgive us, what did we do? – we must have been *mad*.

Principles.

Presumably they, the rabble who had followed in the bak

ın, had had them also. It was impossible for fallible, mortal,
ıcompetent, self-loving humans to have principles without
ıso causing pain. He said to Brenda, 'You cannot go,' or, 'You
ıust not do this or that,' and her eyes suffered, pain went on,
ıslike, temporary cessation of love.

The woman said, 'Well, y'got to stand up for your rights.'

Why not, he thought frivolously, sit down for them? Or
ıeel? Listen, Jesus, listen, he pleaded in the mind, I try to do
ght. I must use vehicles that are weaker, fools like this woman;
have to operate in the terms of the twentieth century – bits of
ımplate and wires and now this spatial impulse selector.

Man, and woman, assuming this monstrous sordid equality:
want, therefore you must surrender, give, be destroyed. It was
priceless joke, killingly funny – hundred megaton bombs to
ıange the minds of the House of Lords! He sniggered use-
ssly.

'Listen!' the woman, too, pleaded. 'Did you bring it?'

'No.'

'Why not, Mr Filmer?'

'Why d'y'think?' he asked angrily. ''Cause I couldn't.'

She was polite, subservient, must placate this dangerous vain
ıol; the whole world depended on him.

'They're relying on you.'

'I can't be rushed.'

'Don't you think – you see, a boat. I shouldn't talk, but
ısten, we're reasonable. We want it badly next Saturday. It's
ıportant. You can have *anything*,' she concluded hopelessly,
ınowing he desired nothing. He didn't even crave equality; it
as not politics with him, just principles, hatred, acid in the
ıul.

'This blasted dog. Oh, she does pull. Sixty-five pounds she
ʻeighs. It's not fair. I get tired. *Anything*.'

'I don't want anything.'

It wasn't true.

The purity of Brenda, Ted, and Bull, and Mrs Farthingale
ımbled, must plead (*did* in his mind under the bedclothes)
harles Filmer, *Mister* Filmer to you, was right. That was all
e wanted. Some cleanliness in the world. There's a bugger over
ıe road trying to save your bleedin' soul. He flushed whenever

he thought – and he thought often. Men like that were low
than animals.

It made one believe in hell. There was a hell all right. But y
had to try *now* to put it all right, convince with devastation
Mister Filmer, and my principles are right. You couldn't w
for the long queues after death, the endless Old Baileys, Nure
bergs beyond the grave. If you believed, if you were Char
Filmer, you had to *act*.

He said, 'I'll try.'

'Believe me,' the woman assured him, 'the last thing we w
is trouble. This lets you out, Mr Filmer. You've been splend
Just this once more. As I said, they told me, *anything*. W
don't you,' she said foully, surrendering to what she was su
posed to hate, 'take 'em up on it? Ask for a thousand. Yo
get it.'

'Ta,' he thanked her politely. 'It would be nice, but it wo
feel wrong.'

'You're a good man,' she asserted eagerly, but he doubted
sincerity. It was just the desperate anxiety to have that spa
impulse selector next Saturday for a ship; she did say sh
Boat.

It filled him with warmth, like Keuscher's whisky: a s
would move across the sea, in a gale perhaps, formalities, lo
ing, flags, men, taps running, oil – all because Charles Filr
had said *I will*.

He went back to Canterbury Station and the journey hom
the dirty electric train, filthy lavatories, grime; the very se
oozed disease. A crowd got on at some small-town stati
louts by the dozen, no grace, politeness, no sense of quiet – fo
ball supporters or something; he hated them. They crashed
and down corridors, left doors open, smoked in non-smok
compartments, sniggered at girls, one or two wrestled, and f
words were shouted for anyone to hear. It was satisfying to
there, nothing in their perspective of the world, knowing t
were doomed. They removed doubt.

Home, to a sullen silence, the solitary question, 'Where
you been?' and the single-syllable reply, 'Out.'

He no longer went to Dawson's little meetings. He was c
verting the world on his own terms, far beyond Daws

powers or imagination. Sunday passed in tiredness; he sat as one stunned, a heavy toll taken by these weeks of what others would call 'treason'. 'Dinner's ready,' the tender voice of Brenda called. 'Dad, come on!' But he had little appetite, felt terror as he walked the few yards to gravy and Yorkshire pudding and the gramophone records on the radio, too loud for conversation. What to do? Nothing had occurred in these weeks and months to alter opinion. Nothing. The work and the people and the contents of newspapers. But he was exhausted by fear. He felt the longing to be liked, loved, by his small family, but it was too late now.

He was wet with fear when he thought of the Random Selector. Monday, dull, wet, a tired day. At lunch time the two hundred and fifty of them filed out through the turnstile to E Gate and the larger crowd. Two hundred and fifty thumbs pressed the button of the Random Selector. They'd signed; it was permissible; if it came on red they could strip you, laugh, go through the formality. It wasn't abused. About one man a week pressed the button and it came on red instead of green. In five minutes he would be out again. 'Y'know what they did?' Filmer listened intently. Many times he'd been through, saturated, with little guilty pieces of the spatial impulse selector in his pocket. It might not have mattered. A featherweight template wouldn't damn him. 'Oh, I put that bloody thing in my pocket when I went to the bogs this morning.' But the spatial impulse selector – you couldn't put *that* in your pocket by accident. It was very small, to be sure, but heavy, two or three pounds.

He listened and watched. He couldn't ask, but once or twice in conversation he'd picked up useful information. The Random Selector, he knew now, had four tumblers. He wasn't supposed to know this; all he was allowed to know was that now and again a man was stopped by the red light, searched. About once a week. No one so far searched had, of course, been guilty of theft, let alone espionage. It was a formality because of the importance of the spatial impulse selector and Billiards. Four tumblers, you see, and a Security man who couldn't care less flicked them early on the first working day of each month. Each tumbler went up to nine. So you had a total of 9999 pos-

sibilities each month. There were 250 men; they went out of th
turnstile twice a day – lunch and home – for five days a week
Four weeks, 500 thumbs a day, 2,500 a week, meant 10,000 exit
in the four-week month. As far as Filmer knew the thing wa
set for each *calendar* month, so there was, this being Marcl
not February, an overlap of three days. But it was perhap
counterbalanced by men away ill.

The 10,000 thumb depressions, then, in one month, and th
tumblers were preset to select only four. Last week the Ran
dom Selector had come up – on 3791, although he could hardl
know that – and a man had been searched. Quite normal. N
comment. But it was worrying. Today they were beginning th
third week of the month. It had three more selections to mak
in ten working days, and on the fifth of those ten, next Friday
Filmer must steal a spatial impulse selector.

Monday passed slowly – careful assembly, eyestrain; the 25
thumbs on the way to fish and chips, sandwiches, beer, por
pies, pressed the white button and the light showed green, green
green all the way. The button was white, but going grey, an
was slippery with the tiny bits of grease and dirt of each thumb
The Security man stood like a big fat pompous pig, thumb
in belt, watching as though Random Selector had been his idea
invention. Filmer didn't like him: inflated, self-importan
ignoramus. 'Rice pudding,' Filmer ordered at the hotel, an
the waitress/barmaid sniggered as usual. It was hard to shove
the pudding down. The wind was against him as he cycle
back, and he felt desperately weak. Oh, God, he beseeched, le
it come on today, get it over with. The siren blew and the after
noon ended. He was tired, wanted to go home, rest, sleep. H
reserved the right to change his mind. 'We don't want an
trouble, Mr Filmer, believe me.' If they could send one shij
they could send another. Or a plane or a man in a car. But h
had to take it on a Friday, so that the factory was silent, th
theft unknown, all through Saturday and Sunday while th
stolen object moved farther and farther away from the Elec
tronics Division of Mayger Electric.

He was in thought about this when the queue stopped. Th
red light. Random Selector had claimed its second search of th
month. A bit of laughter, an impatient plea, 'Come on, get

bloody move on!' and the selected man amused. 'I hope they don't take me clothes off; I ain't had me annual bath!' The tumblers had been preset on March 2 and had come up on 5340. There were two exits a day now for Tuesday, Wednesday, Thursday, and Friday this week and the five days of next, and he knew that Random Selector had two more selections to make. At this moment the odds against Charles Filmer being selected were 4569 to 2. Unless another man had been selected by this Friday afternoon the odds would be less but still over 2500 to 2.

The days went by; the spheres were carefully manoeuvred about on trolleys, the components fitted. They averaged three spatial impulse selectors a day, which didn't make it easier; if they'd been lying about in thousands, like rivets . . .

Ted and Marion came on the Wednesday evening; nothing better to do, he supposed. He listened dully to the stupid talk. 'We're going to Switzerland this summer. Y'got to spend your money when you make it, see the world, get your mind broadened, eh?' Ted sniggered to the assembled attentive audience of four. Filmer felt pity for the porters, waitresses, people on trains: a long itinerary of hatred, unless Ted encountered other fools. It was hard to imagine a sensible little country like Switzerland having its quota of Teds and Marions.

He listened without hatred, for he had long since achieved the process which eliminated fools; this Friday would see the levelling completed. They'd never know, would still stare at the headlines, not believing, because they must inevitably remain in character, fools. It made the week easier to bear. But even so he sweated in sleep, bit fingernails to pieces, bit his lips, was desperately tired by fear, for Random Selector let the thumbs signal green five hundred times on Tuesday, Wednesday, and Thursday.

A man called Bent was away on Friday. It left whole square yards of bench empty, a partial privacy, conditions excellent. If only Random Selector would pick its third worker of the month as the 249 went out to lunch. It could even pick *him*, for his pockets were empty. But it was green, green, a hurrying queue, the click, click of the turnstile and the Security man's red, gross face yawning.

In the afternoon, because of the missing Bent, there was pile-up of work beside Filmer. Three trolleys with spatial impulse-selector equipment stood in a line by him.

He had to do it.

The risk was terrifying, but that ship waited. The opportunity was from God; there was a kind of inevitability, justice, in that small assembly of trolleys that not only had three spatial impulse selectors but in themselves partly hid Filmer.

At half past four he put one in his pocket. His skin was hot in the terror of the simple movement of his hands. His breathing was bad, his heart so fast he was afraid in terms of illness, collapse. Then it was in the pocket, small but surprisingly heavy. If he bumped, jostled, in the exit queue would anyone say, 'What have you got there?' Or would officialdom come along in the remaining time, send the trolleys past Filmer, and a cry go up, 'One's missing!'? Or, equally and absolutely frightening, would the same officialdom, management, come to some silly decision about those trolleys? 'We can't leave 'em lying about, can we'.

The siren blew and he was so weak he could scarcely move. His hands were wet in fear, his face rigid. Thank God this was the last thing he had to do to save or change the world. He wasn't brave enough, strong enough to carry the world. Never mind, if they didn't catch him in the next five minutes they'd never catch him. By Sunday that piece of metal would be on the North Sea.

What position to take in the 249 men leaving work? He felt the panicky urge to rush, get it over with, get his bike, and get the hell out of here. He deserved money, a thousand; perhaps even now he could ask for cash gratitude. No. He'd feel good, superior to them all – Ted, Bull, Dawson, the Government, the fools, the selfish, the weak, the blasphemers, the dirty ones – as soon as his saturated pores breathed fresh air.

He also felt the terrified, weak tendency to hang back, be the last man out, see if Random Selector chose anyone. In the end he was merely jostled into position somewhere about halfway.

Click, click, click went the turnstile. Friday afternoon, freedom for two days – you could sense it – parole from civilization's requirements. Football, beer, horses, screw the wife, girlfriend. In some ways you couldn't blame them. It was an insult

ing, boring, degrading existence at Mayger. Green, green, green
went the visual signal to proceed.

Then a halt.

'Come on, you buggers!'

Laughter.

'They're gonna check Percy.'

'My God, Percy!'

The red light and the locked turnstile had stopped the queue.
Random Selector had picked its third person for the month. Filmer's body, under tremendous tension, went light, felt weightless, floated. He wanted to laugh, cry, scream, so great was
pleasure. To think he might have taken that man's place! He
was safe now. It was odds of about 2,600 to one against his own
selection. But it was more than that. The machine never picked
more than one man on one day. It was as if Random Selector
had a kind of fairness, thought to itself: You mustn't press
these blokes too hard – they've been good enough to sign their
freedom away, their dignity. Four a month, that's all. And
spread, so it doesn't feel like a damn prison or a customs search.
The tumblers were supposed to be spun at random, with indifference, but, despite his small knowledge, Filmer wondered if the
management and security, in an attempt to spread the indignity,
didn't perhaps space it out themselves to once a week or so
before going through the rigmarole of locking the preset
tumblers.

The queue moved on – green, green, green, click, click, click.
The man called Percy had entered a cubicle, was unheard, out of
sight. There would of course, be trouble on Monday, but
Filmer could face that. The spatial impulse selector would be
scores and even hundreds of miles away. It was over. He was
very glad; the weeks and months had tired him; he slept badly,
had the stomach-ache.

The stomach-ache . . .

Something pressed into his belly. It was an iron horizontal
bar of the turnstile. He felt a flash of irritation. Machines,
machines, bloody machines. They were made for man, not man
for them. Why didn't the cow function? He was tired, in a
hurry.

'What's the matter with the damn thing?' he asked.

The thought entered his head, shattered all calm : *It's come* (
red again.

He couldn't, he couldn't, lift his head and eyes to see; the
were too tired, afraid.

The fat pig who was Security, said, 'Wait a minute!'

Filmer raised his frightened eyes. Yes, it was all right; t
green light shone.

He was, in anxiety, seconds away from freedom, furious . . .

'Turn it! Make it move! Have I got to stand here all night

He addressed his panicky thoughts aloud to the gross, comi
opera uniformed Security man, a man who was loved by no on
he had all the characteristics of a pompous park keeper, li
operator, traffic warden . . .

'It'll move when I'm ready to rotate it,' the man said, flushin

Filmer's terror turned his exhausted body into an athlete's. H
was over the turnstile in one movement. Others followed, laug
ing; two or three others were ready to leap.

'*Wait!*'

Thus the Security man in the face of this proof of his nothin
ness.

'To hell with you!' said the younger man, and was off. The f
hands grasped but missed him, seized Filmer instead.

'Just a minute!' the Security man shouted. 'Who are y(
shoving?'

'I'm in a hurry,' Filmer pleaded. 'Wife ill –'

'*Wait!*' repeated the Security man in a bellow. He, too, w
sweating. His panic was that of others' contempt, his own us
lessness, dismissal . . .

'Who are you touching?' Filmer asked in hatred. 'Take yo
damn hands off.' The lout was interfering with the purpose (
God, the world . . .

'I'm Security here –'

'The light's on green.'

Men were laughing at them. Someone had to be humiliate
lose, him or this sod Filmer. He had authority, must prove it,
dismissal : I understand, Stevens, there was some disturbance (
Friday? Yes, sir. And the long search in the newspapers : nig
watchman wanted, some police experience useful, some clea
ing work, free meals, holidays with pay, small pension . . .

'*I'm* Security,' he shouted, sweat rolling down the suet-pudding face. 'The light's a game, a check. *I* am Security.'

Filmer made the worst mistake of all. It didn't matter. A polite word, Sorry, wait a few minutes. I see what you mean . . . But no, it was too much. Panic prodded, the world in his pocket, ship waiting, and this fool . . .

'You?' he sneered. 'You're just a man for a cinema queue! You're *nothing*!'

The fat face hardened, became mean. Filmer saw in terror that it had a certain authority, a toughness. Everybody had a toughness when they confronted Charles Filmer.

'Mr Mason,' he called over the impatient heads. 'Mr Mason, want this man searched.' His fat hand gripped Filmer's arm like a vice.

A clerk said from behind a glass partition, 'What's a matter, Bert? He's through the green, isn't he? Come on, Bert, get the blasted thing moving. It's Friday. Don't keep the lads waiting. Let him go.'

Filmer was weak, sick, feeling the irresolution in the gripping hand. But the voice was still offended. 'All right, when I can, but want this one searched. I'm Security, see? And I say he's gotta be searched.'

They were very kind about it, courteous, because he was, of course, innocent; but the Security man, Bert, had rights, a card in his pocket that said he'd been given authority to search, question, refer a man to others. But the clerks were hesitant, and in this was Filmer's final hope. Was it fair? And, because it was a British factory and not a Soviet or Chinese one, there was comic confusion . . .

'Where's Mr Pepper?'

'Gone home.'

'He didn't ought –'

'Don't tell *me* –'

All the time the three or four of them, clerks, *fools*, had a minor, indifferent eye on him, the queue was still growling. He heard their pleasurable analysis.

'It's that prick, Filmer.'

'Oh, him. Wouldn't fancy stripping *him*, myself!'

Too many eyes were on him. The spatial impulse selector wa̶
like a two-pound block of chocolate in his pocket. Not meltin̶
Fright came back like a powerful disease of the nerves, paraly̶
ing him. He could scarcely think of anything. He heard his ow̶
silly castrated voice, 'It isn't fair, searching *two* in one afte̶
noon.'

The clerks were inclined to agree. 'If we can find Mr Pepp̶
... You'd better move out of the way, in here.'

He was outside the safety of mass, an individual now, to b̶
dealt with by Mr Pepper if they could find that office manage̶

'I'm in a hurry,' he pleaded. 'My wife's ill. Couldn't you do̶
on Monday?'

They had the sympathy but not the authority; it was beyon̶
them, in Mr Pepper's department. 'It won't take a minute.'

Out came the other man, Percy, hair untidy, straightening h̶
tie – 'The things they do!' – and he was off, homeward, free.

Mr Pepper, self-important, harassed by fools: 'Well, w̶
thought, being as he'd got through the green light, he was e̶
titled –'

'Thought?' Mr Pepper was hot. 'He signed the thing, didn̶
he?' His eye fell on Filmer. Nothing, his indifferent expressio̶
said, nothing, no claims on Harold Pepper.

Filmer said bitterly, not that they'd care if it was true, 'M̶
wife's very ill. The shops close in a quarter of an hour. I've g̶
to –'

'But you signed, didn't you?'

'I'm asking you to be reasonable. Two in one afternoon –'

'Reasonable? Me? Am I to be dissuaded from my duty?'

Rubbish, of course. He was annoyed because he'd been on h̶
way home, had been dragged back by fools who couldn't mak̶
a decision without him.

'Step in here.'

'I feel ill ...'

'Only a minute,' said the clerk.

The big windbag Security man in brass buttons and self-im̶
portance came in the cubicle, too. Hope died. He could hav̶
petitioned the clerk, 'I wanted to show my kid ...' but not th̶
man.

He had to go through the motions, pretend, hope. Coat off.

'It's heavy.'

'I got my glasses –'

A wave of genuine shock, eyes that stared at him in disbelief.
'What's this?'

The sweat rolled. His face was white. His revealed shirt was
ending off waves of fear; the smell filled the cubicle. Every bit
of him was trembling. The clerk had the world in his hands.
Filmer couldn't brazen it out, was scarcely able to say anything.
'Mr Pepper!'

He heard the manager's irritation, 'Oh, my God, *now* what?'
and the exasperated face altered, was startled, but made decisions; it was why he was manager.

'What's this?'

'It's a spatial impulse selector.'

'Where was it?'

'In his pocket.'

'An explanation?'

'Somebody musta put it there,' said Filmer, but the shaking,
sweating, and the guilt on his face conveyed the truth.

'Why did you take it?'

'To show my kid.'

'It's worth tens of thousands, is an official object, of immense
secrecy. You signed. *Why did you take it?*'

'I wanted to study it.'

'All *you* have to do is assemble it.'

Silence, voices further away, the news spreading. Someone's
punched an S.I.S. Pepper's in there now. Who? That religious
prick, Filmer.

'Get Mr Shaw.'

It was too big even for Mr Pepper.

Filmer stood there, life over, decisions ended; there was even
a tiny feeling of relief in it. Others could take on the burden of
the world now. He'd tried.

'He's gone home.'

'Get him. And the police.'

Minutes passed. He was tired, wanted to sit down; they'd
forgotten he was human, under a strain. It was all new, exciting,
for them; they were tireless.

'Can I sit down?'

They stared at him as if he was mad.

The comedy went on. Mr Shaw's wife said her husband h[...] gone to Oxford direct from Mayger's. A constable arriv[...] didn't quite know what to do. A sergeant came. They talk[...] discussed it: 'You'll have to get a Special Branch bloke' – 'W[...] not Mr Smith?' – 'I wish to God you'd just do as you're bloo[...] told.'

On and on, tireless, while he felt sick with fear and exha[...] tion. People hung about, waiting to be important, part of he[...] lines.

After two hours they wearied of it.

'You're not under arrest, but you'd better not go anywhere.[...]

He was baffled.

'You mean I can go home?'

'Yes. Don't go anywhere.'

The Security windbag was justifiably annoyed. 'You can't[...] him go just like that. All the trouble I had in finding him.'

'*You* had!' a clerk sneered.

It was nearly dark. He was faint with tiredness, followed t[...] small group outside. He made his way to the bicycle sheds, he[...] tated. There were half a dozen of them there; Bull's voice sa[...] 'Here he comes,' and then, in animal identification, 'That y[...] Filmer?'

He sought his bicycle. 'I'm going home.'

They took his bike, smashed it to pieces. He'd had it for [...] years; it hurt to see it destroyed. He cried out in genuine gri[...] 'You've smashed my bike. I'll have the law on you,' still beli[...] ing that there was a law and he could appeal to it – in his sm[...] world of bicycles, rice pudding, Brenda, the newspapers. ...

'You've been questioned?' Bull asserted. 'You've pinch[...] something?'

They weren't quite sure. He had only to deny it, say, 'A m[...] take,' and they'd let him go. But so deep in guilt was he that [...] never thought of it.

'Answer, you bastard!'

Bull pulled him, and at once his sacrosanct person, his remo[...] ness (for he was so strange, different, they feared him slight[...] was lost; he was what they'd half believed: human, weak, wi[...] out their physical toughness.

They didn't hate him for his betrayal – they would have sold ngland, God, for a couple of pounds. They hated him for his pinions, his implied condemnation of them, his daughter who as pure, his contempt of football, beer, sex, unions, of where e ought to know he belonged. So they beat him while the stification was available, beat him up with fists and feet and a hain, and felt good: they were men.

He got home somehow.

Vi was out.

Brenda sat there, pure, beautiful; his heart wept.

'*Dad!* What's happened?'

'Where's your mum?'

'Gone to Mrs Harris's. Oh, Dad, Dad!' She had stood up, the ne person in the world who loved him, his values, his tired, ured mind. 'What's the matter? You look ill.'

He sat down, near to collapse, breaking point. The smell of mething – cottage pie or stew – filled the room, made him tch. She came to him, touched his grey hair with shyness. ou've been hurt.'

'Brenda, kid, I'm in trouble.'

She began to cry, sensed the importance, the necessity, the end f something.

'What happened to me, kid? Why did I do it?'

'Dad, what did you do?'

He was too exhausted to explain it logically.

'When you were a little kid I used to pick you up, rub my face to yours, stroke your chubby cheeks in wonder. Now look t me. I've no charity. I'm without love. I've betrayed the orld.'

She went on crying, the end of something, perhaps every-ing; her Dad shattered; the man of pure iron appealing to her, st, confused.

'Listen. I'm in trouble. Remember that when you lose me. ou'll know when you have a baby and you love it. Remember e then. I don't mean a thing to you now –'

'You do!' she cried vehemently. 'You're my dad.'

'Don't despise me –'

'What have you done?'

'You'll hate me. I betrayed all of you, I was so *sure*.'

'What's going to happen to you?'

'I'll go to prison.'

'Oh, Dad.' He felt the spots of tears on his head, was aw⟨e⟩ moved, overcome. 'I'll stand by you. And Mum,' she add⟨ed⟩ more doubtfully. 'I don't care *what* you've done.'

'What,' he asked like a child, 'do you want out of life?'

'I dunno. To meet a boy, dance, sing, go to the pictures, s⟨e⟩ side . . .'

'Is that all?' he asked her with a flash of the old intoleran⟨ce⟩ 'To meet boys? The sum total of life?'

'I thought you asked what I wanted *out* of life . . .'

'I dunno what I meant. Its purpose. What,' he asked painful⟨ly⟩ 'do you do with these boys?'

She blushed and asked shakily, 'What's all this about?'

'Be a good kid and tell me the truth. I got to understand.'

'We dance and walk, drink coffee, you know –'

'Nothing happens?'

'I dunno what you mean. He held my hand.'

She saw that whatever it was, it had the power to hurt as mu⟨ch⟩ as this other, larger thing; there was an acute, painful impact if it had value that she should or should not drink coffee, h⟨old⟩ hands, walk by a dirty canal. She was aware of his despera⟨te⟩ need of a relationship, a fear that this one might be lost, or ex⟨ist⟩ differently, to give pain.

'I betrayed my country,' he explained with brutal simplici⟨ty⟩ 'because its values seemed dirty, arrogant, evil, insulting God⟨.'⟩

'What d'you mean, you betrayed your country?'

'It was against my principles to help manufacture a rocket . ⟨.⟩ he began, but stopped, in doubt. That might be the hypocrisy ⟨in⟩ the mind's eye; it had even fooled *him*. 'I gave away secrets ⟨at⟩ the factory because I despised them.'

She was stunned, terrified; the tears stopped.

'But, Dad, you'll go to prison.'

'I just said –'

'Oh, Dad, *why*?'

'I've been trying to tell you. Because it's a dirty, godl⟨ess⟩ country I live in. Was I wrong?'

'How do I know? I'm too young.'

'Because I'd forgotten that, if I was caught, *you'd* suffer; they'll condemn and hate you, too.'

'You did what you thought was right, didn't you?'

'Oh yes. I don't know even now if I was wrong. Do you?'

It was hard to think about it, decide for him.

'You asked *me*, didn't you?' she said, remembering now. 'You asked if you ought to give up work because of your principles. And I was selfish because I didn't want to live anywhere else, and I said if you didn't really know what it was *for* you could turn a blind eye.'

'I made the decision myself,' he acknowledged. 'Don't try to share the burden, kid. I knew what the rocket was for.'

A door opened, breath, feet, Vi's movements, a rush of street air.

Brenda said quickly, 'I'm on your side because you're my lad.'

He was grateful but said wretchedly, 'I'm going to bed. I feel ill.'

And he lay in bed, sweating and restless, heard the agitated voices downstairs, Brenda trying to explain, justify. Hours seemed to go by. Then Vi came to bed, conscious of it, overwhelmed, full of self, ready to weep for herself, the violent alteration of her way of life. He tried hard not to despise her for it; she was simple, ordinary, frightened of decisions and principles.

'Charlie,' she whined in a broken voice, 'what have you done?'

How could he answer a question so simple?

'Has she told you?'

'I can't make head or tail –'

'I'm sorry, Vi. I'm bloody sorry –'

'Sorry?' She couldn't think of any way to talk about it except in terms of self-pity, a row. 'You shoulda thought about me. It's difficult enough here without *principles*.'

Someone was ringing the front-door bell. He was frightened. Whatever it was, it would be relative to his destruction.

'I'm too tired,' he claimed. 'I feel ill.'

'I can't go like this,' Vi said in a shadow of her normal, respectable self. 'It's not proper.'

Filmer went down the stairs – eleven o'clock at night. He had tried to alter the world; now the world was going to decide what to do with him.

Two men, one young and tough, intelligent, the other middle-aged, medium-sized, a kind face – ridiculous, but it was true: the man had a kind sort of face. Rather to Filmer's surprise, the men could not entirely disguise their relief that he was still here despite the idiocy of the local Security and police.

'Mr Charles Filmer?'

'Yes,' he acknowledged, wishing with all his heart that it were not so. It was going to be hard to be Charles Filmer; it always had been pretty difficult.

The same man, the medium-size one, spoke again. 'My name's Bellamy. I'm a police officer. I'd like to talk to you.'

It was, Filmer knew, with a last flicker of humour, the understatement of the year.

'Come in,' he said.

When the telephone call came to request assistance in the case of a man who'd stolen a spatial impulse selector – just like that, the most secret thing in Britain, and here was a man taking one home! – Bellamy felt, not elated, but defeated, confused. It was, presumably, the periphery of yet another conspiracy. Or was it part of the same one? Or some sordid little solitary theft for money? He blushed in agonized embarrassment at the hopeless handling of the situation at that factory. They'd let the man go home! He could make a dozen phone calls, send radio signals to Moscow, even, with moderate luck, escape himself. Yes, indeed, the press would soon be having a high old time!

He was therefore slightly astonished and very relieved to find the man Filmer at home, tired, beaten up by the look of it, in a shabby dressing gown, shaking with fear at his front door.

The atmosphere in that small house was curious: there was no hatred of the police generated, ready. The woman, also in a dressing gown, sat weeping in a chair, explained like the suburban housewife she presumably was, 'He didn't mean any harm, Mister. It was his principles.'

And Bellamy was conscious of someone behind a door. He opened it violently, and a child was there, a pretty girl of about fifteen who blushed and blushed because she was in pyjamas.

He said, smiling, 'You'd better come in,' deciding that it might good psychology to harass the man with the opinions of his own family. The child ran first to put on a raincoat.

It was obvious to Bellamy that Filmer was a man of good, perhaps fanatical, intentions, who had, because of prejudice, principles his wife seemed to regard as peculiar, gone beyond the usual outlets of opinionated persons. There were many societies and minor religions that condemned the way of life they saw around them, sought to mend it in words, hymns, prayers, written articles. This man had felt words weren't enough; he'd had to do something. Bellamy wondered if he knew just what he had been about to do. Filmer was a minor, suburban Fuchs. Fuchs had betrayed the West because of his conscience, had in so doing given Russia the atomic bomb. This man Filmer had been about, Bellamy presumed, to hand over the answer to nuclear rocket attack.

It was, however, obvious that Filmer was near to the breaking point. There were several ways he could break. One was the sullen, defiant 'To hell with the world' and a blank refusal to talk, to go to prison without a word. Another was for him to realize what he'd done, try to make amends. It was this one that Bellamy desired, and he hoped to get it by treating Filmer as a human being whose good intentions had been mistaken.

'Mr Filmer, you took a spatial impulse selector today, didn't you?'

'Yes.'

'Have you taken other things from Mayger Electric?'

The man hesitated. 'A few.'

'But this was the most important?'

'They were all parts of it.'

'What have you done with these other things?'

No answer. The woman was already out of her depth, head down, blubbering quietly. The child sat there like a jury.

'Why did you take those things?'

'What difference does *that* make?'

'It was your conscience, was it not?'

Somewhere in the room a clock ticked: Friday had become Saturday.

'What does it matter *now*?'

'Do you think we don't care? That we're just going to show you in prison, get you out of the way? What was so wrong with our society that you were prepared to betray it? Perhaps it can be put right!'

Filmer squirmed in his chair, was actually embarrassed. 'Every bloody thing.'

'In what way?'

He raged suddenly, 'Can't you *see*? Dirty, selfish, arrogant, stinking, evil –'

'You're a religious man?'

'I believe in God.'

'Did you consult your priest before taking this mighty decision?'

The man waved an arm in impatience. 'How could I with such secrets? I was alone by choice but also of necessity.'

'I think you deceive yourself.'

'You know all about it? You've been here ten minutes and you know all about it?'

'Do you go to church?'

'I never did think much of the clergy.'

'You are prepared to take on the power of the attorney of God, yet you never go near His house? You don't fancy the people who go there? You'd feel self-conscious? It's something the working-class man doesn't do?'

'You know it all, don't you? Clever. I went to Christian Doorstep for years. And I asked *him*, Dawson.'

'If you could betray your country?'

'Well, no. If I should work on a weapon of war at the factory.'

'What did he say?'

'I dunno. Some mealymouthed rubbish. No use to me. Talk.'

'What about your wife? Has she no value to you? And your daughter?'

'Leave 'em out, see?' Filmer said angrily. 'It's nothing to do with them. Do what you like with me, but leave them alone.'

'You deceived them?'

'No, I did not.'

'You didn't consult them. Is that not the same thing?'

'You're too clever with words.'

'Charlie,' pleaded the woman, 'you shoulda told me.'

'You wouldn't understand. You'd talk it over with Ted and arion, as though they cared twopence, valued anything ex-pt pork!'

'And why not? He's my brother.'

'He's a bag of wind,' shouted Filmer. 'A bag of wind. No ve, no conscience, no charity, no cleanliness. Money, just the oney, success.'

He was shaking with the intensity, a lifetime's hatred spewed at last.

Bellamy said, 'What about your mates at the factory? You re prepared to destroy them?'

'Destroy? This is a weapon of defence.'

'It is you who play with words now, Mr Filmer.'

'I only wanted equality of defence, the balance of terror bilized.'

'Oh, come now, Mr Filmer, do not presume me a fool. That as the justification, the excuse, was it not, not the reason?'

Filmer was silent.

Mrs Filmer said, 'I can't understand it. Ted's always gener-s; he's always got a laugh.'

Bellamy persisted, 'What about this evil, dirty, selfish, arro-nt society, Mr Filmer? Are we all like that? And if we are, it not because we have the freedom and the free will?'

'They don't care,' the man said wretchedly. 'They wallow in e physical, what exists, what cannot be disputed, what is easy: oney, property, cars, clothes, vanity, sex, arrogance . . .'

'And you think the citizens of Communist countries do not ve these human weaknesses? Mr Filmer how can you be so ive? Crime and sin, which seem to be what concern you, exist Russia and China. Does not the murder and imprisonment millions mean anything to you?'

'I can only condemn what I *see*.'

'I suggest to you that your decision was as evil as anything u condemn and that you made it because you believed there'd ver be a reckoning; you'd never be found out. A judge and ry will confirm this ⟶

'They'll be partial. They'll only be concerned with whether I d it or not, not *why*.'

'If they cannot be allowed to judge you, then who can?'

'I don't know,' the man admitted. 'I'm tired. They're all pr
judiced, dirtied.'

'You'd like someone pure and untouched to judge?'

'I agree,' Filmer conceded wearily, 'that we couldn't find su
a person.'

'On the contrary,' said Bellamy. 'We have one here. Yo
daughter.'

Filmer was startled.

'It wouldn't be fair to *her*.'

'Why not? She loves you?'

'I think so.'

'Miss Filmer, do you understand what your father's don
What we've been talking about?'

She had paled before the responsibility but said, 'Yes.'

'Did he do right?'

'He wanted to.'

'But did he in fact do an evil thing or not?'

'If his conscience had been entirely clear his action wou
have been morally right.'

'You are saying that a man has the right to act against t
society he lives in?' Bellamy asked in astonishment.

'Yes, if his conscience is absolutely clear.'

'And was your father's?'

She began to cry. 'I'm afraid not. It was bound up wi
hatreds, personal dislikes.'

Filmer stared at his daughter and began to sob.

They waited a long time in pity and embarrassment.

Then Filmer said, 'I accept the word of my child. I mu
believe she's right. It's not easy to believe. I couldn't accept
from any other person. I am an evil person. Mr Bellamy,
God's name, what do I do?'

'What you do,' said Bellamy, 'is even harder. You try to p
things right. What were you going to do with that spatial in
pulse selector?'

'I was going to take it to Canterbury.'

'Then that,' Bellamy decided, 'is what you must do.'

Despite Filmer's surrender and cooperation, twenty-fo

urs later, as Saturday became Sunday, Bellamy found him-
f – tired, in need of sleep, harassed by superiors, eating the
ong foods at mistaken hours – just as anxious as ever.

Stuhler and his wife had been arrested. Their arrest had been
cipitated by the ambulance and the shrieking Sheila An-
ov. The one arrest had necessitated, made immediate the
ers – before escapes, telephone calls, the burning of papers.
eila Antonov was under guard in the hospital. Mr Keuscher,
en arrested, had been acid. 'I am an old man who is a cripple.
ollect stamps and I drink whisky. Do you think such an in-
acitated person is capable of the gymnastics of spies?' Bel-
ny said, 'I think you are an old man who would destroy the
ilized world. I have evidence to prove it.' Keuscher made no
ther comment, answered no questions. But Bellamy's men
ind microdots and other evidence among Keuscher's col-
tion of stamps. Bellamy, looking at the attractive stamps,
d the weak urge to take them home, give them to Simon,
o collected them. A mountain of letters from all over the
rld to be investigated – the majority innocent, but at least
e of those foreign addresses would be that of a guilty person,
erson who'd change his name, his or her way of life, when he
v tomorrow's newspaper in that foreign country.

Three things worried Bellamy, kept him in an acute condi-
n of anxiety despite the arrests, the accumulating evidence
ind. Antonov had vanished. Deliberately. He'd used the
hnique of jumping on and off tube trains, taking taxis, and
half an hour got rid of the small number of persons who had
en assigned to follow him. Henry Derber, too, had shaken
the men and women who followed him. His Morris Oxford,
lowed for some time, had evaded them. At the time they had
en following in three other vehicles, Sheila Antonov's screams
I not begun, and it had been essential that Derber shouldn't
ow he was being followed. But now, eight hours beyond that,
ther he nor his car had been traced.

But the most peculiar, disturbing item of the twenty-four
urs had been the behaviour of the woman in Canterbury.
e had accepted the small parcel of meaningless radio equip-
nt from Filmer. She'd done some shopping, strolled about,
I tea in a cheap café, gone home. The girl who looked like

a warehouse secretary had sat within feet of her in the ca
and the woman had not passed the small parcel to anyon
Indeed, she had taken it home. And she'd stayed at home – s
was there *now*, and no one had called. Bellamy's superiors we
not so patient as he was, urged him to question Filmer, not
trust him, interrogate him to bits. Bellamy had no doubts abo
Filmer. He did indeed question Filmer, ask why the woman d
not pass on the parcel. But Filmer didn't know, and Bellar
believed him.

At three in the morning they brought in Maggie Preston.
was satisfying to have another person in the conspiracy wl
admitted participation, but Maggie Preston hadn't heard
Alexei Antonov, and an hour's questioning only reduced h
to hysteria, confirmed ignorance.

Then, very much to Bellamy's relief, Henry Derber's Mor.
Oxford was seen travelling in London. It was followed ar
rather to Bellamy's disappointment, simply stopped outsi
Derber's home. Henry was arrested, the car, the house, and hi
self searched. But he travelled very light indeed. And he, bei
a professional spy and Communist, refused to answer question
There was even some satisfaction on his face, as if he'd accor
plished something and there was nothing they could do about

This situation existed hour after hour, in a condition
excitement, phones, statements, an endless cataloguing
things found.

The little woman in Canterbury took the bulldog for
morning walk and sixteen people followed. She came bac
peeled potatoes, prepared Sunday dinner. Bellamy's urge was
go in and arrest her, but he waited, waited, and was at la
rewarded. The woman came out, without the dog, strolli
leisurely to Canterbury East railway station, stood on the pla
form, holding a small paper carrier. Eight men and wom
waited also. One was behind her in the small queue for ticke
and heard her say, 'Rochester, day return,' and her irritatio
when the clerk said, 'No day returns on Sundays.'

She sat in a compartment opposite the tall Special Bran
girl and made conversation. 'Not a bad day, is it?' 'Do y
mind if I smoke?' 'I bet you're going to meet your boy friend
'Do you know how old I am? I'm sixty-seven.'

In Rochester she walked with slight unfamiliarity, searching
r something. She stood outside Marks and Spencer's stores
d yawned, watched the traffic. At three o'clock a Polish sailor
r, at any rate, a man dressed as one – talked to her, took the
g off her.

Bellamy ran in front of them; other policemen and the
man appeared. At one moment they were separate parts of a
ving mass along a pavement and the next they coalesced,
came an official group.

'I am a police officer,' Bellamy said. 'You are under arrest.'
The woman said, 'He wasn't accosting, dearie, only asking
time.'

But the sailor struggled, and it needed three men and some
gh treatment to hold him.

The man was taken to the local police station. Bellamy and
policemen approached his ship.

Their reception was hostile, but there was no violence.

When they found Antonov there was a man with him who
ved a pistol, but a policeman hit him and knocked him un-
scious.

The little man looked tired and had been knocked about a
.

My wife,' he pleaded at once. 'Where is my wife?'

And Bellamy told him as gently as such a thing was possible.
do so diminished any elation in the victory.

11

EPILOGUE

OU'RE beautiful, dear,' the woman in the opposite bed told
r. 'Is that why such a lot of people come and see you?'

She was gross, smashed, ugly; she smelled, was without teeth.
e was very ugly. I'm glad I'm not like that, Sheila thought,
t knowing – because they'd kept mirrors, even shining knives,
ay from her – unaware that one half of her own face was
rse.

What the woman said in the small ward was true. Peop
came, saw her, left grapes, oranges, this month's *Bizarre*, *Vogu*
the scents of better places, things; they left behind opinio
sweetened air, dull depression.

Her mother and father sat on two wooden chairs like peop
whose spines had been snapped just below the shoulder blade

It was unbelievable, in her father's dazed view. Every tim
he'd written to her, thought, caught a bus, stroked a do
saddled a horse – it was hard to shake off this perspective of h
daughter, to hear about some girl who slept with men, almo
anybody, committed treason, who writhed there with half h
face burned away. Her father belonged to a generation whi
could still talk of honour, country, God, without embarras
ment, and he didn't understand. He tried to be sympatheti
thought, She's plucky, as Sheila said not a word about the pai
just answered, 'Oh, not bad. Pass me a cigarette, darling.'

Her mother said – no tears, but a sniff at a flawless handke
chief – the scent of eau de Cologne drifted about – 'It will b
all right, you see. You were blackmailed into all these thing
Everything will be fine, of course.'

Neither mentioned Alexei.

When they'd gone the slab woman in the other bed said, 'O
I liked them. She's a lady. And he had such a kind face.'

Audrey came, with Elizabeth and Ann for moral support.

'There's the dimmest little policeman out there,' Elizabe
said. 'I think he thought *we* were spies.'

She flushed wretchedly. 'Sorry, poppet. I'm nervous.'

Ann couldn't take the spectacle of Sheila's face. She wept in
her handkerchief, and a more fashionable scent filled the sma
room.

Audrey said, 'Why not open a boutique when –'

She had been about to say 'when you come out of prison'.

'The new summer colour's called semolina,' Ann manage
to say. 'Isn't it *crazy*? And another's custard. Too depressing

When they'd departed the woman, who'd watched an
listened, enjoyed herself, commented, 'What lovely wome
Where d'you meet them, dear?'

'They're models.'

'Very beautiful.'

't was the first indication given to Sheila that she was no
ger beautiful. She lay there in agony, frightened about it.
Some flowers arrived from Captain Dean, with a cautious
uiry about his sabre.

The nurse said someone called David had phoned and asked
)ut her. He sent good wishes.

Sheila thought, I can still drive a fast car, breed horses. There
ist be something a mess like me can live for.

A policeman called Bellamy sat on the end of the bed.

How do you feel now?'

Pretty bloody.'

I want you to tell me all you know.'

I'm not interested in your dirty politics.'

Do you know what damage you may have done?'

She was silent.

Don't you know your husband is still missing?'

I didn't want to hurt him.'

Why did you become involved in the first place?'

I was bored. Bored, bored, *bored*,' she shouted.

Rubbish,' the man said. 'You just had an itch in your fanny.'

How vulgar can you be?' she asked with scorn. 'A genuine
foot!'

Bellamy knew he'd made a mistake. 'I'm sorry. That was
le,' he admitted, aware that, reported in an account of some
l, it would detract from the value of himself. 'And did you
 to the accused, "You just had an itch in your fanny"?'
ported in the *Daily Globe*. Read by millions. A tiny whiff of
like implanted in the jury's minds.

You don't seem,' he said, 'to have the slightest interest or
ling about what you've done.'

Mr Bellamy,' she said with candour, 'I'm at the bad end of a
e affair. For the man it was an affair; for me it was love.
w you want me to betray him, to *talk*, don't you? I can't.
u wouldn't. I'm dirty enough. Don't ask me to become
tier.'

This man Jones sold the world down the drain.'

Please go away.'

Don't you know Jones had had seven other women before
1? His wife took the dirty photographs.'

'You keep talking about a man called Jones. I don't kn⊙ anyone of that name.'

'I'm sorry. I thought you knew.'

'I'm tired.'

'He called himself Max Stuhler, but he was a Welshman fr⊙ Swansea called Jones. Maxwell Jones.'

'I don't believe you.'

'Perhaps you'd like to meet his sister, see the family pho⊙ graphs?'

It hurt. She knew it was true and it slashed her fibre, induc⊙ tears, self-pity.

'Such a clever little man, aren't you?' she sneered. 'Like schoolboy. Is it all you can do – follow people about like so⊙ kid's game?'

He was angry, she was pleased to note; he could be hu⊙ Ridiculous little policeman!

Bellamy said, 'Can't you picture a world in which th⊙ doesn't have to be a result involving yourself? Do you around with your eyes closed, fail to see people on buses, trai⊙ in this very place? You risked their lives, threw them away, ⊙ Jones.'

She wanted to hurt him, penetrate, sting. He was ordinary, *stupid*, he couldn't *see* . . .

'I hate ordinary people. They're ugly and they smell.'

He answered without anger, '*You smell, Mrs Anton⊙* You'll smell of suppuration for a long time to come. Yo⊙ need the pity you're incapable of.'

She wouldn't weep for him. Her deathly face flushed. '⊙ away, you cheap bastard.'

Surprisingly he went away.

The slab woman in the other bed still didn't compreher⊙ she was a bit dim or something.

'Don't you believe him, dear,' the silly cow said. 'You're s⊙ beautiful.' A long, long pause, and then she added, 'I ne⊙ had anything to lose.'

Hours went by, meals, nurses who clearly were torn betwe⊙ the mercy of duty and the dislike of treason. Sheila slept, ⊙ awakened. There were things they had to do. She refus⊙ to weep. Her breath hissed in the agony; the sweat roll⊙

e felt sick, returned to bed exhausted, refused food, pt.

Another day came, proceeded similarly.

She hoped she would die, didn't know what she waited for. It ould be unfair to her parents if she committed suicide. The in was endurable, accepted as part of punishment.

She awoke, not knowing whether it was day or night. There as a man sitting in a wooden chair, tired, waiting. It was her sband, Alexei.

Sheila was embarrassed, pleased, ashamed, guilty, concerned. e felt weak, the unfamiliar urge to weep. What a silly little an he was, but she was glad he had survived all this.

'You look worried,' he said with a tiny, knowledgeable ile.

'You can pity me now,' she said with a trace of anger. 'I sup- se you know everything.'

'I knew a long time ago,' he claimed.

'Don't be stupid,' she said. 'We were too clever. How did you ow?'

'You came back and your face was sunburned.'

'You never asked.'

'I didn't dare.'

'Why not?'

'I was afraid of losing you.'

'You'll lose me now,' she said bitterly. 'But, then, even you n't find me attractive any more. They tell me I smell.'

'One half of your face is very beautiful,' he said. 'Even half you is enough for me.'

'I shall go to prison,' she said defiantly. 'Two, three, even e years.'

'I will wait,' he offered gladly.

She knew it was true. He was among the fools of the world, e sentimental, the faithful, the dumb, the obedient, who aited for destruction, pain, any responsibility, however dious, accepted willingly, without cynicism, without pride, thout conceit, without arrogance. She wanted in a last flicker her former self – the mirror and the clothes, the adoration, e glamour – to rage against him. He was silly, non-U, un- phisticated; he was pathetic, absurd, like an old film or book,

like a spaniel dog. Instead she began to weep – hurt, foolish
weak, not liking surrender, participation, the responsibilit
even one person, beyond self; and she wept not only for him b
for all of them, the meek, the ugly, the unknowing, the unluck
the ordinary of the earth: the long casualty list that w:
humanity. I never had anything to lose.

Frank Preston read the newspaper column again. It was un
believable, raving mad. Maggie a traitor, involved in some con
spiracy about a rocket. It was laughable, absurd. She hadn't g
the brains. He stirred his morning tea, felt good, read mor
There was no doubt about it. It wasn't some other Magg
Preston; it was the one who worked as a telephone operator :
World Mechanical.

It warmed him more than the tea, made him feel he had wo
something, a hard, bitter victory, but it was his. He was just
fied. If it had been a fever, this then must surely be recovery. H
was right. He usually was. All that stuff about frigidity an
viciousness, and here she was, a cheap (or was it expensive?
did he have to revise the adjective?) whore. She'd even sold h
country for money. A couple of hundred, five hundred, wha
ever it was, chicken feed. If it had been thousands then sh
couldn't have been blamed. A man had a right to sell anythin
when thousands were involved; conscience wasn't involved. H
sniggered, ate a biscuit.

It was not his responsibility. He had been very clever to hav
got rid of her, thrown her out. (For this now, in his mind, wa
how their marriage had ended.) He felt no pity, just a glow i
the stomach where pain normally resided, satisfaction, bett
than booze. Now he wouldn't have to pay that bloody flatfoo
Evans. Thirty quid. He'd been saving it week by week. H
could go on the beer, have fun with some woman, go to Soutr
end.

Love, he'd never understood that, was incapable of it; bu
now, unexpectedly, as he finished breakfast, stood up, and pai
returned – the reminder of himself, the failure – he felt sorrov
A lot of it was self-pity, but some was for her; he wallowed i
it as deeply as minutes ago he'd immersed himself in satisfa
tion. It was true no one would have her now. She'd be pr

ay for years; the brightness in the eyes and the quick, crazy
ovements would die or grow old, useless. Was it really satis-
ng? For if no one else could have her, neither could he. And
wanted, he longed, the indefinable misery that was physical,
rt of pain, returned, and he felt ready to weep.

Eggy walked along the dirty pavements, exhausted by the
ring air. He had too many clothes on for the temperature and
midity of the day and felt stale; the sweat came out of his
ary body, and he knew in some embarrassment that he would
offensive to the doctor's nostrils. But to hell with him; it
s his job.

Half past five when he rang the bell, but he saw in depression
at despite his arriving forty-five minutes before the doctor
ould even consider seeing his first patient the surgery had a
all crowd outside. Sixteen people. He would be seventeenth.
lowing five minutes a patient – and some of the buggers took
quarter of an hour – and adding on the forty-five minutes
fore the evening game would begin, it meant that it would
– Oh, it was unbearable. And the indifference, bordering on
tright insult, when the man finally saw him. He was one of
ose doctors who have always just come back from important
atters to attend to this triviality, *him*.

Most of the patients were women who sat there, talked,
itted, their vegetable minds having the patience and capabil-
to overcome those chunks of time before the doctor saw
em. Eggy's time was no longer valuable, but he longed to
end it somewhere else. Ah, Maggie, if only she hadn't gone.
only she'd been a bit more clever, more fortunate. He was
serable over her loss. There was no satisfaction for him – as
ere seemed to be for Vera – in being a small part of a sensa-
n, not sufficiently involved to be hurt. He was wretched with-
t her lightness of heart. A kid, just a kid, who wanted things,
t much, didn't really know what she was doing. He was filled
th pure terror. I'm ill, fifty-four; with this lot I'll be dead by
ty, and getting worse day by day, month by month, despite
s bloke.

He picked up a magazine to struggle with time. There was a
t on the cover, only the face, but arrogant, beautiful, inso-

lent. It stirred him faintly, a desire to humiliate such beauty.
trick, of course, with cameras and things; there weren't rea
women like that in the world. Expensive whore. His han
turned the pages to see if there were other pictures of t
woman, but there weren't. Too thin, he thought with satisfa
tion. Got a glamorous face but a body like a bean pole, so th
could only photograph the face. Serve her right, he thoug
oddly, glad that there were qualifications. It was unbearable
have someone win everything. Ah, Maggie, you were the o
I'd have liked. He threw the magazine down. An old one an
way. The quack probably bought them second hand from
dentist!

A young man with pale pimpled face picked up the magazir
hesitated, self-conscious. It was a woman's magazine; he'd fe
a fool if one of these old bags sniggered or asked him som
thing. But the face on the cover was so beautiful he had to loo
to hold, to touch the paper as if it had reality. Were there su
people as these? Was there such beauty? He looked very car
fully at the photograph. Every pore in the skin, marking of t
lips, line around the young eyes was there, so it was not a li
Somewhere last year this perfection had existed. He could n
bear to put the magazine down. It would be to insult her. F
looked at it again and again in what felt like guilt. He ha
fallen in love with a photograph.

FROM DIRECTOR TO PROKHOR.
Assignment to the Prosser group.

1. To write out material on the characteristics and history of t
Liberal Party, with notes on the pre-election struggle. Show its sigr
ficance and present relationships, political platform, who finances
and whose circle it represents, and suggest how and at what level
can be infiltrated.

2. Spatial impulse selector. One or more members of group shou
change his/her job, move to Cricklewood with view to working
spatial impulse selector.

3. Bosambo and some of his group have returned to Oogla Prc
ince with specific instructions. Bosambo will request 'Technic
assistance' in a few weeks, and Naja Ridge Airport will be reopene

Bosambo was not, of course, arrested with Keuscher's group, b
his material was sent for safety to the embassy. It will be forward
in due course to the Prosser group. Contact with surviving membe

Keuscher's and Bosambo's groups must be made with extreme
e.

. Give more detailed information on the Steel Concentration Re-
rch Council at Swansea, right down to the sections, their directors,
what they are engaged on. Obtain telephone directory of this
ncil. General details of apparatus, where it is used, its funda-
ntal features.

. Assigned to Prosser personally:

(a) Try to find out particulars of the Graff rotational shell,
especially its batteries. How do these batteries withstand
the discharge of the shell and the rotational speed?

(b) Answer last letter regarding graphs As/RAD213.

(c) Give or borrow the following literature for photographing:
JND 10302; B D 14001; G L (Asv) 5571.

. More data with respect to Williams. Did he really work in the
teorological Station in Greenland? Why did he leave? Try to draw
.liams into frank discussion about himself and put the question to
, what does he want from us, what will he do for us? Do not take
material from Williams yet, and do not show any interest in any
ormation whatever. Does he have access to files and documents of
ret nature?

. Dock strike. Dowell is right to be uneasy about the possibility
secret ballot. If secret ballot repeatedly confirmed that the men
express a point of view in favour of returning to work, which
y are afraid to express in the normal show of hands, then *all*
kes will become much more difficult to foment. These are my
ructions. . . .

MORE ABOUT PENGUINS

Penguinews, which appears every month, contains details of all the new books issued by Penguins as they are published. From time to time it is supplemented by *Penguins in Print*, which is a complete list of all available books published by Penguins. (There are well over three thousand of these.)

A specimen copy of *Penguinews* will be sent to you free on request, and you can become a subscriber for the price of the postage. For a year's issues (including the complete lists) please send 30p if you live in the United Kingdom, or 60p if you live elsewhere. Just write to Dept EP, Penguin Books Ltd, Harmondsworth, Middlesex, enclosing a cheque or postal order, and your name will be added to the mailing list.

Note: *Penguinews* and *Penguins in Print* are not available in the U.S.A. or Canada

ONE DAY IN THE LIFE OF
IVAN DENISOVICH*

Alexander Solzhenitsyn

A sensation was caused by the publication of this astounding first novel in Russia in late 1962. Rumoured to have been authorized by Khrushchev in person, its appearance was hailed as a literary and political event of the greatest magnitude.

Solzhenitsyn's spare description of life in a Siberian labour camp under Stalin has naturally and deservedly been likened to Dostoyevsky's *Memoirs from the House of the Dead*, published a century ago under the Tsars. It yields, somewhat in the manner of Hemingway, a crisp, shattering glimpse of the fate of millions of Russians before the Khrushchev thaw. This translation is by Ralph Parker.

'A masterpiece in the great Russian tradition' – Leonard Schapiro in the *New Statesman*

'Like Dostoyevsky's work, Solzhenitsyn's story is also a major artistic accomplishment' – *The Times*

'It is a blow struck for human freedom all over the world ... and it is gloriously readable' – Cyril Connolly in the *Sunday Times*

also available

CANCER WARD*

THE LOVE-GIRL AND THE INNOCENT*

and

SOLZHENITSYN
A DOCUMENTARY RECORD
Edited by Leopold Labedz

*NOT FOR SALE IN THE U.S.A.

THE RUSSIAN INTERPRETER

Michael Frayn

Winner of the Hawthornden Prize for 1967

'Manning's old friend Proctor-Gould was in Moscow and anxious to get in touch with him. Or so Manning was informed. He looked forward to the meeting. He had few friends in Moscow, none of them old friends, and no friends at all, old or new, in Moscow or anywhere else, called Proctor-Gould . . .'

These are the opening words of Michael Frayn's brilliant second novel, for which he was awarded the 1967 Hawthornden Prize.

'Altogether a notable book . . . Mr Frayn is now our best equipped younger prose-writer as well as being a very sane and very funny one . . ." – *The Times Literary Supplement*

also available

TOWARDS THE END OF THE MORNING
A VERY PRIVATE LIFE

A TRAVELLING WOMAN

John Wain

orge Links, married four years and with one unsuccessful
empt at adultery already behind him, was listless, moody,
d bored. But when his wife suggested psychoanalysis it
k George's rakish friend Captax to see opportunities for
 in the frequent overnight trips to London. And it was
otax, too, who thought up Ruth Cowley – pretty, intelli-
t, sensual, with a far from passionate husband – as a likely
dlady. Everything goes swimmingly in this novel by the
hor of *Hurry On Down* until George's self-indulgent phil-
dering has unexpected and disastrous results, and what
an as light-hearted Restoration comedy in modern dress
omes a grim tragedy of emotional immaturity.

 impossible for Mr Wain to be dull' – *Time and Tide*

hat gives this book its brisk surface animation is, once
in, Wain's inventiveness and his purposeful, lively attack
 a modern theme' – *Guardian*

 John Wain's most accomplished novel' – *New Statesman*

also available

THE CONTENDERS

DEATH OF THE HIND
LEGS *and* OTHER STORIES

HURRY ON DOWN

THE SMALLER SKY

THE YOUNG VISITORS

NOT FOR SALE IN THE U.S.A.

Also by James Barlow

TERM OF TRIAL

Graham Weir, a timid middle-aged teacher, still tortures him
self with the memory of a wartime incident when he w
called a coward. His mind is rotted by self-disgust and t
discontent of his acidic wife, and as he faces the juven
mobsters of the Railway Street Secondary School he
principally conscious of fear. The public house beckons
him.

But at the climax of this tense yet compassionate stu
there emerges another Graham Weir. He is accused of
indecent assault against a girl pupil in whom his interest h
been nothing but professional. In the humiliation of a pub
trial Weir suddenly recovers the courage of his ideals.

By its dramatic and convincing action James Barlow's p
vious novel, *The Patriots*, made an extraordinary impa
Term of Trial harnesses the same force on to a growi
insight.

'A terrifically good story' – *Sunday Times*

'A tense and exciting novel on a very serious and topic
subject' – *The Times Literary Supplement*

also available

THE PATRIOTS
THIS SIDE OF THE SKY

NOT FOR SALE IN THE U.S.A.